Saint's Progress by John Galsworthy

John Galsworthy was born at Kingston Upon Thames in Surrey, England, on August 14th 1867 to a wealthy and well established family. His schooling was at Harrow and New College, Oxford before training as a barrister and being called to the bar in 1890. However, Law was not attractive to him and he travelled abroad becoming great friends with the novelist Joseph Conrad, then a first mate on a sailing ship.

In 1895 Galsworthy began an affair with Ada Nemesis Pearson Cooper, the wife of his cousin Major Arthur Galsworthy. The affair was kept a secret for 10 years till she at last divorced and they married on 23rd September 1905.

Galsworthy first published in 1897 with a collection of short stories entitled "The Four Winds". For the next 7 years he published these and all works under his pen name John Sinjohn. It was only upon the death of his father and the publication of "The Island Pharisees" in 1904 that he published as John Galsworthy.

His first play, The Silver Box in 1906 was a success and was followed by "The Man of Property" later that same year and was the first in the Forsyte trilogy. Whilst today he is far more well know as a Nobel Prize winning novelist then he was considered a playwright dealing with social issues and the class system. Here we publish Villa Rubein, a very fine story that captures Galsworthy's unique narrative and take on life of the time.

He is now far better known for his novels, particularly The Forsyte Saga, his trilogy about the eponymous family of the same name. These books, as with many of his other works, deal with social class, upper-middle class lives in particular. Although always sympathetic to his characters, he reveals their insular, snobbish, and somewhat greedy attitudes and suffocating moral codes. He is now viewed as one of the first from the Edwardian era to challenge some of the ideals of society depicted in the literature of Victorian England.

In his writings he campaigns for a variety of causes, including prison reform, women's rights, animal welfare, and the opposition of censorship as well as a recurring theme of an unhappy marriage from the women's side. During World War I he worked in a hospital in France as an orderly after being passed over for military service.

He was appointed to the Order of Merit in 1929, after earlier turning down a knighthood, and awarded the Nobel Prize in 1932 though he was too ill to attend.

John Galsworthy died from a brain tumour at his London home, Grove Lodge, Hampstead on January 31st 1933. In accordance with his will he was cremated at Woking with his ashes then being scattered over the South Downs from an aeroplane.

Index of Contents

PART I

CHAPTER I

Such a day made glad the heart. All the flags of July were waving; the sun and the poppies flaming; white butterflies spiring up and twining, and the bees busy on the snapdragons. The lime-trees were coming into flower. Tall white lilies in the garden beds already rivaled the delphiniums; the York and Lancaster roses were full-blown round their golden hearts. There was a gentle breeze, and a swish and stir and hum rose and fell above the head of Edward Pierson, coming back from his lonely ramble over Tintern Abbey. He had arrived at Kestrel, his brother Robert's home on the bank of the Wye only that morning, having stayed at Bath on the way down; and now he had got his face burnt in that parti-coloured way peculiar to the faces of those who have been too long in London. As he came along the narrow, rather overgrown avenue, the sound of a waltz thrummed out on a piano fell on his ears, and he smiled, for music was the greatest passion he had. His dark grizzled hair was pushed back off his hot brow, which he fanned with his straw hat. Though not broad, that brow was the broadest part of a narrow oval face whose length was increased by a short, dark, pointed beard—a visage such as Vandyk might have painted, grave and gentle, but for its bright grey eyes, cinder-lashed and crow's-footed, and its strange look of not seeing what was before it. He walked quickly, though he was tired and hot; tall, upright, and thin, in a grey parsonical suit, on whose black kerseymere vest a little gold cross dangled.

Above his brother's house, whose sloping garden ran down to the railway line and river, a large room had been built out apart. Pierson stood where the avenue forked, enjoying the sound of the waltz, and the cool whipping of the breeze in the sycamores and birches. A man of fifty, with a sense of beauty, born and bred in the country, suffers fearfully from nostalgia during a long unbroken spell of London; so that his afternoon in the old Abbey had been almost holy. He had let his senses sink into the sunlit greenery of the towering woods opposite; he had watched the spiders and the little shining beetles, the flycatchers, and sparrows in the ivy; touched the mosses and the lichens; looked the speedwells in the eye; dreamed of he knew not what. A hawk had been wheeling up there above the woods, and he had been up there with it in the blue. He had taken a real spiritual bath, and washed the dusty fret of London off his soul.

For a year he had been working his parish single-handed—no joke—for his curate had gone for a chaplain; and this was his first real holiday since the war began, two years ago; his first visit, too, to his brother's home. He looked down at the garden, and up at the trees of the avenue. Bob had found a perfect retreat after his quarter of a century in Ceylon. Dear old Bob! And he smiled at the thought of his elder brother, whose burnt face and fierce grey whiskers somewhat recalled a Bengal tiger; the kindest fellow that ever breathed! Yes, he had found a perfect home for Thirza and himself. And Edward Pierson sighed. He too had once had a perfect home, a perfect wife; the wound of whose death, fifteen years ago, still bled a little in his heart. Their two daughters, Gratian and Noel, had not "taken after" her; Gratian was like his own mother, and Noel's fair hair and big grey eyes always reminded him of his cousin Leila, who—poor thing!—had made that sad mess of her life, and now, he had heard, was singing for a living, in South Africa. Ah! What a pretty girl she had been!

Drawn by that eternal waltz tune he reached the doorway of the music-room. A chintz curtain hung there, and to the sound of feet slipping on polished boards, he saw his daughter Noel waltzing slowly in the arms of a young officer in khaki: Round and round they went, circling, backing, moving sideways with curious steps which seemed to have come in recently, for he did not recognise them. At the piano sat his niece Eve, with a teasing smile on her rosy face. But it was at his young daughter that Edward Pierson looked. Her eyes were half-closed, her cheeks rather pale, and her fair hair, cut quite short, curled into her slim round neck. Quite cool she seemed, though the young man in whose arms she was gliding along looked fiery hot; a handsome boy, with blue eyes and a little golden down on the upper lip of his sunny red-cheeked face. Edward Pierson thought: 'Nice couple!' And had a moment's vision of himself and Leila, dancing at that long-ago Cambridge May Week—on her seventeenth birthday, he remembered, so that she must have been a year younger than Nollie was now! This would be the young man she had talked of in her letters during the last three weeks. Were they never going to stop?

He passed into view of those within, and said:

"Aren't you very hot, Nollie?"

She blew him a kiss; the young man looked startled and self-conscious, and Eve called out:

"It's a bet, Uncle. They've got to dance me down."

Pierson said mildly:

"A bet? My dears!"

Noel murmured over her shoulder:

"It's all right, Daddy!" And the young man gasped:

"She's bet us one of her puppies against one of mine, sir!"

Pierson sat down, a little hypnotized by the sleepy strumming, the slow giddy movement of the dancers, and those half-closed swimming eyes of his young daughter, looking at him over her shoulder as she went by. He sat with a smile on his lips. Nollie was growing up! Now that Gratian was married, she had become a great responsibility. If only his dear wife had lived! The smile faded from his lips; he looked suddenly very tired. The struggle, physical and spiritual, he had been through, these fifteen years, sometimes weighed him almost to the ground: Most men would have married again, but he had always felt it would be sacrilege. Real unions were for ever, even though the Church permitted remarriage.

He watched his young daughter with a mixture of aesthetic pleasure and perplexity. Could this be good for her? To go on dancing indefinitely with one young man could that possibly be good for her? But they looked very happy; and there was so much in young creatures that he did not understand. Noel, so affectionate, and dreamy, seemed sometimes possessed of a little devil. Edward Pierson was naïf; attributed those outbursts of demonic possession to the loss of her mother when she was such a mite; Gratian, but two years older, had never taken a mother's place. That had been left to himself, and he was more or less conscious of failure.

He sat there looking up at her with a sort of whimsical distress. And, suddenly, in that dainty voice of hers, which seemed to spurn each word a little, she said:

"I'm going to stop!" and, sitting down beside him, took up his hat to fan herself.

Eve struck a triumphant chord. "Hurrah I've won!"

The young man muttered:

"I say, Noel, we weren't half done!"

"I know; but Daddy was getting bored, weren't you, dear? This is Cyril Morland."

Pierson shook the young man's hand.

"Daddy, your nose is burnt!"

"My dear; I know."

"I can give you some white stuff for it. You have to sleep with it on all night. Uncle and Auntie both use it."

"Nollie!"

"Well, Eve says so. If you're going to bathe, Cyril, look out for that current!"

The young man, gazing at her with undisguised adoration, muttered:

"Rather!" and went out.

Noel's eyes lingered after him; Eve broke a silence.

"If you're going to have a bath before tea, Nollie, you'd better hurry up."

"All right. Was it jolly in the Abbey, Daddy?"

"Lovely; like a great piece of music."

"Daddy always puts everything into music. You ought to see it by moonlight; it's gorgeous then. All right, Eve; I'm coming." But she did not get up, and when Eve was gone, cuddled her arm through her father's and murmured:

"What d'you think of Cyril?"

"My dear, how can I tell? He seems a nice-looking young man."

"All right, Daddy; don't strain yourself. It's jolly down here, isn't it?" She got up, stretched herself a little, and moved away, looking like a very tall child, with her short hair curling in round her head.

Pierson, watching her vanish past the curtain, thought: 'What a lovely thing she is!' And he got up too, but instead of following, went to the piano, and began to play Mendelssohn's Prelude and Fugue in E minor. He had a fine touch, and played with a sort of dreamy passion. It was his way out of perplexities, regrets, and longings; a way which never quite failed him.

At Cambridge, he had intended to take up music as a profession, but family tradition had destined him for Holy Orders, and an emotional Church revival of that day had caught him in its stream. He had always had private means, and those early years before he married had passed happily in an East-End parish. To have not only opportunity but power to help in the lives of the poor had been fascinating; simple himself, the simple folk of his parish had taken hold of his heart. When, however, he married Agnes Heriot, he was given a parish of his own on the borders of East and West, where he had been ever since, even after her death had nearly killed him. It was better to go on where work and all reminded him of one whom he had resolved never to forget in other ties. But he knew that his work had not the zest it used to have in her day, or even before her day. It may well be doubted whether he, who had been in Holy Orders twenty-six years, quite knew now what he believed. Everything had become circumscribed, and fixed, by thousands of his own utterances; to have taken fresh stock of his faith, to have gone deep into its roots, would have been like taking up the foundations of a still-standing house. Some men naturally root themselves in the inexpressible—for which one formula is much the same as another; though Edward Pierson, gently dogmatic, undoubtedly preferred his High-Church statement of the inexpressible to that of, say, the Zoroastrians. The subtleties of change, the modifications by science, left little sense of inconsistency or treason on his soul. Sensitive, charitable, and only combative deep down, he instinctively avoided discussion on matters where he might hurt others or they hurt him. And, since explanation was the last thing which o could be expected of one who did not base himself on Reason, he had found but scant occasion ever to examine anything. Just as in the old Abbey he had soared off into the infinite with the hawk, the beetles, and the grasses, so now, at the piano, by these sounds of his own making, he was caught away again into emotionalism, without realising that he was in one of his, most religious moods.

"Aren't you coming to tea, Edward?"

The woman standing behind him, in a lilac-coloured gown, had one of those faces which remain innocent to the end of the chapter, in spite of the complete knowledge of life which appertains to mothers. In days of suffering and anxiety, like these of the great war, Thirza Pierson was a valuable person. Without ever expressing an opinion on cosmic matters, she reconfirmed certain cosmic truths, such as that though the whole world was at war, there was such a thing as peace; that though all the sons of mothers were being killed, there remained such a thing as motherhood; that while everybody was living for the future, the present still existed. Her tranquil, tender, matter-of-fact busyness, and the dew in her eyes, had been proof against twenty-three years of life on a tea-plantation in the hot part of Ceylon; against Bob Pierson; against the anxiety of having two sons at the front, and the confidences of nearly every one she came across. Nothing disturbed her. She was like a painting of "Goodness" by an Old Master, restored by Kate Greenaway. She never went to meet life, but when it came, made the best of it. This was her secret, and Pierson always felt rested in her presence.

He rose, and moved by her side, over the lawn, towards the big tree at the bottom of the garden.

"How d'you think Noel is looking, Edward?"

"Very pretty. That young man, Thirza?"

"Yes; I'm afraid he's over head and ears in love with her."

At the dismayed sound he uttered, she slipped her soft round arm within his. "He's going to the front soon, poor boy!"

"Have they talked to you?"

"He has. Nollie hasn't yet."

"Nollie is a queer child, Thirza."

"Nollie is a darling, but rather a desperate character, Edward."

Pierson sighed.

In a swing under the tree, where the tea-things were set out, the "rather desperate character" was swaying. "What a picture she is!" he said, and sighed again.

The voice of his brother came to them,—high and steamy, as though corrupted by the climate of Ceylon:

"You incorrigible dreamy chap, Ted! We've eaten all the raspberries. Eve, give him some jam; he must be dead! Phew! the heat! Come on, my dear, and pour out his tea. Hallo, Cyril! Had a good bathe? By George, wish my head was wet! Squattez-vous down over there, by Nollie; she'll swing, and keep the flies off you."

"Give me a cigarette, Uncle Bob—"

"What! Your father doesn't—"

"Just for the flies. You don't mind, Daddy?"

"Not if it's necessary, my dear."

Noel smiled, showing her upper teeth, and her eyes seemed to swim under their long lashes.

"It isn't necessary, but it's nice."

"Ah, ha!" said Bob Pierson. "Here you are, Nollie!"

But Noel shook her head. At that moment she struck her father as startlingly grown-up-so composed, swaying above that young man at her feet, whose sunny face was all adoration. 'No longer a child!' he thought. 'Dear Nollie!'

CHAPTER II

1

Awakened by that daily cruelty, the advent of hot water, Edward Pierson lay in his chintz-curtained room, fancying himself back in London. A wild bee hunting honey from the bowl of flowers on the window-sill, and the scent of sweetbrier, shattered that illusion. He drew the curtain, and, kneeling on the window-seat thrust his head out into the morning. The air was intoxicatingly sweet. Haze clung over the river and the woods beyond; the lawn sparkled with dew, and two wagtails strutted in the dewy sunshine. 'Thank God for loveliness!' he thought. 'Those poor boys at the front!' And kneeling with his elbows on the sill, he began to say his prayers. The same feeling which made him beautify his church, use vestments, good music, and incense, filled him now. God was in the loveliness of His world, as well as in His churches. One could worship Him in a grove of beech trees, in a beautiful garden, on a high hill, by the banks of a bright river. God was in the rustle of the leaves, and the hum of a bee, in the dew on the grass, and the scent of flowers; God was in everything! And he added to his usual prayer this whisper: "I give Thee thanks for my senses, O Lord. In all of us, keep them bright, and grateful for beauty." Then he remained motionless, prey to a sort of happy yearning very near, to melancholy. Great beauty ever had that effect on him. One could capture so little of it—could never enjoy it enough! Who was it had said not long ago: "Love of beauty is really only the sex instinct, which nothing but complete union satisfies." Ah! yes, George—Gratian's husband. George Laird! And a little frown came between his brows, as though at some thorn in the flesh. Poor George! But then, all doctors were materialists at heart—splendid fellows, though; a fine fellow, George, working himself to death out there in France. One must not take them too seriously. He plucked a bit of sweetbrier and put it to his nose, which still retained the shine of that bleaching ointment Noel had insisted on his using. The sweet smell of those little rough leaves stirred up an acute aching. He dropped them, and drew back. No longings, no melancholy; one ought to be out, this beautiful morning!

It was Sunday; but he had not to take three Services and preach at least one sermon; this day of rest was really to be his own, for once. It was almost disconcerting; he had so long felt like the cab horse who could not be taken out of the shafts lest he should fall down. He dressed with extraordinary deliberation, and had not quite finished when there came a knock on his door, and Noel's voice said: "Can I come in, Daddy?"

In her flax-blue frock, with a Gloire de Dijon rose pinned where it met on her faintly browned neck, she seemed to her father a perfect vision of freshness.

"Here's a letter from Gratian; George has been sent home ill, and he's gone to our house. She's got leave from her hospital to come home and nurse him."

Pierson read the letter. "Poor George!"

"When are you going to let me be a nurse, Daddy?"

"We must wait till you're eighteen, Nollie."

"I could easily say I was. It's only a month; and I look much more."

Pierson smiled.

"Don't I?"

"You might be anything from fifteen to twenty-five, my dear, according as you behave."

"I want to go out as near the front as possible."

Her head was poised so that the sunlight framed her face, which was rather broad—the brow rather too broad—under the waving light-brown hair, the nose short and indeterminate; cheeks still round from youth, almost waxen-pale, and faintly hollowed under the eyes. It was her lips, dainty yet loving, and above all her grey eyes, big and dreamily alive, which made her a swan. He could not imagine her in nurse's garb.

"This is new, isn't it, Nollie?"

"Cyril Morland's sisters are both out; and he'll be going soon. Everybody goes."

"Gratian hasn't got out yet: It takes a long time to get trained."

"I know; all the more reason to begin."

She got up, looked at him, looked at her hands, seemed about to speak, but did not. A little colour had come into her cheeks. Then, obviously making conversation, she asked:

"Are you going to church? It's worth anything to hear Uncle Bob read the Lessons, especially when he loses his place. No; you're not to put on your long coat till just before church time. I won't have it!"

Obediently Pierson resigned his long coat.

"Now, you see, you can have my rose. Your nose is better!" She kissed his nose, and transferred her rose to the buttonhole of his short coat. "That's all. Come along!" And with her arm through his, they went down. But he knew she had come to say something which she had not said.

2

Bob Pierson, in virtue of greater wealth than the rest of the congregation, always read the Lessons, in his high steamy voice, his breathing never adjusted to the length of any period. The congregation, accustomed, heard nothing peculiar; he was the necessary gentry with the necessary finger in the pie. It was his own family whom he perturbed. In the second row, Noel, staring solemnly at the profile of her father in the front row, was thinking: 'Poor Daddy! His eyes look as if they were coming out. Oh, Daddy! Smile! or it'll hurt you!' Young Morland beside her, rigid in his tunic, was thinking: 'She isn't thinking of me!' And just then her little finger crooked into his. Edward Pierson was thinking: 'Oh! My dear old Bob! Oh!' And, beside him, Thirza thought: 'Poor dear Ted I how nice for him to be having a complete rest! I must make him eat he's so thin!' And Eve was thinking: 'Oh, Father! Mercy!' But Bob Pierson was thinking: 'Cheer oh! Only another three verses!' Noel's little finger unhooked itself, but her eyes stole round to young Morland's eyes, and there was a light in them which lingered through the singing and the prayers. At last, in the reverential rustle of the settling congregation, a surpliced figure mounted the pulpit.

"I come not to bring Peace, but a sword."

Pierson looked up. He felt deep restfulness. There was a pleasant light in this church; the hum of a country bluebottle made all the difference to the quality of silence. No critical thought stirred within him, nor any excitement. He was thinking: 'Now I shall hear something for my good; a fine text; when did I preach from it last?' Turned a little away from the others, he saw nothing but the preacher's homely face up there above the carved oak; it was so long since he had been preached to, so long since he had had a rest! The words came forth, dropped on his forehead, penetrated, met something which absorbed them, and disappeared. 'A good plain sermon!' he thought. 'I suppose I'm stale; I don't seem—' "Let us not, dear brethren," droned the preacher's earnest voice, "think that our dear Lord, in saying that He brought a sword, referred to a physical sword. It was the sword of the spirit to which He was undoubtedly referring, that bright sword of the spirit which in all ages has cleaved its way through the fetters imposed on men themselves by their own desires, imposed by men on other men in gratification of their ambitions, as we have had so striking an example in the invasion by our cruel enemies of a little neighbouring country which had done them no harm. Dear brethren, we may all bring swords." Pierson's chin jerked; he raised his hand quickly and passed it over his face. 'All bring swords,' he thought, 'swords—I wasn't asleep—surely!' "But let us be sure that our swords are bright; bright with hope, and bright with faith, that we may see them flashing among the carnal desires of this mortal life, carving a path for us towards that heavenly kingdom where alone is peace, perfect peace. Let us pray."

Pierson did not shut his eyes; he opened them as he fell on his knees. In the seat behind, Noel and young Morland had also fallen on their knees their faces covered each with a single hand; but her left hand and his right hung at their sides. They prayed a little longer than any others and, on rising, sang the hymn a little louder.

3

No paper came on Sundays—not even the local paper, which had so long and so nobly done its bit with headlines to win the war. No news whatever came, of men blown up, to enliven the hush of the hot July afternoon, or the sense of drugging—which followed Aunt Thirza's Sunday lunch. Some slept, some thought they were awake; but Noel and young Morland walked upward through the woods towards a high common of heath and furze, crowned by what was known as Kestrel rocks. Between these two young people no actual word of love had yet been spoken. Their lovering had advanced by glance and touch alone.

Young Morland was a school and college friend of the two Pierson boys now at the front. He had no home of his own, for his parents were dead; and this was not his first visit to Kestrel. Arriving three weeks ago, for his final leave before he should go out, he had found a girl sitting in a little wagonette outside the station, and had known his fate at once. But who knows when Noel fell in love? She was— one supposes—just ready for that sensation. For the last two years she had been at one of those high-class finishing establishments where, in spite of the healthy curriculum, perhaps because of it, there is ever an undercurrent of interest in the opposing sex; and not even the gravest efforts to eliminate instinct are quite successful. The disappearance of every young male thing into the maw of the military machine put a premium on instinct. The thoughts of Noel and her school companions were turned, perforce, to that which, in pre-war freedom of opportunity they could afford to regard as of secondary interest. Love and Marriage and Motherhood, fixed as the lot of women by the countless ages, were threatened for these young creatures. They not unnaturally pursued what they felt to be receding.

When young Morland showed, by following her about with his eyes, what was happening to him, Noel was pleased. From being pleased, she became a little excited; from being excited she became dreamy. Then, about a week before her father's arrival, she secretly began to follow the young man about with her eyes; became capricious too, and a little cruel. If there had been another young man to favour—but there was not; and she favoured Uncle Bob's red setter. Cyril Morland grew desperate. During those three days the demon her father dreaded certainly possessed her. And then, one evening, while they walked back together from the hay-fields, she gave him a sidelong glance; and he gasped out: "Oh! Noel, what have I done?" She caught his hand, and gave it a quick squeeze. What a change! What blissful alteration ever since!

Through the wood young Morland mounted silently, screwing himself up to put things to the touch. Noel too mounted silently, thinking: 'I will kiss him if he kisses me!' Eagerness, and a sort of languor, were running in her veins; she did not look at him from under her shady hat. Sun light poured down through every chink in the foliage; made the greenness of the steep wood marvellously vivid and alive; flashed on beech leaves, ash leaves, birch leaves; fell on the ground in little runlets; painted bright patches on trunks and grass, the beech mast, the ferns; butterflies chased each other in that sunlight, and myriads of ants and gnats and flies seemed possessed by a frenzy of life. The whole wood seemed possessed, as if the sunshine were a happy Being which had come to dwell therein. At a half-way spot, where the trees opened and they could see, far below them, the gleam of the river, she sat down on the bole of a beech-tree, and young Morland stood looking at her. Why should one face and not an other, this voice and not that, make a heart beat; why should a touch from one hand awaken rapture, and a touch from another awaken nothing? He knelt down and pressed his lips to her foot. Her eyes grew very bright; but she got up and ran on—she had not expected him to kiss her foot. She heard him hurrying after her, and stopped, leaning against a birch trunk. He rushed to her, and, without a word spoken, his lips were on her lips. The moment in life, which no words can render, had come for them. They had found their enchanted spot, and they moved no further, but sat with their arms round each other, while the happy Being of the wood watched. A marvellous speeder-up of Love is War. What might have taken six months, was thus accomplished in three weeks.

A short hour passed, then Noel said:

"I must tell Daddy, Cyril. I meant to tell him something this morning, only I thought I'd better wait, in case you didn't."

Morland answered: "Oh, Noel!" It was the staple of his conversation while they sat there.

Again a short hour passed, and Morland said:

"I shall go off my chump if we're not married before I go out."

"How long does it take?"

"No time, if we hurry up. I've got six days before I rejoin, and perhaps the Chief will give me another week, if I tell him."

"Poor Daddy! Kiss me again; a long one."

When the long one was over, she said:

"Then I can come and be near you till you go out? Oh, Cyril!"

"Oh, Noel!"

"Perhaps you won't go so soon. Don't go if you can help it!"

"Not if I can help it, darling; but I shan't be able."

"No, of course not; I know."

Young Morland clutched his hair. "Everyone's in the same boat, but it can't last for ever; and now we're engaged we can be together all the time till I've got the licence or whatever it is. And then—!"

"Daddy won't like our not being married in a church; but I don't care!"

Looking down at her closed eyes, and their lashes resting on her cheeks, young Morland thought:

'My God! I'm in heaven!'

Another short hour passed before she freed herself.

"We must go, Cyril. Kiss me once more!"

It was nearly dinner-time, and they ran down.

4

Edward Pierson, returning from the Evening Service, where he had read the Lessons, saw them in the distance, and compressed his lips. Their long absence had vexed him. What ought he to do? In the presence of Love's young dream, he felt strange and helpless. That night, when he opened the door of his room, he saw Noel on the window-seat, in her dressing-gown, with the moonlight streaming in on her.

"Don't light up, Daddy; I've got something to say."

She took hold of the little gold cross on his vest, and turned it over.

"I'm engaged to Cyril; we want to be married this week."

It was exactly as if someone had punched him in the ribs; and at the sound he made she hurried on:

"You see, we must be; he may be going out any day."

In the midst of his aching consternation, he admitted a kind of reason in her words. But he said:

"My dear, you're only a child. Marriage is the most serious thing in life; you've only known him three weeks."

"I know all that, Daddy" her voice sounded so ridiculously calm; "but we can't afford to wait. He might never come back, you see, and then I should have missed him."

"But, Noel, suppose he never did come back; it would only be much worse for you."

She dropped the little cross, and took hold of his hand, pressing it against her heart. But still her voice was calm:

"No; much better, Daddy; you think I don't know my own feelings, but I do."

The man in Pierson softened; the priest hardened.

"Nollie, true marriage is the union of souls; and for that, time is wanted. Time to know that you feel and think the same, and love the same things."

"Yes, I know; but we do."

"You can't tell that, my dear; no one could in three weeks."

"But these aren't ordinary times, are they? People have to do things in a hurry. Oh, Daddy! Be an angel! Mother would have understood, and let me, I know!"

Pierson drew away his hand; the words hurt, from reminder of his loss, from reminder of the poor substitute he was.

"Look, Nollie!" he said. "After all these years since she left us, I'm as lonely as ever, because we were really one. If you marry this young man without knowing more of your own hearts than you can in such a little time, you may regret it dreadfully; you may find it turn out, after all, nothing but a little empty passion; or again, if anything happens to him before you've had any real married life together, you'll have a much greater grief and sense of loss to put up with than if you simply stay engaged till after the war. Besides, my child, you're much too young."

She sat so still that he looked at her in alarm. "But I must!"

He bit his lips, and said sharply: "You can't, Nollie!"

She got up, and before he could stop her, was gone. With the closing of the door, his anger evaporated, and distress took its place. Poor child! What to do with this wayward chicken just out of the egg, and wanting to be full-fledged at once? The thought that she would be lying miserable, crying, perhaps, beset him so that he went out into the passage and tapped on her door. Getting no answer, he went in. It was dark but for a streak of moonlight, and in that he saw her, lying on her bed, face down; and stealing up laid his hand on her head. She did not move; and, stroking her hair, he said gently:

"Nollie dear, I didn't mean to be harsh. If I were your mother, I should know how to make you see, but I'm only an old bumble-daddy."

She rolled over, scrambling into a cross-legged posture on the bed. He could see her eyes shining. But she did not speak; she seemed to know that in silence was her strength.

He said with a sort of despair:

"You must let me talk it over with your aunt. She has a lot of good sense."

"Yes."

He bent over and kissed her hot forehead.

"Good night, my dear; don't cry. Promise me!"

She nodded, and lifted her face; he felt her hot soft lips on his forehead, and went away a little comforted.

But Noel sat on her bed, hugging her knees, listening to the night, to the emptiness and silence; each minute so much lost of the little, little time left, that she might have been with him.

CHAPTER III

Pierson woke after a troubled and dreamful night, in which he had thought himself wandering in heaven like a lost soul.

After regaining his room last night nothing had struck him more forcibly than the needlessness of his words: "Don't cry, Nollie!" for he had realised with uneasiness that she had not been near crying. No; there was in her some emotion very different from the tearful. He kept seeing her cross-legged figure on the bed in that dim light; tense, enigmatic, almost Chinese; kept feeling the feverish touch of her lips. A good girlish burst of tears would have done her good, and been a guarantee. He had the uncomfortable conviction that his refusal had passed her by, as if unspoken. And, since he could not go and make music at that time of night, he had ended on his knees, in a long search for guidance, which was not vouchsafed him.

The culprits were demure at breakfast; no one could have told that for the last hour they had been sitting with their arms round each other, watching the river flow by, talking but little, through lips too busy. Pierson pursued his sister-in-law to the room where she did her flowers every morning. He watched her for a minute dividing ramblers from pansies, cornflowers from sweet peas, before he said:

"I'm very troubled, Thirza. Nollie came to me last night. Imagine! They want to get married—those two!"

Accepting life as it came, Thirza showed no dismay, but her cheeks grew a little pinker, and her eyes a little rounder. She took up a sprig of mignonette, and said placidly:

"Oh, my dear!"

"Think of it, Thirza—that child! Why, it's only a year or two since she used to sit on my knee and tickle my face with her hair."

Thirza went on arranging her flowers.

"Noel is older than you think, Edward; she is more than her age. And real married life wouldn't begin for them till after—if it ever began."

Pierson experienced a sort of shock. His sister-in-law's words seemed criminally light-hearted.

"But—but—" he stammered; "the union, Thirza! Who can tell what will happen before they come together again!"

She looked at his quivering face, and said gently:

"I know, Edward; but if you refuse, I should be afraid, in these days, of what Noel might do. I told you there's a streak of desperation in her."

"Noel will obey me."

"I wonder! There are so many of these war marriages now."

Pierson turned away.

"I think they're dreadful. What do they mean—Just a momentary gratification of passion. They might just as well not be."

"They mean pensions, as a rule," said Thirza calmly.

"Thirza, that is cynical; besides, it doesn't affect this case. I can't bear to think of my little Nollie giving herself for a moment which may come to nothing, or may turn out the beginning of an unhappy marriage. Who is this boy—what is he? I know nothing of him. How can I give her to him—it's impossible! If they had been engaged some time and I knew something of him—yes, perhaps; even at her age. But this hasty passionateness—it isn't right, it isn't decent. I don't understand, I really don't—how a child like that can want it. The fact is, she doesn't know what she's asking, poor little Nollie. She can't know the nature of marriage, and she can't realise its sacredness. If only her mother were here! Talk to her, Thirza; you can say things that I can't!"

Thirza looked after the retreating figure. In spite of his cloth, perhaps a little because of it, he seemed to her like a child who had come to show her his sore finger. And, having finished the arrangement of her flowers, she went out to find her niece. She had not far to go; for Noel was standing in the hall, quite evidently lying in wait. They went out together to the avenue.

The girl began at once:

"It isn't any use talking to me, Auntie; Cyril is going to get a license."

"Oh! So you've made up your minds?"

"Quite."

"Do you think that's fair by me, Nollie? Should I have asked him here if I'd thought this was going to happen?"

Noel only smiled.

"Have you the least idea what marriage means?"

Noel nodded.

"Really?"

"Of course. Gratian is married. Besides, at school—"

"Your father is dead against it. This is a sad thing for him. He's a perfect saint, and you oughtn't to hurt him. Can't you wait, at least till Cyril's next leave?"

"He might never have one, you see."

The heart of her whose boys were out there too, and might also never have another leave; could not but be responsive to those words. She looked at her niece, and a dim appreciation of this revolt of life menaced by death, of youth threatened with extinction, stirred in her. Noel's teeth were clenched, her lips drawn back, and she was staring in front of her.

"Daddy oughtn't to mind. Old people haven't to fight, and get killed; they oughtn't to mind us taking what we can. They've had their good time."

It was such a just little speech that Thirza answered:

"Yes; perhaps he hasn't quite realised that."

"I want to make sure of Cyril, Auntie; I want everything I can have with him while there's the chance. I don't think it's much to ask, when perhaps I'll never have any more of him again."

Thirza slipped her hand through the girl's arm.

"I understand," she said. "Only, Nollie, suppose, when all this is over, and we breathe and live naturally once more, you found you'd made a mistake?"

Noel shook her head. "I haven't."

"We all think that, my dear; but thousands of mistakes are made by people who no more dream they're making them than you do now; and then it's a very horrible business. It would be especially horrible for you; your father believes heart and soul in marriage being for ever."

"Daddy's a darling; but I don't always believe what he believes, you know. Besides, I'm not making a mistake, Auntie! I love Cyril ever so."

Thirza gave her waist a squeeze.

"You mustn't make a mistake. We love you too much, Nollie. I wish we had Gratian here."

"Gratian would back me up," said Noel; "she knows what the war is. And you ought to, Auntie. If Rex or Harry wanted to be married, I'm sure you'd never oppose them. And they're no older than Cyril. You must understand what it means to me Auntie dear, to feel that we belong to each other properly before—before it all begins for him, and—and there may be no more. Daddy doesn't realise. I know he's awfully good, but—he's forgotten."

"My dear, I think he remembers only too well. He was desperately attached to your mother."

Noel clenched her hands.

"Was he? Well, so am I to Cyril, and he to me. We wouldn't be unreasonable if it wasn't—wasn't necessary. Talk, to Cyril, Auntie; then you'll understand. There he is; only, don't keep him long, because I want him. Oh! Auntie; I want him so badly!"

She turned; and slipped back into the house; and Thirza, conscious of having been decoyed to this young man, who stood there with his arms folded, like Napoleon before a battle, smiled and said:

"Well, Cyril, so you've betrayed me!"

Even in speaking she was conscious of the really momentous change in this sunburnt, blue-eyed, lazily impudent youth since the day he arrived, three weeks ago, in their little wagonette. He took her arm, just as Noel had, and made her sit down beside him on the rustic bench, where he had evidently been told to wait.

"You see, Mrs. Pierson," he said, "it's not as if Noel were an ordinary girl in an ordinary time, is it? Noel is the sort of girl one would knock one's brains out for; and to send me out there knowing that I could have been married to her and wasn't, will take all the heart out of me. Of course I mean to come back, but chaps do get knocked over, and I think it's cruel that we can't take what we can while we can. Besides, I've got money; and that would be hers anyway. So, do be a darling, won't you?" He put his arm round her waist, just as if he had been her son, and her heart, which wanted her own boys so badly, felt warmed within her.

"You see, I don't know Mr. Pierson, but he seems awfully gentle and jolly, and if he could see into me he wouldn't mind, I know. We don't mind risking our lives and all that, but we do think we ought to have the run of them while we're alive. I'll give him my dying oath or anything, that I could never change towards Noel, and she'll do the same. Oh! Mrs. Pierson, do be a jolly brick, and put in a word for me, quick! We've got so few days!"

"But, my dear boy," said Thirza feebly, "do you think it's fair to such a child as Noel?"

"Yes, I do. You don't understand; she's simply had to grow up. She is grown-up—all in this week; she's quite as old as I am, really—and I'm twenty-two. And you know it's going to be—it's got to be—a young world, from now on; people will begin doing things much earlier. What's the use of pretending it's like what it was, and being cautious, and all that? If I'm going to be killed, I think we've got a right to be married first; and if I'm not, then what does it matter?"

"You've known each other twenty-one days, Cyril."

"No; twenty-one years! Every day's a year when—Oh! Mrs. Pierson, this isn't like you, is it? You never go to meet trouble, do you?"

At that shrewd remark, Thirza put her hand on the hand which still clasped her waist, and pressed it closer.

"Well, my dear," she said softly, "we must see what can be done."

Cyril Morland kissed her cheek. "I will bless you for ever," he said. "I haven't got any people, you know, except my two sisters."

And something like tears started up on Thirza's eyelashes. They seemed to her like the babes in the wood—those two!

CHAPTER IV

1

In the dining-room of her father's house in that old London Square between East and West, Gratian Laird, in the outdoor garb of a nurse, was writing a telegram: "Reverend Edward Pierson, Kestrel, Tintern, Monmouthshire. George terribly ill. Please come if you can. Gratian." Giving it to a maid, she took off her long coat and sat down for a moment. She had been travelling all night, after a full day's work, and had only just arrived, to find her husband between life and death. She was very different from Noel; not quite so tall, but of a stronger build; with dark chestnut-coloured hair, clear hazel eyes, and a broad brow. The expression of her face was earnest, with a sort of constant spiritual enquiry; and a singularly truthful look: She was just twenty; and of the year that she had been married, had only spent six weeks with her husband; they had not even a house of their own as yet. After resting five minutes, she passed her hand vigorously over her face, threw back her head, and walked up stairs to the room where he lay. He was not conscious, and there was nothing to be done but sit and watch him.

'If he dies,' she thought, 'I shall hate God for His cruelty. I have had six weeks with George; some people have sixty years.' She fixed her eyes on his face, short and broad, with bumps of "observation" on the brows. He had been sunburnt. The dark lashes of his closed eyes lay on deathly yellow cheeks; his thick hair grew rather low on his broad forehead. The lips were just open and showed strong white teeth. He had a little clipped moustache, and hair had grown on his clean-cut jaw. His pyjama jacket had fallen open. Gratian drew it close. It was curiously still, for a London day, though the window was wide open. Anything to break this heavy stupor, which was not only George's, but her own, and the very world's! The cruelty of it—when she might be going to lose him for ever, in a few hours or days! She thought of their last parting. It had not been very loving, had come too soon after one of those arguments they were inclined to have, in which they could not as yet disagree with suavity. George had said there was no future life for the individual; she had maintained there was. They had grown hot and impatient. Even in the cab on the way to his train they had pursued the wretched discussion, and the last kiss had been from lips on lips yet warm from disagreement.

Ever since, as if in compunction, she had been wavering towards his point of view; and now, when he was perhaps to solve the problem—find out for certain—she had come to feel that if he died, she would never see him after. It was cruel that such a blight should have come on her belief at this, of all moments.

She laid her hand on his. It was warm, felt strong, although so motionless and helpless. George was so vigorous, so alive, and strong-willed; it seemed impossible that life might be going to play him false. She recalled the unflinching look of his steel-bright eyes, his deep, queerly vibrating voice, which had no trace of self-consciousness or pretence. She slipped her hand on to his heart, and began very slowly, gently rubbing it. He, as doctor, and she, as nurse, had both seen so much of death these last two years! Yet it seemed suddenly as if she had never seen death, and that the young faces she had seen, empty and white, in the hospital wards, had just been a show. Death would appear to her for the first time, if this face which she loved were to be drained for ever of light and colour and movement and meaning.

A humblebee from the Square Garden boomed in and buzzed idly round the room. She caught her breath in a little sob....

2

Pierson received that telegram at midday, returning from a lonely walk after his talk with Thirza. Coming from Gratian so self-reliant—it meant the worst. He prepared at once to catch the next train. Noel was out, no one knew where: so with a sick feeling he wrote:

"DEAREST CHILD,

"I am going up to Gratian; poor George is desperately ill. If it goes badly you should be with your sister. I will wire to-morrow morning early. I leave you in your aunt's hands, my dear. Be reasonable and patient. God bless you.

"Your devoted

"DADDY."

He was alone in his third-class compartment, and, leaning forward, watched the ruined Abbey across the river till it was out of sight. Those old monks had lived in an age surely not so sad as this. They must have had peaceful lives, remote down here, in days when the Church was great and lovely, and men laid down their lives for their belief in her, and built everlasting fanes to the glory of God! What a change to this age of rush and hurry, of science, trade, material profit, and this terrible war! He tried to read his paper, but it was full of horrors and hate. 'When will it end?' he thought. And the train with its rhythmic jolting seemed grinding out the answer: "Never—never!"

At Chepstow a soldier got in, followed by a woman with a very flushed face and curious, swimmy eyes; her hair was in disorder, and her lip bleeding, as if she had bitten it through. The soldier, too, looked strained and desperate. They sat down, far apart, on the seat opposite. Pierson, feeling that he was in their way, tried to hide himself behind his paper; when he looked again, the soldier had taken off his tunic and cap and was leaning out of the window. The woman, on the seat's edge, sniffing and wiping her face, met his glance with resentful eyes, then, getting up, she pulled the man's sleeve.

"Sit dahn; don't 'ang out o' there."

The soldier flung himself back on the seat and looked at Pierson.

"The wife an' me's 'ad a bit of a row," he said companionably. "Gits on me nerves; I'm not used to it. She was in a raid, and 'er nerves are all gone funny; ain't they, old girl? Makes me feel me 'ead. I've been wounded there, you know; can't stand much now. I might do somethin' if she was to go on like this for long."

Pierson looked at the woman, but her eyes still met his resentfully. The soldier held out a packet of cigarettes. "Take one," he said. Pierson took one and, feeling that the soldier wanted him to speak, murmured: "We all have these troubles with those we're fond of; the fonder we are of people, the more we feel them, don't we? I had one with my daughter last night."

"Ah!" said the soldier; "that's right. The wife and me'll make it up. 'Ere, come orf it, old girl."

From behind his paper he soon became conscious of the sounds of reconciliation—reproaches because someone had been offered a drink, kisses mixed with mild slappings, and abuse. When they got out at Bristol the soldier shook his hand warmly, but the woman still gave him her resentful stare, and he thought dreamily: 'The war! How it affects everyone!' His carriage was invaded by a swarm of soldiers, and the rest of the journey was passed in making himself small. When at last he reached home, Gratian met him in the hall.

"Just the same. The doctor says we shall know in a few hours now. How sweet of you to come! You must be tired, in this heat. It was dreadful to spoil your holiday."

"My dear! As if—May I go up and see him?"

George Laird was still lying in that stupor. And Pierson stood gazing down at him compassionately. Like most parsons, he had a wide acquaintance with the sick and dying; and one remorseless fellowship with death. Death! The commonest thing in the world, now—commoner than life! This young doctor must have seen many die in these last two years, saved many from death; and there he lay, not able to lift a finger to save himself. Pierson looked at his daughter; what a strong, promising young couple they were! And putting his arm round her, he led her away to the sofa, whence they could see the sick man.

"If he dies, Dad—" she whispered.

"He will have died for the Country, my love, as much as ever our soldiers do."

"I know; but that's no comfort. I've been watching here all day; I've been thinking; men will be just as brutal afterwards—more brutal. The world will go on the same."

"We must hope not. Shall we pray, Gracie?"

Gratian shook her head.

"If I could believe that the world—if I could believe anything! I've lost the power, Dad; I don't even believe in a future life. If George dies, we shall never meet again."

Pierson stared at her without a word.

Gratian went on: "The last time we talked, I was angry with George because he laughed at my belief; now that I really want belief, I feel that he was right."

Pierson said tremulously:

"No, no, my dear; it's only that you're overwrought. God in His mercy will give you back belief."

"There is no God, Dad"

"My darling child, what are you saying?"

"No God who can help us; I feel it. If there were any God who could take part in our lives, alter anything without our will, knew or cared what we did—He wouldn't let the world go on as it does."

"But, my dear, His purposes are inscrutable. We dare not say He should not do this or that, or try to fathom to what ends He is working."

"Then He's no good to us. It's the same as if He didn't exist. Why should I pray for George's life to One whose ends are just His own? I know George oughtn't to die. If there's a God who can help, it will be a wicked shame if George dies; if there's a God who can help, it's a wicked shame when babies die, and all these millions of poor boys. I would rather think there's no God than a helpless or a wicked God—"

Her father had suddenly thrown up his hands to his ears. She moved closer, and put her arm round him.

"Dad dear, I'm sorry. I didn't mean to hurt you."

Pierson pressed her face down to his shoulder; and said in a dull voice:

"What do you think would have happened to me, Gracie, if I had lost belief when your mother died? I have never lost belief. Pray God I never shall!"

Gratian murmured:

"George would not wish me to pretend I believe—he would want me to be honest. If I'm not honest, I shan't deserve that he should live. I don't believe, and I can't pray."

"My darling, you're overtired."

"No, Dad." She raised her head from his shoulder and, clasping her hands round her knees, looked straight before her. "We can only help ourselves; and I can only bear it if I rebel."

Pierson sat with trembling lips, feeling that nothing he could say would touch her just then. The sick man's face was hardly visible now in the twilight, and Gratian went over to his bed. She stood looking down at him a long time.

"Go and rest, Dad; the doctor's coming again at eleven. I'll call you if I want anything. I shall lie down a little, beside him."

Pierson kissed her, and went out. To lie there beside him would be the greatest comfort she could get. He went to the bare narrow little room he had occupied ever since his wife died; and, taking off his boots, walked up and down, with a feeling of almost crushing loneliness. Both his daughters in such trouble, and he of no use to them! It was as if Life were pushing him utterly aside! He felt confused, helpless, bewildered. Surely if Gratian loved George, she had not left God's side, whatever she might say. Then, conscious of the profound heresy of this thought, he stood still at the open window.

Earthly love—heavenly love; was there any analogy between them?

From the Square Gardens the indifferent whisper of the leaves answered; and a newsvendor at the far end, bawling his nightly tale of murder.

3

George Laird passed the crisis of his illness that night, and in the morning was pronounced out of danger. He had a splendid constitution, and—Scotsman on his father's side—a fighting character. He came back to life very weak, but avid of recovery; and his first words were: "I've been hanging over the edge, Gracie!"

A very high cliff, and his body half over, balancing; one inch, the merest fraction of an inch more, and over he would have gone. Deuced rum sensation! But not so horrible as it would have been in real life. With the slip of that last inch he felt he would have passed at once into oblivion, without the long horror of a fall. So this was what it was for all the poor fellows he had seen slip in the past two years! Mercifully, at the end, one was not alive enough to be conscious of what one was leaving, not alive enough even to care. If he had been able to take in the presence of his young wife, able to realise that he was looking at her face, touching her for the last time—it would have been hell; if he had been up to realising sunlight, moonlight, the sound of the world's life outside, the softness of the bed he lay on—it would have meant the most poignant anguish of defraudment. Life was a rare good thing, and to be squashed out of it with your powers at full, a wretched mistake in Nature's arrangements, a wretched villainy on the part of Man—for his own death, like all those other millions of premature deaths, would have been due to the idiocy and brutality of men! He could smile now, with Gratian looking down at him, but the experience had heaped fuel on a fire which had always smouldered in his doctor's soul against that half emancipated breed of apes, the human race. Well, now he would get a few days off from his death-carnival! And he lay, feasting his returning senses on his wife. She made a pretty nurse, and his practised eye judged her a good one—firm and quiet.

George Laird was thirty. At the opening of the war he was in an East-End practice, and had volunteered at once for service with the Army. For the first nine months he had been right up in the thick of it. A poisoned arm; rather than the authorities, had sent him home. During that leave he married Gratian. He had known the Piersons some time; and, made conscious of the instability of life, had resolved to marry her at the first chance he got. For his father-in-law he had respect and liking, ever mixed with what was not quite contempt and not quite pity. The blend of authority with humility, cleric with dreamer, monk with artist, mystic with man of action, in Pierson, excited in him an interested, but often irritated, wonder. He saw things so differently himself, and had little of the humorous curiosity which enjoys what is strange simply because it is strange. They could never talk together without soon reaching a point when he wanted to say: "If we're not to trust our reason and our senses for what they're worth, sir—will you kindly tell me what we are to trust? How can we exert them to the utmost in some matters, and in others suddenly turn our backs on them?" Once, in one of their discussions, which often bordered on acrimony, he had expounded himself at length.

"I grant," he had said, "that there's a great ultimate Mystery, that we shall never know anything for certain about the origin of life and the principle of the Universe; but why should we suddenly shut up our enquiring apparatus and deny all the evidence of our reason—say, about the story of Christ, or the question of a future life, or our moral code? If you want me to enter a temple of little mysteries, leaving my reason and senses behind—as a Mohammedan leaves his shoes—it won't do to say to me simply: 'There it is! Enter!' You must show me the door; and you can't! And I'll tell you why, sir. Because in your brain there's a little twist which is not in mine, or the lack of a little twist which is in mine. Nothing more than that divides us into the two main species of mankind, one of whom worships, and one of whom doesn't. Oh, yes! I know; you won't admit that, because it makes your religions natural instead of what you call supernatural. But I assure you there's nothing more to it. Your eyes look up or they look down— they never look straight before them. Well, mine do just the opposite."

That day Pierson had been feeling very tired, and though to meet this attack was vital, he had been unable to meet it. His brain had stammered. He had turned a little away, leaning his cheek on his hand, as if to cover that momentary break in his defences. Some days later he had said:

"I am able now to answer your questions, George. I think I can make you understand."

Laird had answered: "All right, sir; go ahead."

"You begin by assuming that the human reason is the final test of all things. What right have you to assume that? Suppose you were an ant. You would take your ant's reason as the final test, wouldn't you? Would that be the truth?" And a smile had fixed itself on his lips above his little grave beard.

George Laird also had smiled.

"That seems a good point, sir," he said, "until you recognise that I don't take, the human reason as final test in any absolute sense. I only say it's the highest test we can apply; and that, behind that test all is quite dark and unknowable."

"Revelation, then, means nothing to you?"

"Nothing, sir."

"I don't think we can usefully go on, George."

"I don't think we can, sir. In talking with you, I always feel like fighting a man with one hand tied behind his back."

"And I, perhaps, feel that I am arguing with one who was blind from birth."

For all that, they had often argued since; but never without those peculiar smiles coming on their faces. Still, they respected each other, and Pierson had not opposed his daughter's marriage to this heretic, whom he knew to be an honest and trustworthy man. It had taken place before Laird's arm was well, and the two had snatched a month's honeymoon before he went back to France, and she to her hospital in Manchester. Since then, just one February fortnight by the sea had been all their time together....

In the afternoon he had asked for beef tea, and, having drunk a cup, said:

"I've got something to tell your father."

But warned by the pallor of his smiling lips, Gratian answered:

"Tell me first, George."

"Our last talk, Gracie; well—there's nothing—on the other side. I looked over; it's as black as your hat."

Gratian shivered.

"I know. While you were lying here last night, I told father."

He squeezed her hand, and said: "I also want to tell him."

"Dad will say the motive for life is gone."

"I say it leaps out all the more, Gracie. What a mess we make of it—we angel-apes! When shall we be men, I wonder? You and I, Gracie, will fight for a decent life for everybody. No hands-upping about that! Bend down! It's good to touch you again; everything's good. I'm going to have a sleep...."

After the relief of the doctor's report in the early morning Pierson had gone through a hard struggle. What should he wire to Noel? He longed to get her back home, away from temptation to the burning indiscretion of this marriage. But ought he to suppress reference to George's progress? Would that be honest? At last he sent this telegram: "George out of danger but very weak. Come up." By the afternoon post, however, he received a letter from Thirza:

"I have had two long talks with Noel and Cyril. It is impossible to budge them. And I really think, dear Edward, that it will be a mistake to oppose it rigidly. He may not go out as soon as we think. How would it be to consent to their having banns published?—that would mean another three weeks anyway, and in absence from each other they might be influenced to put it off. I'm afraid this is the only chance, for if you simply forbid it, I feel they will run off and get married somewhere at a registrar's."

Pierson took this letter out with him into the Square Garden, for painful cogitation. No man can hold a position of spiritual authority for long years without developing the habit of judgment. He judged Noel's conduct to be headlong and undisciplined, and the vein of stubbornness in his character fortified the father and the priest within him. Thirza disappointed him; she did not seem to see the irretrievable gravity of this hasty marriage. She seemed to look on it as something much lighter than it was, to consider that it might be left to Chance, and that if Chance turned out unfavourable, there would still be a way out. To him there would be no way out. He looked up at the sky, as if for inspiration. It was such a beautiful day, and so bitter to hurt his child, even for her good! What would her mother have advised? Surely Agnes had felt at least as deeply as himself the utter solemnity of marriage! And, sitting there in the sunlight, he painfully hardened his heart. He must do what he thought right, no matter what the consequences. So he went in and wrote that he could not agree, and wished Noel to come back home at once.

CHAPTER V

1

But on the same afternoon, just about that hour, Noel was sitting on the river-bank with her arms folded tight across her chest, and by her side Cyril Morland, with despair in his face, was twisting a telegram "Rejoin tonight. Regiment leaves to-morrow."

What consolation that a million such telegrams had been read and sorrowed over these last two years! What comfort that the sun was daily blotted dim for hundreds of bright eyes; the joy of life poured out and sopped up by the sands of desolation!

"How long have we got, Cyril?"

"I've engaged a car from the Inn, so I needn't leave till midnight. I've packed already, to have more time."

"Let's have it to ourselves, then. Let's go off somewhere. I've got some chocolate."

Morland answered miserably:

"I can send the car up here for my things, and have it pick me up at the Inn, if you'll say goodbye to them for me, afterwards. We'll walk down the line, then we shan't meet anyone."

And in the bright sunlight they walked hand in hand on each side of a shining rail. About six they reached the Abbey.

"Let's get a boat," said Noel. "We can come back here when it's moonlight. I know a way of getting in, after the gate's shut."

They hired a boat, rowed over to the far bank, and sat on the stern seat, side by side under the trees where the water was stained deep green by the high woods. If they talked, it was but a word of love now and then, or to draw each other's attention to a fish, a bird, a dragon-fly. What use making plans— for lovers the chief theme? Longing paralysed their brains. They could do nothing but press close to each other, their hands enlaced, their lips meeting now and then. On Noel's face was a strange fixed stillness, as if she were waiting—expecting! They ate their chocolates. The sun set, dew began to fall; the river changed, and grew whiter; the sky paled to the colour of an amethyst; shadows lengthened, dissolved slowly. It was past nine already; a water-rat came out, a white owl flew over the river, towards the

Abbey. The moon had come up, but shed no light as yet. They saw no beauty in all this—too young, too passionate, too unhappy.

Noel said: "When she's over those trees, Cyril, let's go. It'll be half dark."

They waited, watching the moon, which crept with infinite slowness up and up, brightening ever so little every minute.

"Now!" said Noel. And Morland rowed across.

They left the boat, and she led the way past an empty cottage, to a shed with a roof sloping up to the Abbey's low outer wall.

"We can get over here," she whispered.

They clambered up, and over, to a piece of grassy courtyard, and passed on to an inner court, under the black shadow of the high walls.

"What's the time?" said Noel.

"Half-past ten."

"Already! Let's sit here in the dark, and watch for the moon."

They sat down close together. Noel's face still had on it that strange look of waiting; and Morland sat obedient, with his hand on her heart, and his own heart beating almost to suffocation. They sat, still as mice, and the moon crept up. It laid a first vague greyness on the high wall, which spread slowly down, and brightened till the lichen and the grasses up there were visible; then crept on, silvering the dark above their heads. Noel pulled his sleeve, and whispered: "See!" There came the white owl, soft as a snowflake, drifting across in that unearthly light, as if flying to the moon. And just then the top of the moon itself looked over the wall, a shaving of silvery gold. It grew, became a bright spread fan, then balanced there, full and round, the colour of pale honey.

"Ours!" Noel whispered.

2

From the side of the road Noel listened till the sound of the car was lost in the folds of the valley. She did not cry, but passed her hands over her face, and began to walk home, keeping to the shadow of the trees. How many years had been added to her age in those six hours since the telegram came! Several times in that mile and a half she stepped into a patch of brighter moonlight, to take out and kiss a little photograph, then slip it back next her heart, heedless that so warm a place must destroy any effigy. She felt not the faintest compunction for the recklessness of her love—it was her only comfort against the crushing loneliness of the night. It kept her up, made her walk on with a sort of pride, as if she had got the best of Fate. He was hers for ever now, in spite of anything that could be done. She did not even think what she would say when she got in. She came to the avenue, and passed up it still in a sort of dream. Her uncle was standing before the porch; she could hear his mutterings. She moved out of the shadow of the trees, went straight up to him, and, looking in his perturbed face, said calmly:

"Cyril asked me to say good-bye to you all, Uncle. Good night!"

"But, I say, Nollie look here you!"

She had passed on. She went up to her room. There, by the door, her aunt was standing, and would have kissed her. She drew back:

"No, Auntie. Not to-night!" And, slipping by, she locked her door.

Bob and Thirza Pierson, meeting in their own room, looked at each other askance. Relief at their niece's safe return was confused by other emotions. Bob Pierson expressed his first:

"Phew! I was beginning to think we should w have to drag the river. What girls are coming to!"

"It's the war, Bob."

"I didn't like her face, old girl. I don't know what it was, but I didn't like her face."

Neither did Thirza, but she would not admit it, and encourage Bob to take it to heart. He took things so hardly, and with such a noise!

She only said: "Poor young things! I suppose it will be a relief to Edward!"

"I love Nollie!" said Bob Pierson suddenly. "She's an affectionate creature. D-nit, I'm sorry about this. It's not so bad for young Morland; he's got the excitement—though I shouldn't like to be leaving Nollie, if I were young again. Thank God, neither of our boys is engaged. By George! when I think of them out there, and myself here, I feel as if the top of my head would come off. And those politician chaps spouting away in every country—how they can have the cheek!"

Thirza looked at him anxiously.

"And no dinner!" he said suddenly. "What d'you think they've been doing with themselves?"

"Holding each other's hands, poor dears! D'you know what time it is, Bob? Nearly one o'clock."

"Well, all I can say is, I've had a wretched evening. Get to bed, old girl. You'll be fit for nothing."

He was soon asleep, but Thirza lay awake, not exactly worrying, for that was not her nature, but seeing Noel's face, pale, languid, passionate, possessed by memory.

CHAPTER VI

1

Noel reached her father's house next day late in the afternoon. There was a letter in the hall for her. She tore it open, and read:

"MY DARLING LOVE,

"I got back all right, and am posting this at once to tell you we shall pass through London, and go from Charing Cross, I expect about nine o'clock to-night. I shall look out for you, there, in case you are up in time. Every minute I think of you, and of last night. Oh! Noel!

"Your devoted lover,

"C."

She looked at the wrist-watch which, like every other little patriot, she possessed. Past seven! If she waited, Gratian or her father would seize on her.

"Take my things up, Dinah. I've got a headache from travelling; I'm going to walk it off. Perhaps I shan't be in till past nine or so. Give my love to them all."

"Oh, Miss Noel, you can't,—"

But Noel was gone. She walked towards Charing Cross; and, to kill time, went into a restaurant and had that simple repast, coffee and a bun, which those in love would always take if Society did not forcibly feed them on other things. Food was ridiculous to her. She sat there in the midst of a perfect hive of creatures eating hideously. The place was shaped like a modern prison, having tiers of gallery round an open space, and in the air was the smell of viands and the clatter of plates and the music of a band. Men in khaki everywhere, and Noel glanced from form to form to see if by chance one might be that which represented, for her, Life and the British Army. At half-past eight she went out and made her way: through the crowd, still mechanically searching "khaki" for what she wanted; and it was perhaps fortunate that there was about her face and walk something which touched people. At the station she went up to an old porter, and, putting a shilling into his astonished hand, asked him to find out for her whence Morland's regiment would start. He came back presently, and said:

"Come with me, miss."

Noel went. He was rather lame, had grey whiskers, and a ghostly thin resemblance to her uncle Bob, which perhaps had been the reason why she had chosen him.

"Brother goin' out, miss?"

Noel nodded.

"Ah! It's a crool war. I shan't be sorry when it's over. Goin' out and comin' in, we see some sad sights 'ere. Wonderful spirit they've got, too. I never look at the clock now but what I think: 'There you go, slow-coach! I'd like to set you on to the day the boys come back!' When I puts a bag in: 'Another for 'ell' I thinks. And so it is, miss, from all I can 'ear. I've got a son out there meself. It's 'ere they'll come along. You stand quiet and keep a lookout, and you'll get a few minutes with him when he's done with 'is men.

I wouldn't move, if I were you; he'll come to you, all right—can't miss you, there.' And, looking at her face, he thought: 'Astonishin' what a lot o' brothers go. Wot oh! Poor little missy! A little lady, too. Wonderful collected she is. It's 'ard!'.rdquo; And trying to find something consoling to say, he mumbled out: "You couldn't be in a better place for seen'im off. Good night, miss; anything else I can do for you?"

"No, thank you; you're very kind."

He looked back once or twice at her blue-clad figure standing very still. He had left her against a little oasis of piled-up empty milk-cans, far down the platform where a few civilians in similar case were scattered. The trainway was empty as yet. In the grey immensity of the station and the turmoil of its noise, she felt neither lonely nor conscious of others waiting; too absorbed in the one thought of seeing him and touching him again. The empty train began backing in, stopped, and telescoped with a series of little clattering bangs, backed on again, and subsided to rest. Noel turned her eyes towards the station arch ways. Already she felt tremulous, as though the regiment were sending before it the vibration of its march.

She had not as yet seen a troop-train start, and vague images of brave array, of a flag fluttering, and the stir of drums, beset her. Suddenly she saw a brown swirling mass down there at the very edge, out of which a thin brown trickle emerged towards her; no sound of music, no waved flag. She had a longing to rush down to the barrier, but remembering the words of the porter, stayed where she was, with her hands tightly squeezed together. The trickle became a stream, a flood, the head of which began to reach her. With a turbulence of voices, sunburnt men, burdened up to the nose, passed, with rifles jutting at all angles; she strained her eyes, staring into that stream as one might into a walking wood, to isolate a single tree. Her head reeled with the strain of it, and the effort to catch his voice among the hubbub of all those cheery, common, happy-go-lucky sounds. Some who saw her clucked their tongues, some went by silent, others seemed to scan her as though she might be what they were looking for. And ever the stream and the hubbub melted into the train, and yet came pouring on. And still she waited motionless, with an awful fear. How could he ever find her, or she him? Then she saw that others of those waiting had found their men. And the longing to rush up and down the platform almost overcame her; but still she waited. And suddenly she saw him with two other officer boys, close to the carriages, coming slowly down towards her. She stood with her eyes fixed on his face; they passed, and she nearly cried out. Then he turned, broke away from the other two, and came straight to her. He had seen her before she had seen him. He was very flushed, had a little fixed frown between his blue eyes and a set jaw. They stood looking at each other, their hands hard gripped; all the emotion of last night welling up within them, so that to speak would have been to break down. The milk-cans formed a kind of shelter, and they stood so close together that none could see their faces. Noel was the first to master her power of speech; her words came out, dainty as ever, through trembling lips:

"Write to me as much as ever you can, Cyril. I'm going to be a nurse at once. And the first leave you get, I shall come to you—don't forget."

"Forget! Move a little back, darling; they can't see us here. Kiss me!" She moved back, thrust her face forward so that he need not stoop, and put her lips up to his. Then, feeling that she might swoon and fall over among the cans, she withdrew her mouth, leaving her forehead against his lips. He murmured:

"Was it all right when you got in last night?"

"Yes; I said good-bye for you."

"Oh! Noel—I've been afraid—I oughtn't—I oughtn't—"

"Yes, yes; nothing can take you from me now."

"You have got pluck. More than!"

Along whistle sounded. Morland grasped her hands convulsively:

"Good-bye, my little wife! Don't fret. Goodbye! I must go. God bless you, Noel!"

"I love you."

They looked at each other, just another moment, then she took her hands from his and stood back in the shadow of the milk-cans, rigid, following him with her eyes till he was lost in the train.

Every carriage window was full of those brown figures and red-brown faces, hands were waving vaguely, voices calling vaguely, here and there one cheered; someone leaning far out started to sing: "If auld acquaintance—" But Noel stood quite still in the shadow of the milk-cans, her lips drawn in, her hands hard clenched in front of her; and young Morland at his window gazed back at her.

2

How she came to be sitting in Trafalgar Square she did not know. Tears had formed a mist between her and all that seething, summer-evening crowd. Her eyes mechanically followed the wandering search-lights, those new milky ways, quartering the heavens and leading nowhere. All was wonderfully beautiful, the sky a deep dark blue, the moonlight whitening the spire of St. Martin's, and everywhere endowing the great blacked-out buildings with dream-life. Even the lions had come to life, and stared out over this moonlit desert of little human figures too small to be worth the stretching out of a paw. She sat there, aching dreadfully, as if the longing of every bereaved heart in all the town had settled in her. She felt it tonight a thousand times worse; for last night she had been drugged on the new sensation of love triumphantly fulfilled. Now she felt as if life had placed her in the corner of a huge silent room, blown out the flame of joy, and locked the door. A little dry sob came from her. The hay-fields and Cyril, with shirt unbuttoned at the neck, pitching hay and gazing at her while she dabbled her fork in the thin leavings. The bright river, and their boat grounded on the shallows, and the swallows flitting over them. And that long dance, with the feel of his hand between her shoulder-blades! Memories so sweet and sharp that she almost cried out. She saw again their dark grassy courtyard in the Abbey, and the white owl flying over them. The white owl! Flying there again to-night, with no lovers on the grass below! She could only picture Cyril now as a brown atom in that swirling brown flood of men, flowing to a huge brown sea. Those cruel minutes on the platform, when she had searched and searched the walking wood for her, one tree, seemed to have burned themselves into her eyes. Cyril was lost, she could not single him out, all blurred among those thousand other shapes. And suddenly she thought: 'And I—I'm lost to him; he's never seen me at home, never seen me in London; he won't be able to imagine me. It's all in the past, only the past—for both of us. Is there anybody so unhappy?' And the town's voices-wheels, and passing feet, whistles, talk, laughter—seemed to answer callously: 'Not one.' She looked at her wrist-watch; like his, it had luminous hands: 'Half-past ten' was greenishly imprinted there. She got up in dismay. They would think she was lost, or run over, or something silly! She could not find an empty taxi, and began to walk, uncertain of her way at night. At last she stopped a policeman, and said:

"Which is the way towards Bloomsbury, please? I can't find a taxi." The man looked at her, and took time to think it over; then he said:

"They're linin' up for the theatres," and looked at her again. Something seemed to move in his mechanism:

"I'm goin' that way, miss. If you like, you can step along with me." Noel stepped along.

"The streets aren't what they ought to be," the policeman said. "What with the darkness, and the war turning the girls heads—you'd be surprised the number of them that comes out. It's the soldiers, of course."

Noel felt her cheeks burning.

"I daresay you wouldn't have noticed it," the policeman went on: "but this war's a funny thing. The streets are gayer and more crowded at night than I've ever seen them; it's a fair picnic all the time. What we're goin' to settle down to when peace comes, I don't know. I suppose you find it quiet enough up your way, miss?"

"Yes," said Noel; "quite quiet."

"No soldiers up in Bloomsbury. You got anyone in the Army, miss?"

Noel nodded.

"Ah! It's anxious times for ladies. What with the Zeps, and their brothers and all in France, it's 'arassin'. I've lost a brother meself, and I've got a boy out there in the Garden of Eden; his mother carries on dreadful about him. What we shall think of it when it's all over, I can't tell. These Huns are a wicked tough lot!"

Noel looked at him; a tall man, regular and orderly, with one of those perfectly decent faces so often seen in the London police.

"I'm sorry you've lost someone," she said. "I haven't lost anyone very near, yet."

"Well, let's 'ope you won't, miss. These times make you feel for others, an' that's something. I've noticed a great change in folks you'd never think would feel for anyone. And yet I've seen some wicked things too; we do, in the police. Some of these English wives of aliens, and 'armless little German bakers, an' Austrians, and what-not: they get a crool time. It's their misfortune, not their fault, that's what I think; and the way they get served—well, it makes you ashamed o' bein' English sometimes—it does straight: And the women are the worst. I said to my wife only last night, I said: 'They call themselves Christians,' I said, 'but for all the charity that's in 'em they might as well be Huns.' She couldn't see it-not she! Well, why do they drop bombs?' she says. 'What!' I said, 'those English wives and bakers drop bombs? Don't be silly,' I said. 'They're as innocent as we.' It's the innocent that gets punished for the guilty. 'But they're all spies,' she says. 'Oh!' I said, 'old lady! Now really! At your time of life!' But there it is; you can't get a woman to see reason. It's readin' the papers. I often think they must be written by women—beggin' your pardon, miss—but reely, the 'ysterics and the 'atred—they're a fair knockout. D'you find much hatred in your household, miss?"

Noel shook her head. "No; my father's a clergyman, you see."

"Ah!" said the policeman. And in the glance he bestowed on her could be seen an added respect.

"Of course," he went on, "you're bound to have a sense of justice against these Huns; some of their ways of goin' on have been above the limit. But what I always think is—of course I don't say these things—no use to make yourself unpopular—but to meself I often think: Take 'em man for man, and you'd find 'em much the same as we are, I daresay. It's the vicious way they're brought up, of actin' in the mass, that's made 'em such a crool lot. I see a good bit of crowds in my profession, and I've a very low opinion of them. Crowds are the most blunderin' blighted things that ever was. They're like an angry woman with a bandage over her eyes, an' you can't have anything more dangerous than that. These Germans, it seems, are always in a crowd. They get a state o' mind read out to them by Bill Kaser and all that bloody-minded lot, an' they never stop to think for themselves."

"I suppose they'd be shot if they did," said Noel.

"Well, there is that," said the policeman reflectively. "They've brought discipline to an 'igh pitch, no doubt. An' if you ask me,"—he lowered his voice till it was almost lost in his chin-strap, "we'll be runnin' 'em a good second 'ere, before long. The things we 'ave to protect now are gettin' beyond a joke. There's the City against lights, there's the streets against darkness, there's the aliens, there's the aliens' shops, there's the Belgians, there's the British wives, there's the soldiers against the women, there's the women against the soldiers, there's the Peace Party, there's 'orses against croolty, there's a Cabinet Minister every now an' then; and now we've got these Conchies. And, mind you, they haven't raised our pay; no war wages in the police. So far as I can see, there's only one good result of the war—the burglaries are off. But there again, you wait a bit and see if we don't have a prize crop of 'm, or my name's not 'Arris."

"You must have an awfully exciting life!" said Noel.

The policeman looked down at her sideways, without lowering his face, as only a policeman can, and said indulgently:

"We're used to it, you see; there's no excitement in what you're used to. They find that in the trenches, I'm told. Take our seamen—there's lots of 'em been blown up over and over again, and there they go and sign on again next day. That's where the Germans make their mistake! England in war-time! I think a lot, you know, on my go; you can't 'elp it—the mind will work—an' the more I think, the more I see the fightin' spirit in the people. We don't make a fuss about it like Bill Kaser. But you watch a little shopman, one o' those fellows who's had his house bombed; you watch the way he looks at the mess—sort of disgusted. You watch his face, and you see he's got his teeth into it. You watch one of our Tommies on 'is crutches, with the sweat pourin' off his forehead an' 'is eyes all strainy, stumpin' along—that gives you an idea! I pity these Peace fellows, reely I pity them; they don't know what they're up against. I expect there's times when you wish you was a man, don't you, miss? I'm sure there's times when I feel I'd like to go in the trenches. That's the worst o' my job; you can't be a human bein'—not in the full sense of the word. You mustn't let your passions rise, you mustn't drink, you mustn't talk; it's a narrow walk o' life. Well, here you are, miss; your Square's the next turnin' to the right. Good night and thank you for your conversation."

Noel held out her hand. "Good night!" she said.

The policeman took her hand with a queer, flattered embarrassment.

"Good night, miss," he said again. "I see you've got a trouble; and I'm sure I hope it'll turn out for the best."

Noel gave his huge hand a squeeze; her eyes had filled with tears, and she turned quickly up towards the Square, where a dark figure was coming towards her, in whom she recognised her father. His face was worn and harassed; he walked irresolutely, like a man who has lost something.

"Nollie!" he said. "Thank God!" In his voice was an infinite relief. "My child, where have you been?"

"It's all right, Daddy. Cyril has just gone to the front. I've been seeing him off from Charing Cross."

Pierson slipped his arm round her. They entered the house without speaking....

3

By the rail of his transport, as far—about two feet—as he could get from anyone, Cyril Morland stood watching Calais, a dream city, brighten out of the heat and grow solid. He could hear the guns already, the voice of his new life-talking in the distance. It came with its strange excitement into a being held by soft and marvellous memories, by one long vision of Noel and the moonlit grass, under the dark Abbey wall. This moment of passage from wonder to wonder was quite too much for a boy unused to introspection, and he stood staring stupidly at Calais, while the thunder of his new life came rolling in on that passionate moonlit dream.

CHAPTER VII

After the emotions of those last three days Pierson woke with the feeling a ship must have when it makes landfall. Such reliefs are natural, and as a rule delusive; for events are as much the parents of the future as they were the children of the past. To be at home with both his girls, and resting—for his holiday would not be over for ten days—was like old times. Now George was going on so well Gratian would be herself again; now Cyril Morland was gone Noel would lose that sudden youthful love fever. Perhaps in two or three days if George continued to progress, one might go off with Noel somewhere for one's last week. In the meantime the old house, wherein was gathered so much remembrance of happiness and pain, was just as restful as anywhere else, and the companionship of his girls would be as sweet as on any of their past rambling holidays in Wales or Ireland. And that first morning of perfect idleness—for no one knew he was back in London—pottering, and playing the piano in the homely drawing-room where nothing to speak of was changed since his wife's day, was very pleasant. He had not yet seen the girls, for Noel did not come down to breakfast, and Gratian was with George.

Discovery that there was still a barrier between him and them came but slowly in the next two days. He would not acknowledge it, yet it was there, in their voices, in their movements—rather an absence of something old than the presence of something new. It was as if each had said to him: "We love you, but you are not in our secrets—and you must not be, for you would try to destroy them." They showed no fear of him, but seemed to be pushing him unconsciously away, lest he should restrain or alter what was very dear to them. They were both fond of him, but their natures had set foot on definitely diverging paths. The closer the affection, the more watchful they were against interference by that affection. Noel had a look on her face, half dazed, half proud, which touched, yet vexed him. What had he done to forfeit her confidence—surely she must see how natural and right his opposition had been! He made one great effort to show the real sympathy he felt for her. But she only said: "I can't talk of Cyril, Daddy; I simply can't!" And he, who easily shrank into his shell, could not but acquiesce in her reserve.

With Gratian it was different. He knew that an encounter was before him; a struggle between him and her husband—for characteristically he set the change in her, the defection of her faith, down to George, not to spontaneous thought and feeling in herself. He dreaded and yet looked forward to this encounter. It came on the third day, when Laird was up, lying on that very sofa where Pierson had sat listening to Gratian's confession of disbelief. Except for putting in his head to say good morning, he had not yet seen his son-in-law: The young doctor could not look fragile, the build of his face, with that law and those heavy cheekbones was too much against it, but there was about him enough of the look of having come through a hard fight to give Pierson's heart a squeeze.

"Well, George," he said, "you gave us a dreadful fright! I thank God's mercy." With that half-mechanical phrase he had flung an unconscious challenge. Laird looked up whimsically.

"So you really think God merciful, sir?"

"Don't let us argue, George; you're not strong enough."

"Oh! I'm pining for something to bite on."

Pierson looked at Gratian, and said softly:

"God's mercy is infinite, and you know it is."

Laird also looked at Gratian, before he answered:

"God's mercy is surely the amount of mercy man has succeeded in arriving at. How much that is, this war tells you, sir."

Pierson flushed. "I don't follow you," he said painfully. "How can you say such things, when you yourself are only just—No; I refuse to argue, George; I refuse."

Laird stretched out his hand to his wife, who came to him, and stood clasping it with her own. "Well, I'm going to argue," he said; "I'm simply bursting with it. I challenge you, sir, to show me where there's any sign of altruistic pity, except in man. Mother love doesn't count—mother and child are too much one."

The curious smile had come already, on both their faces.

"My dear George, is not man the highest work of God, and mercy the highest quality in man?"

"Not a bit. If geological time be taken as twenty-four hours, man's existence on earth so far equals just two seconds of it; after a few more seconds, when man has been frozen off the earth, geological time will stretch for as long again, before the earth bumps into something, and becomes nebula once more. God's hands haven't been particularly full, sir, have they—two seconds out of twenty-four hours—if man is His pet concern? And as to mercy being the highest quality in, man, that's only a modern fashion of talking. Man's highest quality is the sense of proportion, for that's what keeps him alive; and mercy, logically pursued, would kill him off. It's a sort of a luxury or by-product."

"George! You can have no music in your soul! Science is such a little thing, if you could only see."

"Show me a bigger, sir."

"Faith."

"In what?"

"In what has been revealed to us."

"Ah! There it is again! By whom—how?

"By God Himself—through our Lord."

A faint flush rose in Laird's yellow face, and his eyes brightened.

"Christ," he said; "if He existed, which some people, as you know, doubt, was a very beautiful character; there have been others. But to ask us to believe in His supernaturalness or divinity at this time of day is to ask us to walk through the world blindfold. And that's what you do, don't you?"

Again Pierson looked at his daughter's face. She was standing quite still, with her eyes fixed on her husband. Somehow he was aware that all these words of the sick man's were for her benefit. Anger, and a sort of despair rose within him, and he said painfully:

"I cannot explain. There are things that I can't make clear, because you are wilfully blind to all that I believe in. For what do you imagine we are fighting this great war, if it is not to reestablish the belief in love as the guiding principle of life?"

Laird shook his head. "We are fighting to redress a balance, which was in danger of being lost."

"The balance of power?"

"Heavens!—no! The balance of philosophy."

Pierson smiled. "That sounds very clever, George; but again, I don't follow you."

"The balance between the sayings: 'Might is Right,' and 'Right is Might.' They're both half-truth, but the first was beating the other out of the field. All the rest of it is cant, you know. And by the way, sir, your

Church is solid for punishment of the evildoer. Where's mercy there? Either its God is not merciful, or else it doesn't believe in its God."

"Just punishment does not preclude mercy, George."

"It does in Nature."

"Ah! Nature, George—always Nature. God transcends Nature."

"Then why does He give it a free rein? A man too fond of drink, or women—how much mercy does he get from Nature? His overindulgence brings its exact equivalent of penalty; let him pray to God as much as he likes—unless he alters his ways he gets no mercy. If he does alter his ways, he gets no mercy either; he just gets Nature's due reward. We English who have neglected brain and education—how much mercy are we getting in this war? Mercy's a man-made ornament, disease, or luxury—call it what you will. Except that, I've nothing to say against it. On the contrary, I am all for it."

Once more Pierson looked at his daughter. Something in her face hurt him—the silent intensity with which she was hanging on her husband's words, the eager search of her eyes. And he turned to the door, saying:

"This is bad for you, George."

He saw Gratian put her hand on her husband's forehead, and thought—jealously: 'How can I save my poor girl from this infidelity? Are my twenty years of care to go for nothing, against this modern spirit?'

Down in his study, the words went through his mind: "Holy, holy, holy, Merciful and Mighty!" And going to the little piano in the corner, he opened it, and began playing the hymn. He played it softly on the shabby keys of this thirty-year old friend, which had been with him since College days; and sang it softly in his worn voice.

A sound made him look up. Gratian had come in. She put her hand on his shoulder, and said:

"I know it hurts you, Dad. But we've got to find out for ourselves, haven't we? All the time you and George were talking, I felt that you didn't see that it's I who've changed. It's not what he thinks, but what I've come to think of my own accord. I wish you'd understand that I've got a mind of my own, Dad."

Pierson looked up with amazement.

"Of course you have a mind."

Gratian shook her head. "No, you thought my mind was yours; and now you think it's George's. But it's my own. When you were my age weren't you trying hard to find the truth yourself, and differing from your father?"

Pierson did not answer. He could not remember. It was like stirring a stick amongst a drift of last year's leaves, to awaken but a dry rustling, a vague sense of unsubstantiality. Searched? No doubt he had searched, but the process had brought him nothing. Knowledge was all smoke! Emotional faith alone was truth—reality!

"Ah, Gracie!" he said, "search if you must, but where will you find bottom? The well is too deep for us. You will come back to God, my child, when you're tired out; the only rest is there."

"I don't want to rest. Some people search all their lives, and die searching. Why shouldn't I.

"You will be most unhappy, my child."

"If I'm unhappy, Dad, it'll be because the world's unhappy. I don't believe it ought to be; I think it only is, because it shuts its eyes."

Pierson got up. "You think I shut my eyes?"

Gratian nodded.

"If I do, it is because there is no other way to happiness."

"Are you happy; Dad?"

"As happy as my nature will let me be. I miss your mother. If I lose you and Noel—"

"Oh, but we won't let you!"

Pierson smiled. "My dear," he said, "I think I have!"

CHAPTER VIII

1

Some wag, with a bit of chalk, had written the word "Peace" on three successive doors of a little street opposite Buckingham Palace.

It caught the eye of Jimmy Fort, limping home to his rooms from a very late discussion at his Club, and twisted his lean shaven lips into a sort of smile. He was one of those rolling-stone Englishmen, whose early lives are spent in all parts of the world, and in all kinds of physical conflict—a man like a hickory stick, tall, thin, bolt-upright, knotty, hard as nails, with a curved fighting back to his head and a straight fighting front to his brown face. His was the type which becomes, in a generation or so, typically Colonial or American; but no one could possibly have taken Jimmy Fort for anything but an Englishman. Though he was nearly forty, there was still something of the boy in his face, something frank and curly-headed, gallant and full of steam, and his small steady grey eyes looked out on life with a sort of combative humour. He was still in uniform, though they had given him up as a bad job after keeping him nine months trying to mend a wounded leg which would never be sound again; and he was now in the War Office in connection with horses, about which he knew. He did not like it, having lived too long with all sorts and conditions of men who were neither English nor official, a combination which he found trying.

His life indeed, just now, bored him to distraction, and he would ten times rather have been back in France. This was why he found the word "Peace" so exceptionally tantalising.

Reaching his rooms, he threw off his tunic, to whose stiff regularity he still had a rooted aversion; and, pulling out a pipe, filled it and sat down at his window.

Moonshine could not cool the hot town, and it seemed sleeping badly—the seven million sleepers in their million homes. Sound lingered on, never quite ceased; the stale odours clung in the narrow street below, though a little wind was creeping about to sweeten the air. 'Curse the war!' he thought. 'What wouldn't I give to be sleeping out, instead of in this damned city!' They who slept in the open, neglecting morality, would certainly have the best of it tonight, for no more dew was falling than fell into Jimmy Fort's heart to cool the fret of that ceaseless thought: 'The war! The cursed war!' In the unending rows of little grey houses, in huge caravanserais, and the mansions of the great, in villas, and high slum tenements; in the government offices, and factories, and railway stations where they worked all night; in the long hospitals where they lay in rows; in the camp prisons of the interned; in bar racks, work-houses, palaces—no head, sleeping or waking, would be free of that thought: 'The cursed war!' A spire caught his eye, rising ghostly over the roofs. Ah! churches alone, void of the human soul, would be unconscious! But for the rest, even sleep would not free them! Here a mother would be whispering the name of her boy; there a merchant would snore and dream he was drowning, weighted with gold; and a wife would be turning to stretch out her arms to-no one; and a wounded soldier wake out of a dream trench with sweat on his brow; and a newsvendor in his garret mutter hoarsely. By thousands the bereaved would be tossing, stifling their moans; by thousands the ruined would be gazing into the dark future; and housewives struggling with sums; and soldiers sleeping like logs—for to morrow they died; and children dreaming of them; and prostitutes lying in stale wonder at the busyness of their lives; and journalists sleeping the sleep of the just. And over them all, in the moonlight that thought 'The cursed war!' flapped its black wings, like an old crow! "If Christ were real," he mused, "He'd reach that moon down, and go chalking 'Peace' with it on every door of every house, all over Europe. But Christ's not real, and Hindenburg and Harmsworth are!" As real they were as two great bulls he had once seen in South Africa, fighting. He seemed to hear again the stamp and snort and crash of those thick skulls, to see the beasts recoiling and driving at each other, and the little red eyes of them. And pulling a letter out of his pocket, he read it again by the light of the moon:

"15, Camelot Mansions,

"St. John's Wood.

"DEAR MR. FORT, "I came across your Club address to-night, looking at some old letters. Did you know that I was in London? I left Steenbok when my husband died, five years ago. I've had a simply terrific time since. While the German South West campaign was on I was nursing out there, but came back about a year ago to lend a hand here. It would be awfully nice to meet you again, if by any chance you are in England. I'm working in a V. A. D. hospital in these parts, but my evenings are usually free. Do you remember that moonlit night at grape harvest? The nights here aren't scented quite like that. Listerine! Oh! This war! "With all good remembrances,

"LEILA LYNCH."

A terrific time! If he did not mistake, Leila Lynch had always had a terrific time. And he smiled, seeing again the stoep of an old Dutch house at High Constantia, and a woman sitting there under the white flowers of a sweet-scented creeper—a pretty woman, with eyes which could put a spell on you, a woman he would have got entangled with if he had not cut and run for it! Ten years ago, and here she was again, refreshing him out of the past. He sniffed the fragrance of the little letter. How everybody always managed to work into a letter what they were doing in the war! If he answered her he would be sure to say: "Since I got lamed, I've been at the War Office, working on remounts, and a dull job it is!" Leila Lynch! Women didn't get younger, and he suspected her of being older than himself. But he remembered agreeably her white shoulders and that turn of her neck when she looked at you with those big grey eyes of hers. Only a five-day acquaintanceship, but they had crowded much into it as one did in a strange land. The episode had been a green and dangerous spot, like one of those bright mossy bits of bog when you were snipe-shooting, to set foot on which was to let you down up to the neck, at least. Well, there was none of that danger now, for her husband was dead-poor chap! It would be nice, in these dismal days, when nobody spent any time whatever except in the service of the country, to improve his powers of service by a few hours' recreation in her society. 'What humbugs we are!' he thought: 'To read the newspapers and the speeches you'd believe everybody thought of nothing but how to get killed for the sake of the future. Drunk on verbiage! What heads and mouths we shall all have when we wake up some fine morning with Peace shining in at the window! Ah! If only we could; and enjoy ourselves again!' And he gazed at the moon. She was dipping already, reeling away into the dawn. Water carts and street sweepers had come out into the glimmer; sparrows twittered in the eaves. The city was raising a strange unknown face to the grey light, shuttered and deserted as Babylon. Jimmy Fort tapped out his pipe, sighed, and got into bed.

2

Coming off duty at that very moment, Leila Lynch decided to have her hour's walk before she went home. She was in charge of two wards, and as a rule took the day watches; but some slight upset had given her this extra spell. She was, therefore, at her worst, or perhaps at her best, after eighteen hours in hospital. Her cheeks were pale, and about her eyes were little lines, normally in hiding. There was in this face a puzzling blend of the soft and hard, for the eyes, the rather full lips, and pale cheeks, were naturally soft; but they were hardened by the self-containment which grows on women who have to face life for themselves, and, conscious of beauty, intent to keep it, in spite of age. Her figure was contradictory, also; its soft modelling a little too rigidified by stays. In this desert of the dawn she let her long blue overcoat flap loose, and swung her hat on a finger, so that her light-brown, touched-up hair took the morning breeze with fluffy freedom. Though she could not see herself, she appreciated her appearance, swaying along like that, past lonely trees and houses. A pity there was no one to see her in that round of Regent's Park, which took her the best part of an hour, walking in meditation, enjoying the colour coming back into the world, as if especially for her.

There was character in Leila Lynch, and she had lived an interesting life from a certain point of view. In her girlhood she had fluttered the hearts of many besides Cousin Edward Pierson, and at eighteen had made a passionate love match with a good-looking young Indian civilian, named Fane. They had loved each other to a standstill in twelve months. Then had begun five years of petulance, boredom, and growing cynicism, with increasing spells of Simla, and voyages home for her health which was really harmed by the heat. All had culminated, of course, in another passion for a rifleman called Lynch. Divorce had followed, remarriage, and then the Boer War, in which he had been badly wounded. She had gone out and nursed him back to half his robust health, and, at twenty-eight, taken up life with him on an up-country farm in Cape Colony. This middle period had lasted ten years, between the lonely farm and an old Dutch house at High Constantia. Lynch was not a bad fellow, but, like most soldiers of the old

Army, had been quite carefully divested of an aesthetic sense. And it was Leila's misfortune to have moments when aesthetic sense seemed necessary. She had struggled to overcome this weakness, and that other weakness of hers—a liking for men's admiration; but there had certainly been intervals when she had not properly succeeded. Her acquaintance with Jimmy Fort had occurred during one of these intervals, and when he went back to England so abruptly, she had been feeling very tenderly towards him. She still remembered him with a certain pleasure. Before Lynch died, these "intervals" had been interrupted by a spell of returning warmth for the invalided man to whom she had joined her life under the romantic conditions of divorce. He had failed, of course, as a farmer, and his death left her with nothing but her own settled income of a hundred and fifty pounds a year. Faced by the prospect of having almost to make her living, at thirty-eight, she felt but momentary dismay—for she had real pluck. Like many who have played with amateur theatricals, she fancied herself as an actress; but, after much effort, found that only her voice and the perfect preservation of her legs were appreciated by the discerning managers and public of South Africa; and for three chequered years she made face against fortune with the help of them, under an assumed name. What she did—keeping a certain bloom of refinement, was far better than the achievements of many more respectable ladies in her shoes. At least she never bemoaned her "reduced circumstances," and if her life was irregular and had at least three episodes, it was very human. She bravely took the rough with the smooth, never lost the power of enjoying herself, and grew in sympathy with the hardships of others. But she became deadly tired. When the war broke out, remembering that she was a good nurse, she took her real name again and a change of occupation. For one who liked to please men, and to be pleased by them, there was a certain attraction about that life in war-time; and after two years of it she could still appreciate the way her Tommies turned their heads to look at her when she passed their beds. But in a hard school she had learned perfect self-control; and though the sour and puritanical perceived her attraction, they knew her to be forty-three. Besides, the soldiers liked her; and there was little trouble in her wards. The war moved her in simple ways; for she was patriotic in the direct fashion of her class. Her father had been a sailor, her husbands an official and a soldier; the issue for her was uncomplicated by any abstract meditation. The Country before everything! And though she had tended during those two years so many young wrecked bodies, she had taken it as all in the a day's work, lavishing her sympathy on the individual, without much general sense of pity and waste. Yes, she had worked really hard, had "done her bit"; but of late she had felt rising within her the old vague craving for "life," for pleasure, for something more than the mere negative admiration bestowed on her by her "Tommies." Those old letters—to look them through them had been a sure sign of this vague craving—had sharpened to poignancy the feeling that life was slipping away from her while she was still comely. She had been long out of England, and so hard-worked since she came back that there were not many threads she could pick up suddenly. Two letters out of that little budget of the past, with a far cry between them, had awakened within her certain sentimental longings.

"DEAR LADY OF THE STARRY FLOWERS,

"Exiturus (sic) to saluto! The tender carries you this message of good-bye. Simply speaking, I hate leaving South Africa. And of all my memories, the last will live the longest. Grape harvest at Constantia, and you singing: 'If I could be the falling dew: If ever you and your husband come to England, do let me know, that I may try and repay a little the happiest five days I've spent out here.

"Your very faithful servant,

"TIMMY FORT."

She remembered a very brown face, a tall slim figure, and something gallant about the whole of him. What was he like after ten years? Grizzled, married, with a large family? An odious thing—Time! And Cousin Edward's little yellow letter.

Good heavens! Twenty-six years ago—before he was a parson, or married or anything! Such a good partner, really musical; a queer, dear fellow, devoted, absentminded, easily shocked, yet with flame burning in him somewhere.

'DEAR LEILA,

"After our last dance I went straight off'—I couldn't go in. I went down to the river, and walked along the bank; it was beautiful, all grey and hazy, and the trees whispered, and the cows looked holy; and I walked along and thought of you. And a farmer took me for a lunatic, in my dress clothes. Dear Leila, you were so pretty last night, and I did love our dances. I hope you are not tired, and that I shall see you soon again:

"Your affectionate cousin,

"EDWARD PIERSON."

And then he had gone and become a parson, and married, and been a widower fifteen years. She remembered the death of his wife, just before she left for South Africa, at that period of disgrace when she had so shocked her family by her divorce. Poor Edward—quite the nicest of her cousins! The only one she would care to see again. He would be very old and terribly good and proper, by now.

Her wheel of Regent's Park was coming full circle, and the sun was up behind the houses, but still no sound of traffic stirred. She stopped before a flower-bed where was some heliotrope, and took a long, luxurious sniff: She could not resist plucking a sprig, too, and holding it to her nose. A sudden want of love had run through every nerve and fibre of her; she shivered, standing there with her eyes half closed, above the pale violet blossom. Then, noting by her wrist-watch that it was four o'clock, she hurried on, to get to her bed, for she would have to be on duty again at noon. Oh! the war! She was tired! If only it were over, and one could live!...

Somewhere by Twickenham the moon had floated down; somewhere up from Kentish Town the sun came soaring; wheels rolled again, and the seven million sleepers in their million houses woke from morning sleep to that same thought....

CHAPTER IX

Edward Pierson, dreaming over an egg at breakfast, opened a letter in a handwriting which he did not recognise.

"V. A. D. Hospital,

"Mulberry Road, St. John's Wood N. W.

"DEAR COUSIN EDWARD,

"Do you remember me, or have I gone too far into the shades of night? I was Leila Pierson once upon a time, and I often think of you and wonder what you are like now, and what your girls are like. I have been here nearly a year, working for our wounded, and for a year before that was nursing in South Africa. My husband died five years ago out there. Though we haven't met for I dare not think how long, I should awfully like to see you again. Would you care to come some day and look over my hospital? I have two wards under me; our men are rather dears.

"Your forgotten but still affectionate cousin

"LEILA LYNCH."

"P. S. I came across a little letter you once wrote me; it brought back old days."

No! He had not forgotten. There was a reminder in the house. And he looked up at Noel sitting opposite. How like the eyes were! And he thought: 'I wonder what Leila has become. One mustn't be uncharitable. That man is dead; she has been nursing two years. She must be greatly changed; I should certainly like to see her. I will go!' Again he looked at Noel. Only yesterday she had renewed her request to be allowed to begin her training as a nurse.

"I'm going to see a hospital to-day, Nollie," he said; "if you like, I'll make enquiries. I'm afraid it'll mean you have to begin by washing up."

"I know; anything, so long as I do begin."

"Very well; I'll see about it." And he went back to his egg.

Noel's voice roused him. "Do you feel the war much, Daddy? Does it hurt you here?" She had put her hand on her heart. "Perhaps it doesn't, because you live half in the next world, don't you?"

The words: "God forbid," sprang to Pierson's lips; he did not speak them, but put his egg-spoon down, hurt and bewildered. What did the child mean? Not feel the war! He smiled.

"I hope I'm able to help people sometimes, Nollie," and was conscious that he had answered his own thoughts, not her words. He finished his breakfast quickly, and very soon went out. He crossed the Square, and passed East, down two crowded streets to his church. In the traffic of those streets, all slipshod and confused, his black-clothed figure and grave face, with its Vandyk beard, had a curious remote appearance, like a moving remnant of a past civilisation. He went in by the side door. Only five days he had been away, but they had been so full of emotion that the empty familiar building seemed almost strange to him. He had come there unconsciously, groping for anchorage and guidance in this sudden change of relationship between him and his daughters. He stood by the pale brazen eagle, staring into the chancel. The choir were wanting new hymn-books—he must not forget to order them! His eyes sought the stained-glass window he had put in to the memory of his wife. The sun, too high to slant, was burnishing its base, till it glowed of a deep sherry colour. "In the next world!" What strange words of Noel's! His eyes caught the glimmer of the organ-pipes; and, mounting to the loft, he began to play soft chords wandering into each other. He finished, and stood gazing down. This space within high walls, under high vaulted roof, where light was toned to a perpetual twilight, broken here and there by a little glow of colour from glass and flowers, metal, and dark wood, was his home, his charge, his refuge. Nothing moved down there, and yet—was not emptiness mysteriously living, the closed-in air imprinted in strange sort, as though the drone of music and voices in prayer and praise clung there still? Had not sanctity a presence? Outside, a barrel-organ drove its tune along; a wagon staggered on the paved street, and the driver shouted to his horses; some distant guns boomed out in practice, and the rolling of wheels on wheels formed a net of sound. But those invading noises were transmuted to a mere murmuring in here; only the silence and the twilight were real to Pierson, standing there, a little black figure in a great empty space.

When he left the church, it was still rather early to go to Leila's hospital; and, having ordered the new hymn-books, he called in at the house of a parishioner whose son had been killed in France. He found her in her kitchen; an oldish woman who lived by charing. She wiped a seat for the Vicar.

"I was just makin' meself a cup o' tea, sir."

"Ah! What a comfort tea is, Mrs. Soles!" And he sat down, so that she should feel "at home."

"Yes; it gives me 'eart-burn; I take eight or ten cups a day, now. I take 'em strong, too. I don't seem able to get on without it. I 'ope the young ladies are well, sir?"

"Very well, thank you. Miss Noel is going to begin nursing, too."

"Deary-me! She's very young; but all the young gells are doin' something these days. I've got a niece in munitions-makin' a pretty penny she is. I've been meanin' to tell you—I don't come to church now; since my son was killed, I don't seem to 'ave the 'eart to go anywhere—'aven't been to a picture-palace these three months. Any excitement starts me cryin'."

"I know; but you'd find rest in church."

Mrs. Soles shook her head, and the small twisted bob of her discoloured hair wobbled vaguely.

"I can't take any recreation," she said. "I'd rather sit 'ere, or be at work. My son was a real son to me. This tea's the only thing that does me any good. I can make you a fresh cup in a minute."

"Thank you, Mrs. Soles, but I must be getting on. We must all look forward to meeting our beloved again, in God's mercy. And one of these days soon I shall be seeing you in church, shan't I."

Mrs. Soles shifted her weight from one slippered foot to the other.

"Well! let's 'ope so," she said. "But I dunno when I shall 'ave the spirit. Good day, sir, and thank you kindly for calling, I'm sure."

Pierson walked away with a very faint smile. Poor queer old soul!—she was no older than himself, but he thought of her as ancient—cut off from her son, like so many—so many; and how good and patient! The melody of an anthem began running in his head. His fingers moved on the air beside him, and he stood still, waiting for an omnibus to take him to St. John's Wood. A thousand people went by while he was waiting, but he did not notice them, thinking of that anthem, of his daughters, and the mercy of God; and on the top of his 'bus, when it came along, he looked lonely and apart, though the man beside him was so fat that there was hardly any seat left to sit on. Getting down at Lord's Cricket-ground, he asked his way of a lady in a nurse's dress.

"If you'll come with me," she said, "I'm just going there."

"Oh! Do you happen to know a Mrs. Lynch who nurses"

"I am Mrs. Lynch. Why, you're Edward Pierson!"

He looked into her face, which he had not yet observed.

"Leila!" he said.

"Yes, Leila! How awfully nice of you to come, Edward!"

They continued to stand, searching each for the other's youth, till she murmured:

"In spite of your beard, I should have known you anywhere!" But she thought: 'Poor Edward! He is old, and monk-like!'

And Pierson, in answer, murmured:

"You're very little changed, Leila! We haven't, seen each other since my youngest girl was born. She's just a little like you." But he thought: 'My Nollie! So much more dewy; poor Leila!'

They walked on, talking of his daughters, till they reached the hospital.

"If you'll wait here a minute, I'll take you over my wards."

She had left him in a bare hall, holding his hat in one hand and touching his gold cross with the other; but she soon came hack, and a little warmth crept about his heart. How works of mercy suited women! She looked so different, so much softer, beneath the white coif, with a white apron over the bluish frock.

At the change in his face, a little warmth crept about Leila, too, just where the bib of her apron stopped; and her eyes slid round at him while they went towards what had once been a billiard-room.

"My men are dears," she said; "they love to be talked to."

Under a skylight six beds jutted out from a green distempered wall, opposite to six beds jutting out from another green distempered wall, and from each bed a face was turned towards them young faces, with but little expression in them. A nurse, at the far end, looked round, and went on with her work. The sight of the ward was no more new to Pierson than to anyone else in these days. It was so familiar, indeed, that it had practically no significance. He stood by the first bed, and Leila stood alongside. The man smiled up when she spoke, and did not smile when he spoke, and that again was familiar to him. They passed from bed to bed, with exactly the same result, till she was called away, and he sat down by a young soldier with a long, very narrow head and face, and a heavily bandaged shoulder. Touching the bandage reverently, Pierson said:

"Well, my dear fellow-still bad?"

"Ah!" replied the soldier. "Shrapnel wound: It's cut the flesh properly."

"But not the spirit, I can see!"

The young soldier gave him a quaint look, as much as to say: "Not 'arf bad!" and a gramophone close to the last bed began to play: "God bless Daddy at the war!"

"Are you fond of music?"

"I like it well enough. Passes the time."

"I'm afraid the time hangs heavy in hospital."

"Yes; it hangs a bit 'eavy; it's just 'orspital life. I've been wounded before, you see. It's better than bein' out there. I expect I'll lose the proper use o' this arm. I don't worry; I'll get my discharge."

"You've got some good nurses here."

"Yes; I like Mrs. Lynch; she's the lady I like."

"My cousin."

"I see you come in together. I see everything 'ere. I think a lot, too. Passes the time."

"Do they let you smoke?"

"Oh, yes! They let us smoke."

"Have one of mine?"

The young soldier smiled for the first time. "Thank you; I've got plenty."

The nurse came by, and smiled at Pierson.

"He's one of our blase ones; been in before, haven't you, Simson?"

Pierson looked at the young man, whose long, narrow face; where one sandy-lashed eyelid drooped just a little, seemed armoured with a sort of limited omniscience. The gramophone had whirred and grunted into "Sidi Brahim." The nurse passed on.

"'Seedy Abram,'.rdquo; said the young soldier. "The Frenchies sing it; they takes it up one after the other, ye know."

"Ah!" murmured Pierson; "it's pretty." And his fingers drummed on the counterpane, for the tune was new to him. Something seemed to move in the young man's face, as if a blind had been drawn up a little.

"I don't mind France," he said abruptly; "I don't mind the shells and that; but I can't stick the mud. There's a lot o' wounded die in the mud; can't get up—smothered." His unwounded arm made a restless movement. "I was nearly smothered myself. Just managed to keep me nose up."

Pierson shuddered. "Thank God you did!"

"Yes; I didn't like that. I told Mrs. Lynch about that one day when I had the fever. She's a nice lady; she's seen a lot of us boys: That mud's not right, you know." And again his unwounded arm made that restless movement; while the gramophone struck up: "The boys in brown." The movement of the arm affected Pierson horribly; he rose and, touching the bandaged shoulder, said:

"Good-bye; I hope you'll soon be quite recovered."

The young soldier's lips twisted in the semblance of a smile; his drooped eyelid seemed to try and raise itself.

"Good day, sir," he said; "and thank you."

Pierson went back to the hall. The sunlight fell in a pool just inside the open door, and an uncontrollable impulse made him move into it, so that it warmed him up to the waist. The mud! How ugly life was! Life and Death! Both ugly! Poor boys! Poor boys!

A voice behind him said:

"Oh! There you are, Edward! Would you like to see the other ward, or shall I show you our kitchen?"

Pierson took her hand impulsively. "You're doing a noble work, Leila. I wanted to ask you: Could you arrange for Noel to come and get trained here? She wants to begin at once. The fact is, a boy she is attracted to has just gone out to the Front."

"Ah!" murmured Leila, and her eyes looked very soft. "Poor child! We shall be wanting an extra hand next week. I'll see if she could come now. I'll speak to our Matron, and let you know to-night." She squeezed his hand hard.

"Dear Edward, I'm so glad to see you again. You're the first of our family I've seen for sixteen years. I wonder if you'd bring Noel to have supper at my flat to-night—Just nothing to eat, you know! It's a tiny place. There's a Captain Fort coming; a nice man."

Pierson accepted, and as he walked away he thought: 'Dear Leila! I believe it was Providence. She wants sympathy. She wants to feel the past is the past. How good women are!'

And the sun, blazing suddenly out of a cloud, shone on his black figure and the little gold cross, in the middle of Portland Place.

Men, even if they are not artistic, who have been in strange places and known many nooks of the world, get the scenic habit, become open to pictorial sensation. It was as a picture or series of pictures that Jimmy Fort ever afterwards remembered his first supper at Leila's. He happened to have been all day in the open, motoring about to horse farms under a hot sun; and Leila's hock cup possessed a bland and subtle strength. The scenic sense derived therefrom had a certain poignancy, the more so because the tall child whom he met there did not drink it, and her father seemed but to wet his lips, so that Leila and he had all the rest. Rather a wonderful little scene it made in his mind, very warm, glowing, yet with a strange dark sharpness to it, which came perhaps from the black walls.

The flat had belonged to an artist who was at the war. It was but a pocket dwelling on the third floor. The two windows of the little square sitting-room looked out on some trees and a church. But Leila, who hated dining by daylight, had soon drawn curtains of a deep blue over them. The picture which Fort remembered was this: A little four-square table of dark wood, with a Chinese mat of vivid blue in the centre, whereon stood a silver lustre bowl of clove carnations; some greenish glasses with hock cup in them; on his left, Leila in a low lilac frock, her neck and shoulders very white, her face a little powdered, her eyes large, her lips smiling; opposite him a black-clothed padre with a little gold cross, over whose thin darkish face, with its grave pointed beard, passed little gentle smiles, but whose deep sunk grey eyes were burnt and bright; on his right, a girl in a high grey frock, almost white, just hollowed at the neck, with full sleeves to the elbow, so that her slim arms escaped; her short fair hair a little tumbled; her big grey eyes grave; her full lips shaping with a strange daintiness round every word—and they not many; brilliant red shades over golden lights dotting the black walls; a blue divan; a little black piano flush with the wall; a dark polished floor; four Japanese prints; a white ceiling. He was conscious that his own khaki spoiled something as curious and rare as some old Chinese tea-chest. He even remembered what they ate; lobster; cold pigeon pie; asparagus; St. Ivel cheese; raspberries and cream. He did not remember half so well what they talked of, except that he himself told them stories of the Boer War, in which he had served in the Yeomanry, and while he was telling them, the girl, like a child listening to a fairy-tale, never moved her eyes from his face. He remembered that after supper they all smoked cigarettes, even the tall child, after the padre had said to her mildly, "My dear!" and she had answered: "I simply must, Daddy, just one." He remembered Leila brewing Turkish coffee—very good, and how beautiful her white arms looked, hovering about the cups. He remembered her making the padre sit down at the piano, and play to them. And she and the girl on the divan together, side by side, a strange contrast; with just as strange a likeness to each other. He always remembered how fine and rare that music sounded in the little room, flooding him with a dreamy beatitude. Then—he remembered—Leila sang, the padre standing-by; and the tall child on the divan bending forward over her knees, with her chin on her hands. He remembered rather vividly how Leila turned her neck and looked up, now at the padre, now at himself; and, all through, the delightful sense of colour and warmth, a sort of glamour over all the evening; and the lingering pressure of Leila's hand when he said good-bye and they went away, for they all went together. He remembered talking a great deal to the padre in the cab, about the public school they had both been at, and thinking: 'It's a good padre—this!' He remembered how their taxi took them to an old Square which he did not know, where the garden trees looked densely black in the starshine. He remembered that a man outside the house had engaged the padre in earnest talk, while the tall child and himself stood in the open doorway, where the hall beyond was dark. Very exactly he remembered the little conversation which then took place between them, while they waited for her father.

"Is it very horrid in the trenches, Captain Fort?"

"Yes, Miss Pierson; it is very horrid, as a rule."

"Is it dangerous all the time?"

"Pretty well."

"Do officers run more risks than the men?"

"Not unless there's an attack."

"Are there attacks very often?"

It had seemed to him so strangely primitive a little catechism, that he had smiled. And, though it was so dark, she had seen that smile, for her face went proud and close all of a sudden. He had cursed himself, and said gently:

"Have you a brother out there?"

She shook her head.

"But someone?"

"Yes."

Someone! He had heard that answer with a little shock. This child—this fairy princess of a child already to have someone! He wondered if she went about asking everyone these questions, with that someone in her thoughts. Poor child! And quickly he said:

"After all, look at me! I was out there a year, and here I am with only half a game leg; times were a lot worse, then, too. I often wish I were back there. Anything's better than London and the War Office." But just then he saw the padre coming, and took her hand. "Good night, Miss Pierson. Don't worry. That does no good, and there isn't half the risk you think."

Her hand stirred, squeezed his gratefully, as a child's would squeeze.

"Good night," she murmured; "thank you awfully."

And, in the dark cab again, he remembered thinking: 'Fancy that child! A jolly lucky boy, out there! Too bad! Poor little fairy princess!'

PART II

CHAPTER I

To wash up is not an exciting operation. To wash up in August became for Noel a process which taxed her strength and enthusiasm. She combined it with other forms of instruction in the art of nursing, had very little leisure, and in the evenings at home would often fall asleep curled up in a large chintz-covered chair.

George and Gratian had long gone back to their respective hospitals, and she and her father had the house to themselves. She received many letters from Cyril which she carried about with her and read on her way to and from the hospital; and every other day she wrote to him. He was not yet in the firing line; his letters were descriptive of his men, his food, or the natives, or reminiscent of Kestrel; hers descriptive of washing up, or reminiscent of Kestrel. But in both there was always some little word of the longing within them.

It was towards the end of August when she had the letter which said that he had been moved up. From now on he would be in hourly danger! That evening after dinner she did not go to sleep in the chair, but sat under the open window, clenching her hands, and reading "Pride and Prejudice" without understanding a word. While she was so engaged her father came up and said:

"Captain Fort, Nollie. Will you give him some coffee? I'm afraid I must go out."

When he had gone, Noel looked at her visitor drinking his coffee. He had been out there, too, and he was alive; with only a little limp. The visitor smiled and said:

"What were you thinking about when we came in?"

"Only the war."

"Any news of him?"

Noel frowned, she hated to show her feelings.

"Yes! he's gone to the Front. Won't you have a cigarette?"

"Thanks. Will you?"

"I want one awfully. I think sitting still and waiting is more dreadful than anything in the world."

"Except, knowing that others are waiting. When I was out there I used to worry horribly over my mother. She was ill at the time. The cruelest thing in war is the anxiety of people about each other—nothing touches that."

The words exactly summed up Noel's hourly thought. He said nice things, this man with the long legs and the thin brown bumpy face!

"I wish I were a man," she said, "I think women have much the worst time in the war. Is your mother old?" But of course she was old why he was old himself!

"She died last Christmas."

"Oh! I'm so sorry!"

"You lost your mother when you were a babe, didn't you?"

"Yes. That's her portrait." At the end of the room, hanging on a strip of black velvet was a pastel, very faint in colouring, as though faded, of a young woman, with an eager, sweet face, dark eyes, and bent a little forward, as if questioning her painter. Fort went up to it.

"It's not a bit like you. But she must have been a very sweet woman."

"It's a sort of presence in the room. I wish I were like her!"

Fort turned. "No," he said; "no. Better as you are. It would only have spoiled a complete thing."

"She was good."

"And aren't you?"

"Oh! no. I get a devil."

"You! Why, you're out of a fairy-tale!"

"It comes from Daddy—only he doesn't know, because he's a perfect saint; but I know he's had a devil somewhere, or he couldn't be the saint he is."

"H'm!" said Fort. "That's very deep: and I believe it's true—the saints did have devils."

"Poor Daddy's devil has been dead ages. It's been starved out of him, I think."

"Does your devil ever get away with you?"

Noel felt her cheeks growing red under his stare, and she turned to the window:

"Yes. It's a real devil."

Vividly there had come before her the dark Abbey, and the moon balancing over the top of the crumbling wall, and the white owl flying across. And, speaking to the air, she said:

"It makes you do things that you want to do."

She wondered if he would laugh—it sounded so silly. But he did not.

"And damn the consequences? I know. It's rather a jolly thing to have."

Noel shook her head. "Here's Daddy coming back!"

Fort held out his hand.

"I won't stay. Good night; and don't worry too much, will you?"

He kept her hand rather a long time, and gave it a hard squeeze.

Don't worry! What advice! Ah! if she could see Cyril just for a minute!

2

In September, 1916, Saturday still came before Sunday, in spite of the war. For Edward Pierson this Saturday had been a strenuous day, and even now, at nearly midnight, he was still conning his just-completed sermon.

A patriot of patriots, he had often a passionate longing to resign his parish, and go like his curate for a chaplain at the Front. It seemed to him that people must think his life idle and sheltered and useless. Even in times of peace he had been sensitive enough to feel the cold draughty blasts which the Church encounters in a material age. He knew that nine people out of ten looked on him as something of a parasite, with no real work in the world. And since he was nothing if not conscientious, he always worked himself to the bone.

To-day he had risen at half-past six, and after his bath and exercises, had sat down to his sermon—for, even now, he wrote a new sermon once a month, though he had the fruits of twenty-six years to choose from. True, these new sermons were rather compiled than written, because, bereft of his curate, he had not time enough for fresh thought on old subjects. At eight he had breakfasted with Noel, before she went off to her hospital, whence she would return at eight in the evening. Nine to ten was his hour for seeing parishioners who had troubles, or wanted help or advice, and he had received three to-day who all wanted help, which he had given. From ten to eleven he had gone back to his sermon, and had spent from eleven to one at his church, attending to small matters, writing notices, fixing hymns, holding the daily half-hour Service instituted during wartime, to which but few ever came. He had hurried back to lunch, scamping it so that he might get to his piano for an hour of forgetfulness. At three he had christened a very noisy baby, and been detained by its parents who wished for information on a variety of topics. At half-past four he had snatched a cup of tea, reading the paper; and had spent from five to seven visiting two Parish Clubs, and those whose war-pension matters he had in hand, and filling up forms which would be kept in official places till such time as the system should be changed and a fresh set of forms issued. From seven to eight he was at home again, in case his flock wanted to see him; to-day four sheep had come, and gone away, he was afraid, but little the wiser. From half-past eight to half-past nine he had spent in choir practice, because the organist was on his holiday. Slowly in the cool of the evening he had walked home, and fallen asleep in his chair on getting in. At eleven he had woken with a start, and, hardening his heart, had gone back to his sermon. And now, at nearly midnight, it was still less than twenty minutes long. He lighted one of his rare cigarettes, and let thought wander. How beautiful those pale pink roses were in that old silver bowl-like a little strange poem, or a piece of Debussy music, or a Mathieu Maris picture-reminding him oddly of the word Leila. Was he wrong in letting Noel see so much of Leila? But then she was so improved—dear Leila!... The pink roses were just going to fall! And yet how beautiful!... It was quiet to-night; he felt very drowsy.... Did Nollie still think of that young man, or had it passed? She had never confided in him since! After the war, it would be nice to take her to Italy, to all the little towns. They would see the Assisi of St. Francis. The Little Flowers of St. Francis. The Little Flowers!... His hand dropped, the cigarette went out. He slept with his face in shadow. Slowly into the silence of his sleep little sinister sounds intruded. Short concussions, dragging him back out of that deep slumber. He started up. Noel was standing at the door, in a long coat. She said in her calm voice:

"Zeps, Daddy!"

"Yes, my dear. Where are the maids?"

An Irish voice answered from the hall: "Here, sir; trustin' in God; but 'tis better on the ground floor."

He saw a huddle of three figures, queerly costumed, against the stairs.

"Yes, Yes, Bridgie; you're safe down here." Then he noticed that Noel was gone. He followed her out into the Square, alive with faces faintly luminous in the darkness, and found her against the garden railings.

"You must come back in, Nollie."

"Oh, no! Cyril has this every day."

He stood beside her; not loth, for excitement had begun to stir his blood. They stayed there for some minutes, straining their eyes for sight of anything save the little zagged splashes of bursting shrapnel, while voices buzzed, and muttered: "Look! There! There! There it is!"

But the seers had eyes of greater faith than Pierson's, for he saw nothing: He took her arm at last, and led her in. In the hall she broke from him.

"Let's go up on the roof, Daddy!" and ran upstairs.

Again he followed, mounting by a ladder, through a trapdoor on to the roof.

"It's splendid up here!" she cried.

He could see her eyes blazing, and thought: 'How my child does love excitement—it's almost terrible!'

Over the wide, dark, star-strewn sky travelling searchlights, were lighting up the few little clouds; the domes and spires rose from among the spread-out roofs, all fine and ghostly. The guns had ceased firing, as though puzzled. One distant bang rumbled out.

"A bomb! Oh! If we could only get one of the Zeps!"

A furious outburst of firing followed, lasting perhaps a minute, then ceased as if by magic. They saw two searchlights converge and meet right overhead.

"It's above us!" murmured Noel.

Pierson put his arm round her waist. 'She feels no fear!' he thought. The search-lights switched apart; and suddenly, from far away, came a confusion of weird sounds.

"What is it? They're cheering. Oh! Daddy, look!" There in the heavens, towards the east, hung a dull red thing, lengthening as they gazed.

"They've got it. It's on fire! Hurrah!"

Through the dark firmament that fiery orange shape began canting downward; and the cheering swelled in a savage frenzy of sound. And Pierson's arm tightened on her waist.

"Thank God!" he muttered.

The bright oblong seemed to break and spread, tilted down below the level of the roofs; and suddenly the heavens flared, as if some huge jug of crimson light had been flung out on them. Something turned over in Pierson's heart; he flung up his hand to his eyes.

"The poor men in it!" he said. "How terrible!"

Noel's voice answered, hard and pitiless:

"They needn't have come. They're murderers!"

Yes, they were murderers—but how terrible! And he stood quivering, with his hands pressed to his face, till the cheering had died out into silence.

"Let's pray, Nollie!" he whispered. "O God, Who in Thy great mercy hath delivered us from peril, take into Thy keeping the souls of these our enemies, consumed by Thy wrath before our eyes; give us the power to pity them—men like ourselves."

But even while he prayed he could see Noel's face flame-white in the darkness; and, as that glow in the sky faded out, he felt once more the thrill of triumph.

They went down to tell the maids, and for some time after sat up together, talking over what they had seen, eating biscuits and drinking milk, which they warmed on an etna. It was nearly two o'clock before they went to bed. Pierson fell asleep at once, and never turned till awakened at half-past six by his alarum. He had Holy Communion to administer at eight, and he hurried to get early to his church and see that nothing untoward had happened to it. There it stood in the sunlight; tall, grey, quiet, unharmed, with bell gently ringing.

3

And at that hour Cyril Morland, under the parapet of his trench, tightening his belt, was looking at his wrist-watch for the hundredth time, calculating exactly where he meant to put foot and hand for the going over: 'I absolutely mustn't let those chaps get in front of me,' he thought. So many yards before the first line of trenches, so many yards to the second line, and there stop. So his rehearsals had gone; it was the performance now! Another minute before the terrific racket of the drum-fire should become the curtain-fire, which would advance before them. He ran his eye down the trench. The man next him was licking his two first fingers, as if he might be going to bowl at cricket. Further down, a man was feeling his puttees. A voice said: "Wot price the orchestra nah!" He saw teeth gleam in faces burnt almost black. Then he looked up; the sky was blue beyond the brownish film of dust raised by the striking shells. Noel! Noel! Noel!... He dug his fingers deep into the left side of his tunic till he could feel the outline of her photograph between his dispatch-case and his heart. His heart fluttered just as it used when he was stretched out with hand touching the ground, before the start of the "hundred yards" at school. Out of the corner of his eye he caught the flash of a man's "briquet" lighting a cigarette. All right for those chaps, but not for him; he wanted all his breath—this rifle, and kit were handicap enough! Two days ago he had been reading in some paper how men felt just before an attack. And now he knew. He just felt nervous. If only the moment would come, and get itself over! For all the thought he gave to the enemy there might have been none—nothing but shells and bullets, with lives of their own. He heard the whistle; his foot was on the spot he had marked down; his hand where he had seen it; he called out: "Now, boys!" His head was over the top, his body over; he was conscious of someone falling, and two men neck and neck beside him. Not to try and run, not to break out of a walk; to go steady, and yet keep ahead! D—n these holes! A bullet tore through his sleeve, grazing his arm—a red-hot sensation, like the touch of an iron. A British shell from close over his head burst sixty yards ahead; he stumbled, fell flat, picked himself up. Three ahead of him now! He walked faster, and drew alongside. Two of them fell. 'What luck!' he thought; and gripping his rifle harder, pitched headlong into a declivity. Dead bodies lay there! The first German trench line, and nothing alive in it, nothing to clean up, nothing of it left! He stopped, getting his wind; watching the men panting and stumbling in. The roar of the guns was louder than ever again, barraging the second line. So far, good! And here was his captain!

"Ready, boys? On, then!"

This time he moved more slowly still, over terrible going, all holes and hummocks. Half consciously he took cover all he could. The air was alive with the whistle from machine-gun fire storming across zigzag fashion-alive it was with bullets, dust, and smoke. 'How shall I tell her?' he thought. There would be nothing to tell but just a sort of jagged brown sensation. He kept his eyes steadily before him, not wanting to seethe men falling, not wanting anything to divert him from getting there. He felt the faint fanning of the passing bullets. The second line must be close now. Why didn't that barrage lift? Was this new dodge of firing till the last second going to do them in? Another hundred yards and he would be bang into it. He flung himself flat and waited; looking at his wrist-watch he noted that his arm was soaked with blood. He thought: 'A wound! Now I shall go home. Thank God! Oh, Noel!' The passing bullets whirled above him; he could hear them even through the screech and thunder of the shell-fire. 'The beastly things!' he thought: A voice beside him gasped out:

"It's lifted, sir."

He called: "Come on, boys!" and went forward, stooping. A bullet struck his rifle. The shock made him stagger and sent an electric shock spinning up his arm. 'Luck again!' he thought. 'Now for it! I haven't seen a German yet!' He leaped forward, spun round, flung up his arms, and fell on his back, shot through and through....

The position was consolidated, as they say, and in the darkness stretcher-bearers were out over the half-mile. Like will-o'-the-wisps, with their shaded lanterns, they moved, hour after hour, slowly quartering the black honeycomb which lay behind the new British line. Now and then in the light of some star-shell their figures were disclosed, bending and raising the forms of the wounded, or wielding pick and shovel.

"Officer."

"Dead?"

"Sure."

"Search."

From the shaded lantern, lowered to just above the body, a yellowish glare fell on face and breast. The hands of the searcher moved in that little pool of light. The bearer who was taking notes bent down.

"Another boy," he said. "That all he has?"

The searcher raised himself.

"Just those, and a photo."

"Dispatch-case; pound loose; cigarette-case; wristwatch; photo. Let's see it."

The searcher placed the photo in the pool of light. The tiny face of a girl stared up at them, unmoved, from its short hair.

"Noel," said the searcher, reading.

"H'm! Take care of it. Stick it in his case. Come on!"

The pool of light dissolved, and darkness for ever covered Cyril Morland.

CHAPTER II

When those four took their seats in the Grand Circle at Queen's Hall the programme was already at the second number, which, in spite of all the efforts of patriotism, was of German origin—a Brandenburg concerto by Bach. More curious still, it was encored. Pierson did not applaud, he was too far gone in pleasure, and sat with a rapt smile on his face, oblivious of his surroundings. He remained thus removed from mortal joys and sorrows till the last applause had died away, and Leila's voice said in his ear:

"Isn't it a wonderful audience, Edward? Look at all that khaki. Who'd have thought those young men cared for music—good music—German music, too?"

Pierson looked down at the patient mass of standing figures in straw hats and military caps, with faces turned all one way, and sighed.

"I wish I could get an audience like that in my church."

A smile crept out at the corner of Leila's lips. She was thinking: 'Ah! Your Church is out of date, my dear, and so are you! Your Church, with its smell of mould and incense, its stained-glass, and narrowed length and droning organ. Poor Edward, so out of the world!' But she only pressed his arm, and whispered:

"Look at Noel!"

The girl was talking to Jimmy Fort. Her cheeks were gushed, and she looked prettier than Pierson had seen her look for a long time now, ever since Kestrel, indeed. He heard Leila sigh.

"Does she get news of her boy? Do you remember that May Week, Edward? We were very young then; even you were young. That was such a pretty little letter you wrote me. I can see you still-wandering in your dress clothes along the river, among the 'holy' cows."

But her eyes slid round again, watching her other neighbour and the girl. A violinist had begun to play the Cesar Franck Sonata. It was Pierson's favourite piece of music, bringing him, as it were, a view of heaven, of devotional blue air where devout stars were shining in a sunlit noon, above ecstatic trees and waters where ecstatic swans were swimming.

"Queer world, Mr. Pierson! Fancy those boys having to go back to barrack life after listening to that! What's your feeling? Are we moving back to the apes? Did we touch top note with that Sonata?"

Pierson turned and contemplated his questioner shrewdly.

"No, Captain Fort, I do not think we are moving back to the apes; if we ever came from them. Those boys have the souls of heroes!"

"I know that, sir, perhaps better than you do."

"Ah! yes," said Pierson humbly, "I forgot, of course." But he still looked at his neighbour doubtfully. This Captain Fort, who was a friend of Leila's, and who had twice been to see them, puzzled him. He had a frank face, a frank voice, but queer opinions, or so it seemed to, Pierson—little bits of Moslemism, little bits of the backwoods, and the veldt; queer unexpected cynicisms, all sorts of side views on England had lodged in him, and he did not hide them. They came from him like bullets, in that frank voice, and drilled little holes in the listener. Those critical sayings flew so much more poignantly from one who had been through the same educational mill as himself, than if they had merely come from some rough diamond, some artist, some foreigner, even from a doctor like George. And they always made him uncomfortable, like the touch of a prickly leaf; they did not amuse him. Certainly Edward Pierson shrank from the rough touches of a knock-about philosophy. After all, it was but natural that he should.

He and Noel left after the first part of the concert, parting from the other two at the door. He slipped his hand through her arm; and, following out those thoughts of his in the concert-hall, asked:

"Do you like Captain Fort, Nollie?"

"Yes; he's a nice man."

"He seems a nice man, certainly; he has a nice smile, but strange views, I'm afraid."

"He thinks the Germans are not much worse than we are; he says that a good many of us are bullies too."

"Yes, that is the sort of thing I mean."

"But are we, Daddy?"

"Surely not."

"A policeman I talked to once said the same. Captain Fort says that very few men can stand having power put into their hands without being spoiled. He told me some dreadful stories. He says we have no imagination, so that we often do things without seeing how brutal they are."

"We're not perfect, Nollie; but on the whole I think we're a kind people."

Noel was silent a moment, then said suddenly:

"Kind people often think others are kind too, when they really aren't. Captain Fort doesn't make that mistake."

"I think he's a little cynical, and a little dangerous."

"Are all people dangerous who don't think like others, Daddy?"

Pierson, incapable of mockery, was not incapable of seeing when he was being mocked. He looked at his daughter with a smile.

"Not quite so bad as that, Nollie; but Mr. Fort is certainly subversive. I think perhaps he has seen too many queer sides of life."

"I like him the better for that."

"Well, well," Pierson answered absently. He had work to do in preparation for a Confirmation Class, and sought his study on getting in.

Noel went to the dining-room to drink her hot milk. The curtains were not drawn, and bright moonlight was coming in. Without lighting up, she set the etna going, and stood looking at the moon-full for the second time since she and Cyril had waited for it in the Abbey. And pressing her hands to her breast, she shivered. If only she could summon him from the moonlight out there; if only she were a witch-could see him, know where he was, what doing! For a fortnight now she had received no letter. Every day since he had left her she had read the casualty lists, with the superstitious feeling that to do so would keep him out of them. She took up the Times. There was just enough light, and she read the roll of honour—till the moon shone in on her, lying on the floor, with the dropped journal....

But she was proud, and soon took grief to her room, as on that night after he left her, she had taken love. No sign betrayed to the house her disaster; the journal on the floor, and the smell of the burnt milk which had boiled over, revealed nothing. After all, she was but one of a thousand hearts which spent that moonlit night in agony. Each night, year in, year out, a thousand faces were buried in pillows to smother that first awful sense of desolation, and grope for the secret spirit-place where bereaved souls go, to receive some feeble touch of healing from knowledge of each other's trouble....

In the morning she got up from her sleepless bed, seemed to eat her breakfast, and went off to her hospital. There she washed up plates and dishes, with a stony face, dark under the eyes.

The news came to Pierson in a letter from Thirza, received at lunch-time. He read it with a dreadful aching. Poor, poor little Nollie! What an awful trouble for her! And he, too, went about his work with the nightmare thought that he had to break the news to her that evening. Never had he felt more lonely, more dreadfully in want of the mother of his children. She would have known how to soothe, how to comfort. On her heart the child could have sobbed away grief. And all that hour, from seven to eight, when he was usually in readiness to fulfil the functions of God's substitute to his parishioners, he spent in prayer of his own, for guidance how to inflict and heal this blow. When, at last, Noel came, he opened the door to her himself, and, putting back the hair from her forehead, said: "Come in here a moment, my darling!" Noel followed him into the study, and sat down. "I know already, Daddy." Pierson was more dismayed by this stoicism than he would have been by any natural out burst. He stood, timidly stroking her hair, murmuring to her what he had said to Gratian, and to so many others in these days: "There is no death; look forward to seeing him again; God is merciful" And he marvelled at the calmness of that pale face—so young.

"You are very brave, my child!" he said.

"There's nothing else to be, is there?"

"Isn't there anything I can do for you, Nollie?"

"No, Daddy."

"When did you see it?"

"Last night." She had already known for twenty-four hours without telling him!

"Have you prayed, my darling?"

"No."

"Try, Nollie!"

"No."

"Ah, try!"

"It would be ridiculous, Daddy; you don't know."

Grievously upset and bewildered, Pierson moved away from her, and said:

"You look dreadfully tired. Would you like a hot bath, and your dinner in bed?"

"I'd like some tea; that's all." And she went out.

When he had seen that the tea had gone up to her, he too went out; and, moved by a longing for woman's help, took a cab to Leila's flat.

On leaving the concert Leila and Jimmy Fort had secured a taxi; a vehicle which, at night, in wartime, has certain advantages for those who desire to become better acquainted. Vibration, sufficient noise, darkness, are guaranteed; and all that is lacking for the furtherance of emotion is the scent of honeysuckle and roses, or even of the white flowering creeper which on the stoep at High Constantia had smelled so much sweeter than petrol.

When Leila found herself with Fort in that loneliness to which she had been looking forward, she was overcome by an access of nervous silence. She had been passing through a strange time for weeks past. Every night she examined her sensations without quite understanding them as yet. When a woman comes to her age, the world-force is liable to take possession, saying:

"You were young, you were beautiful, you still have beauty, you are not, cannot be, old. Cling to youth, cling to beauty; take all you can get, before your face gets lines and your hair grey; it is impossible that you have been loved for the last time."

To see Jimmy Fort at the concert, talking to Noel, had brought this emotion to a head. She was not of a grudging nature, and could genuinely admire Noel, but the idea that Jimmy Fort might also admire disturbed her greatly. He must not; it was not fair; he was too old—besides, the girl had her boy; and she had taken care that he should know it. So, leaning towards him, while a bare-shouldered young lady sang, she had whispered:

"Penny?"

And he had whispered back:

"Tell you afterwards."

That had comforted her. She would make him take her home. It was time she showed her heart.

And now, in the cab, resolved to make her feelings known, in sudden shyness she found it very difficult. Love, to which for quite three years she had been a stranger, was come to life within her. The knowledge was at once so sweet, and so disturbing, that she sat with face averted, unable to turn the precious minutes to account. They arrived at the flat without having done more than agree that the streets were dark, and the moon bright. She got out with a sense of bewilderment, and said rather desperately:

"You must come up and have a cigarette. It's quite early, still."

He went up.

"Wait just a minute," said Leila.

Sitting there with his drink and his cigarette, he stared at some sunflowers in a bowl—Famille Rose—and waited just ten; smiling a little, recalling the nose of the fairy princess, and the dainty way her lips shaped the words she spoke. If she had not had that lucky young devil of a soldier boy, one would have wanted to buckle her shoes, lay one's coat in the mud for her, or whatever they did in fairytales. One would have wanted—ah! what would one not have wanted! Hang that soldier boy! Leila said he was twenty-two. By George! how old it made a man feel who was rising forty, and tender on the off-fore! No fairy princesses for him! Then a whiff of perfume came to his nostrils; and, looking up, he saw Leila standing before him, in a long garment of dark silk, whence her white arms peeped out.

"Another penny? Do you remember these things, Jimmy? The Malay women used to wear them in Cape Town. You can't think what a relief it is to get out of my slave's dress. Oh! I'm so sick of nursing! Jimmy, I want to live again a little!"

The garment had taken fifteen years off her age, and a gardenia, just where the silk crossed on her breast, seemed no whiter than her skin. He wondered whimsically whether it had dropped to her out of the dark!

"Live?" he said. "Why! Don't you always?"

She raised her hands so that the dark silk fell, back from the whole length of those white arms.

"I haven't lived for two years. Oh, Jimmy! Help me to live a little! Life's so short, now."

Her eyes disturbed him, strained and pathetic; the sight of her arms; the scent of the flower disturbed him; he felt his cheeks growing warm, and looked down.

She slipped suddenly forward on to her knees at his feet, took his hand, pressed it with both of hers, and murmured:

"Love me a little! What else is there? Oh! Jimmy, what else is there?"

And with the scent of the flower, crushed by their hands, stirring his senses, Fort thought: 'Ah, what else is there, in these forsaken days?'

To Jimmy Fort, who had a sense of humour, and was in some sort a philosopher, the haphazard way life settled things seldom failed to seem amusing. But when he walked away from Leila's he was pensive. She was a good sort, a pretty creature, a sportswoman, an enchantress; but—she was decidedly mature. And here he was—involved in helping her to "live"; involved almost alarmingly, for there had been no mistaking the fact that she had really fallen in love with him.

This was flattering and sweet. Times were sad, and pleasure scarce, but—! The roving instinct which had kept him, from his youth up, rolling about the world, shied instinctively at bonds, however pleasant, the strength and thickness of which he could not gauge; or, was it that perhaps for the first time in his life he had been peeping into fairyland of late, and this affair with Leila was by no means fairyland? He had another reason, more unconscious, for uneasiness. His heart, for all his wanderings, was soft, he had always found it difficult to hurt anyone, especially anyone who did him the honour to love him. A sort of presentiment weighed on him while he walked the moonlit streets at this most empty hour, when even the late taxis had ceased to run. Would she want him to marry her? Would it be his duty, if she did? And then he found himself thinking of the concert, and that girl's face, listening to the tales he was telling her. 'Deuced queer world,' he thought, 'the way things go! I wonder what she would think of us, if she knew—and that good padre! Phew!'

He made such very slow progress, for fear of giving way in his leg, and having to spend the night on a door-step, that he had plenty of time for rumination; but since it brought him no confidence whatever, he began at last to feel: 'Well; it might be a lot worse. Take the goods the gods send you and don't fuss!' And suddenly he remembered with extreme vividness that night on the stoep at High Constantia, and thought with dismay: 'I could have plunged in over head and ears then; and now—I can't! That's life all over! Poor Leila! Me miserum, too, perhaps—who knows!'

CHAPTER IV

When Leila opened her door to Edward Pierson, her eyes were smiling, and her lips were soft. She seemed to smile and be soft all over, and she took both his hands. Everything was a pleasure to her that day, even the sight of this sad face. She was in love and was loved again; had a present and a future once more, not only her own full past; and she must finish with Edward in half an hour, for Jimmy was coming. She sat down on the divan, took his hand in a sisterly way, and said:

"Tell me, Edward; I can see you're in trouble. What is it?"

"Noel. The boy she was fond of has been killed."

She dropped his hand.

"Oh, no! Poor child! It's too cruel!" Tears started up in her grey eyes, and she touched them with a tiny handkerchief. "Poor, poor little Noel! Was she very fond of him?"

"A very sudden, short engagement; but I'm afraid she takes it desperately to heart. I don't know how to comfort her; only a woman could. I came to ask you: Do you think she ought to go on with her work? What do you think, Leila? I feel lost!"

Leila, gazing at him, thought: 'Lost? Yes, you look lost, my poor Edward!'

"I should let her go on," she said: "it helps; it's the only thing that does help. I'll see if I can get them to let her come into the wards. She ought to be in touch with suffering and the men; that kitchen work will try her awfully just now: Was he very young?"

"Yes. They wanted to get married. I was opposed to it."

Leila's lip curled ever so little. 'You would be!' she thought.

"I couldn't bear to think of Nollie giving herself hastily, like that; they had only known each other three weeks. It was very hard for me, Leila. And then suddenly he was sent to the front."

Resentment welled up in Leila. The kill-Joys! As if life didn't kill joy fast enough! Her cousin's face at that moment was almost abhorrent to her, its gentle perplexed goodness darkened and warped by that monkish look. She turned away, glanced at the clock over the hearth, and thought: 'Yes, and he would stop Jimmy and me! He would say: "Oh, no! dear Leila—you mustn't love—it's sin!" How I hate that word!'

"I think the most dreadful thing in life," she said abruptly, "is the way people suppress their natural instincts; what they suppress in themselves they make other people suppress too, if they can; and that's the cause of half the misery in this world."

Then at the surprise on his face at this little outburst, whose cause he could not know, she added hastily: "I hope Noel will get over it quickly, and find someone else."

"Yes. If they had been married—how much worse it would have been. Thank God, they weren't!"

"I don't know. They would have had an hour of bliss. Even an hour of bliss is worth something in these days."

"To those who only believe in this 'life—perhaps."

'Ten minutes more!' she thought: 'Oh, why doesn't he go?' But at that very moment he got up, and instantly her heart went out to him again.

"I'm so sorry, Edward. If I can help in any way—I'll try my best with Noel to-morrow; and do come to me whenever you feel inclined."

She took his hand in hers; afraid that he would sit down again, she yet could not help a soft glance into his eyes, and a little rush of pitying warmth in the pressure of her hand.

Pierson smiled; the smile which always made her sorry for him.

"Good-bye, Leila; you're very good and kind to me. Good-bye."

Her bosom swelled with relief and compassion; and—she let him out.

Running upstairs again she thought: 'I've just time. What shall I put on? Poor Edward, poor Noel! What colour does Jimmy like? Oh! Why didn't I keep him those ten years ago—what utter waste!' And, feverishly adorning herself, she came back to the window, and stood there in the dark to watch, while some jasmine which grew below sent up its scent to her. 'Would I marry him?' she thought, 'if he asked me? But he won't ask me—why should he now? Besides, I couldn't bear him to feel I wanted position or money from him. I only want love—love—love!' The silent repetition of that word gave her a wonderful sense of solidity and comfort. So long as she only wanted love, surely he would give it.

A tall figure turned down past the church, coming towards her. It was he! And suddenly she bethought herself. She went to the little black piano, sat down, and began to sing the song she had sung to him ten years ago: "If I could be the falling dew and fall on thee all day!" She did not even look round when he came in, but continued to croon out the words, conscious of him just behind her shoulder in the dark. But when she had finished, she got up and threw her arms round him, strained him to her, and burst into tears on his shoulder; thinking of Noel and that dead boy, thinking of the millions of other boys, thinking of her own happiness, thinking of those ten years wasted, of how short was life, and love; thinking—hardly knowing what she thought! And Jimmy Fort, very moved by this emotion which he only half understood, pressed her tightly in his arms, and kissed her wet cheeks and her neck, pale and warm in the darkness.

CHAPTER V

1

Noel went on with her work for a month, and then, one morning, fainted over a pile of dishes. The noise attracted attention, and Mrs. Lynch was summoned.

The sight of her lying there so deadly white taxed Leila's nerves severely. But the girl revived quickly, and a cab was sent for. Leila went with her, and told the driver to stop at Camelot Mansions. Why take her home in this state, why not save the jolting, and let her recover properly? They went upstairs arm in arm. Leila made her lie down on the divan, and put a hot-water bottle to her feet. Noel was still so passive and pale that even to speak to her seemed a cruelty. And, going to her little sideboard, Leila stealthily extracted a pint bottle of some champagne which Jimmy Fort had sent in, and took it with two glasses and a corkscrew into her bedroom. She drank a little herself, and came out bearing a glass to the girl. Noel shook her head, and her eyes seemed to say: "Do you really think I'm so easily mended?" But Leila had been through too much in her time to despise earthly remedies, and she held it to the girl's lips until she drank. It was excellent champagne, and, since Noel had never yet touched alcohol, had an instantaneous effect. Her eyes brightened; little red spots came up in her cheeks. And suddenly she rolled over and buried her face deep in a cushion. With her short hair, she looked so like a child lying there, that Leila knelt down, stroking her head, and saying: "There, there; my love! There, there!"

At last the girl raised herself; now that the pallid, masklike despair of the last month was broken, she seemed on fire, and her face had a wild look. She withdrew herself from Leila's touch, and, crossing her arms tightly across her chest, said:

"I can't bear it; I can't sleep. I want him back; I hate life—I hate the world. We hadn't done anything—only just loved each other. God likes punishing; just because we loved each other; we had only one day to love each other—only one day—only one!"

Leila could see the long white throat above those rigid arms straining and swallowing; it gave her a choky feeling to watch it. The voice, uncannily dainty for all the wildness of the words and face, went on:

"I won't—I don't want to live. If there's another life, I shall go to him. And if there isn't—it's just sleep."

Leila put out her hand to ward of these wild wanderings. Like most women who live simply the life of their senses and emotions, she was orthodox; or rather never speculated on such things.

"Tell me about yourself and him," she said.

Noel fastened her great eyes on her cousin. "We loved each other; and children are born, aren't they, after you've loved? But mine won't be!" From the look on her face rather than from her words, the full reality of her meaning came to Leila, vanished, came again. Nonsense! But—what an awful thing, if true! That which had always seemed to her such an exaggerated occurrence in the common walks of life— why! now, it was a tragedy! Instinctively she raised herself and put her arms round the girl.

"My poor dear!" she said; "you're fancying things!"

The colour had faded out of Noel's face, and, with her head thrown back and her eyelids half-closed, she looked like a scornful young ghost.

"If it is—I shan't live. I don't mean to—it's easy to die. I don't mean Daddy to know."

"Oh! my dear, my dear!" was all Leila could stammer.

"Was it wrong, Leila?"

"Wrong? I don't know—wrong? If it really is so—it was—unfortunate. But surely, surely—you're mistaken?"

Noel shook her head. "I did it so that we should belong to each other. Nothing could have taken him from me."

Leila caught at the girl's words.

"Then, my dear—he hasn't quite gone from you, you see?"

Noel's lips formed a "No" which was inaudible. "But Daddy!" she whispered.

Edward's face came before Leila so vividly that she could hardly see the girl for the tortured shape of it. Then the hedonist in her revolted against that ascetic vision. Her worldly judgment condemned and deplored this calamity, her instinct could not help applauding that hour of life and love, snatched out of the jaws of death. "Need he ever know?" she said.

"I could never lie to Daddy. But it doesn't matter. Why should one go on living, when life is rotten?"

Outside the sun was shining brightly, though it was late October. Leila got up from her knees. She stood at the window thinking hard.

"My dear," she said at last, "you mustn't get morbid. Look at me! I've had two husbands, and—and— well, a pretty stormy up and down time of it; and I daresay I've got lots of trouble before me. But I'm not going to cave in. Nor must you. The Piersons have plenty of pluck; you mustn't be a traitor to your blood. That's the last thing. Your boy would have told you to stick it. These are your 'trenches,' and you're not going to be downed, are you?"

After she had spoken there was a long silence, before Noel said:

"Give me a cigarette, Leila."

Leila produced the little flat case she carried.

"That's brave," she said. "Nothing's incurable at your age. Only one thing's incurable—getting old."

Noel laughed. "That's curable too, isn't it?"

"Not without surrender."

Again there was a silence, while the blue fume from two cigarettes fast-smoked, rose towards the low ceiling. Then Noel got up from the divan, and went over to the piano. She was still in her hospital dress of lilac-coloured linen, and while she stood there touching the keys, playing a chord now, and then, Leila's heart felt hollow from compassion; she was so happy herself just now, and this child so very wretched!

"Play to me," she said; "no—don't; I'll play to you." And sitting down, she began to play and sing a little French song, whose first line ran: "Si on est jolie, jolie comme vous." It was soft, gay, charming. If the girl cried, so much the better. But Noel did not cry. She seemed suddenly to have recovered all her self-possession. She spoke calmly, answered Leila's questions without emotion, and said she would go home. Leila went out with her, and walked some way in the direction of her home; distressed, but frankly at a loss. At the bottom of Portland Place Noel stopped and said: "I'm quite all right now, Leila; thank you awfully. I shall just go home and lie down. And I shall come to-morrow, the same as usual. Goodbye!" Leila could only grasp the girl's hand, and say: "My dear, that's splendid. There's many a slip—besides, it's war-time."

With that saying, enigmatic even to herself, she watched the girl moving slowly away; and turned back herself towards her hospital, with a disturbed and compassionate heart.

2

But Noel did not go east; she walked down Regent Street. She had received a certain measure of comfort, been steadied by her experienced cousin's vitality, and the new thoughts suggested by those words: "He hasn't quite gone from you, has he?" "Besides, it's war-time." Leila had spoken freely, too, and the physical ignorance in which the girl had been groping these last weeks was now removed. Like most proud natures, she did not naturally think much about the opinion of other people; besides, she knew nothing of the world, its feelings and judgments. Her nightmare was the thought of her father's horror and grief. She tried to lessen that nightmare by remembering his opposition to her marriage, and the resentment she had felt. He had never realised, never understood, how she and Cyril loved. Now, if she were really going to have a child, it would be Cyril's—Cyril's son—Cyril over again. The instinct stronger than reason, refinement, tradition, upbringing, which had pushed her on in such haste to make sure of union—the irrepressible pulse of life faced with annihilation—seemed to revive within her, and make her terrible secret almost precious. She had read about "War babies" in the papers, read with a dull curiosity; but now the atmosphere, as it were, of those writings was illumined for her. These babies were wrong, were a "problem," and yet, behind all that, she seemed now to know that people were glad of them; they made up, they filled the gaps. Perhaps, when she had one, she would be proud, secretly proud, in spite of everyone, in spite of her father! They had tried to kill Cyril—God and everyone; but they hadn't been able, he was alive within her! A glow came into her face, walking among the busy shopping crowd, and people turned to look at her; she had that appearance of seeing no one, nothing, which is strange and attractive to those who have a moment to spare from contemplation of their own affairs. Fully two hours she wandered thus, before going in, and only lost that exalted feeling when, in her own little room, she had taken up his photograph, and was sitting on her bed gazing at it. She had a bad breakdown then. Locked in there, she lay on her bed, crying, dreadfully lonely, till she fell asleep exhausted, with the tear-stained photograph clutched in her twitching fingers. She woke with a start. It was dark, and someone was knocking on her door.

"Miss Noel!"

Childish perversity kept her silent. Why couldn't they leave her alone? They would leave her alone if they knew. Then she heard another kind of knocking, and her father's voice:

"Nollie! Nollie!"

She scrambled up, and opened. He looked scared, and her heart smote her.

"It's all right, Daddy; I was asleep."

"My dear, I'm sorry, but dinner's ready."

"I don't want any dinner; I think I'll go to bed."

The frown between his brows deepened.

"You shouldn't lock your door, Nollie: I was quite frightened. I went round to the hospital to bring you home, and they told me about your fainting. I want you to see a doctor."

Noel shook her head vigorously. "Oh, no! It's nothing!"

"Nothing? To faint like that? Come, my child. To please me." He took her face in his hands. Noel shrank away.

"No, Daddy. I won't see a doctor. Extravagance in wartime! I won't. It's no good trying to make me. I'll come down if you like; I shall be all right to-morrow."

With this Pierson had to be content; but, often that evening, she saw him looking at her anxiously. And when she went up, he came out of his study, followed to her room, and insisted on lighting her fire. Kissing her at the door, he said very quietly:

"I wish I could be a mother to you, my child!"

For a moment it flashed through Noel: 'He knows!' then, by the puzzled look on his face, she knew that he did not. If only he did know; what a weight it would be off her mind! But she answered quietly too; "Good night, Daddy dear!" kissed him, and shut the door.

She sat down before the little new fire, and spread her hands out to it; all was so cold and wintry in her heart. And the firelight flickered on her face, where shadows lay thick under her eyes, for all the roundness of her cheeks, and on her slim pale hands, and the supple grace of her young body. And out in the night, clouds raced over the moon, which had come full once more.

CHAPTER VI

1

Pierson went back to his study, and wrote to Gratian.

"If you can get leave for a few days, my dear, I want you at home. I am troubled about Nollie. Ever since that disaster happened to her she has been getting paler; and to-day she fainted. She won't see a doctor, but perhaps you could get her to see George. If you come up, he will surely be able to run up to us for a day or two. If not, you must take her down to him at the sea. I have just seen the news of your second cousin Charlie Pierson's death; he was killed in one of the last attacks on the Somme; he was nephew of my cousin Leila whom, as you know, Noel sees every day at her hospital. Bertram has the D. S. O. I have been less hard-pressed lately; Lauder has been home on leave and has taken some Services for me. And now the colder weather has come, I am feeling much fresher. Try your best to come. I am seriously concerned for our beloved child.

"Your affectionate father

"EDWARD PIERSON."

Gratian answered that she could get week-end leave, and would come on Friday. He met her at the station, and they drove thence straight to the hospital, to pick up Noel. Leila came to them in the waiting-room, and Pierson, thinking they would talk more freely about Noel's health if he left them alone, went into the recreation room, and stood watching a game of bagatelle between two convalescents. When he returned to the little sitting-room they were still standing by the hearth, talking in low voices. Gratian must surely have been stooping over the fire, for her face was red, almost swollen, and her eyes looked as if she had scorched them.

Leila said lightly:

"Well, Edward, aren't the men delightful? When are we going to another concert together?"

She, too, was flushed and looking almost young.

"Ah! If we could do the things we want to.

"That's very pretty, Edward; but you should, you know—for a tonic." He shook his head and smiled.

"You're a temptress, Leila. Will you let Nollie know, please, that we can take her back with us? Can you let her off to-morrow?"

"For as long as you like; she wants a rest. I've been talking to Gratian. We oughtn't to have let her go on after a shock like that—my fault, I'm afraid. I thought that work might be best."

Pierson was conscious of Gratian walking past him out of the room. He held out his hand to Leila, and followed. A small noise occurred behind him such as a woman makes when she has put a foot through her own skirt, or has other powerful cause for dismay. Then he saw Noel in the hall, and was vaguely aware of being the centre of a triangle of women whose eyes were playing catch-glance. His daughters kissed each other; and he became seated between them in the taxi. The most unobservant of men, he parted from them in the hall without having perceived anything except that they were rather silent; and, going to his study, he took up a Life of Sir Thomas More. There was a passage therein which he itched to show George Laird, who was coming up that evening.

Gratian and Noel had mounted the stairs with lips tight set, and eyes averted; both were very pale. When they reached the door of Gratian's room the room which had been their mother's—Noel was for passing on, but Gratian caught her by the arm, and said: "Come in." The fire was burning brightly in there, and the two sisters stood in front of it, one on each side, their hands clutching the mantel-shelf, staring at the flames. At last Noel put one hand in front of her eyes, and said:

"I asked her to tell you."

Gratian made the movement of one who is gripped by two strong emotions, and longs to surrender to one or to the other.

"It's too horrible," was all she said.

Noel turned towards the door.

"Stop, Nollie!"

Noel stopped with her hand on the door knob. "I don't want to be forgiven and sympathised with. I just want to be let alone."

"How can you be let alone?"

The tide of misery surged up in Noel, and she cried out passionately:

"I hate sympathy from people who can't understand. I don't want anyone's. I can always go away, and lose myself."

The words "can't understand" gave Gratian a shock.

"I can understand," she said.

"You can't; you never saw him. You never saw—" her lips quivered so that she had to stop and bite them, to keep back a rush of tears.

"Besides you would never have done it yourself."

Gratian went towards her, but stopped, and sat down on the bed. It was true. She would never have done it herself; it was just that which, for all her longing to help her sister, iced her love and sympathy. How terrible, wretched, humiliating! Her own sister, her only sister, in the position of all those poor, badly brought up girls, who forgot themselves! And her father—their father! Till that moment she had hardly thought of him, too preoccupied by the shock to her own pride. The word: "Dad!" was forced from her.

Noel shuddered.

"That boy!" said Gratian suddenly; "I can't forgive him. If you didn't know—he did. It was—it was—" She stopped at the sight of Noel's face.

"I did know," she said. "It was I. He was my husband, as much as yours is. If you say a word against him, I'll never speak to you again: I'm glad, and you would be, if you were going to have one. What's the difference, except that you've had luck, and I—haven't." Her lips quivered again, and she was silent.

Gratian stared up at her. She had a longing for George—to know what he thought and felt.

"Do you mind if I tell George?" she said.

Noel shook her head. "No! not now. Tell anybody." And suddenly the misery behind the mask of her face went straight to Gratian's heart. She got up and put her arms round her sister.

"Nollie dear, don't look like that!"

Noel suffered the embrace without response, but when it was over, went to her own room.

Gratian stayed, sorry, sore and vexed, uncertain, anxious. Her pride was deeply wounded, her heart torn; she was angry with herself. Why couldn't she have been more sympathetic? And yet, now that Noel was no longer there, she again condemned the dead. What he had done was unpardonable. Nollie was such—a child! He had committed sacrilege. If only George would come, and she could talk it all out with him! She, who had married for love and known passion, had insight enough to feel that Noel's love had been deep—so far as anything, of course, could be deep in such a child. Gratian was at the mature age of twenty. But to have forgotten herself like that! And this boy! If she had known him, that feeling might have been mitigated by the personal element, so important to all human judgment; but never having seen him, she thought of his conduct as "caddish." And she knew that this was, and would be, the trouble between her and her sister. However she might disguise it, Noel would feel that judgment underneath.

She stripped off her nurse's garb, put on an evening frock, and fidgeted about the room. Anything rather than go down and see her father again before she must. This, which had happened, was beyond words terrible for him; she dreaded the talk with him about Noel's health which would have to come. She could say nothing, of course, until Noel wished; and, very truthful by nature, the idea, of having to act a lie distressed her.

She went down at last, and found them both in the drawing-room already; Noel in a frilly evening frock, sitting by the fire with her chin on her hand, while her father was reading out the war news from the evening paper. At sight of that cool, dainty, girlish figure brooding over the fire, and of her father's worn face, the tragedy of this business thrust itself on her with redoubled force. Poor Dad! Poor Nollie! Awful! Then Noel turned, and gave a little shake of her head, and her eyes said, almost as plainly as lips could have said it: 'Silence!' Gratian nodded, and came forward to the fire. And so began one of those calm, domestic evenings, which cover sometimes such depths of heartache.

2

Noel stayed up until her father went to bed, then went upstairs at once. She had evidently determined that they should not talk about her. Gratian sat on alone, waiting for her husband! It was nearly midnight when he came, and she did not tell him the family news till next morning. He received it with a curious little grunt. Gratian saw his eyes contract, as they might have, perhaps, looking at some bad and complicated wound, and then stare steadily at the ceiling. Though they had been married over a year, she did not yet know what he thought about many things, and she waited with a queer sinking at her heart. This skeleton in the family cupboard was a test of his affection for herself, a test of the quality of the man she had married. He did not speak for a little, and her anxiety grew. Then his hand sought hers, and gave it a hard squeeze.

"Poor little Nollie! This is a case for Mark Tapleyism. But cheer up, Gracie! We'll get her through somehow."

"But father! It's impossible to keep it from him, and impossible to tell him! Oh George! I never knew what family pride was till now. It's incredible. That wretched boy!"

"'De mortuis.' Come, Gracie! In the midst of death we are in life! Nollie was a plumb little idiot. But it's the war—the war! Your father must get used to it; it's a rare chance for his Christianity."

"Dad will be as sweet as anything—that's what makes it so horrible!"

George Laird redoubled his squeeze. "Quite right! The old-fashioned father could let himself go. But need he know? We can get her away from London, and later on, we must manage somehow. If he does hear, we must make him feel that Nollie was 'doing her bit.'.rdquo;

Gratian withdrew her hand. "Don't!" she said in a muffled voice.

George Laird turned and looked at her. He was greatly upset himself, realising perhaps more truly than his young wife the violence of this disaster; he was quite capable, too, of feeling how deeply she was stirred and hurt; but, a born pragmatist, confronting life always in the experimental spirit, he was impatient of the: "How awful!" attitude. And this streak of her father's ascetic traditionalism in Gratian always roused in him a wish to break it up. If she had not been his wife he would have admitted at once that he might just as well try and alter the bone-formation of her head, as break down such a fundamental trait of character, but, being his wife, he naturally considered alteration as possible as putting a new staircase in a house, or throwing two rooms into one. And, taking her in his arms, he said: "I know; but it'll all come right, if we put a good face on it. Shall I talk to Nollie?"

Gratian assented, from the desire to be able to say to her father: "George is seeing her!" and so stay the need for a discussion. But the whole thing seemed to her more and more a calamity which nothing could lessen or smooth away.

George Laird had plenty of cool courage, invaluable in men who have to inflict as well as to alleviate pain, but he did not like his mission "a little bit" as he would have said; and he proposed a walk because he dreaded a scene. Noel accepted for the same reason. She liked George, and with the disinterested detachment of a sister-in-law, and the shrewdness of extreme youth, knew him perhaps better than did his wife. She was sure, at all events, of being neither condemned nor sympathised with.

They might have gone, of course, in any direction, but chose to make for the City. Such deep decisions are subconscious. They sought, no doubt, a dry, unemotional region; or perhaps one where George, who was in uniform, might rest his arm from the automatic-toy game which the military play. They had reached Cheapside before he was conscious to the full of the bizarre nature of this walk with his pretty young sister-in-law among all the bustling, black-coated mob of money-makers. 'I wish the devil we hadn't come out!' he thought; 'it would have been easier indoors, after all.'

He cleared his throat, however, and squeezing her arm gently, began: "Gratian's told me, Nollie. The great thing is to keep your spirit up, and not worry."

"I suppose you couldn't cure me."

The words, in that delicate spurning voice, absolutely staggered George; but he said quickly:

"Out of the question, Nollie; impossible! What are you thinking of?"

"Daddy."

The words: "D—n Daddy!" rose to his teeth; he bit them off, and said: "Bless him! We shall have to see to all that. Do you really want to keep it from him? It must be one way or the other; no use concealing it, if it's to come out later."

"No."

He stole a look at her. She was gazing straight before her. How damnably young she was, how pretty! A lump came up in his throat.

"I shouldn't do anything yet," he said; "too early. Later on, if you'd like me to tell him. But that's entirely up to you, my dear; he need never know."

"No."

He could not follow her thought. Then she said:

"Gratian condemns Cyril. Don't let her. I won't have him badly thought of. It was my doing. I wanted to make sure of him."

George answered stoutly:

"Gracie's upset, of course, but she'll soon be all right. You mustn't let it come between you. The thing you've got to keep steadily before you is that life's a huge wide adaptable thing. Look at all these people! There's hardly one of them who hasn't got now, or hasn't had, some personal difficulty or trouble before them as big as yours almost; bigger perhaps. And here they are as lively as fleas. That's what makes the fascination of life—the jolly irony of it all. It would do you good to have a turn in France, and see yourself in proportion to the whole." He felt her fingers suddenly slip under his arm, and went on with greater confidence:

"Life's going to be the important thing in the future, Nollie; not comfort and cloistered virtue and security; but living, and pressure to the square inch. Do you twig? All the old hard-and-fast traditions and drags on life are in the melting-pot. Death's boiling their bones, and they'll make excellent stock for the new soup. When you prune and dock things, the sap flows quicker. Regrets and repinings and repressions are going out of fashion; we shall have no time or use for them in the future. You're going to make life—well, that's something to be thankful for, anyway. You've kept Cyril Morland alive. And— well, you know, we've all been born; some of us properly, and some improperly, and there isn't a ha'porth of difference in the value of the article, or the trouble of bringing it into the world. The cheerier you are the better your child will be, and that's all you've got to think about. You needn't begin to trouble at all for another couple of months, at least; after that, just let us know where you'd like to go, and I'll arrange it somehow."

She looked round at him, and under that young, clear, brooding gaze he had the sudden uncomfortable feeling of having spoken like a charlatan. Had he really touched the heart of the matter? What good were his generalities to this young, fastidiously nurtured girl, brought up to tell the truth, by a father so old-fashioned and devoted, whom she loved? It was George's nature, too, to despise words; and the conditions of his life these last two years had given him a sort of horror of those who act by talking. He felt inclined to say: 'Don't pay the slightest attention to me; it's all humbug; what will be will be, and there's an end of it:

Then she said quietly:

"Shall I tell Daddy or not?"

He wanted to say: "No," but somehow couldn't. After all, the straightforward course was probably the best. For this would have to be a lifelong concealment. It was impossible to conceal a thing for ever; sooner or later he would find out. But the doctor rose up in him, and he said:

"Don't go to meet trouble, Nollie; it'll be time enough in two months. Then tell him, or let me."

She shook her head. "No; I will, if it is to be done."

He put his hand on hers, within his arm, and gave it a squeeze.

"What shall I do till then?" she asked.

"Take a week's complete rest, and then go on where you are."

Noel was silent a minute, then said: "Yes; I will."

They spoke no more on the subject, and George exerted himself to talk about hospital experiences, and that phenomenon, the British soldier. But just before they reached home he said:

"Look here, Nollie! If you're not ashamed of yourself, no one will be ashamed of you. If you put ashes on your own head, your fellow-beings will, assist you; for of such is their charity."

And, receiving another of those clear, brooding looks, he left her with the thought: 'A lonely child!'

CHAPTER VII

Noel went back to her hospital after a week's rest. George had done more for her than he suspected, for his saying: "Life's a huge wide adaptable thing!" had stuck in her mind. Did it matter what happened to her? And she used to look into the faces of the people she met, and wonder what was absorbing them. What secret griefs and joys were they carrying about with them? The loneliness of her own life now forced her to this speculation concerning others, for she was extraordinarily lonely; Gratian and George were back at work, her father must be kept at bay; with Leila she felt ill at ease, for the confession had hurt her pride; and family friends and acquaintances of all sorts she shunned like the plague. The only person she did not succeed in avoiding was Jimmy Fort, who came in one evening after dinner, bringing her a large bunch of hothouse violets. But then, he did not seem to matter—too new an acquaintance, too detached. Something he said made her aware that he had heard of her loss, and that the violets were a token of sympathy. He seemed awfully kind that evening, telling her "tales of Araby," and saying nothing which would shock her father. It was wonderful to be a man and roll about the world as he had, and see all life, and queer places, and people—Chinamen, and Gauchos, and Boers, and Mexicans. It gave her a kind of thirst. And she liked to watch his brown, humorous face; which seemed made of dried leather. It gave her the feeling that life and experience were all that mattered, doing and seeing things; it made her own trouble seem smaller; less important. She squeezed his hand when she said good night: "Thank you for my violets and for coming; it was awfully kind of you! I wish I could have adventures!" And he answered: "You will, my dear fairy princess!" He said it queerly and very kindly.

Fairy Princess! What a funny thing to call her! If he had only known!

There were not many adventures to be had in those regions where she washed up. Not much "wide and adaptable life" to take her thoughts off herself. But on her journeys to and from the hospital she had more than one odd little experience. One morning she noticed a poorly dressed woman with a red and swollen face, flapping along Regent Street like a wounded bird, and biting strangely at her hand. Hearing her groan, Noel asked her what the matter was. The woman held out the hand. "Oh!" she moaned, "I was scrubbin' the floor and I got this great needle stuck through my 'and, and it's broke off, and I can't get it out. Oh! Oh!" She bit at the needle-end, not quite visible, but almost within reach of teeth, and suddenly went very white. In dismay, Noel put an arm round her, and turned her into a fine chemist's shop. Several ladies were in there, buying perfumes, and they looked with acerbity at this disordered dirty female entering among them. Noel went up to a man behind the counter. "Please give me something quick, for this poor woman, I think she's going to faint. She's run a needle through her hand, and can't get it out." The man gave her "something quick," and Noel pushed past two of the dames back to where the woman was sitting. She was still obstinately biting at her hand, and suddenly her chin flew up, and there, between her teeth, was the needle. She took it from them with her other hand, stuck it proudly in the front of her dress, and out tumbled the words: "Oh! there—I've got it!"

When she had swallowed the draught, she looked round her, bewildered, and said:

"Thank you kindly, miss!" and shuffled out. Noel paid for the draught, and followed; and, behind her, the shining shop seemed to exhale a perfumed breath of relief.

"You can't go back to work," she said to the woman. "Where do you live?"

"'Ornsey, miss."

"You must take a 'bus and go straight home, and put your hand at once into weak Condy's fluid and water. It's swelling. Here's five shillings."

"Yes, miss; thank you, miss, I'm sure. It's very kind of you. It does ache cruel."

"If it's not better this afternoon, you must go to a doctor. Promise!"

"Oh, dear, yes. 'Ere's my 'bus. Thank you kindly, miss."

Noel saw her borne away, still sucking at her dirty swollen hand. She walked on in a glow of love for the poor woman, and hate for the ladies in the chemist's shop, and forgot her own trouble till she had almost reached the hospital.

Another November day, a Saturday, leaving early, she walked to Hyde Park. The plane-trees were just at the height of their spotted beauty. Few—very few-yellow leaves still hung; and the slender pretty trees seemed rejoicing in their freedom from summer foliage. All their delicate boughs and twigs were shaking and dancing in the wind; and their rain-washed leopard-like bodies had a lithe un-English gaiety. Noel passed down their line, and seated herself on a bench. Close by, an artist was painting. His easel was only some three yards away from her, and she could see the picture; a vista of the Park Lane houses through, the gay plane-tree screen. He was a tall man, about forty, evidently foreign, with a thin, long, oval, beardless face, high brow, large grey eyes which looked as if he suffered from headaches and lived much within himself. He cast many glances at her, and, pursuant of her new interest in "life" she watched him discreetly; a little startled however, when, taking off his broad-brimmed squash hat, he said in a broken accent:

"Forgive me the liberty I take, mademoiselle, but would you so very kindly allow me to make a sketch of you sitting there? I work very quick. I beg you will let me. I am Belgian, and have no manners, you see." And he smiled.

"If you like," said Noel.

"I thank you very much:"

He shifted his easel, and began to draw. She felt flattered, and a little fluttered. He was so pale, and had a curious, half-fed look, which moved her.

"Have you been long in England?" she said presently.

"Ever since the first months of the war."

"Do you like it?"

"I was very homesick at first. But I live in my pictures; there are wonderful things in London."

"Why did you want to sketch me?"

The painter smiled again. "Mademoiselle, youth is so mysterious. Those young trees I have been painting mean so much more than the old big trees. Your eyes are seeing things that have not yet happened. There is Fate in them, and a look of defending us others from seeing it. We have not such faces in my country; we are simpler; we do not defend our expressions. The English are very mysterious. We are like children to them. Yet in some ways you are like children to us. You are not people of the world at all. You English have been good to us, but you do not like us."

"And I suppose you do not like us, either?"

He smiled again, and she noticed how white his teeth were.

"Well, not very much. The English do things from duty, but their hearts they keep to themselves. And their Art—well, that is really amusing!"

"I don't know much about Art," Noel murmured.

"It is the world to me," said the painter, and was silent, drawing with increased pace and passion.

"It is so difficult to get subjects," he remarked abruptly. "I cannot afford to pay models, and they are not fond of me painting out of doors. If I had always a subject like you! You—you have a grief, have you not?"

At that startling little question, Noel looked up, frowning.

"Everybody has, now."

The painter grasped his chin; his eyes had suddenly become tragical.

"Yes," he said, "everybody. Tragedy is daily bread. I have lost my family; they are in Belgium. How they live I do not know."

"I'm sorry; very sorry, too, if we aren't nice to you, here. We ought to be."

He shrugged his shoulders. "What would you have? We are different. That is unpardonable. An artist is always lonely, too; he has a skin fewer than other people, and he sees things that they do not. People do not like you to be different. If ever in your life you act differently from others, you will find it so, mademoiselle."

Noel felt herself flushing. Was he reading her secret? His eyes had such a peculiar, secondsighted look.

"Have you nearly finished?" she asked.

"No, mademoiselle; I could go on for hours; but I do not wish to keep you. It is cold for you, sitting there."

Noel got up. "May I look?"

"Certainly."

She did not quite recognise herself—who does?—but she saw a face which affected her oddly, of a girl looking at something which was, and yet was not, in front of her.

"My name is Lavendie," the painter said; "my wife and I live here," and he gave her a card.

Noel could not help answering: "My name is Noel Pierson; I live with my father; here's the address"— she found her case, and fished out a card. "My father is a clergyman; would you care to come and see him? He loves music and painting."

"It would be a great pleasure; and perhaps I might be allowed to paint you. Alas! I have no studio."

Noel drew back. "I'm afraid that I work in a hospital all day, and—and I don't want to be painted, thank you. But, Daddy would like to meet you, I'm sure."

The painter bowed again; she saw that he was hurt.

"Of course I can see that you're a very fine painter," she said quickly; "only—only—I don't want to, you see. Perhaps you'd like to paint Daddy; he's got a most interesting face."

The painter smiled. "He is your father, mademoiselle. May I ask you one question? Why do you not want to be painted?"

"Because—because I don't, I'm afraid." She held out her hand. The painter bowed over it. "Au revoir, mademoiselle."

"Thank you," said Noel; "it was awfully interesting." And she walked away. The sky had become full of clouds round the westerly sun; and the foreign crinkled tracery of the plane-tree branches against that French-grey, golden-edged mass, was very lovely. Beauty, and the troubles of others, soothed her. She felt sorry for the painter, but his eyes saw too much! And his words: "If ever you act differently from others," made her feel him uncanny. Was it true that people always disliked and condemned those who acted differently? If her old school-fellows now knew what was before her, how would they treat her? In her father's study hung a little reproduction of a tiny picture in the Louvre, a "Rape of Europa," by an unknown painter—a humorous delicate thing, of an enraptured; fair-haired girl mounted on a prancing white bull, crossing a shallow stream, while on the bank all her white girl-companions were gathered, turning half-sour, half-envious faces away from that too-fearful spectacle, while one of them tried with timid desperation to mount astride of a sitting cow, and follow. The face of the girl on the bull had once been compared by someone with her own. She thought of this picture now, and saw her school fellows- a throng of shocked and wondering girls. Suppose one of them had been in her position! 'Should I have been turning my face away, like the rest? I wouldn't no, I wouldn't,' she thought; 'I should have understood!' But she knew there was a kind of false emphasis in her thought. Instinctively she felt the painter right. One who acted differently from others, was lost.

She told her father of the encounter, adding:

"I expect he'll come, Daddy."

Pierson answered dreamily: "Poor fellow, I shall be glad to see him if he does."

"And you'll sit to him, won't you?"

"My dear—I?"

"He's lonely, you know, and people aren't nice to him. Isn't it hateful that people should hurt others, because they're foreign or different?"

She saw his eyes open with mild surprise, and went on: "I know you think people are charitable, Daddy, but they aren't, of course."

"That's not exactly charitable, Nollie."

"You know they're not. I think sin often just means doing things differently. It's not real sin when it only hurts yourself; but that doesn't prevent people condemning you, does it?"

"I don't know what you mean, Nollie."

Noel bit her lips, and murmured: "Are you sure we're really Christians, Daddy?"

The question was so startling, from his own daughter, that Pierson took refuge in an attempt at wit. "I should like notice of that question, Nollie, as they say in Parliament."

"That means you don't."

Pierson flushed. "We're fallible enough; but, don't get such ideas into your head, my child. There's a lot of rebellious talk and writing in these days...."

Noel clasped her hands behind her head. "I think," she said, looking straight before her, and speaking to the air, "that Christianity is what you do, not what you think or say. And I don't believe people can be Christians when they act like others—I mean, when they join together to judge and hurt people."

Pierson rose and paced the room. "You have not seen enough of life to talk like that," he said. But Noel went on:

"One of the men in her hospital told Gratian about the treatment of conscientious objectors—it was horrible. Why do they treat them like that, just because they disagree? Captain Fort says it's fear which makes people bullies. But how can it be fear when they're hundreds to one? He says man has domesticated his animals but has never succeeded in domesticating himself. Man must be a wild beast, you know, or the world couldn't be so awfully brutal. I don't see much difference between being brutal for good reasons, and being brutal for bad ones."

Pierson looked down at her with a troubled smile. There was something fantastic to him in this sudden philosophising by one whom he had watched grow up from a tiny thing. Out of the mouths of babes and sucklings—sometimes! But then the young generation was always something of a sealed book to him; his sensitive shyness, and, still more, his cloth, placed a sort of invisible barrier between him and the hearts of others, especially the young. There were so many things of which he was compelled to disapprove, or which at least he couldn't discuss. And they knew it too well. Until these last few months he had never realised that his own daughters had remained as undiscovered by him as the interior of Brazil. And now that he perceived this, he was bewildered, yet could not imagine how to get on terms with them.

And he stood looking at Noel, intensely puzzled, suspecting nothing of the hard fact which was altering her—vaguely jealous, anxious, pained. And when she had gone up to bed, he roamed up and down the room a long time, thinking. He longed for a friend to confide in, and consult; but he knew no one. He shrank from them all, as too downright, bluff, and active; too worldly and unaesthetic; or too stiff and narrow. Amongst the younger men in his profession he was often aware of faces which attracted him, but one could not confide deep personal questions to men half one's age. But of his own generation, or his elders, he knew not one to whom he could have gone.

CHAPTER VIII

Leila was deep in her new draught of life. When she fell in love it had always been over head and ears, and so far her passion had always burnt itself out before that of her partner. This had been, of course, a great advantage to her. Not that Leila had ever expected her passions to burn themselves out. When she fell in love she had always thought it was for always. This time she was sure it was, surer than she had ever been. Jimmy Fort seemed to her the man she had been looking for all her life. He was not so good-looking as either Farie or Lynch, but beside him these others seemed to her now almost ridiculous. Indeed they did not figure at all, they shrank, they withered, they were husks, together with the others for whom she had known passing weaknesses. There was only one man in the world for her now, and would be for evermore. She did not idealise him either, it was more serious than that; she was thrilled by his voice, and his touch, she dreamed of him, longed for him when he was not with her. She worried, too, for she was perfectly aware that he was not half as fond of her as she was of him. Such a new experience puzzled her, kept her instincts painfully on the alert. It was perhaps just this uncertainty about his affection which made him seem more precious than any of the others. But there was ever the other reason, too-consciousness that Time was after her, and this her last grand passion. She watched him as a mother-cat watches her kitten, without seeming to, of course, for she had much experience. She had begun to have a curious secret jealousy of Noel though why she could not have said. It was perhaps merely incidental to her age, or sprang from that vague resemblance between her and one who outrivalled even what she had been as a girl; or from the occasional allusions Fort made to what he called "that little fairy princess." Something intangible, instinctive, gave her that jealousy. Until the death of her young cousin's lover she had felt safe, for she knew that Jimmy Fort would not hanker after another man's property; had he not proved that in old days, with herself, by running away from her? And she had often regretted having told him of Cyril Morland's death. One day she determined to repair that error. It was at the Zoo, where they often went on Sunday afternoons. They were standing before a creature called the meercat, which reminded them both of old days on the veldt. Without turning her head she said, as if to the little animal: "Do you know that your fairy princess, as you call her, is going to have what is known as a war-baby?"

The sound of his "What!" gave her quite a stab. It was so utterly horrified.

She said stubbornly: "She came and told me all about it. The boy is dead, as you know. Yes, terrible, isn't it?" And she looked at him. His face was almost comic, so wrinkled up with incredulity.

"That lovely child! But it's impossible!"

"The impossible is sometimes true, Jimmy."

"I refuse to believe it."

"I tell you it is so," she said angrily.

"What a ghastly shame!"

"It was her own doing; she said so, herself."

"And her father—the padre! My God!"

Leila was suddenly smitten with a horrible doubt. She had thought it would disgust him, cure him of any little tendency to romanticise that child; and now she perceived that it was rousing in him, instead, a dangerous compassion. She could have bitten her tongue out for having spoken. When he got on the high horse of some championship, he was not to be trusted, she had found that out; was even finding it out bitterly in her own relations with him, constantly aware that half her hold on him, at least, lay in his sense of chivalry, aware that he knew her lurking dread of being flung on the beach, by age. Only ten minutes ago he had uttered a tirade before the cage of a monkey which seemed unhappy. And now she had roused that dangerous side of him in favour of Noel. What an idiot she had been!

"Don't look like that, Jimmy. I'm sorry I told you."

His hand did not answer her pressure in the least, but he muttered:

"Well, I do think that's the limit. What's to be done for her?"

Leila answered softly: "Nothing, I'm afraid. Do you love me?" And she pressed his hand hard.

"Of course."

But Leila thought: 'If I were that meercat he'd have taken more notice of my paw!' Her heart began suddenly to ache, and she walked on to the next cage with head up, and her mouth hard set.

Jimmy Fort walked away from Camelot Mansions that evening in extreme discomfort of mind. Leila had been so queer that he had taken leave immediately after supper. She had refused to talk about Noel; had even seemed angry when he had tried to. How extraordinary some women were! Did they think that a man could hear of a thing like that about such a dainty young creature without being upset! It was the most perfectly damnable news! What on earth would she do—poor little fairy princess! Down had come her house of cards with a vengeance! The whole of her life—the whole of her life! With her bringing-up and her father and all—it seemed inconceivable that she could ever survive it. And Leila had been almost callous about the monstrous business. Women were hard to each other! Bad enough, these things, when it was a simple working girl, but this dainty, sheltered, beautiful child! No, it was altogether too strong—too painful! And following an impulse which he could not resist, he made his way to the old Square. But having reached the house, he nearly went away again. While he stood hesitating with his hand on the bell, a girl and a soldier passed, appearing as if by magic out of the moonlit November mist, blurred and solid shapes embraced, then vanished into it again, leaving the sound of footsteps. Fort jerked the bell. He was shown into what seemed, to one coming out of that mist, to be a brilliant, crowded room, though in truth there were but two lamps and five people in it. They were sitting round the fire, talking, and paused when he came in. When he had shaken hands with Pierson and been introduced to "my daughter Gratian" and a man in khaki "my son-in-law George Laird," to a tall thin-faced, foreign-looking man in a black stock and seemingly no collar, he went up to Noel, who had risen from a chair before the fire. 'No!' he thought, 'I've dreamed it, or Leila has lied!' She was so perfectly the self-possessed, dainty maiden he remembered. Even the feel of her hand was the same-warm and confident; and sinking into a chair, he said: "Please go on, and let me chip in."

"We were quarrelling about the Universe, Captain Fort," said the man in khaki; "delighted to have your help. I was just saying that this particular world has no particular importance, no more than a newspaper-seller would accord to it if it were completely destroyed tomorrow—''.rrible catastrophe, total destruction of the world—six o'clock edition-pyper!' I say that it will become again the nebula out of which it was formed, and by friction with other nebula re-form into a fresh shape and so on ad infinitum—but I can't explain why. My wife wonders if it exists at all except in the human mind—but she can't explain what the human mind is. My father-in-law thinks that it is God's hobby—but he can't explain who or what God is. Nollie is silent. And Monsieur Lavendie hasn't yet told us what he thinks. What do you think, monsieur?" The thin-faced, big-eyed man put up his hand to his high, veined brow as if he had a headache, reddened, and began to speak in French, which Fort followed with difficulty.

"For me the Universe is a limitless artist, monsieur, who from all time and to all time is ever expressing himself in differing forms—always trying to make a masterpiece, and generally failing. For me this world, and all the worlds, are like ourselves, and the flowers and trees—little separate works of art, more or less perfect, whose little lives run their course, and are spilled or powdered back into this Creative Artist, whence issue ever fresh attempts at art. I agree with Monsieur Laird, if I understand him right; but I agree also with Madame Laird, if I understand her. You see, I think mind and matter are one, or perhaps there is no such thing as either mind or matter, only growth and decay and growth again, for ever and ever; but always conscious growth—an artist expressing himself in millions of ever-changing forms; decay and death as we call them, being but rest and sleep, the ebbing of the tide, which must ever come between two rising tides, or the night which comes between two days. But the next day is never the same as the day before, nor the tide as the last tide; so the little shapes of the world and of ourselves, these works of art by the Eternal Artist, are never renewed in the same form, are never twice alike, but always fresh-fresh worlds, fresh individuals, fresh flowers, fresh everything. I do not see anything depressing in that. To me it would be depressing to think that I would go on living after death, or live again in a new body, myself yet not myself. How stale that would be! When I finish a picture it is inconceivable to me that this picture should ever become another picture, or that one can divide the expression from the mind-stuff it has expressed. The Great Artist who is the whole of Everything, is ever in fresh effort to achieve new things. He is as a fountain who throws up new drops, no two ever alike, which fall back into the water, flow into the pipe, and so are thrown up again in fresh-shaped drops. But I cannot explain why there should be this Eternal Energy, ever expressing itself in fresh individual shapes, this Eternal Working Artist, instead of nothing at all—just empty dark for always; except indeed that it must be one thing or the other, either all or nothing; and it happens to be this and not that, the all and not the nothing."

He stopped speaking, and his big eyes, which had fixed themselves on Fort's face, seemed to the latter not to be seeing him at all, but to rest on something beyond. The man in khaki, who had risen and was standing with his hand on his wife's shoulder, said:

"Bravo, monsieur; Jolly well put from the artist's point of view. The idea is pretty, anyway; but is there any need for an idea at all? Things are; and we have just to take them." Fort had the impression of something dark and writhing; the thin black form of his host, who had risen and come close to the fire.

"I cannot admit," he was saying, "the identity of the Creator with the created. God exists outside ourselves. Nor can I admit that there is no defnite purpose and fulfilment. All is shaped to His great ends. I think we are too given to spiritual pride. The world has lost reverence; I regret it, I bitterly regret it."

"I rejoice at it," said the man in khaki. "Now, Captain Fort, your turn to bat!"

Fort, who had been looking at Noel, gave himself a shake, and said: "I think what monsieur calls expression, I call fighting. I suspect the Universe of being simply a long fight, a sum of conquests and defeats. Conquests leading to defeats, defeats to conquests. I want to win while I'm alive, and because I want to win, I want to live on after death. Death is a defeat. I don't want to admit it. While I have that instinct, I don't think I shall really die; when I lose it, I think I shall." He was conscious of Noel's face turning towards him, but had the feeling that she wasn't really listening. "I suspect that what we call spirit is just the fighting instinct; that what we call matter is the mood of lying down. Whether, as Mr. Pierson says, God is outside us, or, as monsieur thinks, we are all part of God, I don't know, I'm sure."

"Ah! There we are!" said the man in khaki. "We all speak after our temperaments, and none of us know. The religions of the world are just the poetic expressions of certain strongly marked temperaments. Monsieur was a poet just now, and his is the only temperament which has never yet been rammed down the world's throat in the form of religion. Go out and proclaim your views from the housetops, monsieur, and see what happens."

The painter shook his head with a smile which seemed to Fort very bright on the surface, and very sad underneath.

"Non, monsieur," he said; "the artist does not wish to impose his temperament. Difference of temperament is the very essence of his joy, and his belief in life. Without difference there would be no life for him. 'Tout casse, tout lasse,' but change goes on for ever: We artists reverence change, monsieur; we reverence the newness of each morning, of each night, of each person, of each expression of energy. Nothing is final for us; we are eager for all and always for more. We are in love, you see, even with-death."

There was a silence; then Fort heard Pierson murmur:

"That is beautiful, monsieur; but oh! how wrong!" "And what do you think, Nollie?" said the man in khaki suddenly. The girl had been sitting very still in her low chair, with her hands crossed in her lap, her eyes on the fire, and the lamplight shining down on her fair hair; she looked up, startled, and her eyes met Fort's.

"I don't know; I wasn't listening." Something moved in him, a kind of burning pity, a rage of protection. He said quickly:

"These are times of action. Philosophy seems to mean nothing nowadays. The one thing is to hate tyranny and cruelty, and protect everything that's weak and lonely. It's all that's left to make life worth living, when all the packs of all the world are out for blood."

Noel was listening now, and he went on fervently: "Why! Even we who started out to fight this Prussian pack, have caught the pack feeling—so that it's hunting all over the country, on every sort of scent. It's a most infectious thing."

"I cannot see that we are being infected, Captain Fort."

"I'm afraid we are, Mr. Pierson. The great majority of people are always inclined to run with the hounds; the pressure's great just now; the pack spirit's in the air."

Pierson shook his head. "No, I cannot see it," he repeated; "it seems to me that we are all more brotherly, and more tolerant."

"Ah! monsieur le cure," Fort heard the painter say very gently, "it is difficult for a good man to see the evil round him. There are those whom the world's march leaves apart, and reality cannot touch. They walk with God, and the bestialities of us animals are fantastic to them. The spirit of the pack, as monsieur says, is in the air. I see all human nature now, running with gaping mouths and red tongues lolling out, their breath and their cries spouting thick before them. On whom they will fall next—one never knows; the innocent with the guilty. Perhaps if you were to see some one dear to you devoured before your eyes, monsieur le cure, you would feel it too; and yet I do not know."

Fort saw Noel turn her face towards her father; her expression at that moment was very strange, searching, half frightened. No! Leila had not lied, and he had not dreamed! That thing was true!

When presently he took his leave, and was out again in the Square, he could see nothing but her face and form before him in the moonlight: its soft outline, fair colouring, slender delicacy, and the brooding of the big grey eyes. He had already crossed New Oxford Street and was some way down towards the Strand, when a voice behind him murmured: "Ah! c'est vous, monsieur!" and the painter loomed up at his elbow.

"Are you going my way?" said Fort. "I go slowly, I'm afraid."

"The slower the better, monsieur. London is so beautiful in the dark. It is the despair of the painter—these moonlit nights. There are moments when one feels that reality does not exist. All is in dreams—like the face of that young lady."

Fort stared sharply round at him. "Oh! She strikes you like that, does she?"

"Ah! What a charming figure! What an atmosphere of the past and future round her! And she will not let me paint her! Well, perhaps only Mathieu Maris." He raised his broad Bohemian hat, and ran his fingers through his hair.

"Yes," said Fort, "she'd make a wonderful picture. I'm not a judge of Art, but I can see that."

The painter smiled, and went on in his rapid French:

"She has youth and age all at once—that is rare. Her father is an interesting man, too; I am trying to paint him; he is very difficult. He sits lost in some kind of vacancy of his own; a man whose soul has gone before him somewhere, like that of his Church, escaped from this age of machines, leaving its body behind—is it not? He is so kind; a saint, I think. The other clergymen I see passing in the street are not at all like him; they look buttoned-up and busy, with faces of men who might be schoolmasters or lawyers, or even soldiers—men of this world. Do you know this, monsieur—it is ironical, but it is true, I think a man cannot be a successful priest unless he is a man of this world. I do not see any with that look of Monsieur Pierson, a little tortured within, and not quite present. He is half an artist, really a lover of music, that man. I am painting him at the piano; when he is playing his face is alive, but even then, so far away. To me, monsieur, he is exactly like a beautiful church which knows it is being deserted. I find him pathetic. Je suis socialiste, but I have always an aesthetic admiration for that old Church, which held its children by simple emotion. The times have changed; it can no longer hold them so; it stands in the dusk, with its spire to a heaven which exists no more, its bells, still beautiful but out of tune with the music of the streets. It is something of that which I wish to get into my picture of Monsieur Pierson; and sapristi! it is difficult!" Fort grunted assent. So far as he could make out the painter's words, it seemed to him a large order.

"To do it, you see," went on the painter, "one should have the proper background—these currents of modern life and modern types, passing him and leaving him untouched. There is no illusion, and no dreaming, in modern life. Look at this street. La, la!"

In the darkened Strand, hundreds of khaki-clad figures and girls were streaming by, and all their voices had a hard, half-jovial vulgarity. The motor-cabs and buses pushed along remorselessly; newspaper-sellers muttered their ceaseless invitations. Again the painter made his gesture of despair: "How am I to get into my picture this modern life, which washes round him as round that church, there, standing in the middle of the street? See how the currents sweep round it, as if to wash it away; yet it stands, seeming not to see them. If I were a phantasist, it would be easy enough: but to be a phantasist is too simple for me—those romantic gentlemen bring what they like from anywhere, to serve their ends. Moi, je suis realiste. And so, monsieur, I have invented an idea. I am painting over his head while he sits there at the piano a picture hanging on the wall—of one of these young town girls who have no mysteriousness at all, no youth; nothing but a cheap knowledge and defiance, and good humour. He is looking up at it, but he does not see it. I will make the face of that girl the face of modern life, and he shall sit staring at it, seeing nothing. What do you think of my idea?"

But Fort had begun to feel something of the revolt which the man of action so soon experiences when he listens to an artist talking.

"It sounds all right," he said abruptly; "all the same, monsieur, all my sympathy is with modern life. Take these young girls, and these Tommies. For all their feather-pated vulgarity and they are damned vulgar, I must say—they're marvellous people; they do take the rough with the smooth; they're all 'doing their bit,' you know, and facing this particularly beastly world. Aesthetically, I daresay, they're deplorable, but can you say that on the whole their philosophy isn't an advance on anything we've had up till now? They worship nothing, it's true; but they keep their ends up marvellously."

The painter, who seemed to feel the wind blowing cold on his ideas, shrugged his shoulders.

"I am not concerned with that, monsieur; I set down what I see; better or worse, I do not know. But look at this!" And he pointed down the darkened and moonlit street. It was all jewelled and enamelled with little spots and splashes of subdued red and green-blue light, and the downward orange glow of the high lamps—like an enchanted dream-street peopled by countless moving shapes, which only came to earth-reality when seen close to. The painter drew his breath in with a hiss.

"Ah!" he said, "what beauty! And they don't see it—not one in a thousand! Pity, isn't it? Beauty is the holy thing!"

Fort, in his turn, shrugged his shoulders. "Every man to his vision!" he said. "My leg's beginning to bother me; I'm afraid I must take a cab. Here's my address; any time you like to come. I'm often in about seven. I can't take you anywhere, I suppose?"

"A thousand thanks, monsieur; but I go north. I loved your words about the pack. I often wake at night and hear the howling of all the packs of the world. Those who are by nature gentle nowadays feel they are strangers in a far land. Good night, monsieur!"

He took off his queer hat, bowed low, and crossed out into the Strand, like one who had come in a dream, and faded out with the waking. Fort hailed a cab, and went home, still seeing Noel's face. There was one, if you liked, waiting to be thrown to the wolves, waiting for the world's pack to begin howling round her—that lovely child; and the first, the loudest of all the pack, perhaps, must be her own father, the lean, dark figure with the gentle face, and the burnt bright eyes. What a ghastly business! His dreams that night were not such as Leila would have approved.

CHAPTER IX

When in the cupboard there is a real and very bony skeleton, carefully kept from the sight of a single member of the family, the position of that member is liable to become lonely. But Pierson, who had been lonely fifteen years, did not feel it so much, perhaps, as most men would have. In his dreamy nature there was a curious self-sufficiency, which only violent shocks disturbed, and he went on with his routine of duty, which had become for him as set as the pavements he trod on his way to and from it. It was not exactly true, as the painter had said, that this routine did not bring him into touch with life. After all he saw people when they were born, when they married, when they died. He helped them when they wanted money, and when they were ill; he told their children Bible stories on Sunday afternoons; he served those who were in need with soup and bread from his soup kitchen. He never spared himself in any way, and his ears were always at the service of their woes. And yet he did not understand them, and they knew that. It was as though he, or they, were colour-blind. The values were all different. He was seeing one set of objects, they another.

One street of his parish touched a main line of thoroughfare, and formed a little part of the new hunting-grounds of women, who, chased forth from their usual haunts by the Authorities under pressure of the country's danger, now pursued their calling in the dark. This particular evil had always been a sort of nightmare to Pierson. The starvation which ruled his own existence inclined him to a particularly severe view and severity was not his strong point. In consequence there was ever within him a sort of very personal and poignant struggle going on beneath that seeming attitude of rigid disapproval. He joined the hunters, as it were, because he was afraid-not, of course, of his own instincts, for he was fastidious, a gentleman, and a priest, but of being lenient to a sin, to something which God abhorred: He was, as it were, bound to take a professional view of this particular offence. When in his walks abroad he passed one of these women, he would unconsciously purse his lips, and frown. The darkness of the streets seemed to lend them such power, such unholy sovereignty over the night. They were such a danger to the soldiers, too; and in turn, the soldiers were such a danger to the lambs of his flock. Domestic disasters in his parish came to his ears from time to time; cases of young girls whose heads were turned by soldiers, so that they were about to become mothers. They seemed to him pitiful indeed; but he could not forgive them for their giddiness, for putting temptation in the way of brave young men, fighting, or about to fight. The glamour which surrounded soldiers was not excuse enough. When the babies were born, and came to his notice, he consulted a Committee he had formed, of three married and two maiden ladies, who visited the mothers, and if necessary took the babies into a creche; for those babies had a new value to the country, and were not—poor little things!—to be held responsible for their mothers' faults. He himself saw little of the young mothers; shy of them, secretly afraid, perhaps, of not being censorious enough. But once in a way Life set him face to face with one.

On New Year's Eve he was sitting in his study after tea, at that hour which he tried to keep for his parishioners, when a Mrs. Mitchett was announced, a small bookseller's wife, whom he knew for an occasional Communicant. She came in, accompanied by a young dark-eyed girl in a loose mouse-coloured coat. At his invitation they sat down in front of the long bookcase on the two green leather chairs which had grown worn in the service of the parish; and, screwed round in his chair at the bureau, with his long musician's fingers pressed together, he looked at them and waited. The woman had taken out her handkerchief, and was wiping her eyes; but the girl sat quiet, as the mouse she somewhat resembled in that coat.

"Yes, Mrs. Mitchett?" He said gently, at last.

The woman put away her handkerchief, sniffed resolutely, and began:

"It's 'Ilda, sir. Such a thing Mitchett and me never could 'ave expected, comin' on us so sudden. I thought it best to bring 'er round, poor girl. Of course, it's all the war. I've warned 'er a dozen times; but there it is, comin' next month, and the man in France." Pierson instinctively averted his gaze from the girl, who had not moved her eyes from his face, which she scanned with a seeming absence of interest, as if she had long given up thinking over her lot, and left it now to others.

"That is sad," he said; "very, very sad."

"Yes," murmured Mrs. Mitchett; "that's what I tell 'Ilda."

The girl's glance, lowered for a second, resumed its impersonal scrutiny of Pierson's face.

"What is the man's name and regiment? Perhaps we can get leave for him to come home and marry Hilda at once."

Mrs. Mitchett sniffed. "She won't give it, sir. Now, 'Ilda, give it to Mr. Pierson." And her voice had a real note of entreaty. The girl shook her head. Mrs. Mitchett murmured dolefully: "That's 'ow she is, sir; not a word will she say. And as I tell her, we can only think there must 'ave been more than one. And that does put us to shame so!"

But still the girl made no sign.

"You speak to her, sir; I'm really at my wit's end."

"Why won't you tell us?" said Pierson. "The man will want to do the right thing, 'I'm sure."

The girl shook her head, and spoke for the first time.

"I don't know his name."

Mrs. Mitchett's face twitched.

"Oh, dear!" she said: "Think of that! She's never said as much to us."

"Not know his name?" Pierson murmured. "But how—how could you—" he stopped, but his face had darkened. "Surely you would never have done such a thing without affection? Come, tell me!"

"I don't know it," the girl repeated.

"It's these Parks," said Mrs. Mitchett, from behind her handkerchief. "And to think that this'll be our first grandchild and all! 'Ilda is difficult; as quiet, as quiet; but that stubborn—"

Pierson looked at the girl, who seemed, if anything, less interested than ever. This impenetrability and something mulish in her attitude annoyed him. "I can't think," he said, "how you could so have forgotten yourself. It's truly grievous."

Mrs. Mitchett murmured: "Yes, sir; the girls gets it into their heads that there's going to be no young men for them."

"That's right," said the girl sullenly.

Pierson's lips grew tighter. "Well, what can I do for you, Mrs. Mitchett?" he said. "Does your daughter come to church?"

Mrs. Mitchett shook her head mournfully. "Never since she had her byke."

Pierson rose from his chair. The old story! Control and discipline undermined, and these bitter apples the result!

"Well," he said, "if you need our creche, you have only to come to me," and he turned to the girl. "And you—won't you let this dreadful experience move your heart? My dear girl, we must all master ourselves, our passions, and our foolish wilfulness, especially in these times when our country needs us strong, and self-disciplined, not thinking of ourselves. I'm sure you're a good girl at heart."

The girl's dark eyes, unmoved from his face, roused in him a spasm of nervous irritation. "Your soul is in great danger, and you're very unhappy, I can see. Turn to God for help, and in His mercy everything will be made so different for you—so very different! Come!"

The girl said with a sort of surprising quietness: "I don't want the baby!"

The remark staggered him, almost as if she had uttered a hideous oath.

"'Ilda was in munitions," said her mother in an explanatory voice: "earnin' a matter of four pound a week. Oh! dear, it is a waste an' all!" A queer, rather terrible little smile curled Pierson's lips.

"A judgment!" he said. "Good evening, Mrs. Mitchett. Good evening, Hilda. If you want me when the time comes, send for me."

They stood up; he shook hands with them; and was suddenly aware that the door was open, and Noel standing there. He had heard no sound; and how long she had been there he could not tell. There was a singular fixity in her face and attitude. She was staring at the girl, who, as she passed, lifted her face, so that the dark eyes and the grey eyes met. The door was shut, and Noel stood there alone with him.

"Aren't you early, my child?" said Pierson. "You came in very quietly."

"Yes; I heard."

A slight shock went through him at the tone of her voice; her face had that possessed look which he always dreaded. "What did you hear?" he said.

"I heard you say: 'A judgment!' You'll say the same to me, won't you? Only, I do want my baby."

She was standing with her back to the door, over which a dark curtain hung; her face looked young and small against its stuff, her eyes very large. With one hand she plucked at her blouse, just over her heart.

Pierson stared at her, and gripped the back of the chair he had been sitting in. A lifetime of repression served him in the half-realised horror of that moment. He stammered out the single word—

"Nollie!"

"It's quite true," she said, turned round, and went out.

Pierson had a sort of vertigo; if he had moved, he must have fallen down. Nollie! He slid round and sank into his chair, and by some horrible cruel fiction of his nerves, he seemed to feel Noel on his knee, as, when a little girl, she had been wont to sit, with her fair hair fluffing against his cheek. He seemed to feel that hair tickling his skin; it used to be the greatest comfort he had known since her mother died. At that moment his pride shrivelled like a flower held to a flame; all that abundant secret pride of a father who loves and admires, who worships still a dead wife in the children she has left him; who, humble by nature, yet never knows how proud he is till the bitter thing happens; all the long pride of the priest who, by dint of exhortation and remonstrance has coated himself in a superiority he hardly suspects—all this pride shrivelled in him. Then something writhed and cried within, as a tortured beast cries, at loss to know why it is being tortured. How many times has not a man used those words: "My God! My God! Why hast Thou forsaken me!" He sprang up and tried to pace his way out of this cage of confusion: His thoughts and feelings made the strangest medley, spiritual and worldly—Social ostracism—her soul in peril—a trial sent by God! The future! Imagination failed him. He went to his little piano, opened it, closed it again; took his hat, and stole out. He walked fast, without knowing where. It was very cold—a clear, bitter evening. Silent rapid motion in the frosty air was some relief. As Noel had fled from him, having uttered her news, so did he fly from her. The afflicted walk fast. He was soon down by the river, and turned West along its wall. The moon was up, bright and nearly full, and the steel-like shimmer of its light burnished the ebbing water. A cruel night! He came to the Obelisk, and leaned against it, overcome by a spasm of realisation. He seemed to see his dead wife's face staring at him out of the past, like an accusation. "How have you cared for Nollie, that she should have come to this?" It became the face of the moonlit sphinx, staring straight at him, the broad dark face with wide nostrils, cruel lips, full eyes blank of pupils, all livened and whitened by the moonlight—an embodiment of the marvellous unseeing energy of Life, twisting and turning hearts without mercy. He gazed into those eyes with a sort of scared defiance. The great clawed paws of the beast, the strength and remorseless serenity of that crouching creature with human head, made living by his imagination and the moonlight, seemed to him like a temptation to deny God, like a refutation of human virtue.

Then, the sense of beauty stirred in him; he moved where he could see its flanks coated in silver by the moonlight, the ribs and the great muscles, and the tail with tip coiled over the haunch, like the head of a serpent. It was weirdly living; fine and cruel, that great man-made thing. It expressed something in the soul of man, pitiless and remote from love—or rather, the remorselessness which man had seen, lurking within man's fate. Pierson recoiled from it, and resumed his march along the Embankment, almost deserted in the bitter cold. He came to where, in the opening of the Underground railway, he could see the little forms of people moving, little orange and red lights glowing. The sight arrested him by its warmth and motion. Was it not all a dream? That woman and her daughter, had they really come? Had not Noel been but an apparition, her words a trick which his nerves had played him? Then, too vividly again, he saw her face against the dark stuff of the curtain, the curve of her hand plucking at her blouse, heard the sound of his own horrified: "Nollie!" No illusion, no deception! The edifice of his life was in the dust. And a queer and ghastly company of faces came about him; faces he had thought friendly, of good men and women whom he knew, yet at that moment did not know, all gathered round Noel, with fingers pointing at her. He staggered back from that vision, could not bear it, could not recognise this calamity. With a sort of comfort, yet an aching sense of unreality, his mind flew to all those summer holidays spent in Scotland, Ireland, Cornwall, Wales, by mountain and lake, with his two girls; what sunsets, and turning leaves, birds, beasts, and insects they had watched together! From their youthful companionship, their eagerness, their confidence in him, he had known so much warmth and pleasure. If all those memories were true, surely this could not be true. He felt suddenly that he must hurry back, go straight to Noel, tell her that she had been cruel to him, or assure himself that, for the moment, she had been insane: His temper rose suddenly, took fire. He felt anger against her, against every one he knew, against life itself. Thrusting his hands deep into the pockets of his thin black overcoat, he plunged into that narrow glowing tunnel of the station booking-office, which led back to the crowded streets. But by the time he reached home his anger had evaporated; he felt nothing but utter lassitude. It was nine o'clock, and the maids had cleared the dining table. In despair Noel had gone up to her room. He had no courage left, and sat down supperless at his little piano, letting his fingers find soft painful harmonies, so that Noel perhaps heard the faint far thrumming of that music through uneasy dreams. And there he stayed, till it became time for him to go forth to the Old Year's Midnight Service.

When he returned, Pierson wrapped himself in a rug and lay down on the old sofa in his study. The maid, coming in next morning to "do" the grate, found him still asleep. She stood contemplating him in awe; a broad-faced, kindly, fresh-coloured girl. He lay with his face resting on his hand, his dark, just grizzling hair unruffled, as if he had not stirred all night; his other hand clutched the rug to his chest, and his booted feet protruded beyond it. To her young eyes he looked rather appallingly neglected. She gazed with interest at the hollows in his cheeks, and the furrows in his brow, and the lips, dark-moustached and bearded, so tightly compressed, even in sleep. Being holy didn't make a man happy, it seemed! What fascinated her were the cindery eyelashes resting on the cheeks, the faint movement of face and body as he breathed, the gentle hiss of breath escaping through the twitching nostrils. She moved nearer, bending down over him, with the childlike notion of counting those lashes. Her lips parted in readiness to say: "Oh!" if he waked. Something in his face, and the little twitches which passed over it, made her feel "that sorry" for him. He was a gentleman, had money, preached to her every Sunday, and was not so very old—what more could a man want? And yet—he looked so tired, with those cheeks.

She pitied him; helpless and lonely he seemed to her, asleep there instead of going to bed properly. And sighing, she tiptoed towards the door.

"Is that you, Bessie?"

The girl turned: "Yes, sir. I'm sorry I woke you, sir. 'Appy New Year, sir!"

"Ah, yes. A Happy New Year, Bessie."

She saw his usual smile, saw it die, and a fixed look come on his face; it scared her, and she hurried away. Pierson had remembered. For full five minutes he lay there staring at nothing. Then he rose, folded the rug mechanically, and looked at the clock. Eight! He went upstairs, knocked on Noel's door, and entered.

The blinds were drawn up, but she was still in bed. He stood looking down at her. "A Happy New Year, my child!" he said; and he trembled all over, shivering visibly. She looked so young and innocent, so round-faced and fresh, after her night's sleep, that the thought sprang up in him again: 'It must have been a dream!' She did not move, but a slow flush came up in her cheeks. No dream—dream! He said tremulously: "I can't realise. I—I hoped I had heard wrong. Didn't I, Nollie? Didn't I?"

She just shook her head.

"Tell me—everything," he said; "for God's sake!"

He saw her lips moving, and caught the murmur: "There 's nothing more. Gratian and George know, and Leila. It can't be undone, Daddy. Perhaps I wouldn't have wanted to make sure, if you hadn't tried to stop Cyril and me—and I'm glad sometimes, because I shall have something of his—" She looked up at him. "After all, it's the same, really; only, there's no ring. It's no good talking to me now, as if I hadn't been thinking of this for ages. I'm used to anything you can say; I've said it to myself, you see. There's nothing but to make the best of it."

Her hot hand came out from under the bedclothes, and clutched his very tight. Her flush had deepened, and her eyes seemed to him to glitter.

"Oh, Daddy! You do look tired! Haven't you been to bed? Poor Daddy!"

That hot clutch, and the words: "Poor Daddy!" brought tears into his eyes. They rolled slowly down to his beard, and he covered his face with the other hand. Her grip tightened convulsively; suddenly she dragged it to her lips, kissed it, and let it drop.

"Don't!" she said, and turned away her face.

Pierson effaced his emotion, and said quite calmly:

"Shall you wish to be at home, my dear, or to go elsewhere?"

Noel had begun to toss her head on her pillow, like a feverish child whose hair gets in its eyes and mouth.

"Oh! I don't know; what does it matter?"

"Kestrel; would you like to go there? Your aunt—I could write to her." Noel stared at him a moment; a struggle seemed going on within her.

"Yes," she said, "I would. Only, not Uncle Bob."

"Perhaps your uncle would come up here, and keep me company."

She turned her face away, and that tossing movement of the limbs beneath the clothes began again. "I don't care," she said; "anywhere—it doesn't matter."

Pierson put his chilly hand on her forehead. "Gently!" he said, and knelt down by the bed. "Merciful Father," he murmured, "give us strength to bear this dreadful trial. Keep my beloved child safe, and bring her peace; and give me to understand how I have done wrong, how I have failed towards Thee, and her. In all things chasten and strengthen her, my child, and me."

His thoughts moved on in the confused, inarticulate suspense of prayer, till he heard her say: "You haven't failed; why do you talk of failing—it isn't true; and don't pray for me, Daddy."

Pierson raised himself, and moved back from the bed. Her words confounded him, yet he was afraid to answer. She pushed her head deep into the pillow, and lay looking up at the ceiling.

"I shall have a son; Cyril won't quite have died. And I don't want to be forgiven."

He dimly perceived what long dumb processes of thought and feeling had gone on in her to produce this hardened state of mind, which to him seemed almost blasphemous. And in the very midst of this turmoil in his heart, he could not help thinking how lovely her face looked, lying back so that the curve of her throat was bared, with the short tendrils of hair coiling about it. That flung-back head, moving restlessly from side to side in the heat of the soft pillow, had such a passion of protesting life in it! And he kept silence.

"I want you to know it was all me. But I can't pretend. Of course I'll try and not let it hurt you more than I possibly can. I'm sorry for you, poor Daddy; oh! I'm sorry for you!" With a movement incredibly lithe and swift, she turned and pressed her face down in the pillow, so that all he could see was her tumbled hair and the bedclothes trembling above her shoulders. He tried to stroke that hair, but she shook her head free, and he stole out.

She did not come to breakfast; and when his own wretched meal was over, the mechanism of his professional life caught him again at once. New Year's Day! He had much to do. He had, before all, to be of a cheerful countenance before his flock, to greet all and any with an air of hope and courage.

CHAPTER X

1

Thirza Pierson, seeing her brother-in-law's handwriting, naturally said: "Here's a letter from Ted."

Bob Pierson, with a mouth full of sausage, as naturally responded:

"What does he say?"

In reading on, she found that to answer that question was one of the most difficult tasks ever set her. Its news moved and disturbed her deeply. Under her wing this disaster had happened! Down here had been wrought this most deplorable miracle, fraught with such dislocation of lives! Noel's face, absorbed and passionate, outside the door of her room on the night when Cyril Morland went away—her instinct had been right!

"He wants you to go up and stay with him, Bob."

"Why not both of us?"

"He wants Nollie to come down to me; she's not well."

"Not well? What's the matter?"

To tell him seemed disloyalty to her sex; not to tell him, disloyalty to her husband. A simple consideration of fact and not of principle, decided her. He would certainly say in a moment: 'Here! Pitch it over!' and she would have to. She said tranquilly:

"You remember that night when Cyril Morland went away, and Noel behaved so strangely. Well, my dear; she is going to have a child at the beginning of April. The poor boy is dead, Bob; he died for the Country."

She saw the red tide flow up into his face.

"What!"

"Poor Edward is dreadfully upset. We must do what we can. I blame myself." By instinct she used those words.

"Blame yourself? Stuff! That young—!" He stopped.

Thirza said quietly: "No, Bob; of the two, I'm sure it was Noel; she was desperate that day. Don't you remember her face? Oh! this war! It's turned the whole world upside down. That's the only comfort; nothing's normal."

Bob Pierson possessed beyond most men the secret of happiness, for he was always absorbed in the moment, to the point of unself-consciousness. Eating an egg, cutting down a tree, sitting on a Tribunal, making up his accounts, planting potatoes, looking at the moon, riding his cob, reading the Lessons—no part of him stood aside to see how he was doing it, or wonder why he was doing it, or not doing it better. He grew like a cork-tree, and acted like a sturdy and well-natured dog. His griefs, angers, and enjoyments were simple as a child's, or as his somewhat noisy slumbers. They were notably well-suited, for Thirza had the same secret of happiness, though her, absorption in the moment did not—as became a woman—prevent her being conscious of others; indeed, such formed the chief subject of her absorptions. One might say that they neither of them had philosophy yet were as philosophic a couple as one could meet on this earth of the self-conscious. Daily life to these two was still of simple savour. To be absorbed in life—the queer endless tissue of moments and things felt and done and said and made, the odd inspiring conjunctions of countless people—was natural to them; but they never thought whether they were absorbed or not, or had any particular attitude to Life or Death—a great blessing at the epoch in which they were living.

Bob Pierson, then, paced the room, so absorbed in his dismay and concern, that he was almost happy.

"By Jove!" he said, "what a ghastly thing!

"Nollie, of all people! I feel perfectly wretched, Thirza; wretched beyond words." But with each repetition his voice grew cheerier, and Thirza felt that he was already over the worst.

"Your coffee's getting cold!" she said.

"What do you advise? Shall I go up, heh?"

"I think you'll be a godsend to poor Ted; you'll keep his spirits up. Eve won't get any leave till Easter; and I can be quite alone, and see to Nollie here. The servants can have a holiday—, Nurse and I will run the house together. I shall enjoy it."

"You're a good woman, Thirza!" Taking his wife's hand, he put it to his lips. "There isn't another woman like you in the world."

Thirza's eyes smiled. "Pass me your cup; I'll give you some fresh coffee."

It was decided to put the plan into operation at mid-month, and she bent all her wits to instilling into her husband the thought that a baby more or less was no great matter in a world which already contained twelve hundred million people. With a man's keener sense of family propriety, he could not see that this baby would be the same as any other baby. "By heaven!" he would say, "I simply can't get used to it; in our family! And Ted a parson! What the devil shall we do with it?"

"If Nollie will let us, why shouldn't we adopt it? It'll be something to take my thoughts off the boys."

"That's an idea! But Ted's a funny fellow. He'll have some doctrine of atonement, or other in his bonnet."

"Oh, bother!" said Thirza with asperity.

The thought of sojourning in town for a spell was not unpleasant to Bob Pierson. His Tribunal work was over, his early, potatoes in, and he had visions of working for the Country, of being a special constable, and dining at his Club. The nearer he was to the front, and the more he could talk about the war, the greater the service he felt he would be doing. He would ask for a job where his brains would be of use. He regretted keenly that Thirza wouldn't be with him; a long separation like this would be a great trial. And he would sigh and run his fingers through his whiskers. Still for the Country, and for Nollie, one must put up with it!

When Thirza finally saw him into the train, tears stood in the eyes of both, for they were honestly attached, and knew well enough that this job, once taken in hand, would have to be seen through; a three months' separation at least.

"I shall write every day."

"So shall I, Bob."

"You won't fret, old girl?"

"Only if you do."

"I shall be up at 5.5, and she'll be down at 4.50. Give us a kiss—damn the porters. God bless you! I suppose she'd mind if—I—were to come down now and then?"

"I'm afraid she would. It's—it's—well, you know."

"Yes, Yes; I do." And he really did; for underneath, he had true delicacy.

Her last words: "You're very sweet, Bob," remained in his ears all the way to Severn Junction.

She went back to the house, emptied of her husband, daughter, boys, and maids; only the dogs left and the old nurse whom she had taken into confidence. Even in that sheltered, wooded valley it was very cold this winter. The birds hid themselves, not one flower bloomed, and the red-brown river was full and swift. The sound of trees being felled for trench props, in the wood above the house resounded all day long in the frosty air. She meant to do the cooking herself; and for the rest of the morning and early afternoon she concocted nice things, and thought out how she herself would feel if she were Noel and

Noel she, so as to smooth out of the way anything which would hurt the girl. In the afternoon she went down to the station in the village car, the same which had borne Cyril Morland away that July night, for their coachman had been taken for the army, and the horses were turned out.

Noel looked tired and white, but calm—too calm. Her face seemed to Thirza to have fined down, and with those brooding eyes, to be more beautiful. In the car she possessed herself of the girl's hand, and squeezed it hard; their only allusion to the situation, except Noel's formal:

"Thank you so much, Auntie, for having me; it's most awfully sweet of you and Uncle Bob."

"There's no one in the house, my dear, except old Nurse. It'll be very dull for you; but I thought I'd teach you to cook; it's rather useful."

The smile which slipped on to Noel's face gave Thirza quite a turn.

She had assigned the girl a different room, and had made it extraordinarily cheerful with a log fire, chrysanthemums, bright copper candlesticks, warming-pans, and such like.

She went up with her at bedtime, and standing before the fire, said:

"You know, Nollie, I absolutely refuse to regard this as any sort of tragedy. To bring life into the worlds in these days, no matter how, ought to make anyone happy. I only wish I could do it again, then I should feel some use. Good night dear; and if you want anything, knock on the wall. I'm next door. Bless you!" She saw that the girl was greatly moved, underneath her pale mask; and went out astonished at her niece's powers of self-control.

But she did not sleep at all well; for in imagination, she kept on seeing Noel turning from side to side in the big bed, and those great eyes of hers staring at the dark.

2

The meeting of the brothers Pierson took place at the dinner-hour, and was characterised by a truly English lack of display. They were so extremely different, and had been together so little since early days in their old Buckinghamshire home, that they were practically strangers, with just the potent link of far-distant memories in common. It was of these they talked, and about the war. On this subject they agreed in the large, and differed in the narrow. For instance, both thought they knew about Germany and other countries, and neither of course had any real knowledge of any country outside their own; for, though both had passed through considerable tracts of foreign ground at one time or another, they had never remarked anything except its surface,—its churches, and its sunsets. Again, both assumed that they were democrats, but neither knew the meaning of the word, nor felt that the working man could be really trusted; and both revered Church and, King: Both disliked conscription, but considered it necessary. Both favoured Home Rule for Ireland, but neither thought it possible to grant it. Both wished for the war to end, but were for prosecuting it to Victory, and neither knew what they meant by that word. So much for the large. On the narrower issues, such as strategy, and the personality of their country's leaders, they were opposed. Edward was a Westerner, Robert an Easterner, as was natural in one who had lived twenty-five years in Ceylon. Edward favoured the fallen government, Robert the risen. Neither had any particular reasons for their partisanship except what he had read in the journals.

After all—what other reasons could they have had? Edward disliked the Harmsworth Press; Robert thought it was doing good. Robert was explosive, and rather vague; Edward dreamy, and a little didactic. Robert thought poor Ted looking like a ghost; Edward thought poor Bob looking like the setting sun. Their faces were indeed as curiously contrasted as their views and voices; the pale-dark, hollowed, narrow face of Edward, with its short, pointed beard, and the red-skinned, broad, full, whiskered face of Robert. They parted for the night with an affectionate hand-clasp. So began a queer partnership which consisted, as the days went on, of half an hour's companionship at breakfast, each reading the paper; and of dinner together perhaps three times a week. Each thought his brother very odd, but continued to hold the highest opinion of him. And, behind it all, the deep tribal sense that they stood together in trouble, grew. But of that trouble they never spoke, though not seldom Robert would lower his journal, and above the glasses perched on his well-shaped nose, contemplate his brother, and a little frown of sympathy would ridge his forehead between his bushy eyebrows. And once in a way he would catch Edward's eyes coming off duty from his journal, to look, not at his brother, but at—the skeleton; when that happened, Robert would adjust his glasses hastily, damn the newspaper type, and apologise to Edward for swearing. And he would think: 'Poor Ted! He ought to drink port, and—and enjoy himself, and forget it. What a pity he's a parson!'

In his letters to Thirza he would deplore Edward's asceticism. "He eats nothing, he drinks nothing, he smokes a miserable cigarette once in a blue moon. He's as lonely as a coot; it's a thousand pities he ever lost his wife. I expect to see his wings sprout any day; but—dash it all I—I don't believe he's got the flesh to grow them on. Send him up some clotted cream; I'll see if I can get him to eat it." When the cream came, he got Edward to eat some the first morning, and at tea time found that he had finished it himself. "We never talk about Nollie," he wrote, "I'm always meaning to have it out with him and tell him to buck up, but when it comes to the point I dry up; because, after all, I feel it too; it sticks in my gizzard horribly. We Piersons are pretty old, and we've always been respectable, ever since St. Bartholomew, when that Huguenot chap came over and founded us. The only black sheep I ever heard of is Cousin Leila. By the way, I saw her the other day; she came round here to see Ted. I remember going to stay with her and her first husband; young Fane, at Simla, when I was coming home, just before we were married. Phew! That was a queer menage; all the young chaps fluttering round her, and young Fane looking like a cynical ghost. Even now she can't help setting her cap a little at Ted, and he swallows her whole; thinks her a devoted creature reformed to the nines with her hospital and all that. Poor old Ted; he is the most dreamy chap that ever was."

"We have had Gratian and her husband up for the week-end," he wrote a little later; "I don't like her so well as Nollie; too serious and downright for me. Her husband seems a sensible fellow, though; but the devil of a free-thinker. He and poor Ted are like cat and dog. We had Leila in to dinner again on Saturday, and a man called Fort came too. She's sweet on him, I could see with half an eye, but poor old Ted can't. The doctor and Ted talked up hill and down dale. The doctor said a thing which struck me. 'What divides us from the beasts? Will power: nothing else. What's this war, really, but a death carnival of proof that man's will is invincible?' I stuck it down to tell you, when I got upstairs. He's a clever fellow. I believe in God, as you know, but I must say when it comes to an argument, poor old Ted does seem a bit weak, with his: 'We're told this,' and 'We're told that: Nobody mentioned Nollie. I must have the whole thing out with Ted; we must know how to act when it's all over."

But not till the middle of March, when the brothers had been sitting opposite each other at meals for two months, was the subject broached between them, and then not by Robert. Edward, standing by the hearth after dinner, in his familiar attitude, one foot on the fender, one hand grasping the mantel-shelf, and his eyes fixed on the flames, said: "I've never asked your forgiveness, Bob."

Robert, lingering at the table over his glass of port, started, looked at Edward's back in its parson's coat, and answered:

"My dear old chap!"

"It has been very difficult to speak of this."

"Of course, of course!" And there was a silence, while Robert's eyes travelled round the walls for inspiration. They encountered only the effigies of past Piersons very oily works, and fell back on the dining-table. Edward went on speaking to the fire:

"It still seems to me incredible. Day and night I think of what it's my duty to do."

"Nothing!" ejaculated Robert. "Leave the baby with Thirza; we'll take care of it, and when Nollie's fit, let her go back to work in a hospital again. She'll soon get over it." He saw his brother shake his head, and thought: 'Ah! yes; now there's going to be some d—d conscientious complication.'

Edward turned round on him: "That is very sweet of you both, but it would be wrong and cowardly for me to allow it."

The resentment which springs up in fathers when other fathers dispose of young lives, rose in Robert.

"Dash it all, my dear Ted, that's for Nollie to say. She's a woman now, remember."

A smile went straying about in the shadows of his brother's face. "A woman? Little Nollie! Bob, I've made a terrible mess of it with my girls." He hid his lips with his hand, and turned again to the flames. Robert felt a lump in his throat. "Oh! Hang it, old boy, I don't think that. What else could you have done? You take too much on yourself. After all, they're fine girls. I'm sure Nollie's a darling. It's these modern notions, and this war. Cheer up! It'll all dry straight." He went up to his brother and put a hand on his shoulder. Edward seemed to stiffen under that touch.

"Nothing comes straight," he said, "unless it's faced; you know that, Bob."

Robert's face was a study at that moment. His cheeks filled and collapsed again like a dog's when it has been rebuked. His colour deepened, and he rattled some money in a trouser pocket.

"Something in that, of course," he said gruffly. "All the same, the decision's with Nollie. We'll see what Thirza says. Anyway, there's no hurry. It's a thousand pities you're a parson; the trouble's enough without that:"

Edward shook his head. "My position is nothing; it's the thought of my child, my wife's child. It's sheer pride; and I can't subdue it. I can't fight it down. God forgive me, I rebel."

And Robert thought: 'By George, he does take it to heart! Well, so should I! I do, as it is!' He took out his pipe, and filled it, pushing the tobacco down and down.

"I'm not a man of the world," he heard his brother say; "I'm out of touch with many things. It's almost unbearable to me to feel that I'm joining with the world to condemn my own daughter; not for their reasons, perhaps—I don't know; I hope not, but still, I'm against her."

Robert lit his pipe.

"Steady, old man!" he said. "It's a misfortune. But if I were you I should feel: 'She's done a wild, silly thing, but, hang it, if anybody says a word against her, I'll wring his neck.' And what's more, you'll feel much the same, when it comes to the point." He emitted a huge puff of smoke, which obscured his brother's face, and the blood, buzzing in his temples, seemed to thicken the sound of Edward's voice.

"I don't know; I've tried to see clearly. I have prayed to be shown what her duty is, and mine. It seems to me there can be no peace for her until she has atoned, by open suffering; that the world's judgment is her cross, and she must bear it; especially in these days, when all the world is facing suffering so nobly. And then it seems so hard-so bitter; my poor little Nollie!"

There was a silence, broken only by the gurgling of Robert's pipe, till he said abruptly:

"I don't follow you, Ted; no, I don't. I think a man should screen his children all he can. Talk to her as you like, but don't let the world do it. Dash it, the world's a rotten gabbling place. I call myself a man of the world, but when it comes to private matters—well, then I draw the line. It seems to me it seems to me inhuman. What does George Laird think about it? He's a knowing chap. I suppose you've—no, I suppose you haven't—" For a peculiar smile had come on Edward's face.

"No," he said, "I should hardly ask George Laird's opinion."

And Robert realised suddenly the stubborn loneliness of that thin black figure, whose fingers were playing with a little gold cross. 'By Jove!' he thought, 'I believe old Ted's like one of those Eastern chaps who go into lonely places. He's got himself surrounded by visions of things that aren't there. He lives in unreality—something we can't understand. I shouldn't be surprised if he heard voices, like—'who was it? Tt, tt! What a pity!' Ted was deceptive. He was gentle and—all that, a gentleman of course, and that disguised him; but underneath; what was there—a regular ascetic, a fakir! And a sense of bewilderment, of dealing with something which he could not grasp, beset Bob Pierson, so that he went back to the table, and sat down again beside his port.

"It seems to me," he said rather gruffly, "that the chicken had better be hatched before we count it." And then, sorry for his brusqueness, emptied his glass. As the fluid passed over his palate, he thought: 'Poor old Ted! He doesn't even drink—hasn't a pleasure in life, so far as I can see, except doing his duty, and doesn't even seem to know what that is. There aren't many like him—luckily! And yet I love him—pathetic chap!'

The "pathetic chap" was still staring at the flames.

3

And at this very hour, when the brothers were talking—for thought and feeling do pass mysteriously over the invisible wires of space Cyril Morland's son was being born of Noel, a little before his time.

PART III

CHAPTER I

Down by the River Wye, among plum-trees in blossom, Noel had laid her baby in a hammock, and stood reading a letter:

"MY DEAREST NOLLIE,

"Now that you are strong again, I feel that I must put before you my feeling as to your duty in this crisis of your life. Your aunt and uncle have made the most kind and generous offer to adopt your little boy. I have known that this was in their minds for some time, and have thought it over day and night for weeks. In the worldly sense it would be the best thing, no doubt. But this is a spiritual matter. The future of our souls depends on how we meet the consequences of our conduct. And painful, dreadful, indeed, as they must be, I am driven to feel that you can only reach true peace by facing them in a spirit of brave humility. I want you to think and think—till you arrive at a certainty which satisfies your conscience. If you decide, as I trust you will, to come back to me here with your boy, I shall do all in my power to make you happy while we face the future together. To do as your aunt and uncle in their kindness wish, would, I am sore afraid, end in depriving you of the inner strength and happiness which God only gives to those who do their duty and try courageously to repair their errors. I have confidence in you, my dear child.

"Ever your most loving father,

"EDWARD PIERSON."

She read it through a second time, and looked at her baby. Daddy seemed to think that she might be willing to part from this wonderful creature! Sunlight fell through the plum blossom, in an extra patchwork quilt over the bundle lying there, touched the baby's nose and mouth, so that he sneezed. Noel laughed, and put her lips close to his face. 'Give you up!' she thought: 'Oh, no! And I'm going to be happy too. They shan't stop me:

In answer to the letter she said simply that she was coming up; and a week later she went, to the dismay of her uncle and aunt. The old nurse went too. Everything had hitherto been so carefully watched and guarded against by Thirza, that Noel did not really come face to face with her position till she reached home.

Gratian, who had managed to get transferred to a London Hospital, was now living at home. She had provided the house with new maids against her sister's return; and though Noel was relieved not to meet her old familiars, she encountered with difficulty the stolid curiosity of new faces. That morning before she left Kestrel, her aunt had come into her room while she was dressing, taken her left hand and slipped a little gold band on to its third finger. "To please me, Nollie, now that you're going, just for the foolish, who know nothing about you."

Noel had suffered it with the thought: 'It's all very silly!' But now, when the new maid was pouring out her hot water, she was suddenly aware of the girl's round blue eyes wandering, as it were, mechanically to her hand. This little hoop of gold, then, had an awful power! A rush of disgust came over her. All life seemed suddenly a thing of forms and sham. Everybody then would look at that little ring; and she was a coward, saving herself from them! When she was alone again, she slipped it off, and laid it on the washstand, where the sunlight fell. Only this little shining band of metal, this little yellow ring, stood between her and the world's hostile scorn! Her lips trembled. She took up the ring, and went to the open window; to throw it out. But she did not, uncertain and unhappy—half realising the cruelty of life. A knock at the door sent her flying back to the washstand. The visitor was Gratian.

"I've been looking at him," she said softly; "he's like you, Nollie, except for his nose."

"He's hardly got one yet. But aren't his eyes intelligent? I think they're wonderful." She held up the ring: "What shall I do about this, Gratian?"

Gratian flushed. "Wear it. I don't see why outsiders should know. For the sake of Dad I think you ought. There's the parish."

Noel slipped the ring back on to her finger. "Would you?"

"I can't tell. I think I would."

Noel laughed suddenly. "I'm going to get cynical; I can feel it in my bones. How is Daddy looking?"

"Very thin; Mr. Lauder is back again from the Front for a bit, and taking some of the work now."

"Do I hurt him very much still?"

"He's awfully pleased that you've come. He's as sweet as he can be about you."

"Yes," murmured Noel, "that's what's dreadful. I'm glad he wasn't in when I came. Has he told anyone?"

Gratian shook her head. "I don't think anybody knows; unless—perhaps Captain Fort. He came in again the other night; and somehow—"

Noel flushed. "Leila!" she said enigmatically. "Have you seen her?"

"I went to her flat last week with Dad—he likes her."

"Delilah is her real name, you know. All men like her. And Captain Fort is her lover."

Gratian gasped. Noel would say things sometimes which made her feel the younger of the two.

"Of course he is," went on Noel in a hard voice. "She has no men friends; her sort never have, only lovers. Why do you think he knows about me?"

"When he asked after you he looked—"

"Yes; I've seen him look like that when he's sorry for anything. I don't care. Has Monsieur Lavendie been in lately?"

"Yes; he looks awfully unhappy."

"His wife drugs."

"Oh, Nollie! How do you know?"

"I saw her once; I'm sure she does; there was a smell; and she's got wandering eyes that go all glassy. He can paint me now, if he likes. I wouldn't let him before. Does he know?"

"Of course not."

"He knows there was something; he's got second sight, I think. But I mind him less than anybody. Is his picture of Daddy good?"

"Powerful, but it hurts, somehow."

"Let's go down and see it."

The picture was hung in the drawing-room, and its intense modernity made that old-fashioned room seem lifeless and strange. The black figure, with long pale fingers touching the paler piano keys, had a frightening actuality. The face, three-quarters full, was raised as if for inspiration, and the eyes rested, dreamy and unseeing, on the face of a girl painted and hung on a background of wall above the piano.

"It's the face of that girl," said Gratian, when they had looked at the picture for some time in silence:

"No," said Noel, "it's the look in his eyes."

"But why did he choose such a horrid, common girl? Isn't she fearfully alive, though? She looks as if she were saying: 'Cheerio!'.rdquo;

"She is; it's awfully pathetic, I think. Poor Daddy!"

"It's a libel," said Gratian stubbornly.

"No. That's what hurts. He isn't quite—quite all there. Will he be coming in soon?"

Gratian took her arm, and pressed it hard. "Would you like me at dinner or not; I can easily be out?"

Noel shook her head. "It's no good to funk it. He wanted me, and now he's got me. Oh! why did he? It'll be awful for him."

Gratian sighed. "I've tried my best, but he always said: 'I've thought so long about it all that I can't think any longer. I can only feel the braver course is the best. When things are bravely and humbly met, there will be charity and forgiveness.'.rdquo;

"There won't," said Noel, "Daddy's a saint, and he doesn't see."

"Yes, he is a saint. But one must think for oneself—one simply must. I can't believe as he does, any more; can you, Nollie?"

"I don't know. When I was going through it, I prayed; but I don't know whether I really believed. I don't think I mind much about that, one way or the other."

"I mind terribly," said Gratian, "I want the truth."

"I don't know what I want," said Noel slowly, "except that sometimes I want—life; awfully."

And the two sisters were silent, looking at each other with a sort of wonder.

Noel had a fancy to put on a bright-coloured blue frock that evening, and at her neck she hung a Breton cross of old paste, which had belonged to her mother. When she had finished dressing she went into the nursery and stood by the baby's cot. The old nurse who was sitting there beside him, got up at once and said:

"He's sleeping beautiful—the lamb. I'll go down and get a cup o' tea, and come up, ma'am, when the gong goes." In the way peculiar to those who have never to initiate, but only to support positions in which they are placed by others, she had adopted for herself the theory that Noel was a real war-widow. She knew the truth perfectly; for she had watched that hurried little romance at Kestrel, but by dint of charity and blurred meditations it was easy for her to imagine the marriage ceremony which would and should have taken place; and she was zealous that other people should imagine it too. It was so much more regular and natural like that, and "her" baby invested with his proper dignity. She went downstairs to get a "cup o' tea," thinking: 'A picture they make—that they do, bless his little heart; and his pretty little mother—no more than a child, all said and done.'

Noel had been standing there some minutes in the failing light, absorbed in the face of the sleeping baby, when, raising her eyes, she saw in a mirror the refection of her father's dark figure by the door. She could hear him breathing as if the ascent of the stairs had tired him; and moving to the head of the cot, she rested her hand on it, and turned her face towards him. He came up and stood beside her, looking silently down at the baby. She saw him make the sign of the Cross above it, and the movement of his lips in prayer. Love for her father, and rebellion against this intercession for her perfect baby fought so hard in the girl's heart that she felt suffocated, and glad of the dark, so that he could not see her eyes. Then he took her hand and put it to his lips, but still without a word; and for the life of her she could not speak either. In silence, he kissed her forehead; and there mounted in Noel a sudden passion of longing to show him her pride and love for her baby. She put her finger down and touched one of his hands. The tiny sleeping fingers uncurled and, like some little sea anemone, clutched round it. She heard her father draw his breath in; saw him turn away quickly, silently, and go out. And she stayed, hardly breathing, with the hand of her baby squeezing her finger.

CHAPTER II

1

When Edward Pierson, afraid of his own emotion, left the twilit nursery, he slipped into his own room, and fell on his knees beside his bed, absorbed in the vision he had seen. That young figure in Madonna blue, with the halo of bright hair; the sleeping babe in the fine dusk; the silence, the adoration in that white room! He saw, too; a vision of the past, when Noel herself had been the sleeping babe within her mother's arm, and he had stood beside them, wondering and giving praise. It passed with its other-worldliness and the fine holiness which belongs to beauty, passed and left the tormenting realism of life. Ah! to live with only the inner meaning, spiritual and beautifed, in a rare wonderment such as he had experienced just now!

His alarum clock, while he knelt in his narrow, monkish little room—ticked the evening hour away into darkness. And still he knelt, dreading to come back into it all, to face the world's eyes, and the sound of the world's tongue, and the touch of the rough, the gross, the unseemly. How could he guard his child? How preserve that vision in her life, in her spirit, about to enter such cold, rough waters? But the gong sounded; he got up, and went downstairs.

But this first family moment, which all had dreaded, was relieved, as dreaded moments so often are, by the unexpected appearance of the Belgian painter. He had a general invitation, of which he often availed himself; but he was so silent, and his thin, beardless face, which seemed all eyes and brow, so mournful, that all three felt in the presence of a sorrow deeper even than their own family grief. During the meal he gazed silently at Noel. Once he said: "You will let me paint you now, mademoiselle, I hope?" and his face brightened a little when she nodded. There was never much talk when he came, for any depth of discussion, even of art, brought out at once too wide a difference. And Pierson could never avoid a vague irritation with one who clearly had spirituality, but of a sort which he could not understand. After dinner he excused himself, and went off to his study. Monsieur would be happier alone with the two girls! Gratian, too, got up. She had remembered Noel's words: "I mind him less than anybody." It was a chance for Nollie to break the ice.

2

"I have not seen you for a long time, mademoiselle," said the painter, when they were alone.

Noel was sitting in front of the empty drawing-room hearth, with her arms stretched out as if there had been a fire there.

"I've been away. How are you going to paint me, monsieur?"

"In that dress, mademoiselle; Just as you are now, warming yourself at the fire of life."

"But it isn't there."

"Yes, fires soon go out. Mademoiselle, will you come and see my wife? She is ill."

"Now?" asked Noel, startled.

"Yes, now. She is really ill, and I have no one there. That is what I came to ask of your sister; but—now you are here, it's even better. She likes you."

Noel got up. "Wait one minute!" she said, and ran upstairs. Her baby was asleep, and the old nurse dozing. Putting on a cloak and cap of grey rabbit's fur, she ran down again to the hall where the painter was waiting; and they went out together.

"I do not know if I am to blame," he said, "my wife has been no real wife to me since she knew I had a mistress and was no real husband to her."

Noel stared round at his face lighted by a queer, smile.

"Yes," he went on, "from that has come her tragedy. But she should have known before I married her. Nothing was concealed. Bon Dieu! she should have known! Why cannot a woman see things as they are? My mistress, mademoiselle, is not a thing of flesh. It is my art. It has always been first with me, and always will. She has never accepted that, she is incapable of accepting it. I am sorry for her. But what would you? I was a fool to marry her. Chere mademoiselle, no troubles are anything beside the trouble which goes on day and night, meal after meal, year, after year, between two people who should never have married, because one loves too much and requires all, and the other loves not at all—no, not at all, now, it is long dead—and can give but little."

"Can't you separate?" asked Noel, wondering.

"It is hard to separate from one who craves for you as she craves her drugs—yes, she takes drugs now, mademoiselle. It is impossible for one who has any compassion in his soul. Besides, what would she do? We live from hand to mouth, in a strange land. She has no friends here, not one. How could I leave her while this war lasts? As well could two persons on a desert island separate. She is killing herself, too, with these drugs, and I cannot stop her."

"Poor madame!" murmured Noel. "Poor monsieur!"

The painter drew his hand across his eyes.

"I cannot change my nature," he said in a stifled voice, "nor she hers. So we go on. But life will stop suddenly some day for one of us. After all, it is much worse for her than for me. Enter, mademoiselle. Do not tell her I am going to paint you; she likes you, because you refused to let me."

Noel went up the stairs, shuddering; she had been there once before, and remembered that sickly scent of drugs. On the third floor they entered a small sitting-room whose walls were covered with paintings and drawings; from one corner a triangular stack of canvases jutted out. There was little furniture save an old red sofa, and on this was seated a stoutish man in the garb of a Belgian soldier, with his elbows on his knees and his bearded cheeks resting on his doubled fists. Beside him on the sofa, nursing a doll, was a little girl, who looked up at Noel. She had a most strange, attractive, pale little face, with pointed chin and large eyes, which never moved from this apparition in grey rabbits' skins.

"Ah, Barra! You here!" said the painter:

"Mademoiselle, this is Monsieur Barra, a friend of ours from the front; and this is our landlady's little girl. A little refugee, too, aren't you, Chica?"

The child gave him a sudden brilliant smile and resumed her grave scrutiny of the visitor. The soldier, who had risen heavily, offered Noel one of his podgy hands, with a sad and heavy giggle.

"Sit down, mademoiselle," said Lavendie, placing a chair for her: "I will bring my wife in," and he went out through some double doors.

Noel sat down. The soldier had resumed his old attitude, and the little girl her nursing of the doll, though her big eyes still watched the visitor. Overcome by strangeness, Noel made no attempt to talk. And presently through the double doors the painter and his wife came in. She was a thin woman in a red wrapper, with hollow cheeks, high cheek-bones, and hungry eyes; her dark hair hung loose, and one hand played restlessly with a fold of her gown. She took Noel's hand; and her uplifted eyes seemed to dig into the girl's face, to let go suddenly, and flutter.

"How do you do?" she said in English. "So Pierre brought you, to see me again. I remember you so well. You would not let him paint you. Ah! que c'est drole! You are so pretty, too. Hein, Monsieur Barra, is not mademoiselle pretty?"

The soldier gave his heavy giggle, and resumed his scrutiny of the floor.

"Henriette," said Lavendie, "sit down beside Chica—you must not stand. Sit down, mademoiselle, I beg."

"I'm so sorry you're not well," said Noel, and sat down again.

The painter stood leaning against the wall, and his wife looked up at his tall, thin figure, with eyes which had in them anger, and a sort of cunning.

"A great painter, my husband, is he not?" she said to Noel. "You would not imagine what that man can do. And how he paints—all day long; and all night in his head. And so you would not let him paint you, after all?"

Lavendie said impatiently: "Voyons, Henriette, causez d'autre chose."

His wife plucked nervously at a fold in her red gown, and gave him the look of a dog that has been rebuked.

"I am a prisoner here, mademoiselle, I never leave the house. Here I live day after day—my husband is always painting. Who would go out alone under this grey sky of yours, and the hatreds of the war in every face? I prefer to keep my room. My husband goes painting; every face he sees interests him, except that which he sees every day. But I am a prisoner. Monsieur Barra is our first visitor for a long time."

The soldier raised his face from his fists. "Prisonnier, madame! What would you say if you were out there?" And he gave his thick giggle. "We are the prisoners, we others. What would you say to imprisonment by explosion day and night; never a minute free. Bom! Bom! Bom! Ah! les tranchees! It's not so free as all that, there."

"Every one has his own prison," said Lavendie bitterly. "Mademoiselle even, has her prison—and little Chica, and her doll. Every one has his prison, Barra. Monsieur Barra is also a painter, mademoiselle."

"Moi!" said Barra, lifting his heavy hairy hand. "I paint puddles, star-bombs, horses' ribs—I paint holes and holes and holes, wire and wire and wire, and water—long white ugly water. I paint splinters, and men's souls naked, and men's bodies dead, and nightmare—nightmare—all day and all night—I paint them in my head." He suddenly ceased speaking and relapsed into contemplation of the carpet, with his bearded cheeks resting on his fists. "And their souls as white as snow, les camarades," he added suddenly and loudly, "millions of Belgians, English, French, even the Boches, with white souls. I paint those souls!"

A little shiver ran through Noel, and she looked appealingly at Lavendie.

"Barra," he said, as if the soldier were not there, "is a great painter, but the Front has turned his head a little. What he says is true, though. There is no hatred out there. It is here that we are prisoners of hatred, mademoiselle; avoid hatreds—they are poison!"

His wife put out her hand and touched the child's shoulder.

"Why should we not hate?" she said. "Who killed Chica's father, and blew her home to-rags? Who threw her out into this horrible England—pardon, mademoiselle, but it is horrible. Ah! les Boches! If my hatred could destroy them there would not be one left. Even my husband was not so mad about his painting when we lived at home. But here—!" Her eyes darted at his face again, and then sank as if rebuked. Noel saw the painter's lips move. The sick woman's whole figure writhed.

"It is mania, your painting!" She looked at Noel with a smile. "Will you have some tea, mademoiselle? Monsieur Barra, some tea?"

The soldier said thickly: "No, madame; in the trenches we have tea enough. It consoles us. But when we get away—give us wine, le bon vin; le bon petit vin!"

"Get some wine, Pierre!"

Noel saw from the painter's face that there was no wine, and perhaps no money to get any; but he went quickly out. She rose and said:

"I must be going, madame."

Madame Lavendie leaned forward and clutched her wrist. "Wait a little, mademoiselle. We shall have some wine, and Pierre shall take you back presently. You cannot go home alone—you are too pretty. Is she not, Monsieur Barra?"

The soldier looked up: "What would you say," he said, "to bottles of wine bursting in the air, bursting red and bursting white, all day long, all night long? Great steel bottles, large as Chica: bits of bottles, carrying off men's heads? Bsum, garra-a-a, and a house comes down, and little bits of people ever so small, ever so small, tiny bits in the air and all over the ground. Great souls out there, madame. But I will tell you a secret," and again he gave his heavy giggle, "all a little, little mad; nothing to speak of—just a little bit mad; like a watch, you know, that you can wind for ever. That is the discovery of this war, mademoiselle," he said, addressing Noel for the first time, "you cannot gain a great soul till you are a little mad." And lowering his piggy grey eyes at once, he resumed his former attitude. "It is that madness

I shall paint some day," he announced to the carpet; "lurking in one tiny corner of each soul of all those millions, as it creeps, as it peeps, ever so sudden, ever so little when we all think it has been put to bed, here—there, now—then, when you least think; in and out like a mouse with bright eyes. Millions of men with white souls, all a little mad. A great subject, I think," he added heavily. Involuntarily Noel put her hand to her heart, which was beating fast. She felt quite sick.

"How long have you been at the Front, monsieur?"

"Two years, mademoiselle. Time to go home and paint, is it not? But art—!" he shrugged his heavy round shoulders, his whole bear-like body. "A little mad," he muttered once more. "I will tell you a story. Once in winter after I had rested a fortnight, I go back to the trenches at night, and I want some earth to fill up a hole in the ground where I was sleeping; when one has slept in a bed one becomes particular. Well, I scratch it from my parapet, and I come to something funny. I strike my briquet, and there is a Boche's face all frozen and earthy and dead and greeny-white in the flame from my briquet."

"Oh, no!"

"Oh! but yes, mademoiselle; true as I sit here. Very useful in the parapet—dead Boche. Once a man like me. But in the morning I could not stand him; we dug him out and buried him, and filled the hole up with other things. But there I stood in the night, and my face as close to his as this"—and he held his thick hand a foot before his face. "We talked of our homes; he had a soul, that man. 'Il me disait des choses', how he had suffered; and I, too, told him my sufferings. Dear God, we know all; we shall never know more than we know out there, we others, for we are mad—nothing to speak of, but just a little, little mad. When you see us, mademoiselle, walking the streets, remember that." And he dropped his face on to his fists again.

A silence had fallen in the room-very queer and complete. The little girl nursed her doll, the soldier gazed at the floor, the woman's mouth moved stealthily, and in Noel the thought rushed continually to the verge of action: 'Couldn't I get up and run downstairs?' But she sat on, hypnotised by that silence, till Lavendie reappeared with a bottle and four glasses.

"To drink our health, and wish us luck, mademoiselle," he said.

Noel raised the glass he had given her. "I wish you all happiness."

"And you, mademoiselle," the two men murmured.

She drank a little, and rose.

"And now, mademoiselle," said Lavendie, "if you must go, I will see you home."

Noel took Madame Lavendie's hand; it was cold, and returned no pressure; her eyes had the glazed look that she remembered. The soldier had put his empty glass down on the floor, and was regarding it unconscious of her. Noel turned quickly to the door; the last thing she saw was the little girl nursing her doll.

In the street the painter began at once in his rapid French:

"I ought not to have asked you to come, mademoiselle; I did not know our friend Barra was there. Besides, my wife is not fit to receive a lady; vous voyez qu'il y a de la manie dans cette pauvre tote. I should not have asked you; but I was so miserable."

"Oh!" murmured Noel, "I know."

"In our home over there she had interests. In this great town she can only nurse her grief against me. Ah! this war! It seems to me we are all in the stomach of a great coiling serpent. We lie there, being digested. In a way it is better out there in the trenches; they are beyond hate, they have attained a height that we have not. It is wonderful how they still can be for going on till they have beaten the Boche; that is curious and it is very great. Did Barra tell you how, when they come back—all these fighters—they are going to rule, and manage the future of the world? But it will not be so. They will mix in with life, separate—be scattered, and they will be ruled as they were before. The tongue and the pen will rule them: those who have not seen the war will rule them."

"Oh!"' cried Noel, "surely they will be the bravest and strongest in the future."

The painter smiled.

"War makes men simple," he said, "elemental; life in peace is neither simple nor elemental, it is subtle, full of changing environments, to which man must adapt himself; the cunning, the astute, the adaptable, will ever rule in times of peace. It is pathetic, the belief of those brave soldiers that the-future is theirs."

"He said, a strange thing," murmured Noel; "that they were all a little mad."

"He is a man of queer genius—Barra; you should see some of his earlier pictures. Mad is not quite the word, but something is loosened, is rattling round in them, they have lost proportion, they are being forced in one direction. I tell you, mademoiselle, this war is one great forcing-house; every living plant is being made to grow too fast, each quality, each passion; hate and love, intolerance and lust and avarice, courage and energy; yes, and self-sacrifice—all are being forced and forced beyond their strength, beyond the natural flow of the sap, forced till there has come a great wild luxuriant crop, and then— Psum! Presto! The change comes, and these plants will wither and rot and stink. But we who see Life in forms of Art are the only ones who feel that; and we are so few. The natural shape of things is lost. There is a mist of blood before all eyes. Men are afraid of being fair. See how we all hate not only our enemies, but those who differ from us. Look at the streets too—see how men and women rush together, how Venus reigns in this forcing-house. Is it not natural that Youth about to die should yearn for pleasure, for love, for union, before death?"

Noel stared up at him. 'Now!' she thought: I will.'

"Yes," she said, "I know that's true, because I rushed, myself. I'd like you to know. We couldn't be married—there wasn't time. And—he was killed. But his son is alive. That's why I've been away so long. I want every one to know." She spoke very calmly, but her cheeks felt burning hot.

The painter had made an upward movement of his hands, as if they had been jerked by an electric current, then he said quite quietly:

"My profound respect, mademoiselle, and my great sympathy. And your father?"

"It's awful for him."

The painter said gently: "Ah! mademoiselle, I am not so sure. Perhaps he does not suffer so greatly. Perhaps not even your trouble can hurt him very much. He lives in a world apart. That, I think, is his true tragedy to be alive, and yet not living enough to feel reality. Do you know Anatole France's description of an old woman: 'Elle vivait, mais si peu.' Would that not be well said of the Church in these days: 'Elle vivait, mais si peu.' I see him always like a rather beautiful dark spire in the night-time when you cannot see how it is attached to the earth. He does not know, he never will know, Life."

Noel looked round at him. "What do you mean by Life, monsieur? I'm always reading about Life, and people talk of seeing Life! What is it—where is it? I never see anything that you could call Life."

The painter smiled.

"To 'see life'." he said. "Ah! that is different. To enjoy yourself! Well, it is my experience that when people are 'seeing life' as they call it, they are not enjoying themselves. You know when one is very thirsty one drinks and drinks, but the thirst remains all the same. There are places where one can see life as it is called, but the only persons you will see enjoying themselves at such places are a few humdrums like myself, who go there for a talk over a cup of coffee. Perhaps at your age, though, it is different."

Noel clasped her hands, and her eyes seemed to shine in the gloom. "I want music and dancing and light, and beautiful things and faces; but I never get them."

"No, there does not exist in this town, or in any other, a place which will give you that. Fox-trots and ragtime and paint and powder and glare and half-drunken young men, and women with red lips you can get them in plenty. But rhythm and beauty and charm never. In Brussels when I was younger I saw much 'life' as they call it, but not one lovely thing unspoiled; it was all as ashes in the mouth. Ah! you may smile, but I know what I am talking of. Happiness never comes when you are looking for it, mademoiselle; beauty is in Nature and in real art, never in these false silly make believes. There is a place just here where we Belgians go; would you like to see how true my words are?"

"Oh, yes!"

"Tres-bien! Let us go in?"

They passed into a revolving doorway with little glass compartments which shot them out into a shining corridor. At the end of this the painter looked at Noel and seemed to hesitate, then he turned off from the room they were about to enter into a room on the right. It was large, full of gilt and plush and marble tables, where couples were seated; young men in khaki and older men in plain clothes, together or with young women. At these last Noel looked, face after face, while they were passing down a long way to an empty table. She saw that some were pretty, and some only trying to be, that nearly all were powdered and had their eyes darkened and their lips reddened, till she felt her own face to be dreadfully ungarnished: Up in a gallery a small band was playing an attractive jingling hollow little tune; and the buzz of talk and laughter was almost deafening.

"What will you have, mademoiselle?" said the painter. "It is just nine o'clock; we must order quickly."

"May I have one of those green things?"

"Deux cremes de menthe," said Lavendie to the waiter.

Noel was too absorbed to see the queer, bitter little smile hovering about his face. She was busy looking at the faces of women whose eyes, furtively cold and enquiring, were fixed on her; and at the faces of men with eyes that were furtively warm and wondering.

"I wonder if Daddy was ever in a place like this?" she said, putting the glass of green stuff to her lips. "Is it nice? It smells of peppermint."

"A beautiful colour. Good luck, mademoiselle!" and he chinked his glass with hers.

Noel sipped, held it away, and sipped again.

"It's nice; but awfully sticky. May I have a cigarette?"

"Des cigarettes," said Lavendie to the waiter, "Et deux cafes noirs. Now, mademoiselle," he murmured when they were brought, "if we imagine that we have drunk a bottle of wine each, we shall have exhausted all the preliminaries of what is called Vice. Amusing, isn't it?" He shrugged his shoulders.

His face struck Noel suddenly as tarnished and almost sullen.

"Don't be angry, monsieur, it's all new to me, you see."

The painter smiled, his bright, skin-deep smile.

"Pardon! I forget myself. Only, it hurts me to see beauty in a place like this. It does not go well with that tune, and these voices, and these faces. Enjoy yourself, mademoiselle; drink it all in! See the way these people look at each other; what love shines in their eyes! A pity, too, we cannot hear what they are saying. Believe me, their talk is most subtle, tres-spirituel. These young women are 'doing their bit,' as you call it; bringing le plaisir to all these who are serving their country. Eat, drink, love, for tomorrow we die. Who cares for the world simple or the world beautiful, in days like these? The house of the spirit is empty."

He was looking at her sidelong as if he would enter her very soul.

Noel got up. "I'm ready to go, monsieur."

He put her cloak on her shoulders, paid the bill, and they went out, threading again through the little tables, through the buzz of talk and laughter and the fumes of tobacco, while another hollow little tune jingled away behind them.

"Through there," said the painter, pointing to another door, "they dance. So it goes. London in war-time! Well, after all, it is never very different; no great town is. Did you enjoy your sight of 'life,' mademoiselle?"

"I think one must dance, to be happy. Is that where your friends go?"

"Oh, no! To a room much rougher, and play dominoes, and drink coffee and beer, and talk. They have no money to throw away."

"Why didn't you show me?"

"Mademoiselle, in that room you might see someone perhaps whom one day you would meet again; in the place we visited you were safe enough at least I hope so."

Noel shrugged. "I suppose it doesn't matter now, what I do."

And a rush of emotion caught at her throat—a wave from the past—the moonlit night, the dark old Abbey, the woods and the river. Two tears rolled down her cheeks.

"I was thinking of—something," she said in a muffled voice. "It's all right."

"Chere mademoiselle!" Lavendie murmured; and all the way home he was timid and distressed. Shaking his hand at the door, she murmured:

"I'm sorry I was such a fool; and thank you awfully, monsieur. Good night."

"Good night; and better dreams. There is a good time coming—Peace and Happiness once more in the world. It will not always be this Forcing-House. Good night, chere mademoiselle!"

Noel went up to the nursery, and stole in. A night-light was burning, Nurse and baby were fast asleep. She tiptoed through into her own room. Once there, she felt suddenly so tired that she could hardly undress; and yet curiously rested, as if with that rush of emotion, Cyril and the past had slipped from her for ever.

CHAPTER III

Noel's first encounter with Opinion took place the following day. The baby had just come in from its airing; she had seen it comfortably snoozing, and was on her way downstairs, when a voice from the hall said:

"How do you do?" and she saw the khaki-clad figure of Adrian Lauder, her father's curate! Hesitating just a moment, she finished her descent, and put her fingers in his. He was a rather heavy, dough-coloured young man of nearly thirty, unsuited by khaki, with a round white collar buttoned behind; but his aspiring eyes redeemed him, proclaiming the best intentions in the world, and an inclination towards sentiment in the presence of beauty.

"I haven't seen you for ages," he said rather fatuously, following her into her father's study.

"No," said Noel. "How—do you like being at the Front?"

"Ah!" he said, "they're wonderful!" And his eyes shone. "It's so nice to see you again."

"Is it?"

He seemed puzzled by that answer; stammered, and said:

"I didn't know your sister had a baby. A jolly baby."

"She hasn't."

Lauder's mouth opened. 'A silly mouth,' she thought.

"Oh!" he said. "Is it a protegee—Belgian or something?"

"No, it's mine; my own." And, turning round, she slipped the little ring off her finger. When she turned back to him, his face had not recovered from her words. It had a hapless look, as of one to whom such a thing ought not to have happened.

"Don't look like that," said Noel. "Didn't you understand? It's mine-mine." She put out her left hand. "Look! There's no ring."

He stammered: "I say, you oughtn't to—you oughtn't to—!"

"What?"

"Joke about—about such things; ought you?"

"One doesn't joke if one's had a baby without being married, you know."

Lauder went suddenly slack. A shell might have burst a few paces from him. And then, just as one would in such a case, he made an effort, braced himself, and said in a curious voice, both stiff and heavy: "I can't—one doesn't—it's not—"

"It is," said Noel. "If you don't believe me, ask Daddy."

He put his hand up to his round collar; and with the wild thought that he was going to tear it off, she cried: "Don't!"

"You!" he said. "You! But—"

Noel turned away from him to the window: She stood looking out, but saw nothing whatever.

"I don't want it hidden," she said without turning round, "I want every one to know. It's stupid as it is— stupid!" and she stamped her foot. "Can't you see how stupid it is—everybody's mouth falling open!"

He uttered a little sound which had pain in it, and she felt a real pang of compunction. He had gripped the back of a chair; his face had lost its heaviness. A dull flush coloured his cheeks. Noel had a feeling, as if she had been convicted of treachery. It was his silence, the curious look of an impersonal pain beyond power of words; she felt in him something much deeper than mere disapproval—something which echoed within herself. She walked quickly past him and escaped. She ran upstairs and threw herself on her bed. He was nothing: it was not that! It was in herself, the awful feeling, for the first time developed and poignant, that she had betrayed her caste, forfeited the right to be thought a lady, betrayed her secret reserve and refinement, repaid with black ingratitude the love lavished on her up bringing, by behaving like any uncared-for common girl. She had never felt this before—not even when Gratian first heard of it, and they had stood one at each end of the hearth, unable to speak. Then she still had her passion, and her grief for the dead. That was gone now as if it had never been; and she had no defence, nothing between her and this crushing humiliation and chagrin. She had been mad! She must have been mad! The Belgian Barra was right: "All a little mad" in this "forcing-house" of a war! She buried her face deep in the pillow, till it almost stopped her power of breathing; her head and cheeks and ears seemed to be on fire. If only he had shown disgust, done something which roused her temper, her sense of justice, her feeling that Fate had been too cruel to her; but he had just stood there, bewilderment incarnate, like a creature with some very deep illusion shattered. It was horrible! Then, feeling that she could not stay still, must walk, run, get away somehow from this feeling of treachery and betrayal, she sprang up. All was quiet below, and she slipped downstairs and out, speeding along with no knowledge of direction, taking the way she had taken day after day to her hospital. It was the last of April, trees and shrubs were luscious with blossom and leaf; the dogs ran gaily; people had almost happy faces in the sunshine. 'If I could get away from myself, I wouldn't care,' she thought. Easy to get away from people, from London, even from England perhaps; but from oneself—impossible! She passed her hospital; and looked at it dully, at the Red Cross flag against its stucco wall, and a soldier in his blue slops and red tie, coming out. She had spent many miserable hours there, but none quite so miserable as this. She passed the church opposite to the flats where Leila lived, and running suddenly into a tall man coming round the corner, saw Fort. She bent her head, and tried to hurry past. But his hand was held out, she could not help putting hers into it; and looking up hardily, she said:

"You know about me, don't you?"

His face, naturally so frank, seemed to clench up, as if he were riding at a fence. 'He'll tell a lie,' she thought bitterly. But he did not.

"Yes, Leila told me."

And she thought: 'I suppose he'll try and pretend that I've not been a beast!'

"I admire your pluck," he said.

"I haven't any."

"We never know ourselves, do we? I suppose you wouldn't walk my pace a minute or two, would you? I'm going the same way."

"I don't know which way I'm going."

"That is my case, too."

They walked on in silence.

"I wish to God I were back in France," said Fort abruptly. "One doesn't feel clean here."

Noel's heart applauded.

Ah! to get away—away from oneself! But at the thought of her baby, her heart fell again. "Is your leg quite hopeless?" she said.

"Quite."

"That must be horrid."

"Hundreds of thousands would look on it as splendid luck; and so it is if you count it better to be alive than dead, which I do, in spite of the blues."

"How is Cousin Leila?"

"Very well. She goes on pegging away at the hospital; she's a brick." But he did not look at her, and again there was silence, till he stopped by Lord's Cricket-ground.

"I mustn't keep you crawling along at this pace."

"Oh, I don't mind!"

"I only wanted to say that if I can be of any service to you at any time in any way whatever, please command me."

He gave her hand a squeeze, took his hat off; and Noel walked slowly on. The little interview, with its suppressions, and its implications, had but exasperated her restlessness, and yet, in a way, it had soothed the soreness of her heart. Captain Fort at all events did not despise her; and he was in trouble like herself. She felt that somehow by the look of his face, and the tone of his voice when he spoke of Leila. She quickened her pace. George's words came back to her: "If you're not ashamed of yourself, no one will be of you!" How easy to say! The old days, her school, the little half grown-up dances she used to go to, when everything was happy. Gone! All gone!

But her meetings with Opinion were not over for the day, for turning again at last into the home Square, tired out by her three hours' ramble, she met an old lady whom she and Gratian had known from babyhood—a handsome dame, the widow of an official, who spent her days, which showed no symptom of declining, in admirable works. Her daughter, the widow of an officer killed at the Marne, was with her, and the two greeted Noel with a shower of cordial questions: So she was back from the country, and was she quite well again? And working at her hospital? And how was her dear father? They had thought him looking very thin and worn. But now Gratian was at home—How dreadfully the war kept husbands and wives apart! And whose was the dear little baby they had in the house?

"Mine," said Noel, walking straight past them with her head up. In every fibre of her being she could feel the hurt, startled, utterly bewildered looks of those firm friendly persons left there on the pavement behind her; could feel the way they would gather themselves together, and walk on, perhaps without a word, and then round the corner begin: "What has come to Noel? What did she mean?" And taking the little gold hoop out of her pocket, she flung it with all her might into the Square Garden. The action saved her from a breakdown; and she went in calmly. Lunch was long over, but her father had not gone out, for he met her in the hall and drew her into the dining-room.

"You must eat, my child," he said. And while she was swallowing down what he had caused to be kept back for her, he stood by the hearth in that favourite attitude of his, one foot on the fender, and one hand gripping the mantel-shelf.

"You've got your wish, Daddy," she said dully: "Everybody knows now. I've told Mr. Lauder, and Monsieur, and the Dinnafords."

She saw his fingers uncrisp, then grip the shelf again. "I'm glad," he said.

"Aunt Thirza gave me a ring to wear, but I've thrown it away."

"My dearest child," he began, but could not go on, for the quivering of his lips.

"I wanted to say once more, Daddy, that I'm fearfully sorry about you. And I am ashamed of myself; I thought I wasn't, but I am—only, I think it was cruel, and I'm not penitent to God; and it's no good trying to make me."

Pierson turned and looked at her. For a long time after, she could not get that look out of her memory.

Jimmy Fort had turned away from Noel feeling particularly wretched. Ever since the day when Leila had told him of the girl's misfortune he had been aware that his liaison had no decent foundation, save a sort of pity. One day, in a queer access of compunction, he had made Leila an offer of marriage. She had refused; and he had respected her the more, realising by the quiver in her voice and the look in her eyes that she refused him, not because she did not love him well enough, but because she was afraid of losing any of his affection. She was a woman of great experience.

To-day he had taken advantage of the luncheon interval to bring her some flowers, with a note to say that he could not come that evening. Letting himself in with his latchkey, he had carefully put those Japanese azaleas in the bowl "Famille Rose," taking water from her bedroom. Then he had sat down on the divan with his head in his hands.

Though he had rolled so much about the world, he had never had much to do with women. And there was nothing in him of the Frenchman, who takes what life puts in his way as so much enjoyment on the credit side, and accepts the ends of such affairs as they naturally and rather rapidly arrive. It had been a pleasure, and was no longer a pleasure; but this apparently did not dissolve it, or absolve him. He felt himself bound by an obscure but deep instinct to go on pretending that he was not tired of her, so long as she was not tired of him. And he sat there trying to remember any sign, however small, of such a consummation, quite without success. On the contrary, he had even the wretched feeling that if only he had loved her, she would have been much more likely to have tired of him by now. For her he was still the unconquered, in spite of his loyal endeavour to seem conquered. He had made a fatal mistake, that evening after the concert at Queen's Hall, to let himself go, on a mixed tide of desire and pity!

His folly came to him with increased poignancy after he had parted from Noel. How could he have been such a base fool, as to have committed himself to Leila on an evening when he had actually been in the company of that child? Was it the vague, unseizable likeness between them which had pushed him over the edge? 'I've been an ass,' he thought; 'a horrible ass.' I would always have given every hour I've ever spent with Leila, for one real smile from that girl.'

This sudden sight of Noel after months during which he had tried loyally to forget her existence, and not succeeded at all, made him realise as he never had yet that he was in love with her; so very much in love with her that the thought of Leila was become nauseating. And yet the instincts of a gentleman seemed to forbid him to betray that secret to either of them. It was an accursed coil! He hailed a cab, for he was late; and all the way back to the War Office he continued to see the girl's figure and her face with its short hair. And a fearful temptation rose within him. Was it not she who was now the real object for chivalry and pity? Had he not the right to consecrate himself to championship of one in such a deplorable position? Leila had lived her life; but this child's life—pretty well wrecked—was all before her. And then he grinned from sheer disgust. For he knew that this was Jesuitry. Not chivalry was moving him, but love! Love! Love of the unattainable! And with a heavy heart, indeed, he entered the great building, where, in a small room, companioned by the telephone, and surrounded by sheets of paper covered with figures, he passed his days. The war made everything seem dreary, hopeless. No wonder he had caught at any distraction which came along—caught at it, till it had caught him!

CHAPTER IV

1

To find out the worst is, for human nature, only a question of time. But where the "worst" is attached to a family haloed, as it were, by the authority and reputation of an institution like the Church, the process of discovery has to break through many a little hedge. Sheer unlikelihood, genuine respect, the defensive instinct in those identified with an institution, who will themselves feel weaker if its strength be diminished, the feeling that the scandal is too good to be true—all these little hedges, and more, had to be broken through. To the Dinnafords, the unholy importance of what Noel had said to them would have continued to keep them dumb, out of self-protection; but its monstrosity had given them the feeling that there must be some mistake, that the girl had been overtaken by a wild desire to "pull their legs" as dear Charlie would say. With the hope of getting this view confirmed, they lay in wait for the old nurse who took the baby out, and obtained the information, shortly imparted: "Oh, yes; Miss Noel's. Her 'usband was killed—poor lamb!" And they felt rewarded. They had been sure there was some mistake. The relief of hearing that word "'usband" was intense. One of these hasty war marriages, of which the dear Vicar had not approved, and so it had been kept dark. Quite intelligible, but so sad! Enough misgiving however remained in their minds, to prevent their going to condole with the dear Vicar; but not enough to prevent their roundly contradicting the rumours and gossip already coming to their ears. And then one day, when their friend Mrs. Curtis had said too positively: "Well, she doesn't wear a wedding-ring, that I'll swear, because I took very good care to look!" they determined to ask Mr. Lauder. He would—indeed must—know; and, of course, would not tell a story. When they asked him it was so manifest that he did know, that they almost withdrew the question. The poor young man had gone the colour of a tomato.

"I prefer not to answer," he said. The rest of a very short interview was passed in exquisite discomfort. Indeed discomfort, exquisite and otherwise, within a few weeks of Noel's return, had begun to pervade all the habitual congregation of Pierson's church. It was noticed that neither of the two sisters attended Service now. Certain people who went in the sincere hope of seeing Noel, only fell off again when she did not appear. After all, she would not have the face! And Gratian was too ashamed, no doubt. It was constantly remarked that the Vicar looked very grave and thin, even for him. As the rumours hardened into certainty, the feeling towards him became a curious medley of sympathy and condemnation. There was about the whole business that which English people especially resent. By the very fact of his presence before them every Sunday, and his public ministrations, he was exhibiting to them, as it were, the seamed and blushing face of his daughter's private life, besides affording one long and glaring demonstration of the failure of the Church to guide its flock: If a man could not keep his own daughter in the straight path—whom could he? Resign! The word began to be thought about, but not yet spoken. He had been there so long; he had spent so much money on the church and the parish; his gentle dreamy manner was greatly liked. He was a gentleman; and had helped many people; and, though his love of music and vestments had always caused heart-burnings, yet it had given a certain cachet to the church. The women, at any rate, were always glad to know that the church they went to was capable of drawing their fellow women away from other churches. Besides, it was war-time, and moral delinquency which in time of peace would have bulked too large to neglect, was now less insistently dwelt on, by minds preoccupied by food and air-raids. Things, of course, could not go on as they were; but as yet they did go on.

The talked-about is always the last to hear the talk; and nothing concrete or tangible came Pierson's way. He went about his usual routine without seeming change. And yet there was a change, secret and creeping. Wounded almost to death himself, he felt as though surrounded by one great wound in others; but it was some weeks before anything occurred to rouse within him the weapon of anger or the protective impulse.

And then one day a little swift brutality shook him to the very soul. He was coming home from a long parish round, and had turned into the Square, when a low voice behind him said:

"Wot price the little barstard?"

A cold, sick feeling stifled his very breathing; he gasped, and spun round, to see two big loutish boys walking fast away. With swift and stealthy passion he sprang after them, and putting his hands on their two neighbouring shoulders, wrenched them round so that they faced him, with mouths fallen open in alarm. Shaking them with all his force, he said:

"How dare you—how dare you use that word?" His face and voice must have been rather terrible, for the scare in their faces brought him to sudden consciousness of his own violence, and he dropped his hands. In two seconds they were at the corner. They stopped there for a second; one of them shouted "Gran'pa"; then they vanished. He was left with lips and hands quivering, and a feeling that he had not known for years—the weak white empty feeling one has after yielding utterly to sudden murderous rage. He crossed over, and stood leaning against the Garden railings, with the thought: 'God forgive me! I could have killed them—I could have killed them!' There had been a devil in him. If he had had something in his hand, he might now have been a murderer: How awful! Only one had spoken; but he could have killed them both! And the word was true, and was in all mouths—all low common mouths, day after day, of his own daughter's child! The ghastliness of this thought, brought home so utterly, made him writhe, and grasp the railings as if he would have bent them.

From that day on, a creeping sensation of being rejected of men, never left him; the sense of identification with Noel and her tiny outcast became ever more poignant, more real; the desire to protect them ever more passionate; and the feeling that round about there were whispering voices, pointing fingers, and a growing malevolence was ever more sickening. He was beginning too to realise the deep and hidden truth: How easily the breath of scandal destroys the influence and sanctity of those endowed therewith by vocation; how invaluable it is to feel untarnished, and how difficult to feel that when others think you tarnished.

He tried to be with Noel as much as possible; and in the evenings they sometimes went walks together, without ever talking of what was always in their minds. Between six and eight the girl was giving sittings to Lavendie in the drawing-room, and sometimes Pierson would come there and play to them. He was always possessed now by a sense of the danger Noel ran from companionship with any man. On three occasions, Jimmy Fort made his appearance after dinner. He had so little to say that it was difficult to understand why he came; but, sharpened by this new dread for his daughter, Pierson noticed his eyes always following her. 'He admires her,' he thought; and often he would try his utmost to grasp the character of this man, who had lived such a roving life. 'Is he—can he be the sort of man I would trust Nollie to?' he would think. 'Oh, that I should have to hope like this that some good man would marry her—my little Nollie, a child only the other day!'

In these sad, painful, lonely weeks he found a spot of something like refuge in Leila's sitting-room, and would go there often for half an hour when she was back from her hospital. That little black-walled room with its Japanese prints and its flowers, soothed him. And Leila soothed him, innocent as he was of any knowledge of her latest aberration, and perhaps conscious that she herself was not too happy. To watch her arranging flowers, singing her little French songs, or to find her beside him, listening to his confidences, was the only real pleasure he knew in these days. And Leila, in turn, would watch him and think: 'Poor Edward! He has never lived; and never will; now!' But sometimes the thought would shoot through her: 'Perhaps he's to be envied. He doesn't feel what I feel, anyway. Why did I fall in love again?'

They did not speak of Noel as a rule, but one evening she expressed her views roundly.

"It was a great mistake to make Noel come back. Edward. It was Quixotic. You'll be lucky if real mischief doesn't come of it. She's not a patient character; one day she'll do something rash. And, mind you, she'll be much more likely to break out if she sees the world treating you badly than if it happens to herself. I should send her back to the country, before she makes bad worse."

"I can't do that, Leila. We must live it down together."

"Wrong, Edward. You should take things as they are."

With a heavy sigh Pierson answered:

"I wish I could see her future. She's so attractive. And her defences are gone. She's lost faith, and belief in all that a good woman should be. The day after she came back she told me she was ashamed of herself. But since—she's not given a sign. She's so proud—my poor little Nollie. I see how men admire her, too. Our Belgian friend is painting her. He's a good man; but he finds her beautiful, and who can wonder. And your friend Captain Fort. Fathers are supposed to be blind, but they see very clear sometimes."

Leila rose and drew down a blind.

"This sun," she said. "Does Jimmy Fort come to you—often?"

"Oh! no; very seldom. But still—I can see."

'You bat—you blunderer!' thought Leila: 'See! You can't even see this beside you!'

"I expect he's sorry for her," she said in a queer voice.

"Why should he be sorry? He doesn't know:"

"Oh, yes! He knows; I told him."

"You told him!"

"Yes," Leila repeated stubbornly; "and he's sorry for her."

And even then "this monk" beside her did not see, and went blundering on.

"No, no; it's not merely that he's sorry. By the way he looks at her, I know I'm not mistaken. I've wondered—what do you think, Leila. He's too old for her; but he seems an honourable, kind man."

"Oh! a most honourable, kind man." But only by pressing her hand against her lips had she smothered a burst of bitter laughter. He, who saw nothing, could yet notice Fort's eyes when he looked at Noel, and be positive that he was in love with her! How plainly those eyes must speak! Her control gave way.

"All this is very interesting," she said, spurning her words like Noel, "considering that he's more than my friend, Edward." It gave her a sort of pleasure to see him wince. 'These blind bats!' she thought, terribly stung that he should so clearly assume her out of the running. Then she was sorry, his face had become so still and wistful. And turning away, she said:

"Oh! I shan't break my heart; I'm a good loser. And I'm a good fighter, too; perhaps I shan't lose." And snapping off a sprig of geranium, she pressed it to her lips.

"Forgive me," said Pierson slowly; "I didn't know. I'm stupid. I thought your love for your poor soldiers had left no room for other feelings."

Leila uttered a shrill laugh. "What have they to do with each other? Did you never hear of passion, Edward? Oh! Don't look at me like that. Do you think a woman can't feel passion at my age? As much as ever, more than ever, because it's all slipping away."

She took her hand from her lips, but a geranium petal was left clinging there, like a bloodstain. "What has your life been all these years," she went on vehemently—"suppression of passion, nothing else! You monks twist Nature up with holy words, and try to disguise what the eeriest simpleton can see. Well, I haven't suppressed passion, Edward. That's all."

"And are you happier for that?"

"I was; and I shall be again."

A little smile curled Pierson's lips. "Shall be?" he said. "I hope so. It's just two ways of looking at things, Leila."

"Oh, Edward! Don't be so gentle! I suppose you don't think a person like me can ever really love?"

He was standing before her with his head down, and a sense that, naive and bat-like as he was, there was something in him she could not reach or understand, made her cry out:

"I've not been nice to you. Forgive me, Edward! I'm so unhappy."

"There was a Greek who used to say: 'God is the helping of man by man.' It isn't true, but it's beautiful. Good-bye, dear Leila, and don't be sorrowful."

She squeezed his hand, and turned to the window.

She stood there watching his black figure cross the road in the sunshine, and pass round the corner by the railings of the church. He walked quickly, very upright; there was something unseeing even about that back view of him; or was it that he saw-another world? She had never lost the mental habits of her orthodox girlhood, and in spite of all impatience, recognised his sanctity. When he had disappeared she went into her bedroom. What he had said, indeed, was no discovery. She had known. Oh! She had known. 'Why didn't I accept Jimmy's offer? Why didn't I marry him? Is it too late?' she thought. 'Could I? Would he—even now?' But then she started away from her own thought. Marry him! knowing his heart was with this girl?

She looked long at her face in the mirror, studying with a fearful interest the little hard lines and markings there beneath their light coating of powder. She examined the cunning touches of colouring matter here and there in her front hair. Were they cunning enough? Did they deceive? They seemed to her suddenly to stare out. She fingered and smoothed the slight looseness and fulness of the skin below her chin. She stretched herself, and passed her hands down over her whole form, searching as it were for slackness, or thickness. And she had the bitter thought: 'I'm all out. I'm doing all I can.' The lines of a little poem Fort had showed her went thrumming through her head:

"Time, you old gipsy man Will you not stay Put up your caravan Just for a day?"

What more could she do? He did not like to see her lips reddened. She had marked his disapprovals, watched him wipe his mouth after a kiss, when he thought she couldn't see him. 'I need'nt!' she thought. 'Noel's lips are no redder, really. What has she better than I? Youth—dew on the grass!' That didn't last long! But long enough to "do her in" as her soldier-men would say. And, suddenly she revolted against herself, against Fort, against this chilled and foggy country; felt a fierce nostalgia for African sun, and the African flowers; the happy-go-lucky, hand-to-mouth existence of those five years before the war began. High Constantia at grape harvest! How many years ago—ten years, eleven years! Ah! To have before her those ten years, with him! Ten years in the sun! He would have loved her then, and gone on loving her! And she would not have tired of him, as she had tired of those others. 'In half an hour,' she thought, 'he'll be here, sit opposite me; I shall see him struggling forcing himself to seem affectionate! It's too humbling! But I don't care; I want him!'

She searched her wardrobe, for some garment or touch of colour, novelty of any sort, to help her. But she had tried them all—those little tricks—was bankrupt. And such a discouraged, heavy mood came on her, that she did not even "change," but went back in her nurse's dress and lay down on the divan, pretending to sleep, while the maid set out the supper. She lay there moody and motionless, trying to summon courage, feeling that if she showed herself beaten she was beaten; knowing that she only held him by pity. But when she heard his footstep on the stairs she swiftly passed her hands over her cheeks, as if to press the blood out of them, and lay absolutely still. She hoped that she was white, and indeed she was, with finger-marks under the eyes, for she had suffered greatly this last hour. Through her lashes she saw him halt, and look at her in surprise. Asleep, or-ill, which? She did not move. She wanted to watch him. He tiptoed across the room and stood looking down at her. There was a furrow between his eyes. 'Ah!' she thought, 'it would suit you, if I were dead, my kind friend.' He bent a little towards her; and she wondered suddenly whether she looked graceful lying there, sorry now that she had not changed her dress. She saw him shrug his shoulders ever so faintly with a puzzled little movement. He had not seen that she was shamming. How nice his face was—not mean, secret, callous! She opened her eyes, which against her will had in them the despair she was feeling. He went on his knees, and lifting her hand to his lips, hid them with it.

"Jimmy," she said gently, "I'm an awful bore to you. Poor Jimmy! No! Don't pretend! I know what I know!" 'Oh, God! What am I saying?' she thought. 'It's fatal-fatal. I ought never!' And drawing his head to her, she put it to her heart. Then, instinctively aware that this moment had been pressed to its uttermost, she scrambled up, kissed his forehead, stretched herself, and laughed.

"I was asleep, dreaming; dreaming you loved me. Wasn't it funny? Come along. There are oysters, for the last time this season."

All that evening, as if both knew they had been looking over a precipice, they seemed to be treading warily, desperately anxious not to rouse emotion in each other, or touch on things which must bring a scene. And Leila talked incessantly of Africa.

"Don't you long for the sun, Jimmy? Couldn't we—couldn't you go? Oh! why doesn't this wretched war end? All that we've got here at home every scrap of wealth, and comfort, and age, and art, and music, I'd give it all for the light and the sun out there. Wouldn't you?"

And Fort said he would, knowing well of one thing which he would not give. And she knew that, as well as he.

They were both gayer than they had been for a long time; so that when he had gone, she fell back once more on to the divan, and burying her face in a cushion, wept bitterly.

CHAPTER V

1

It was not quite disillusionment that Pierson felt while he walked away. Perhaps he had not really believed in Leila's regeneration. It was more an acute discomfort, an increasing loneliness. A soft and restful spot was now denied him; a certain warmth and allurement had gone out of his life. He had not even the feeling that it was his duty to try and save Leila by persuading her to marry Fort. He had always been too sensitive, too much as it were of a gentleman, for the robuster sorts of evangelism. Such delicacy had been a stumbling-block to him all through professional life. In the eight years when his wife was with him, all had been more certain, more direct and simple, with the help of her sympathy, judgment; and companionship. At her death a sort of mist had gathered in his soul. No one had ever spoken plainly to him. To a clergyman, who does? No one had told him in so many words that he should have married again—that to stay unmarried was bad for him, physically and spiritually, fogging and perverting life; not driving him, indeed, as it drove many, to intolerance and cruelty, but to that half-living dreaminess, and the vague unhappy yearnings which so constantly beset him. All these celibate years he had really only been happy in his music, or in far-away country places, taking strong exercise, and losing himself in the beauties of Nature; and since the war began he had only once, for those three days at Kestrel, been out of London.

He walked home, going over in his mind very anxiously all the evidence he had of Fort's feeling for Noel. How many times had he been to them since she came back? Only three times—three evening visits! And he had not been alone with her a single minute! Before this calamity befell his daughter, he would never have observed anything in Fort's demeanour; but, in his new watchfulness, he had seen the almost reverential way he looked at her, noticed the extra softness of his voice when he spoke to her, and once a look of sudden pain, a sort of dulling of his whole self, when Noel had got up and gone out of the room. And the girl herself? Twice he had surprised her gazing at Fort when he was not looking, with a sort of brooding interest. He remembered how, as a little girl, she would watch a grown-up, and then suddenly one day attach herself to him, and be quite devoted. Yes, he must warn her, before she could possibly become entangled. In his fastidious chastity, the opinion he had held of Fort was suddenly lowered. He, already a free-thinker, was now revealed as a free-liver. Poor little Nollie! Endangered again already! Every man a kind of wolf waiting to pounce on her!

He found Lavendie and Noel in the drawing-room, standing before the portrait which was nearing completion. He looked at it for a long minute, and turned away:

"Don't you think it's like me, Daddy?"

"It's like you; but it hurts me. I can't tell why."

He saw the smile of a painter whose picture is being criticised come on Lavendie's face.

"It is perhaps the colouring which does not please you, monsieur?"

"No, no; deeper. The expression; what is she waiting for?"

The defensive smile died on Lavendie's lips.

"It is as I see her, monsieur le cure."

Pierson turned again to the picture, and suddenly covered his eyes. "She looks 'fey,'" he said, and went out of the room.

Lavendie and Noel remained staring at the picture. "Fey? What does that mean, mademoiselle?"

"Possessed, or something."

And they continued to stare at the picture, till Lavendie said:

"I think there is still a little too much light on that ear."

The same evening, at bedtime, Pierson called Noel back.

"Nollie, I want you to know something. In all but the name, Captain Fort is a married man."

He saw her flush, and felt his own face darkening with colour.

She said calmly: "I know; to Leila."

"Do you mean she has told you?"

Noel shook her head.

"Then how?"

"I guessed. Daddy, don't treat me as a child any more. What's the use, now?"

He sat down in the chair before the hearth, and covered his face with his hands. By the quivering of those hands, and the movement of his shoulders, she could tell that he was stifling emotion, perhaps even crying; and sinking down on his knees she pressed his hands and face to her, murmuring: "Oh, Daddy dear! Oh, Daddy dear!"

He put his arms round her, and they sat a long time with their cheeks pressed together, not speaking a word.

CHAPTER VI

1

The day after that silent outburst of emotion in the drawing-room was a Sunday. And, obeying the longing awakened overnight to be as good as she could to her father; Noel said to him:

"Would you like me to come to Church?"

"Of course, Nollie."

How could he have answered otherwise? To him Church was the home of comfort and absolution, where people must bring their sins and troubles—a haven of sinners, the fount of charity, of forgiveness, and love. Not to have believed that, after all these years, would have been to deny all his usefulness in life, and to cast a slur on the House of God.

And so Noel walked there with him, for Gratian had gone down to George, for the week-end. She slipped quietly up the side aisle to their empty pew, under the pulpit. Never turning her eyes from the chancel, she remained unconscious of the stir her presence made, during that hour and twenty minutes. Behind her, the dumb currents of wonder, disapproval, and resentment ran a stealthy course. On her all eyes were fixed sooner or later, and every mind became the play ground of judgments. From every soul, kneeling, standing, or sitting, while the voice of the Service droned, sang, or spoke, a kind of glare radiated on to that one small devoted head, which seemed so ludicrously devout. She disturbed their devotions, this girl who had betrayed her father, her faith, her class. She ought to repent, of course, and Church was the right place; yet there was something brazen in her repenting there before their very eyes; she was too palpable a flaw in the crystal of the Church's authority, too visible a rent in the raiment of their priest. Her figure focused all the uneasy amazement and heart searchings of these last weeks. Mothers quivered with the knowledge that their daughters could see her; wives with the idea that their husbands were seeing her. Men experienced sensations varying from condemnation to a sort of covetousness. Young folk wondered, and felt inclined to giggle. Old maids could hardly bear to look. Here and there a man or woman who had seen life face to face, was simply sorry! The consciousness of all who knew her personally was at stretch how to behave if they came within reach of her in going out. For, though only half a dozen would actually rub shoulders with her, all knew that they might be, and many felt it their duty to be, of that half-dozen, so as to establish their attitude once for all. It was, in fact, too severe a test for human nature and the feelings which Church ought to arouse. The stillness of that young figure, the impossibility of seeing her face and judging of her state of mind thereby; finally, a faint lurking shame that they should be so intrigued and disturbed by something which had to do with sex, in this House of Worship—all combined to produce in every mind that herd-feeling of defence, which so soon becomes, offensive. And, half unconscious, half aware of it all, Noel stood, and sat, and knelt. Once or twice she saw her father's eyes fixed on her; and, still in the glow of last night's pity and remorse, felt a kind of worship for his thin grave face. But for the most part, her own wore the expression Lavendie had translated to his canvas—the look of one ever waiting for the extreme moments of life, for those few and fleeting poignancies which existence holds for the human heart. A look neither hungry nor dissatisfied, but dreamy and expectant, which might blaze into warmth and depth at any moment, and then go back to its dream.

When the last notes of the organ died away she continued to sit very still, without looking round.

There was no second Service, and the congregation melted out behind her, and had dispersed into the streets and squares long before she came forth. After hesitating whether or no to go to the vestry door, she turned away and walked home alone.

It was this deliberate evasion of all contact which probably clinched the business. The absence of vent, of any escape-pipe for the feelings, is always dangerous. They felt cheated. If Noel had come out amongst all those whose devotions her presence had disturbed, if in that exit, some had shown and others had witnessed one knows not what of a manifested ostracism, the outraged sense of social decency might have been appeased and sleeping dogs allowed to lie, for we soon get used to things; and, after all, the war took precedence in every mind even over social decency. But none of this had occurred, and a sense that Sunday after Sunday the same little outrage would happen to them, moved more than a dozen quite unrelated persons, and caused the posting that evening of as many letters, signed and unsigned, to a certain quarter. London is no place for parish conspiracy, and a situation which in the country would have provoked meetings more or less public, and possibly a resolution, could perhaps only thus be dealt with. Besides, in certain folk there is ever a mysterious itch to write an unsigned letter—such missives satisfy some obscure sense of justice, some uncontrollable longing to get even with those who have hurt or disturbed them, without affording the offenders chance for further hurt or disturbance.

Letters which are posted often reach their destination.

On Wednesday morning Pierson was sitting in his study at the hour devoted to the calls of his parishioners, when the maid announced, "Canon Rushbourne, sir," and he saw before him an old College friend whom he had met but seldom in recent years. His visitor was a short, grey-haired man of rather portly figure, whose round, rosy, good-humoured face had a look of sober goodness, and whose light-blue eyes shone a little. He grasped Pierson's hand, and said in a voice to whose natural heavy resonance professional duty had added a certain unction:

"My dear Edward, how many years it is since we met! Do you remember dear old Blakeway? I saw him only yesterday. He's just the same. I'm delighted to see you again," and he laughed a little soft nervous laugh. Then for a few moments he talked of the war and old College days, and Pierson looked at him and thought: 'What has he come for?'

"You've something to say to me, Alec," he said, at last.

Canon Rushbourne leaned forward in his chair, and answered with evident effort: "Yes; I wanted to have a little talk with you, Edward. I hope you won't mind. I do hope you won't."

"Why should I mind?"

Canon Rushbourne's eyes shone more than ever, there was real friendliness in his face.

"I know you've every right to say to me: 'Mind your own business.' But I made up my mind to come as a friend, hoping to save you from—er" he stammered, and began again: "I think you ought to know of the feeling in your parish that—er—that—er—your position is very delicate. Without breach of confidence I may tell you that letters have been sent to headquarters; you can imagine perhaps what I mean. Do believe, my dear friend, that I'm actuated by my old affection for you; nothing else, I do assure you."

In the silence, his breathing could be heard, as of a man a little touched with asthma, while he continually smoothed his thick black knees, his whole face radiating an anxious kindliness. The sun shone brightly on those two black figures, so very different, and drew out of their well-worn garments the faint latent green mossiness which. underlies the clothes of clergymen.

At last Pierson said: "Thank you, Alec; I understand."

The Canon uttered a resounding sigh. "You didn't realise how very easily people misinterpret her being here with you; it seems to them a kind—a kind of challenge. They were bound, I think, to feel that; and I'm afraid, in consequence—" He stopped, moved by the fact that Pierson had closed his eyes.

"I am to choose, you mean, between my daughter and my parish?"

The Canon seemed, with a stammer of words, to try and blunt the edge of that clear question.

"My visit is quite informal, my dear fellow; I can't say at all. But there is evidently much feeling; that is what I wanted you to know. You haven't quite seen, I think, that—"

Pierson raised his hand. "I can't talk of this."

The Canon rose. "Believe me, Edward, I sympathise deeply. I felt I had to warn you." He held out his hand. "Good-bye, my dear friend, do forgive me"; and he went out. In the hall an adventure befell him so plump, and awkward, that he could barely recite it to Mrs. Rushbourne that night.

"Coming out from my poor friend," he said, "I ran into a baby's perambulator and that young mother, whom I remember as a little thing"—he held his hand at the level of his thigh—"arranging it for going out. It startled me; and I fear I asked quite foolishly: 'Is it a boy?' The poor young thing looked up at me. She has very large eyes, quite beautiful, strange eyes. 'Have you been speaking to Daddy about me?' 'My dear young lady,' I said, 'I'm such an old friend, you see. You must forgive me.' And then she said: 'Are they going to ask him to resign?' 'That depends on you,' I said. Why do I say these things, Charlotte? I ought simply to have held my tongue. Poor young thing; so very young! And the little baby!" "She has brought it on herself, Alec," Mrs. Rushbourne replied.

CHAPTER VII

1

The moment his visitor had vanished, Pierson paced up and down the study, with anger rising in his, heart. His daughter or his parish! The old saw, "An Englishman's house is his castle!" was being attacked within him. Must he not then harbour his own daughter, and help her by candid atonement to regain her inward strength and peace? Was he not thereby acting as a true Christian, in by far the hardest course he and she could pursue? To go back on that decision and imperil his daughter's spirit, or else resign his parish—the alternatives were brutal! This was the centre of his world, the only spot where so lonely a man could hope to feel even the semblance of home; a thousand little threads tethered him to his church, his parishioners, and this house—for, to live on here if he gave up his church was out of the question. But his chief feeling was a bewildered anger that for doing what seemed to him his duty, he should be attacked by his parishioners.

A passion of desire to know what they really thought and felt—these parishioners of his, whom he had befriended, and for whom he had worked so long—beset him now, and he went out. But the absurdity of his quest struck him before he had gone the length of the Square. One could not go to people and say: "Stand and deliver me your inmost judgments." And suddenly he was aware of how far away he really was from them. Through all his ministrations had he ever come to know their hearts? And now, in this dire necessity for knowledge, there seemed no way of getting it. He went at random into a stationer's shop; the shopman sang bass in his choir. They had met Sunday after Sunday for the last seven years. But when, with this itch for intimate knowledge on him, he saw the man behind the counter, it was as if he were looking on him for the first time. The Russian proverb, "The heart of another is a dark forest," gashed into his mind, while he said:

"Well, Hodson, what news of your son?"

"Nothing more, Mr. Pierson, thank you, sir, nothing more at present."

And it seemed to Pierson, gazing at the man's face clothed in a short, grizzling beard cut rather like his own, that he must be thinking: 'Ah! sir, but what news of your daughter?' No one would ever tell him to his face what he was thinking. And buying two pencils, he went out. On the other side of the road was a bird-fancier's shop, kept by a woman whose husband had been taken for the Army. She was not friendly towards him, for it was known to her that he had expostulated with her husband for keeping larks, and other wild birds. And quite deliberately he crossed the road, and stood looking in at the window, with the morbid hope that from this unfriendly one he might hear truth. She was in her shop, and came to the door.

"Have you any news of your husband, Mrs. Cherry?"

"No, Mr. Pierson, I 'ave not; not this week."

"He hasn't gone out yet?"

"No, Mr. Pierson; 'e 'as not."

There was no expression on her face, perfectly blank it was—Pierson had a mad longing to say 'For God's sake, woman, speak out what's in your mind; tell me what you think of me and my daughter. Never mind my cloth!' But he could no more say it than the woman could tell him what was in her mind. And with a "Good morning" he passed on. No man or woman would tell him anything, unless, perhaps, they were drunk. He came to a public house, and for a moment even hesitated before it, but the thought of insult aimed at Noel stopped him, and he passed that too. And then reality made itself known to him. Though he had come out to hear what they were thinking, he did not really want to hear it, could not endure it if he did. He had been too long immune from criticism, too long in the position of one who may tell others what he thinks of them. And standing there in the crowded street, he was attacked by that longing for the country which had always come on him when he was hard pressed. He looked at his memoranda. By stupendous luck it was almost a blank day. An omnibus passed close by which would take him far out. He climbed on to it, and travelled as far as Hendon; then getting down, set forth on foot. It was bright and hot, and the May blossom in full foam. He walked fast along the perfectly straight road till he came to the top of Elstree Hill. There for a few moments he stood gazing at the school chapel, the cricket-field, the wide land beyond. All was very quiet, for it was lunch-time. A horse was tethered there, and a strolling cat, as though struck by the tall black incongruity of his figure, paused in her progress, then, slithering under the wicket gate, arched her back and rubbed herself against his leg, crinkling and waving the tip of her tail. Pierson bent down and stroked the creature's head; but uttering a faint miaou, the cat stepped daintily across the road, Pierson too stepped on, past the village, and down over the stile, into a field path. At the edge of the young clover, under a bank of hawthorn, he lay down on his back, with his hat beside him and his arms crossed over his chest, like the effigy of some crusader one may see carved on an old tomb. Though he lay quiet as that old knight, his eyes were not closed, but fixed on the blue, where a lark was singing. Its song refreshed his spirit; its passionate light-heartedness stirred all the love of beauty in him, awoke revolt against a world so murderous and uncharitable. Oh! to pass up with that song into a land of bright spirits, where was nothing ugly, hard, merciless, and the gentle face of the Saviour radiated everlasting love! The scent of the mayflowers, borne down by the sun shine, drenched his senses; he closed his eyes, and, at once, as if resenting that momentary escape, his mind resumed debate with startling intensity. This matter went to the very well-springs, had a terrible and secret significance. If to act as conscience bade him rendered him unfit to keep his parish, all was built on sand, had no deep reality, was but rooted in convention. Charity, and the forgiveness of sins honestly atoned for—what became of them? Either he was wrong to have espoused straightforward confession and atonement for her, or they were wrong in chasing him from that espousal. There could be no making those extremes to meet. But if he were wrong, having done the hardest thing already—where could he turn? His Church stood bankrupt of ideals. He felt as if pushed over the edge of the world, with feet on space, and head in some blinding cloud. 'I cannot have been wrong,' he thought; 'any other course was so much easier. I sacrificed my pride, and my poor girl's pride; I would have loved to let her run away. If for this we are to be stoned and cast forth, what living force is there in the religion I have loved; what does it all come to? Have I served a sham? I cannot and will not believe it. Something is wrong with me, something is wrong—but where—what?' He rolled over, lay on his face, and prayed. He prayed for guidance and deliverance from the gusts of anger which kept sweeping over him; even more for relief from the feeling of personal outrage, and the unfairness of this thing. He had striven to be loyal to what he thought the right, had sacrificed all his sensitiveness, all his secret fastidious pride in his child and himself. For that he was to be thrown out! Whether through prayer, or in the scent and feel of the clover, he found presently a certain rest. Away in the distance he could see the spire of Harrow Church.

The Church! No! She was not, could not be, at fault. The fault was in himself. 'I am unpractical,' he thought. 'It is so, I know. Agnes used to say so, Bob and Thirza think so. They all think me unpractical and dreamy. Is it a sin—I wonder?' There were lambs in the next field; he watched their gambollings and his heart relaxed; brushing the clover dust off his black clothes, he began to retrace his steps. The boys were playing cricket now, and he stood a few minutes watching them. He had not seen cricket played since the war began; it seemed almost otherworldly, with the click of the bats, and the shrill young 'voices, under the distant drone of that sky-hornet threshing along to Hendon. A boy made a good leg hit. "Well played!" he called. Then, suddenly conscious of his own incongruity and strangeness in that green spot, he turned away on the road back to London. To resign; to await events; to send Noel away— of those three courses, the last alone seemed impossible. 'Am I really so far from them,' he thought, 'that they can wish me to go, for this? If so, I had better go. It will be just another failure. But I won't believe it yet; I can't believe it.'

The heat was sweltering, and he became very tired before at last he reached his omnibus, and could sit with the breeze cooling his hot face. He did not reach home till six, having eaten nothing since breakfast. Intending to have a bath and lie down till dinner, he went upstairs.

Unwonted silence reigned. He tapped on the nursery door. It was deserted; he passed through to Noel's room; but that too was empty. The wardrobe stood open as if it had been hastily ransacked, and her dressing-table was bare. In alarm he went to the bell and pulled it sharply. The old-fashioned ring of it jingled out far below. The parlour-maid came up.

"Where are Miss Noel and Nurse, Susan?"

"I didn't know you were in, sir. Miss Noel left me this note to give you. They—I—"

Pierson stopped her with his hand. "Thank you, Susan; get me some tea, please." With the note unopened in his hand, he waited till she was gone. His head was going round, and he sat down on the side of Noel's bed to read:

"DARLING DADDY,

"The man who came this morning told me of what is going to happen. I simply won't have it. I'm sending Nurse and baby down to Kestrel at once, and going to Leila's for the night, until I've made up my mind what to do. I knew it was a mistake my coming back. I don't care what happens to me, but I won't have you hurt. I think it's hateful of people to try and injure you for my fault. I've had to borrow money from Susan—six pounds. Oh! Daddy dear, forgive me.

"Your loving

"NOLLIE."

He read it with unutterable relief; at all events he knew where she was—poor, wilful, rushing, loving-hearted child; knew where she was, and could get at her. After his bath and some tea, he would go to Leila's and bring her back. Poor little Nollie, thinking that by just leaving his house she could settle this deep matter! He did not hurry, feeling decidedly exhausted, and it was nearly eight before he set out, leaving a message for Gratian, who did not as a rule come in from her hospital till past nine.

The day was still glowing, and now, in the cool of evening, his refreshed senses soaked up its beauty. 'God has so made this world,' he thought, 'that, no matter what our struggles and sufferings, it's ever a joy to live when the sun shines, or the moon is bright, or the night starry. Even we can't spoil it.' In Regent's Park the lilacs and laburnums were still in bloom though June had come, and he gazed at them in passing, as a lover might at his lady. His conscience pricked him suddenly. Mrs. Mitchett and the dark-eyed girl she had brought to him on New Year's Eve, the very night he had learned of his own daughter's tragedy—had he ever thought of them since? How had that poor girl fared? He had been too impatient of her impenetrable mood. What did he know of the hearts of others, when he did not even know his own, could not rule his feelings of anger and revolt, had not guided his own daughter into the waters of safety! And Leila! Had he not been too censorious in thought? How powerful, how strange was this instinct of sex, which hovered and swooped on lives, seized them, bore them away, then dropped them exhausted and defenceless! Some munition-wagons, painted a dull grey, lumbered past, driven by sunburned youths in drab. Life-force, Death-force—was it all one; the great unknowable momentum from which there was but the one escape, in the arms of their Heavenly Father? Blake's little old stanzas came into his mind:

"And we are put on earth a little space,
That we may learn to bear the beams of love;
And these black bodies and this sunburnt face
Are but a cloud, and like a shady grove.

"For when our souls have learned the heat to bear,
The cloud will vanish, we shall hear His voice, Saying:
Come out from the grove, my love and care,
And round my golden tent like lambs rejoice!"

Learned the heat to bear! Those lambs he had watched in a field that afternoon, their sudden little leaps and rushes, their funny quivering wriggling tails, their tiny nuzzling black snouts—what little miracles of careless joy among the meadow flowers! Lambs, and flowers, and sunlight! Famine, lust, and the great grey guns! A maze, a wilderness; and but for faith, what issue, what path for man to take which did not keep him wandering hopeless, in its thicket? 'God preserve our faith in love, in charity, and the life to come!' he thought. And a blind man with a dog, to whose neck was tied a little deep dish for pennies, ground a hurdy-gurdy as he passed. Pierson put a shilling in the dish. The man stopped playing, his whitish eyes looked up. "Thank you kindly, sir; I'll go home now. Come on, Dick!" He tapped his way round the corner, with his dog straining in front. A blackbird hidden among the blossoms of an acacia, burst into evening song, and another great grey munition-wagon rumbled out through the Park gate. 2

The Church-clock was striking nine when he reached Leila's flat, went up, and knocked. Sounds from a piano ceased; the door was opened by Noel. She recoiled when she saw who it was, and said:

"Why did you come, Daddy? It was much better not."

"Are you alone here?"

"Yes; Leila gave me her key. She has to be at the hospital till ten to-night."

"You must come home with me, my dear."

Noel closed the piano, and sat down on the divan. Her face had the same expression as when he had told her that she could not marry Cyril Morland.

"Come, Nollie," he said; "don't be unreasonable. We must see this through together."

"No."

"My dear, that's childish. Do you think the mere accident of your being or not being at home can affect my decision as to what my duty is?"

"Yes; it's my being there that matters. Those people don't care, so long as it isn't an open scandal."

"Nollie!"

"But it is so, Daddy. Of course it's so, and you know it. If I'm away they'll just pity you for having a bad daughter. And quite right too. I am a bad daughter."

Pierson smiled. "Just like when you were a tiny."

"I wish I were a tiny again, or ten years older. It's this half age—But I'm not coming back with you, Daddy; so it's no good."

Pierson sat down beside her.

"I've been thinking this over all day," he said quietly. "Perhaps in my pride I made a mistake when I first knew of your trouble. Perhaps I ought to have accepted the consequences of my failure, then, and have given up, and taken you away at once. After all, if a man is not fit to have the care of souls, he should have the grace to know it."

"But you are fit," cried Noel passionately; "Daddy, you are fit!"

"I'm afraid not. There is something wanting in me, I don't know exactly what; but something very wanting."

"There isn't. It's only that you're too good—that's why!"

Pierson shook his head. "Don't, Nollie!"

"I will," cried Noel. "You're too gentle, and you're too good. You're charitable, and you're simple, and you believe in another world; that's what's the matter with you, Daddy. Do you think they do, those people who want to chase us out? They don't even begin to believe, whatever they say or think. I hate them, and sometimes I hate the Church; either it's hard and narrow, or else it's worldly." She stopped at the expression on her father's face, the most strange look of pain, and horror, as if an unspoken treachery of his own had been dragged forth for his inspection.

"You're talking wildly," he said, but his lips were trembling. "You mustn't say things like that; they're blasphemous and wicked."

Noel bit her lips, sitting very stiff and still, against a high blue cushion. Then she burst out again:

"You've slaved for those people years and years, and you've had no pleasure and you've had no love; and they wouldn't care that if you broke your heart. They don't care for anything, so long as it all seems proper. Daddy, if you let them hurt you, I won't forgive you!"

"And what if you hurt me now, Nollie?"

Noel pressed his hand against her warm cheek.

"Oh, no! Oh, no! I don't—I won't. Not again. I've done that already."

"Very well, my dear! then come home with me, and we'll see what's best to be done. It can't be settled by running away."

Noel dropped his hand. "No. Twice I've done what you wanted, and it's been a mistake. If I hadn't gone to Church on Sunday to please you, perhaps it would never have come to this. You don't see things, Daddy. I could tell, though I was sitting right in front. I knew what their faces were like, and what they were thinking."

"One must do right, Nollie, and not mind."

"Yes; but what is right? It's not right for me to hurt you, and I'm not going to."

Pierson understood all at once that it was useless to try and move her.

"What are you going to do, then?"

"I suppose I shall go to Kestrel to-morrow. Auntie will have me, I know; I shall talk to Leila."

"Whatever you do, promise to let me know."

Noel nodded.

"Daddy, you—look awfully, awfully tired. I'm going to give you some medicine." She went to a little three-cornered cupboard, and bent down. Medicine! The medicine he wanted was not for the body; knowledge of what his duty was—that alone could heal him!

The loud popping of a cork roused him. "What are you doing, Nollie?"

Noel rose with a flushed face, holding in one hand a glass of champagne, in the other a biscuit.

"You're to take this; and I'm going to have some myself."

"My dear," said Pierson bewildered; "it's not yours."

"Drink it; Daddy! Don't you know that Leila would never forgive me if I let you go home looking like that. Besides, she told me I was to eat. Drink it. You can send her a nice present. Drink it!" And she stamped her foot.

Pierson took the glass, and sat there nibbling and sipping. It was nice, very! He had not quite realised how much he needed food and drink. Noel returned from the cupboard a second time; she too had a glass and a biscuit.

"There, you look better already. Now you're to go home at once, in a cab if you can get one; and tell Gratian to make you feed up, or you won't have a body at all; you can't do your duty if you haven't one, you know."

Pierson smiled, and finished the champagne.

Noel took the glass from him. "You're my child to-night, and I'm going to send you to bed. Don't worry, Daddy; it'll all come right." And, taking his arm, she went downstairs with him, and blew him a kiss from the doorway.

He walked away in a sort of dream. Daylight was not quite gone, but the moon was up, just past its full, and the search-lights had begun their nightly wanderings. It was a sky of ghosts and shadows, fitting to the thought which came to him. The finger of Providence was in all this, perhaps! Why should he not go out to France! At last; why not? Some better man, who understood men's hearts, who knew the world, would take his place; and he could go where death made all things simple, and he could not fail. He walked faster and faster, full of an intoxicating relief. Thirza and Gratian would take care of Nollie far better than he. Yes, surely it was ordained! Moonlight had the town now; and all was steel blue, the very air steel-blue; a dream-city of marvellous beauty, through which he passed, exalted. Soon he would be where that poor boy, and a million others, had given their lives; with the mud and the shells and the scarred grey ground, and the jagged trees, where Christ was daily crucified—there where he had so often longed to be these three years past. It was ordained!

And two women whom he met looked at each other when he had gone by, and those words 'the blighted crow' which they had been about to speak, died on their lips.

Noel felt light-hearted too, as if she had won a victory. She found some potted meat, spread it on another biscuit, ate it greedily, and finished the pint bottle of champagne. Then she hunted for the cigarettes, and sat down at the piano. She played old tunes—"There is a Tavern in the Town," "Once I Loved a Maiden Fair," "Mowing the Barley," "Clementine," "Lowlands," and sang to them such words as she remembered. There was a delicious running in her veins, and once she got up and danced. She was kneeling at the window, looking out, when she heard the door open, and without getting up, cried out:

"Isn't it a gorgeous night! I've had Daddy here. I gave him some of your champagne, and drank the rest—" then was conscious of a figure far too tall for Leila, and a man's voice saying:

"I'm awfully sorry. It's only I, Jimmy Fort."

Noel scrambled up. "Leila isn't in; but she will be directly—it's past ten."

He was standing stock-still in the middle of the room.

"Won't you sit down? Oh! and won't you have a cigarette?"

"Thanks."

By the flash of his briquette she saw his face clearly; the look on it filled her with a sort of malicious glee.

"I'm going now," she said. "Would you mind telling Leila that I found I couldn't stop?" She made towards the divan to get her hat. When she had put it on, she found him standing just in front of her.

"Noel-if you don't mind me calling you that?"

"Not a bit."

"Don't go; I'm going myself."

"Oh, no! Not for worlds." She tried to slip past, but he took hold of her wrist.

"Please; just one minute!"

Noel stayed motionless, looking at him, while his hand still held her wrist. He said quietly:

"Do you mind telling me why you came here?"

"Oh, just to see Leila."

"Things have come to a head at home, haven't they?"

Noel shrugged her shoulders.

"You came for refuge, didn't you?"

"From whom?"

"Don't be angry; from the need of hurting your father."

She nodded.

"I knew it would come to that. What are you going to do?"

"Enjoy myself." She was saying something fatuous, yet she meant it.

"That's absurd. Don't be angry! You're quite right. Only, you must begin at the right end, mustn't you? Sit down!"

Noel tried to free her wrist.

"No; sit down, please."

Noel sat down; but as he loosed her wrist, she laughed. This was where he sat with Leila, where they would sit when she was gone. "It's awfully funny, isn't it?" she said.

"Funny?" he muttered savagely. "Most things are, in this funny world."

The sound of a taxi stopping not far off had come to her ears, and she gathered her feet under her, planting them firmly. If she sprang up, could she slip by him before he caught her arm again, and get that taxi?

"If I go now," he said, "will you promise me to stop till you've seen Leila?"

"No."

"That's foolish. Come, promise!"

Noel shook her head. She felt a perverse pleasure at his embarrassment.

"Leila's lucky, isn't she? No children, no husband, no father, no anything. Lovely!"

She saw his arm go up as if to ward off a blow. "Poor Leila!" he said.

"Why are you sorry for her? She has freedom! And she has you!"

She knew it would hurt; but she wanted to hurt him.

"You needn't envy her for that."

He had just spoken, when Noel saw a figure over by the door.

She jumped up, and said breathlessly:

"Oh, here you are, Leila! Father's been here, and we've had some of your champagne!"

"Capital! You are in the dark!"

Noel felt the blood rush into her cheeks. The light leaped up, and Leila came forward. She looked extremely pale, calm, and self-contained, in her nurse's dress; her full lips were tightly pressed together, but Noel could see her breast heaving violently. A turmoil of shame and wounded pride began raging in the girl. Why had she not flown long ago? Why had she let herself be trapped like this? Leila would think she had been making up to him! Horrible! Disgusting! Why didn't he—why didn't some one, speak? Then Leila said:

"I didn't expect you, Jimmy; I'm glad you haven't been dull. Noel is staying here to-night. Give me a cigarette. Sit down, both of you. I'm awfully tired!"

She sank into a chair, leaning back, with her knees crossed; and at that moment Noel admired her. She had said it beautifully; she looked so calm. Fort was lighting her cigarette; his hand was shaking, his face all sorry and mortified.

"Give Noel one, too, and draw the curtains, Jimmy. Quick! Not that it makes any difference; it's as light as day. Sit down, dear."

But Noel remained standing.

"What have you been talking of? Love and Chinese lanterns, or only me?"

At those words Fort, who was drawing the last curtain, turned round; his tall figure was poised awkwardly against the wall, his face, unsuited to diplomacy, had a look as of flesh being beaten. If weals had started up across it, Noel would not have been surprised.

He said with painful slowness:

"I don't exactly know; we had hardly begun, had we?"

"The night is young," said Leila. "Go on while I just take off my things."

She rose with the cigarette between her lips, and went into the inner room. In passing, she gave Noel a look. What there was in that look, the girl could never make clear even to herself. Perhaps a creature shot would gaze like that, with a sort of profound and distant questioning, reproach, and anger, with a sort of pride, and the quiver of death. As the door closed, Fort came right across the room.

"Go to her;" cried Noel; "she wants you. Can't you see, she wants you?"

And before he could move, she was at the door. She flew downstairs, and out into the moonlight. The taxi, a little way off, was just beginning to move away; she ran towards it, calling out:

"Anywhere! Piccadilly!" and jumping in, blotted herself against the cushions in the far corner.

She did not come to herself, as it were, for several minutes, and then feeling she 'could no longer bear the cab, stopped it, and got out. Where was she? Bond Street! She began, idly, wandering down its narrow length; the fullest street by day, the emptiest by night. Oh! it had been horrible! Nothing said by any of them—nothing, and yet everything dragged out—of him, of Leila, of herself! She seemed to have no pride or decency left, as if she had been caught stealing. All her happy exhilaration was gone, leaving a miserable recklessness. Nothing she did was right, nothing turned out well, so what did it all matter? The moonlight flooding down between the tall houses gave her a peculiar heady feeling. "Fey" her father had called her. She laughed. 'But I'm not going home,' she thought. Bored with the street's length; she turned off, and was suddenly in Hanover Square. There was the Church, grey-white, where she had been bridesmaid to a second cousin, when she was fifteen. She seemed to see it all again—her frock, the lilies in her hand, the surplices of the choir, the bride's dress, all moonlight-coloured, and unreal. 'I wonder what's become of her!' she thought. 'He's dead, I expect, like Cyril!' She saw her father's face as he was marrying them, heard his voice: "For better, for worse, for richer, for poorer, in sickness and in health, till death do you part." And the moonlight on the Church seemed to shift and quiver-some pigeons perhaps had been disturbed up there. Then instead of that wedding vision, she saw Monsieur Barra, sitting on his chair, gazing at the floor, and Chica nursing her doll. "All mad, mademoiselle, a little mad. Millions of men with white souls, but all a little tiny bit mad, you know." Then Leila's face came before her, with that look in her eyes. She felt again the hot clasp of Fort's fingers on her wrist, and walked on, rubbing it with the other hand. She turned into Regent Street. The wide curve of the Quadrant swept into a sky of unreal blue, and the orange-shaded lamps merely added to the unreality. 'Love and Chinese lanterns! I should like some coffee,' she thought suddenly. She was quite close to the place where Lavendie had taken her. Should she go in there? Why not? She must go somewhere. She turned into the revolving cage of glass. But no sooner was she imprisoned there than in a flash Lavendie's face of disgust; and the red-lipped women, the green stuff that smelled of peppermint came back, filling her with a rush of dismay. She made the full circle in the revolving cage; and came out into the street again with a laugh. A tall young man in khaki stood there: "Hallo!" he said. "Come in and dance!" She started, recoiled from him and began to walk away as fast as ever she could. She passed a woman whose eyes seemed to scorch her. A woman like a swift vision of ruin with those eyes, and thickly powdered cheeks, and loose red mouth. Noel shuddered and fled along, feeling that her only safety lay in speed. But she could not walk about all night. There would be no train for Kestrel till the morning—and did she really want to go there, and eat her heart out? Suddenly she thought of George. Why should she not go down to him? He would know what was best for her to do. At the foot of the steps below the Waterloo Column she stood still. All was quiet there and empty, the great buildings whitened, the trees blurred and blue; and sweeter air was coming across their flowering tops. The queer "fey" moony sensation was still with her; so that she felt small and light, as if she could have floated through a ring. Faint rims of light showed round the windows of the Admiralty. The war! However lovely the night, however sweet the lilac smelt-that never stopped! She turned away and passed out under the arch, making for the station. The train of the wounded had just come in, and she stood in the cheering crowd watching the ambulances run out. Tears of excited emotion filled her eyes, and trickled down. Steady, smooth, grey, one after the other they came gliding, with a little burst of cheers greeting each one. All were gone now, and she could pass in. She went to the buffet and got a large cup of coffee, and a bun. Then, having noted the time of her early morning train, she sought the ladies' waiting-room, and sitting down in a corner, took out her purse and counted her money. Two pounds fifteen-enough to go to the hotel, if she liked. But, without luggage—it was so conspicuous, and she could sleep in this corner all right, if she wanted. What did girls do who had no money, and no friends to go to? Tucked away in the corner of that empty, heavy, varnished room, she seemed to see the cruelty and hardness of life as she had never before seen it, not even when facing her confinement. How lucky she had been, and was! Everyone was good to her. She had no real want or dangers, to face. But, for women—yes, and men too—who had no one to fall back on, nothing but their own hands and health and luck, it must be awful. That girl whose eyes had scorched her—perhaps she had no one—nothing. And people who were born ill, and the millions of poor women, like those whom she had gone visiting with Gratian sometimes in the poorer streets of her father's parish—for the first time she seemed to really know and feel the sort of lives they led. And then, Leila's face came back to her once more—Leila whom she had robbed. And the worst of it was, that, alongside her remorseful sympathy, she felt a sort of satisfaction. She could not help his not loving Leila, she could not help it if he loved herself! And he did—she knew it! To feel that anyone loved her was so comforting. But it was all awful! And she—the cause of it! And yet—she had never done or said anything to attract him. No! She could not have helped it.

She had begun to feel drowsy, and closed her eyes. And gradually there came on her a cosey sensation, as if she were leaning up against someone with her head tucked in against his shoulder, as she had so often leaned as a child against her father, coming back from some long darkening drive in Wales or Scotland. She seemed even to feel the wet soft Westerly air on her face and eyelids, and to sniff the scent of a frieze coat; to hear the jog of hoofs and the rolling of the wheels; to feel the closing in of the darkness. Then, so dimly and drowsily, she seemed to know that it was not her father, but someone—someone—then no more, no more at all.

CHAPTER IX

She was awakened by the scream of an engine, and looked around her amazed. Her neck had fallen sideways while she slept, and felt horridly stiff; her head ached, and she was shivering. She saw by the clock that it was past five. 'If only I could get some tea!' she thought. 'Anyway I won't stay here any longer!' When she had washed, and rubbed some of the stiffness out of her neck, the tea renewed her sense of adventure wonderfully. Her train did not start for an hour; she had time for a walk, to warm herself, and went down to the river. There was an early haze, and all looked a little mysterious; but people were already passing on their way to work. She walked along, looking at the water flowing up under the bright mist to which the gulls gave a sort of hovering life. She went as far as Blackfriars Bridge, and turning back, sat down on a bench under a plane-tree, just as the sun broke through. A little pasty woman with a pinched yellowish face was already sitting there, so still, and seeming to see so little, that Noel wondered of what she could be thinking. While she watched, the woman's face began puckering, and tears rolled slowly, down, trickling from pucker to pucker, till, summoning up her courage, Noel sidled nearer, and said:

"Oh! What's the matter?"

The tears seemed to stop from sheer surprise; little grey eyes gazed round, patient little eyes from above an almost bridgeless nose.

"I'ad a baby. It's dead.... its father's dead in France.... I was goin' in the water, but I didn't like the look of it, and now I never will."

That "Now I never will," moved Noel terribly. She slid her arm along the back of the bench and clasped the skinniest of shoulders.

"Don't cry!"

"It was my first. I'm thirty-eight. I'll never 'ave another. Oh! Why didn't I go in the water?"

The face puckered again, and the squeezed-out tears ran down. 'Of course she must cry,' thought Noel; 'cry and cry till it feels better.' And she stroked the shoulder of the little woman, whose emotion was disengaging the scent of old clothes.

"The father of my baby was killed in France, too," she said at last. The little sad grey eyes looked curiously round.

"Was 'e? 'Ave you got your baby still?"

"Yes, oh, yes!"

"I'm glad of that. It 'urts so bad, it does. I'd rather lose me 'usband than me baby, any day." The sun was shining now on a cheek of that terribly patient face; its brightness seemed cruel perching there.

"Can I do anything to help you?" Noel murmured.

"No, thank you, miss. I'm goin' 'ome now. I don't live far. Thank you kindly." And raising her eyes for one more of those half-bewildered looks, she moved away along the Embankment wall. When she was out of sight, Noel walked back to the station. The train was in, and she took her seat. She had three fellow passengers, all in khaki; very silent and moody, as men are when they have to get up early. One was tall, dark, and perhaps thirty-five; the second small, and about fifty, with cropped, scanty grey hair; the third was of medium height and quite sixty-five, with a long row of little coloured patches on his tunic, and a bald, narrow, well-shaped head, grey hair brushed back at the sides, and the thin, collected features and drooping moustache of the old school. It was at him that Noel looked. When he glanced out of the window, or otherwise retired within himself, she liked his face; but when he turned to the ticket-collector or spoke to the others, she did not like it half so much. It was as if the old fellow had two selves, one of which he used when alone, the other in which he dressed every morning to meet the world. They had begun to talk about some Tribunal on which they had to sit. Noel did not listen, but a word or two carried to her now and then.

"How many to-day?" she heard the old fellow ask, and the little cropped man answering: "Hundred and fourteen."

Fresh from the sight of the poor little shabby woman and her grief, she could not help a sort of shrinking from that trim old soldier, with his thin, regular face, who held the fate of a "Hundred and fourteen" in his firm, narrow grasp, perhaps every day. Would he understand their troubles or wants? Of course he wouldn't! Then, she saw him looking at her critically with his keen eyes. If he had known her secret, he would be thinking: 'A lady and act like that! Oh, no! Quite-quite out of the question!' And she felt as if she could, sink under the seat with shame. But no doubt he was only thinking: 'Very young to be travelling by herself at this hour of the morning. Pretty too!' If he knew the real truth of her—how he would stare! But why should this utter stranger, this old disciplinarian, by a casual glance, by the mere form of his face, make her feel more guilty and ashamed than she had yet felt? That puzzled her. He was, must be, a narrow, conventional old man; but he had this power to make her feel ashamed, because she felt that he had faith in his gods, and was true to them; because she knew he would die sooner than depart from his creed of conduct. She turned to the window, biting her lips-angry and despairing. She would never—never get used to her position; it was no good! And again she had the longing of her dream, to tuck her face away into that coat, smell the scent of the frieze, snuggle in, be protected, and forget. 'If I had been that poor lonely little woman,' she thought, 'and had lost everything, I should have gone into the water. I should have rushed and jumped. It's only luck that I'm alive. I won't look at that old man again: then I shan't feel so bad.'

She had bought some chocolate at the station, and nibbled it, gazing steadily at the fields covered with daisies and the first of the buttercups and cowslips. The three soldiers were talking now in carefully lowered voices. The words: "women," "under control," "perfect plague," came to her, making her ears burn. In the hypersensitive mood caused by the strain of yesterday, her broken night, and the emotional meeting with the little woman, she felt as if they were including her among those "women." 'If we stop, I'll get out,' she thought. But when the train did stop it was they who got out. She felt the old General's keen veiled glance sum her up for the last time, and looked full at him just for a moment. He touched his cap, and said: "Will you have the window up or down?" and lingered to draw it half-way up.' His punctiliousness made her feel worse than ever. When the train had started again she roamed up and down her empty carriage; there was no more a way out of her position than out of this rolling cushioned carriage! And then she seemed to hear Fort's voice saying: 'Sit down, please!' and to feel his fingers clasp her wrist, Oh! he was nice and comforting; he would never reproach or remind her! And now, probably, she would never see him again.

The train drew up at last. She did not know where George lodged, and would have to go to his hospital. She planned to get there at half past nine, and having eaten a sort of breakfast at the station, went forth into the town. The seaside was still wrapped in the early glamour which haunts chalk of a bright morning. But the streets were very much alive. Here was real business of the war. She passed houses which had been wrecked. Trucks clanged and shunted, great lorries rumbled smoothly by. Sea—and Air-planes were moving like great birds far up in the bright haze, and khaki was everywhere. But it was the sea Noel wanted. She made her way westward to a little beach; and, sitting down on a stone, opened her arms to catch the sun on her face and chest. The tide was nearly up, with the wavelets of a blue bright sea. The great fact, the greatest fact in the world, except the sun; vast and free, making everything human seem small and transitory! It did her good, like a tranquillising friend. The sea might be cruel and terrible, awful things it could do, and awful things were being done on it; but its wide level line, its never-ending song, its sane savour, were the best medicine she could possibly have taken. She rubbed the Shelly sand between her fingers in absurd ecstasy; took off her shoes and stockings, paddled, and sat drying her legs in the sun.

When she left the little beach, she felt as if someone had said to her:

'Your troubles are very little. There's the sun, the sea, the air; enjoy them. They can't take those from you.'

At the hospital she had to wait half an hour in a little bare room before George came.

"Nollie! Splendid. I've got an hour. Let's get out of this cemetery. We'll have time for a good stretch on the tops. Jolly of you to have come to me. Tell us all about it."

When she had finished, he squeezed her arm.

"I knew it wouldn't do. Your Dad forgot that he's a public figure, and must expect to be damned accordingly. But though you've cut and run, he'll resign all the same, Nollie."

"Oh, no!" cried Noel.

George shook his head.

"Yes, he'll resign, you'll see, he's got no worldly sense; not a grain."

"Then I shall have spoiled his life, just as if—oh, no!"

"Let's sit down here. I must be back at eleven."

They sat down on a bench, where the green cliff stretched out before them, over a sea quite clear of haze, far down and very blue.

"Why should he resign," cried Noel again, "now that I've gone? He'll be lost without it all."

George smiled.

"Found, my dear. He'll be where he ought to be, Nollie, where the Church is, and the Churchmen are not—in the air!"

"Don't!" cried Noel passionately.

"No, no, I'm not chaffing. There's no room on earth for saints in authority. There's use for a saintly symbol, even if one doesn't hold with it, but there's no mortal use for those who try to have things both ways—to be saints and seers of visions, and yet to come the practical and worldly and rule ordinary men's lives. Saintly example yes; but not saintly governance. You've been his deliverance, Nollie."

"But Daddy loves his Church."

George frowned. "Of course, it'll be a wrench. A man's bound to have a cosey feeling about a place where he's been boss so long; and there is something about a Church—the drone, the scent, the half darkness; there's beauty in it, it's a pleasant drug. But he's not being asked to give up the drug habit; only to stop administering drugs to others. Don't worry, Nollie; I don't believe that's ever suited him, it wants a thicker skin than he's got."

"But all the people he helps?"

"No reason he shouldn't go on helping people, is there?"

"But to go on living there, without—Mother died there, you know!"

George grunted. "Dreams, Nollie, all round him; of the past and the future, of what people are and what he can do with them. I never see him without a skirmish, as you know, and yet I'm fond of him. But I should be twice as fond, and half as likely to skirmish, if he'd drop the habits of authority. Then I believe he'd have some real influence over me; there's something beautiful about him, I know that quite well."

"Yes," murmured Noel fervently.

"He's such a queer mixture," mused George. "Clean out of his age; chalks above most of the parsons in a spiritual sense and chalks below most of them in the worldly. And yet I believe he's in the right of it. The Church ought to be a forlorn hope, Nollie; then we should believe in it. Instead of that, it's a sort of business that no one can take too seriously. You see, the Church spiritual can't make good in this age—has no chance of making good, and so in the main it's given it up for vested interests and social influence. Your father is a symbol of what the Church is not. But what about you, my dear? There's a room at my boarding-house, and only one old lady besides myself, who knits all the time. If Grace can get shifted we'll find a house, and you can have the baby. They'll send your luggage on from Paddington if you write; and in the meantime Gracie's got some things here that you can have."

"I'll have to send a wire to Daddy."

"I'll do that. You come to my diggings at half past one, and I'll settle you in. Until then, you'd better stay up here."

When he had gone she roamed a little farther, and lay down on the short grass, where the chalk broke through in patches. She could hear a distant rumbling, very low, travelling in that grass, the long mutter of the Flanders guns. 'I wonder if it's as beautiful a day there,' she thought. 'How dreadful to see no green, no butterflies, no flowers-not even sky-for the dust of the shells. Oh! won't it ever, ever end?' And a sort of passion for the earth welled up in her, the warm grassy earth along which she lay, pressed so close that she could feel it with every inch of her body, and the soft spikes of the grass against her nose and lips. An aching sweetness tortured her, she wanted the earth to close its arms about her, she wanted the answer to her embrace of it. She was alive, and wanted love. Not death—not loneliness—not death! And out there, where the guns muttered, millions of men would be thinking that same thought!

CHAPTER X

Pierson had passed nearly the whole night with the relics of his past, the records of his stewardship, the tokens of his short married life. The idea which had possessed him walking home in the moonlight sustained him in that melancholy task of docketing and destruction. There was not nearly so much to do as one would have supposed, for, with all his dreaminess, he had been oddly neat and businesslike in all parish matters. But a hundred times that night he stopped, overcome by memories. Every corner, drawer, photograph, paper was a thread in the long-spun web of his life in this house. Some phase of his work, some vision of his wife or daughters started forth from each bit of furniture, picture, doorway. Noiseless, in his slippers, he stole up and down between the study, diningroom, drawing-room, and anyone seeing him at his work in the dim light which visited the staircase from above the front door and the upper-passage window, would have thought: 'A ghost, a ghost gone into mourning for the condition of the world.' He had to make this reckoning to-night, while the exaltation of his new idea was on him;

had to rummage out the very depths of old association, so that once for all he might know whether he had strength to close the door on the past. Five o'clock struck before he had finished, and, almost dropping from fatigue, sat down at his little piano in bright daylight. The last memory to beset him was the first of all; his honeymoon, before they came back to live in this house, already chosen, furnished, and waiting for them. They had spent it in Germany—the first days in Baden-baden, and each morning had been awakened by a Chorale played down in the gardens of the Kurhaus, a gentle, beautiful tune, to remind them that they were in heaven. And softly, so softly that the tunes seemed to be but dreams he began playing those old Chorales, one after another, so that the stilly sounds floated out, through the opened window, puzzling the early birds and cats and those few humans who were abroad as yet.....

He received the telegram from Noel in the afternoon of the same day, just as he was about to set out for Leila's to get news of her; and close on the top of it came Lavendie. He found the painter standing disconsolate in front of his picture.

"Mademoiselle has deserted me?"

"I'm afraid we shall all desert you soon, monsieur."

"You are going?"

"Yes, I am leaving here. I hope to go to France."

"And mademoiselle?"

"She is at the sea with my son-in-law."

The painter ran his hands through his hair, but stopped them half-way, as if aware that he was being guilty of ill-breeding.

"Mon dieu!" he said: "Is this not a calamity for you, monsieur le cure?" But his sense of the calamity was so patently limited to his unfinished picture that Pierson could not help a smile.

"Ah, monsieur!" said the painter, on whom nothing was lost. "Comme je suis egoiste! I show my feelings; it is deplorable. My disappointment must seem a bagatelle to you, who will be so distressed at leaving your old home. This must be a time of great trouble. Believe me; I understand. But to sympathise with a grief which is not shown would be an impertinence, would it not? You English gentlefolk do not let us share your griefs; you keep them to yourselves."

Pierson stared. "True," he said. "Quite true!"

"I am no judge of Christianity, monsieur, but for us artists the doors of the human heart stand open, our own and others. I suppose we have no pride—c'est tres-indelicat. Tell me, monsieur, you would not think it worthy of you to speak to me of your troubles, would you, as I have spoken of mine?"

Pierson bowed his head, abashed.

"You preach of universal charity and love," went on Lavendie; "but how can there be that when you teach also secretly the keeping of your troubles to yourselves? Man responds to example, not to teaching; you set the example of the stranger, not the brother. You expect from others what you do not give. Frankly, monsieur, do you not feel that with every revelation of your soul and feelings, virtue goes out of you? And I will tell you why, if you will not think it an offence. In opening your hearts you feel that you lose authority. You are officers, and must never forget that. Is it not so?"

Pierson grew red. "I hope there is another feeling too. I think we feel that to speak of our sufferings or, deeper feelings is to obtrude oneself, to make a fuss, to be self-concerned, when we might be concerned with others."

"Monsieur, au fond we are all concerned with self. To seem selfless is but your particular way of cultivating the perfection of self. You admit that not to obtrude self is the way to perfect yourself. Eh bien! What is that but a deeper concern with self? To be free of this, there is no way but to forget all about oneself in what one is doing, as I forget everything when I am painting. But," he added, with a sudden smile, "you would not wish to forget the perfecting of self—it would not be right in your profession. So I must take away this picture, must I not? It is one of my best works: I regret much not to have finished it."

"Some day, perhaps—"

"Some day! The picture will stand still, but mademoiselle will not. She will rush at something, and behold! this face will be gone. No; I prefer to keep it as it is. It has truth now." And lifting down the canvas, he stood it against the wall and folded up the easel. "Bon soir, monsieur, you have been very good to me." He wrung Pierson's hand; and his face for a moment seemed all eyes and spirit. "Adieu!"

"Good-bye," Pierson murmured. "God bless you!"

"I don't know if I have great confidence in Him," replied Lavendie, "but I shall ever remember that so good a man as you has wished it. To mademoiselle my distinguished salutations, if you please. If you will permit me, I will come back for my other things to-morrow." And carrying easel and canvas, he departed.

Pierson stayed in the old drawing-room, waiting for Gratian to come in, and thinking over the painter's words. Had his education and position really made it impossible for him to be brotherly? Was this the secret of the impotence which he sometimes felt; the reason why charity and love were not more alive in the hearts of his congregation? 'God knows I've no consciousness of having felt myself superior,' he thought; 'and yet I would be truly ashamed to tell people of my troubles and of my struggles. Can it be that Christ, if he were on earth, would count us Pharisees, believing ourselves not as other men? But surely it is not as Christians but rather as gentlemen that we keep ourselves to ourselves. Officers, he called us. I fear—I fear it is true.' Ah, well! There would not be many more days now. He would learn out there how to open the hearts of others, and his own. Suffering and death levelled all barriers, made all men brothers. He was still sitting there when Gratian came in; and taking her hand, he said:

"Noel has gone down to George, and I want you to get transferred and go to them, Gracie. I'm giving up the parish and asking for a chaplaincy."

"Giving up? After all this time? Is it because of Nollie?"

"No, I think not; I think the time has come. I feel my work here is barren."

"Oh, no! And even if it is, it's only because—"

Pierson smiled. "Because of what, Gracie?"

"Dad, it's what I've felt in myself. We want to think and decide things for ourselves, we want to own our consciences, we can't take things at second-hand any longer."

Pierson's face darkened. "Ah!" he said, "to have lost faith is a grievous thing."

"We're gaining charity," cried Gratian.

"The two things are not opposed, my dear."

"Not in theory; but in practice I think they often are. Oh, Dad! you look so tired. Have you really made up your mind? Won't you feel lost?"

"For a little. I shall find myself, out there."

But the look on his face was too much for Gratian's composure, and she turned away.

Pierson went down to his study to write his letter of resignation. Sitting before that blank sheet of paper, he realised to the full how strongly he had resented the public condemnation passed on his own flesh and blood, how much his action was the expression of a purely mundane championship of his daughter; of a mundane mortification. 'Pride,' he thought. 'Ought I to stay and conquer it?' Twice he set his pen down, twice took it up again. He could not conquer it. To stay where he was not wanted, on a sort of sufferance—never! And while he sat before that empty sheet of paper he tried to do the hardest thing a man can do—to see himself as others see him; and met with such success as one might expect— harking at once to the verdicts, not of others at all, but of his own conscience; and coming soon to that perpetual gnawing sense which had possessed him ever since the war began, that it was his duty to be dead. This feeling that to be alive was unworthy of him when so many of his flock had made the last sacrifice, was reinforced by his domestic tragedy and the bitter disillusionment it had brought. A sense of having lost caste weighed on him, while he sat there with his past receding from him, dusty and unreal. He had the queerest feeling of his old life falling from him, dropping round his feet like the outworn scales of a serpent, rung after rung of tasks and duties performed day after day, year after year. Had they ever been quite real? Well, he had shed them now, and was to move out into life illumined by the great reality-death! And taking up his pen, he wrote his resignation.

CHAPTER XI

1

The last Sunday, sunny and bright! Though he did not ask her to go, Gratian went to every Service that day. And the sight of her, after this long interval, in their old pew, where once he had been wont to see his wife's face, and draw refreshment therefrom, affected Pierson more than anything else. He had told no one of his coming departure, shrinking from the falsity and suppression which must underlie every allusion and expression of regret. In the last minute of his last sermon he would tell them! He went through the day in a sort of dream. Truly proud and sensitive, under this social blight, he shrank from all alike, made no attempt to single out supporters or adherents from those who had fallen away. He knew there would be some, perhaps many, seriously grieved that he was going; but to try and realise who they were, to weigh them in the scales against the rest and so forth, was quite against his nature. It was all or nothing. But when for the last time of all those hundreds, he mounted the steps of his dark pulpit, he showed no trace of finality, did not perhaps even feel it yet. For so beautiful a summer evening the congregation was large. In spite of all reticence, rumour was busy and curiosity still rife. The writers of the letters, anonymous and otherwise, had spent a week, not indeed in proclaiming what they had done, but in justifying to themselves the secret fact that they had done it. And this was best achieved by speaking to their neighbours of the serious and awkward situation of the poor Vicar. The result was visible in a better attendance than had been seen since summer-time began.

Pierson had never been a great preacher, his voice lacked resonance and pliancy, his thought breadth and buoyancy, and he was not free from, the sing-song which mars the utterance of many who have to speak professionally. But he always made an impression of goodness and sincerity. On this last Sunday evening he preached again the first sermon he had ever preached from that pulpit, fresh from the honeymoon with his young wife. "Solomon in all his glory was not arrayed like one of these." It lacked now the happy fervour of that most happy of all his days, yet gained poignancy, coming from so worn a face and voice. Gratian, who knew that he was going to end with his farewell, was in a choke of emotion long before he came to it. She sat winking away her tears, and not till he paused, for so long that she thought his strength had failed, did she look up. He was leaning a little forward, seeming to see nothing; but his hands, grasping the pulpit's edge, were quivering. There was deep silence in the Church, for the look of his face and figure was strange, even to Gratian. When his lips parted again to speak, a mist covered her eyes, and she lost sight of him.

"Friends, I am leaving you; these are the last words I shall ever speak in this place. I go to other work. You have been very good to me. God has been very good to me. I pray with my whole heart that He may bless you all. Amen! Amen!"

The mist cleared into tears, and she could see him again gazing down at her. Was it at her? He was surely seeing something—some vision sweeter than reality, something he loved more dearly. She fell on her knees, and buried her face in her hand. All through the hymn she knelt, and through his clear slow Benediction: "The peace of God, which passeth all understanding, keep your hearts and minds in the knowledge and love of God, and of his Son Jesus Christ our Lord; and the blessing of God Almighty, the Father, the Son, and the Holy Ghost, be amongst you and remain with you always." And still she knelt on; till she was alone in the Church. Then she rose and stole home. He did not come in; she did not expect him. 'It's over,' she kept thinking; 'all over. My beloved Daddy! Now he has no home; Nollie and I have pulled him down. And yet I couldn't help it, and perhaps she couldn't. Poor Nollie!...'

2

Pierson had stayed in the vestry, talking with his choir and wardens; there was no hitch, for his resignation had been accepted, and he had arranged with a friend to carry on till the new Vicar was appointed. When they were gone he went back into the empty Church, and mounted to the organ-loft. A little window up there was open, and he stood leaning against the stone, looking out, resting his whole being. Only now that it was over did he know what stress he had been through. Sparrows were chirping, but sound of traffic had almost ceased, in that quiet Sunday hour of the evening meal. Finished! Incredible that he would never come up here again, never see those roof-lines, that corner of Square Garden, and hear this familiar chirping of the sparrows. He sat down at the organ and began to play. The last time the sound would roll out and echo 'round the emptied House of God. For a long time he played, while the building darkened slowly down there below him. Of all that he would leave, he would miss this most—the right to come and play here in the darkening Church, to release emotional sound in this dim empty space growing ever more beautiful. From chord to chord he let himself go deeper and deeper into the surge and swell of those sound waves, losing all sense of actuality, till the music and the whole dark building were fused in one rapturous solemnity. Away down there the darkness crept over the Church, till the pews, the altar-all was invisible, save the columns; and the walls. He began playing his favourite slow movement from Beethoven's Seventh Symphony—kept to the end, for the visions it ever brought him. And a cat, which had been stalking the sparrows, crept in through the little window, and crouched, startled, staring at him with her green eyes. He closed the organ, went quickly down, and locked up his Church for the last time. It was warmer outside than in, and lighter, for daylight was not quite gone. He moved away a few yards, and stood looking up. Walls, buttresses, and spire were clothed in milky shadowy grey. The top of the spire seemed to touch a star. 'Goodbye, my Church!' he thought. 'Good-bye, good-bye!' He felt his face quiver; clenched his teeth, and turned away.

CHAPTER XII

When Noel fled, Fort had started forward to stop her; then, realising that with his lameness he could never catch her, he went back and entered Leila's bedroom.

She had taken off her dress, and was standing in front of her glass, with the cigarette still in her mouth; and the only movement was the curling of its blue smoke. He could see her face reflected, pale, with a little spot of red in each cheek, and burning red ears. She had not seemed to hear him coming in, but he saw her eyes change when they caught his reflection in the mirror. From lost and blank, they became alive and smouldering.

"Noel's gone!" he said.

She answered, as if to his reflection in the glass

"And you haven't gone too? Ah, no! Of course—your leg! She fled, I suppose? It was rather a jar, my coming in, I'm afraid."

"No; it was my coming in that was the jar."

Leila turned round. "Jimmy! I wonder you could discuss me. The rest—" She shrugged her shoulders— "But that!"

"I was not discussing you. I merely said you were not to be envied for having me. Are you?"

The moment he had spoken, he was sorry. The anger in her eyes changed instantly, first to searching, then to misery. She cried out:

"I was to be envied. Oh! Jimmy; I was!" and flung herself face down on the bed.

Through Fort's mind went the thought: 'Atrocious!' How could he soothe—make her feel that he loved her, when he didn't—that he wanted her, when he wanted Noel. He went up to the bedside and touched her timidly:

"Leila, what is it? You're overtired. What's the matter? I couldn't help the child's being here. Why do you let it upset you? She's gone. It's all right. Things are just as they were."

"Yes!" came the strangled echo; "just!"

He knelt down and stroked her arm. It shivered under the touch, seemed to stop shivering and wait for the next touch, as if hoping it might be warmer; shivered again.

"Look at me!" he said. "What is it you want? I'm ready to do anything."

She turned and drew herself up on the bed, screwing herself back against the pillow as if for support, with her knees drawn under her. He was astonished at the strength of her face and figure, thus entrenched.

"My dear Jimmy!" she said, "I want you to do nothing but get me another cigarette. At my age one expects no more than one gets!" She held out her thumb and finger: "Do you mind?"

Fort turned away to get the cigarette. With what bitter restraint and curious little smile she had said that! But no sooner was he out of the room and hunting blindly for the cigarettes, than his mind was filled with an aching concern for Noel, fleeing like that, reckless and hurt, with nowhere to go. He found the polished birch-wood box which held the cigarettes, and made a desperate effort to dismiss the image of the girl before he again reached Leila. She was still sitting there, with her arms crossed, in the stillness of one whose every nerve and fibre was stretched taut.

"Have one yourself," she said. "The pipe of peace."

Fort lit the cigarettes, and sat down on the edge of the bed; and his mind at once went back to Noel.

"Yes," she said suddenly; "I wonder where she's gone. Can you see her? She might do something reckless a second time. Poor Jimmy! It would be a pity. And so that monk's been here, and drunk champagne. Good idea! Get me some, Jimmy!"

Again Fort went, and with him the image of the girl. When he came back the second time; she had put on that dark silk garment in which she had appeared suddenly radiant the fatal night after the Queen's Hall concert. She took the wineglass, and passed him, going into the sitting-room.

"Come and sit down," she said. "Is your leg hurting you?"

"Not more than usual," and he sat down beside her.

"Won't you have some? 'In vino veritas;' my friend."

He shook his head, and said humbly: "I admire you, Leila."

"That's lucky. I don't know anyone else who, would." And she drank her champagne at a draught.

"Don't you wish," she said suddenly, "that I had been one of those wonderful New Women, all brain and good works. How I should have talked the Universe up and down, and the war, and Causes, drinking tea, and never boring you to try and love me. What a pity!"

But to Fort there had come Noel's words: "It's awfully funny, isn't it?"

"Leila," he said suddenly, "something's got to be done. So long as you don't wish me to, I'll promise never to see that child again."

"My dear boy, she's not a child. She's ripe for love; and—I'm too ripe for love. That's what's the matter, and I've got to lump it." She wrenched her hand out of his and, dropping the empty glass, covered her face. The awful sensation which visits the true Englishman when a scene stares him in the face spun in Fort's brain. Should he seize her hands, drag them down, and kiss her? Should he get up and leave her alone? Speak, or keep silent; try to console; try to pretend? And he did absolutely nothing. So far as a man can understand that moment in a woman's life when she accepts the defeat of Youth and Beauty, he understood perhaps; but it was only a glimmering. He understood much better how she was recognising once for all that she loved where she was not loved.

'And I can't help that,' he thought dumbly; 'simply can't help that!' Nothing he could say or do would alter it. No words can convince a woman when kisses have lost reality. Then, to his infinite relief, she took her hands from her face, and said:

"This is very dull. I think you'd better go, Jimmy."

He made an effort to speak, but was too afraid of falsity in his voice.

"Very nearly a scene!" said Leila. "My God!

"How men hate them! So do I. I've had too many in my time; nothing comes of them but a headache next morning. I've spared you that, Jimmy. Give me a kiss for it."

He bent down and put his lips to hers. With all his heart he tried to answer the passion in her kiss. She pushed him away suddenly, and said faintly:

"Thank you; you did try!"

Fort dashed his hand across his eyes. The sight of her face just then moved him horribly. What a brute he felt! He took her limp hand, put it to his lips, and murmured:

"I shall come in to-morrow. We'll go to the theatre, shall we? Good night, Leila!"

But, in opening the door, he caught sight of her face, staring at him, evidently waiting for him to turn; the eyes had a frightened look. They went suddenly soft, so soft as to give his heart a squeeze.

She lifted her hand, blew him a kiss, and he saw her smiling. Without knowing what his own lips answered, he went out. He could not make up his mind to go away, but, crossing to the railings, stood leaning against them, looking up at her windows. She had been very good to him. He felt like a man who has won at cards, and sneaked away without giving the loser his revenge. If only she hadn't loved him; and it had been a soulless companionship, a quite sordid business. Anything rather than this! English to the backbone, he could not divest himself of a sense of guilt. To see no way of making up to her, of straightening it out, made him feel intensely mean. 'Shall I go up again?' he thought. The window-curtain moved. Then the shreds of light up there vanished. 'She's gone to bed,' he thought. 'I should only upset her worse. Where is Noel, now, I wonder? I shall never see her again, I suppose. Altogether a bad business. My God, yes! A bad-bad business!'

And, painfully, for his leg was hurting him, he walked away.

Leila was only too well aware of a truth that feelings are no less real, poignant, and important to those outside morality's ring fence than to those within. Her feelings were, indeed, probably even more real and poignant, just as a wild fruit's flavour is sharper than that of the tame product. Opinion—she knew—would say, that having wilfully chosen a position outside morality she had not half the case for brokenheartedness she would have had if Fort had been her husband: Opinion—she knew—would say she had no claim on him, and the sooner an illegal tie was broken, the better! But she felt fully as wretched as if she had been married. She had not wanted to be outside morality; never in her life wanted to be that. She was like those who by confession shed their sins and start again with a clear conscience. She never meant to sin, only to love, and when she was in love, nothing else mattered for the moment. But, though a gambler, she had always so far paid up. Only, this time the stakes were the heaviest a woman can put down. It was her last throw; and she knew it. So long as a woman believed in her attraction, there was hope, even when the curtain fell on a love-affair! But for Leila the lamp of belief had suddenly gone out, and when this next curtain dropped she felt that she must sit in the dark until old age made her indifferent. And between forty-four and real old age a gulf is fixed. This was the first time a man had tired of her. Why! he had been tired before he began, or so she felt. In one swift moment as of a drowning person, she saw again all the passages of their companionship, knew with certainty that it had never been a genuine flame. Shame ran, consuming, in her veins. She buried her face in the cushions. This girl had possessed his real heart all the time. With a laugh she thought: 'I put my money on the wrong horse; I ought to have backed Edward. I could have turned that poor monk's head. If only I had never seen Jimmy again; if I had torn his letter up, I could have made poor Edward love me!' Ifs! What folly! Things happened as they must!

And, starting up, she began to roam the little room. Without Jimmy she would be wretched, with him she would be wretched too! 'I can't bear to see his face,' she thought; 'and I can't live here without him! It's really funny!' The thought of her hospital filled her with loathing. To go there day after day with this despair eating at her heart—she simply could not. She went over her resources. She had more money than she thought; Jimmy had given her a Christmas present of five hundred pounds. She had wanted to tear up the cheque, or force him to take it back; but the realities of the previous five years had prevailed with her, and she had banked it. She was glad now. She had not to consider money. Her mind sought to escape in the past. She thought of her first husband, Ronny Fane; of their mosquito-curtained rooms in that ghastly Madras heat. Poor Ronny! What a pale, cynical young ghost started up under that name. She thought of Lynch, his horsey, matter-of-fact solidity. She had loved them both—for a time. She thought of the veldt, of Constantia, and the loom of Table Mountain under the stars; and the first sight of Jimmy, his straight look, the curve of his crisp head, the kind, fighting-schoolboy frankness of his face. Even now, after all those months of their companionship, that long-ago evening at grape harvest, when she sang to him under the scented creepers, was the memory of him most charged with real feeling. That one evening at any rate he had longed for her, eleven: years ago, when she was in her prime. She could have held her own then; Noel would have come in vain. To think that this girl had still fifteen years before she would be even in her prime. Fifteen years of witchery; and then another ten before she was on the shelf. Why! if Noel married Jimmy, he would be an old man doting on her still, by the time she had reached this fatal age of forty-four: She felt as if she must scream, and; stuffing her handkerchief into her mouth, turned out the light. Darkness cooled her, a little. She pulled aside the curtains, and let in the moon light. Jimmy and that girl were out in it some where, seeking each other, if not in body, then in thought. And soon, somehow, somewhere, they would come together—come together because Fate meant them to! Fate which had given her young cousin a likeness to herself; placed her, too, in just such a hopeless position as appealed to Jimmy, and gave him a chance against younger men. She saw it with bitter surety. Good gamblers cut their losses! Yes, and proud women did not keep unwilling lovers! If she had even an outside chance, she would trail her pride, drag it through the mud, through thorns! But she had not. And she clenched her fist, and struck out at the night, as though at the face of that Fate which one could never reach—impalpable, remorseless, surrounding Fate with its faint mocking smile, devoid of all human warmth. Nothing could set back the clock, and give her what this girl had. Time had "done her in," as it "did in" every woman, one by one. And she saw herself going down the years, powdering a little more, painting a little more, touching up her hair, till it was all artifice, holding on by every little device—and all, to what end? To see his face get colder and colder, hear his voice more and more constrained to gentleness; and know that underneath, aversion was growing with the thought 'You are keeping me from life, and love!' till one evening, in sheer nerve-break, she would say or do some fearful thing, and he would come no more. 'No, Jimmy!' she thought; 'find her, and stay with her. You're not worth all that!' And puffing to the curtains, as though with that gesture she could shut out her creeping fate, she turned up the light and sat down at her writing table. She stayed some minutes motionless, her chin resting on her hands, the dark silk fallen down from her arms. A little mirror, framed in curiously carved ivory, picked up by her in an Indian bazaar twenty-five years ago, hung on a level with her face and gave that face back to her. 'I'm not ugly,' she thought passionately, 'I'm not. I still have some looks left. If only that girl hadn't come. And it was all my doing. Oh, what made me write to both of them, Edward and Jimmy?' She turned the mirror aside, and took up a pen.

"MY DEAR JIMMY," she wrote: "It will be better for us both if you take a holiday from here. Don't come again till I write for you. I'm sorry I made you so much disturbance to-night. Have a good time, and a good rest; and don't worry. Your—"

So far she had written when a tear dropped on the page, and she had to tear it up and begin again. This time she wrote to the end—"Your Leila." 'I must post it now,' she thought, 'or he may not get it before to-morrow evening. I couldn't go through with this again.' She hurried out with it and slipped it in a pillar box. The night smelled of flowers; and, hastening back, she lay down, and stayed awake for hours, tossing, and staring at the dark.

CHAPTER XIII

1

Leila had pluck, but little patience. Her one thought was to get away and she at once began settling up her affairs and getting a permit to return to South Africa. The excitements of purchase and preparation were as good an anodyne as she could have taken. The perils of the sea were at full just then, and the prospect of danger gave her a sort of pleasure. 'If I go down,' she thought, 'all the better; brisk, instead of long and dreary.' But when she had the permit and her cabin was booked, the irrevocability of her step came to her with full force. Should she see him again or no? Her boat started in three days, and she must decide. If in compunction he were to be affectionate, she knew she would never keep to her decision, and then the horror would begin again, till again she was forced to this same action. She let the hours go and go till the very day before, when the ache to see him and the dread of it had become so unbearable that she could not keep quiet. Late that afternoon—everything, to the last label, ready—she went out, still undecided. An itch to turn the dagger in her wound, to know what had become of Noel, took her to Edward's house. Almost unconsciously she had put on her prettiest frock, and spent an hour before the glass. A feverishness of soul, more than of body, which had hung about her ever since that night, gave her colour. She looked her prettiest; and she bought a gardenia at a shop in Baker Street and fastened it in her dress. Reaching the old Square, she was astonished to see a board up with the words: "To let," though the house still looked inhabited. She rang, and was shown into the drawing-room. She had only twice been in this house before; and for some reason, perhaps because of her own unhappiness, the old, rather shabby room struck her as pathetic, as if inhabited by the past. 'I wonder what his wife was like,' she thought: And then she saw, hanging against a strip of black velvet on the wall, that faded colour sketch of the slender young woman leaning forward, with her hands crossed in her lap. The colouring was lavender and old ivory, with faint touches of rose. The eyes, so living, were a little like Gratian's; the whole face delicate, eager, good. 'Yes,' she thought, 'he must have loved you very much. To say good-bye must have been hard.' She was still standing before it when Pierson came in.

"That's a dear face, Edward. I've come to say good-bye. I'm leaving for South Africa to-morrow." And, as her hand touched his, she thought: 'I must have been mad to think I could ever have made him love me.'

"Are you—are you leaving him?"

Leila nodded:

"That's very brave, and wonderful."

"Oh! no. Needs must when the devil drives—that's all. I don't give up happiness of my own accord. That's not within a hundred miles of the truth. What I shall become, I don't know, but nothing better, you may be sure. I give up because I can't keep, and you know why. Where is Noel?"

"Down at the sea, with George and Gratian."

He was looking at her in wonder; and the pained, puzzled expression on his face angered her.

"I see the house is to let. Who'd have thought a child like that could root up two fossils like us? Never mind, Edward, there's the same blood in us. We'll keep our ends up in our own ways. Where are you going?"

"They'll give me a chaplaincy in the East, I think."

For a wild moment Leila thought: 'Shall I offer to go with him—the two lost dogs together?'

"What would have happened, Edward, if you had proposed to me that May week, when we were—a little bit in love? Which would it have been, worst for, you or me?"

"You wouldn't have taken me, Leila."

"Oh, one never knows. But you'd never have been a priest then, and you'd never have become a saint."

"Don't use that silly word. If you knew—"

"I do; I can see that you've been half burned alive; half burned and half buried! Well, you have your reward, whatever it is, and I mine. Good-bye, Edward!" She took his hand. "You might give me your blessing; I want it."

Pierson put his other hand on her shoulder and, bending forward, kissed her forehead.

The tears rushed up in Leila's eyes. "Ah me!" she said, "it's a sad world!" And wiping the quivering off her lips with the back of her gloved hand, she went quickly past him to the door. She looked back from there. He had not stirred, but his lips were moving. 'He's praying for me!' she thought. 'How funny!'

2

The moment she was outside, she forgot him; the dreadful ache for Fort seemed to have been whipped up within her, as if that figure of lifelong repression had infuriated the love of life and pleasure in her. She must and would see Jimmy again, if she had to wait and seek for him all night! It was nearly seven, he would surely have finished at the War Office; he might be at his Club or at his rooms. She made for the latter.

The little street near Buckingham Gate, where no wag had chalked "Peace" on the doors for nearly a year now, had an arid look after a hot day's sun. The hair-dresser's shop below his rooms was still open, and the private door ajar: 'I won't ring,' she thought; 'I'll go straight up.' While she was mounting the two flights of stairs, she stopped twice, breathless, from a pain in her side. She often had that pain now, as if the longing in her heart strained it physically. On the modest landing at the top, outside his rooms, she waited, leaning against the wall, which was covered with a red paper. A window at the back was open and the confused sound of singing came in—a chorus "Vive-la, vive-la, vive-la ve. Vive la compagnie." So it came to her. 'O God!' she thought: 'Let him be in, let him be nice to me. It's the last time.' And, sick from anxiety, she opened the door. He was in—lying on a wicker-couch against the wall in the far corner, with his arms crossed behind his head, and a pipe in his mouth; his eyes were closed, and he neither moved, nor opened them, perhaps supposing her to be the servant. Noiseless as a cat, Leila crossed the room till she stood above him. And waiting for him to come out of that defiant lethargy, she took her fill of his thin, bony face, healthy and hollow at the same time. With teeth clenched on the pipe it had a look of hard resistance, as of a man with his head back, his arms pinioned to his sides, stiffened against some creature, clinging and climbing and trying to drag him down. The pipe was alive, and dribbled smoke; and his leg, the injured one, wriggled restlessly, as if worrying him; but the rest of him was as utterly and obstinately still as though he were asleep. His hair grew thick and crisp, not a thread of grey in it, the teeth which held the pipe glinted white and strong. His face was young; so much younger than hers. Why did she love it—the face of a man who couldn't love her? For a second she felt as if she could seize the cushion which had slipped down off the couch, and smother him as he lay there, refusing, so it seemed to her, to come to consciousness. Love despised! Humiliation! She nearly turned and stole away. Then through the door, left open, behind her, the sound of that chorus: "Vive-la, vive-la, vive-la ve!" came in and jolted her nerves unbearably. Tearing the gardenia from her breast, she flung it on to his upturned face.

"Jimmy!"

Fort struggled up, and stared at her. His face was comic from bewilderment, and she broke into a little nervous laugh.

"You weren't dreaming of me, dear Jimmy, that's certain. In what garden were you wandering?"

"Leila! You! How—how jolly!"

"How—how jolly! I wanted to see you, so I came. And I have seen you, as you are, when you aren't with me. I shall remember it; it was good for me—awfully good for me."

"I didn't hear you."

"Far, far away, my dear. Put my gardenia in, your buttonhole. Stop, I'll pin it in. Have you had a good rest all this week? Do you like my dress? It's new. You wouldn't have noticed it, would you?"

"I should have noticed. I think it's charming.

"Jimmy, I believe that nothing—nothing will ever shake your chivalry."

"Chivalry? I have none."

"I am going to shut the door, do you mind?" But he went to the door himself, shut it, and came back to her. Leila looked up at him.

"Jimmy, if ever you loved me a little bit, be nice to me today. And if I say things—if I'm bitter—don't mind; don't notice it. Promise!"

"I promise."

She took off her hat and sat leaning against him on the couch, so that she could not see his face. And with his arm round her, she let herself go, deep into the waters of illusion; down-down, trying to forget there was a surface to which she must return; like a little girl she played that game of make-believe. 'He loves me-he loves me—he loves me!' To lose herself like that for, just an hour, only an hour; she felt that she would give the rest of the time vouchsafed to her; give it all and willingly. Her hand clasped his against her heart, she turned her face backward, up to his, closing her eyes so as still not to see his face; the scent of the gardenia in his coat hurt her, so sweet and strong it was.

3

When with her hat on she stood ready to go, it was getting dark. She had come out of her dream now, was playing at make-believe no more. And she stood with a stony smile, in the half-dark, looking between her lashes at the mortified expression on his unconscious face.

"Poor Jimmy!" she said; "I'm not going to keep you from dinner any longer. No, don't come with me. I'm going alone; and don't light up, for heaven's sake."

She put her hand on the lapel of his coat. "That flower's gone brown at the edges. Throw it away; I can't bear faded flowers. Nor can you. Get yourself a fresh one tomorrow."

She pulled the flower from his buttonhole and, crushing it in her hand, held her face up.

"Well, kiss me once more; it won't hurt you."

For one moment her lips clung to his with all their might. She wrenched them away, felt for the handle blindly, opened the door, and, shutting it in his face, went slowly, swaying a little, down the stairs. She trailed a gloved hand along the wall, as if its solidity could help her. At the last half-landing, where a curtain hung, dividing off back premises, she stopped and listened. There wasn't a sound. 'If I stand here behind this curtain,' she thought, 'I shall see him again.' She slipped behind the curtain, close drawn but for a little chink. It was so dark there that she could not see her own hand. She heard the door open, and his slow footsteps coming down the stairs. His feet, knees, whole figure came into sight, his face just a dim blur. He passed, smoking a cigarette. She crammed her hand against her mouth to stop herself from speaking and the crushed gardenia filled her nostrils with its cold, fragrant velvet. He was gone, the door below was shut. A wild, half-stupid longing came on her to go up again, wait till he came in, throw herself upon him, tell him she was going, beg him to keep her with him. Ah! and he would! He would look at her with that haggard pity she could not bear, and say, "Of course, Leila, of course." No! By God, no! "I am going quietly home," she muttered; "just quietly home! Come along, be brave; don't be a fool! Come along!" And she went down into the street: At the entrance to the Park she saw him, fifty yards in front, dawdling along. And, as if she had been his shadow lengthened out to that far distance, she moved behind him. Slowly, always at that distance, she followed him under the plane-trees, along the Park railings, past St. James's Palace, into Pall Mall. He went up some steps, and vanished into his Club. It was the end. She looked up at the building; a monstrous granite tomb, all dark. An emptied cab was just moving from the door. She got in. "Camelot Mansions, St. John's Wood." And braced against the cushions, panting, and clenching her hands, she thought: 'Well, I've seen him again. Hard crust's better than no bread. Oh, God! All finished—not a crumb, not a crumb! Vive-la, vive-la, vive-la ve. Vive-la compagnie!'

CHAPTER XIV

Fort had been lying there about an hour, sleeping and awake, before that visit: He had dreamed a curious and wonderfully emotionalising dream. A long grey line, in a dim light, neither of night nor morning, the whole length of the battle-front in France, charging in short drives, which carried the line a little forward, with just a tiny pause and suck-back; then on again irresistibly, on and on; and at each rush, every voice, his own among them, shouted "Hooray! the English! Hooray! the English!" The sensation of that advancing tide of dim figures in grey light, the throb and roar, the wonderful, rhythmic steady drive of it, no more to be stopped than the waves of an incoming tide, was gloriously fascinating;

life was nothing, death nothing. "Hooray, the English!" In that dream, he was his country, he was every one of that long charging line, driving forward in. those great heaving pulsations, irresistible, on and on. Out of the very centre of this intoxicating dream he had been dragged by some street noise, and had closed his eyes again, in the vain hope that he might dream it on to its end. But it came no more; and lighting his pipe, he lay there wondering at its fervid, fantastic realism. Death was nothing, if his country lived and won. In waking hours he never had quite that single-hearted knowledge of himself. And what marvellously real touches got mixed into the fantastic stuff of dreams, as if something were at work to convince the dreamer in spite of himself—"Hooray!" not "Hurrah!" Just common "Hooray!" And "the English," not the literary "British." And then the soft flower had struck his forehead, and Leila's voice cried: "Jimmy!"

When she left him, his thought was just a tired: 'Well, so it's begun again!' What did it matter, since common loyalty and compassion cut him off from what his heart desired; and that desire was absurd, as little likely of attainment as the moon. What did it matter? If it gave her any pleasure to love him, let it go on! Yet, all the time that he was walking across under the plane trees, Noel seemed to walk in front of him, just out of reach, so that he ached with the thought that he would never catch her up, and walk beside her.

Two days later, on reaching his rooms in the evening, he found this letter on ship's note-paper, with the Plymouth postmark—

"Fare thee well, and if for ever, Then for ever fare thee well" "Leila"

He read it with a really horrible feeling, for all the world as if he had been accused of a crime and did not know whether he had committed it or not. And, trying to collect his thoughts, he took a cab and drove to her fiat. It was closed, but her address was given him; a bank in Cape Town. He had received his release. In his remorse and relief, so confusing and so poignant, he heard the driver of the cab asking where he wanted to go now. "Oh, back again!" But before they had gone a mile he corrected the address, in an impulse of which next moment he felt thoroughly ashamed. What he was doing indeed, was as indecent as if he were driving from the funeral of his wife to the boudoir of another woman. When he reached the old Square, and the words "To let" stared him in the face, he felt a curious relief, though it meant that he would not see her whom to see for ten minutes he felt he would give a year of life. Dismissing his cab, he stood debating whether to ring the bell. The sight of a maid's face at the window decided him. Mr. Pierson was out, and the young ladies were away. He asked for Mrs. Laird's address, and turned away, almost into the arms of Pierson himself. The greeting was stiff and strange. 'Does he know that Leila's gone?' he thought. 'If so, he must think me the most awful skunk. And am I? Am I?' When he reached home, he sat down to write to Leila. But having stared at the paper for an hour and written these three lines—

"MY DEAR LEILA,

"I cannot express to you the feelings with which I received your letter—"

he tore it up. Nothing would be adequate, nothing would be decent. Let the dead past bury its dead— the dead past which in his heart had never been alive! Why pretend? He had done his best to keep his end up. Why pretend?

PART IV

CHAPTER I

In the boarding-house, whence the Lairds had not yet removed, the old lady who knitted, sat by the fireplace, and light from the setting sun threw her shadow on the wall, moving spidery and grey, over the yellowish distemper, in time to the tune of her needles. She was a very old lady—the oldest lady in the world, Noel thought—and she knitted without stopping, without breathing, so that the girl felt inclined to scream. In the evening when George and Gratian were not in, Noel would often sit watching the needles, brooding over her as yet undecided future. And now and again the old lady would look up above her spectacles; move the corners of her lips ever so slightly, and drop her gaze again. She had pitted herself against Fate; so long as she knitted, the war could not stop—such was the conclusion Noel had come to. This old lady knitted the epic of acquiescence to the tune of her needles; it was she who kept the war going such a thin old lady! 'If I were to hold her elbows from behind,' the girl used to think, 'I believe she'd die. I expect I ought to; then the war would stop. And if the war stopped, there'd be love and life again.' Then the little silvery tune would click itself once more into her brain, and stop her thinking. In her lap this evening lay a letter from her father.

"MY DEAREST NOLLIE,

"I am glad to say I have my chaplaincy, and am to start for Egypt very soon. I should have wished to go to France, but must take what I can get, in view of my age, for they really don't want us who are getting on, I fear. It is a great comfort to me to think that Gratian is with you, and no doubt you will all soon be in a house where my little grandson can join you. I have excellent accounts of him in a letter from your aunt, just received: My child, you must never again think that my resignation has been due to you. It is not so. You know, or perhaps you don't, that ever since the war broke out, I have chafed over staying at home, my heart has been with our boys out there, and sooner or later it must have come to this, apart from anything else. Monsieur Lavendie has been round in the evening, twice; he is a nice man, I like him very much, in spite of our differences of view. He wanted to give me the sketch he made of you in the Park, but what can I do with it now? And to tell you the truth, I like it no better than the oil painting. It is not a likeness, as I know you. I hope I didn't hurt his feelings, the feelings of an artist are so very easily wounded. There is one thing I must tell you. Leila has gone back to South Africa; she came round one evening about ten days ago, to say goodbye. She was very brave, for I fear it means a great wrench for her. I hope and pray she may find comfort and tranquillity out there. And now, my dear, I want you to promise me not to see Captain Fort. I know that he admires you. But, apart from the question of his conduct in regard to Leila, he made the saddest impression on me by coming to our house the very day after her departure. There is something about that which makes me feel he cannot be the sort of man in whom I could feel any confidence. I don't suppose for a moment that he is in your thoughts, and yet before going so far from you, I feel I must warn you. I should rejoice to see you married to a good man; but, though I don't wish to think hardly of anyone, I cannot believe Captain Fort is that.

"I shall come down to you before I start, which may be in quite a short time now. My dear love to you and Gracie, and best wishes to George.

"Your ever loving father,

"EDWARD PIERSON"

Across this letter lying on her knees, Noel gazed at the spidery movement on the wall. Was it acquiescence that the old lady knitted, or was it resistance—a challenge to death itself, a challenge dancing to the tune of the needles like the grey ghost of human resistance to Fate! She wouldn't give in, this oldest lady in the world, she meant to knit till she fell into the grave. And so Leila had gone! It hurt her to know that; and yet it pleased her. Acquiescence—resistance! Why did Daddy always want to choose the way she should go? So gentle he was, yet he always wanted to! And why did he always make her feel that she must go the other way? The sunlight ceased to stream in, the old lady's shadow faded off the wall, but the needles still sang their little tune. And the girl said:

"Do you enjoy knitting, Mrs. Adam?"

The old lady looked at her above the spectacles.

"Enjoy, my dear? It passes the time."

"But do you want the time to pass?"

There was no answer for a moment, and Noel thought: 'How dreadful of me to have said that!'

"Eh?" said the old lady.

"I said: Isn't it very tiring?"

"Not when I don't think about it, my dear."

"What do you think about?"

The old lady cackled gently.

"Oh—well!" she said.

And Noel thought: 'It must be dreadful to grow old, and pass the time!'

She took up her father's letter, and bent it meditatively against her chin. He wanted her to pass the time—not to live, not to enjoy! To pass the time. What else had he been doing himself, all these years, ever since she could remember, ever since her mother died, but just passing the time? Passing the time because he did not believe in this life; not living at all, just preparing for the life he did believe in. Denying himself everything that was exciting and nice, so that when he died he might pass pure and saintly to his other world. He could not believe Captain Fort a good man, because he had not passed the time, and resisted Leila; and Leila was gone! And now it was a sin for him to love someone else; he must pass the time again. 'Daddy doesn't believe in life,' she thought; 'it's monsieur's picture. Daddy's a saint; but I don't want to be a saint, and pass the time. He doesn't mind making people unhappy, because the more they're repressed, the saintlier they'll be. But I can't bear to be unhappy, or to see others unhappy. I wonder if I could bear to be unhappy to save someone else—as Leila is? I admire her! Oh! I admire her! She's not doing it because she thinks it good for her soul; only because she can't bear making him unhappy. She must love him very much. Poor Leila! And she's done it all by herself, of her own accord.' It was like what George said of the soldiers; they didn't know why they were heroes, it was not because they'd been told to be, or because they believed in a future life. They just had to be, from inside somewhere, to save others. 'And they love life as much as I do,' she thought. 'What a beast it makes one feel!' Those needles! Resistance—acquiescence? Both perhaps. The oldest lady in the world, with her lips moving at the corners, keeping things in, had lived her life, and knew it. How dreadful to live on when you were of no more interest to anyone, but must just "pass the time" and die. But how much more dreadful to "pass the time" when you were strong, and life and love were yours for the taking! 'I shan't answer Daddy,' she thought.

CHAPTER II

The maid, who one Saturday in July opened the door to Jimmy Fort, had never heard the name of Laird, for she was but a unit in the ceaseless procession which pass through the boarding-houses of places subject to air-raids. Placing him in a sitting-room, she said she would find Miss 'Allow. There he waited, turning the leaves of an illustrated Journal, wherein Society beauties; starving Servians, actresses with pretty legs, prize dogs, sinking ships, Royalties, shells bursting, and padres reading funeral services, testified to the catholicity of the public taste, but did not assuage his nerves. What if their address were not known here? Why, in his fear of putting things to the test, had he let this month go by? An old lady was sitting by the hearth, knitting, the click of whose needles blended with the buzzing of a large bee on the window-pane. 'She may know,' he thought, 'she looks as if she'd been here for ever.' And approaching her, he said:

"I can assure you those socks are very much appreciated, ma'am."

The old lady bridled over her spectacles.

"It passes the time," she said.

"Oh, more than that; it helps to win the war, ma'am."

The old lady's lips moved at the corners; she did not answer. 'Deaf!' he thought.

"May I ask if you knew my friends, Doctor and Mrs. Laird, and Miss Pierson?"

The old lady cackled gently.

"Oh, yes! A pretty young girl; as pretty as life. She used to sit with me. Quite a pleasure to watch her; such large eyes she had."

"Where have they gone? Can you tell me?"

"Oh, I don't know at all."

It was a little cold douche on his heart. He longed to say: 'Stop knitting a minute, please. It's my life, to know.' But the tune of the needles answered: 'It's my life to knit.' And he turned away to the window.

"She used to sit just there; quite still; quite still."

Fort looked down at the window-seat. So, she used to sit just here, quite still.

"What a dreadful war this is!" said the old lady. "Have you been at the front?"

"Yes."

"To think of the poor young girls who'll never have husbands! I'm sure I think it's dreadful."

"Yes," said Fort; "it's dreadful—" And then a voice from the doorway said:

"Did you want Doctor and Mrs. Laird, sir? East Bungalow their address is; it's a little way out on the North Road. Anyone will tell you."

With a sigh of relief Fort looked gratefully at the old lady who had called Noel as pretty as life. "Good afternoon, ma'am."

"Good afternoon." The needles clicked, and little movements occurred at the corners of her mouth. Fort went out. He could not find a vehicle, and was a long time walking. The Bungalow was ugly, of yellow brick pointed with red. It lay about two-thirds up between the main road and cliffs, and had a rock-garden and a glaring, brand-new look, in the afternoon sunlight. He opened the gate, uttering one of those prayers which come so glibly from unbelievers when they want anything. A baby's crying answered it, and he thought with ecstasy: 'Heaven, she is here!' Passing the rock-garden he could see a lawn at the back of the house and a perambulator out there under a holm-oak tree, and Noel—surely Noel herself! Hardening his heart, he went forward. In a lilac sunbonnet she was bending over the perambulator. He trod softly on the grass, and was quite close before she heard him. He had prepared no words, but just held out his hand. The baby, interested in the shadow failing across its pram, ceased crying. Noel took his hand. Under the sunbonnet, which hid her hair, she seemed older and paler, as if she felt the heat. He had no feeling that she was glad to see him.

"How do you do? Have you seen Gratian; she ought to be in."

"I didn't come to see her; I came to see you."

Noel turned to the baby.

"Here he is."

Fort stood at the end of the perambulator, and looked at that other fellow's baby. In the shade of the hood, with the frilly clothes, it seemed to him lying with its head downhill. It had scratched its snub nose and bumpy forehead, and it stared up at its mother with blue eyes, which seemed to have no underlids so fat were its cheeks.

"I wonder what they think about," he said.

Noel put her finger into the baby's fist.

"They only think when they want some thing."

"That's a deep saying: but his eyes are awfully interested in you."

Noel smiled; and very slowly the baby's curly mouth unclosed, and discovered his toothlessness.

"He's a darling," she said in a whisper.

'And so are you,' he thought, 'if only I dared say it!'

"Daddy is here," she said suddenly, without looking up. "He's sailing for Egypt the day after to-morrow. He doesn't like you."

Fort's heart gave a jump. Why did she tell him that, unless—unless she was just a little on his side?

"I expected that," he said. "I'm a sinner, as you know."

Noel looked up at him. "Sin!" she said, and bent again over her baby. The word, the tone in which she said it, crouching over her baby, gave him the thought: 'If it weren't for that little creature, I shouldn't have a dog's chance.' He said, "I'll go and see your father. Is he in?"

"I think so."

"May I come to-morrow?"

"It's Sunday; and Daddy's last day."

"Ah! Of course." He did not dare look back, to see if her gaze was following him, but he thought: 'Chance or no chance, I'm going to fight for her tooth and nail.'

In a room darkened against the evening sun Pierson was sitting on a sofa reading. The sight of that figure in khaki disconcerted Fort, who had not realised that there would be this metamorphosis. The narrow face, clean-shaven now, with its deep-set eyes and compressed lips, looked more priestly than ever, in spite of this brown garb. He felt his hope suddenly to be very forlorn indeed. And rushing at the fence, he began abruptly:

"I've come to ask you, sir, for your permission to marry Noel, if she will have me."

He had thought Pierson's face gentle; it was not gentle now. "Did you know I was here, then, Captain Fort?"

"I saw Noel in the garden. I've said nothing to her, of course. But she told me you were starting to-morrow for Egypt, so I shall have no other chance."

"I am sorry you have come. It is not for me to judge, but I don't think you will make Noel happy."

"May I ask you why, sir?"

"Captain Fort, the world's judgment of these things is not mine; but since you ask me. I will tell you frankly. My cousin Leila has a claim on you. It is her you should ask to marry you."

"I did ask her; she refused."

"I know. She would not refuse you again if you went out to her."

"I am not free to go out to her; besides, she would refuse. She knows I don't love her, and never have."

"Never have?"

"No."

"Then why—"

"Because I'm a man, I suppose, and a fool"

"If it was simply, 'because you are a man' as you call it, it is clear that no principle or faith governs you. And yet you ask me to give you Noel; my poor Noel, who wants the love and protection not of a 'man' but of a good man. No, Captain Fort, no!"

Fort bit his lips. "I'm clearly not a good man in your sense of the word; but I love her terribly, and I would protect her. I don't in the least know whether she'll have me. I don't expect her to, naturally. But I warn you that I mean to ask her, and to wait for her. I'm so much in love that I can do nothing else."

"The man who is truly in love does what is best for the one he loves." Fort bent his head; he felt as if he were at school again, confronting his head-master. "That's true," he said. "And I shall never trade on her position. If she can't feel anything for me now or in the future, I shan't trouble her, you may be sure of that. But if by some wonderful chance she should, I know I can make her happy, sir."

"She is a child."

"No, she's not a child," said Fort stubbornly.

Pierson touched the lapel of his new tunic. "Captain Fort, I am going far away from her, and leaving her without protection. I trust to your chivalry not to ask her, till I come back."

Fort threw back his head. "No, no, I won't accept that position. With or without your presence the facts will be the same. Either she can love me, or she can't. If she can, she'll be happier with me. If she can't, there's an end of it."

Pierson came slowly up to him. "In my view," he said, "you are as bound to Leila as if you were married to her."

"You can't, expect me to take the priest's view, sir."

Pierson's lips trembled.

"You call it a priest's view; I think it is only the view of a man of honour."

Fort reddened. "That's for my conscience," he said stubbornly. "I can't tell you, and I'm not going to, how things began. I was a fool. But I did my best, and I know that Leila doesn't think I'm bound. If she had, she would never have gone. When there's no feeling—there never was real feeling on my side—and when there's this terribly real feeling for Noel, which I never sought, which I tried to keep down, which I ran away from—"

"Did you?"

"Yes. To go on with the other was foul. I should have thought you might have seen that, sir; but I did go on with it. It was Leila who made an end."

"Leila behaved nobly, I think."

"She was splendid; but that doesn't make me a brute.".

Pierson turned away to the window, whence he must see Noel.

"It is repugnant to me," he said. "Is there never to be any purity in her life?"

"Is there never to be any life for her? At your rate, sir, there will be none. I'm no worse than other men, and I love her more than they could."

For fully a minute Pierson stood silent, before he said: "Forgive me if I've spoken harshly. I didn't mean to. I love her intensely; I wish for nothing but her good. But all my life I have believed that for a man there is only one woman—for a woman only one man."

"Then, Sir," Fort burst out, "you wish her—"

Pierson had put his hand up, as if to ward off a blow; and, angry though he was, Fort stopped.

"We are all made of flesh and blood," he continued coldly, "and it seems to me that you think we aren't."

"We have spirits too, Captain Fort." The voice was suddenly so gentle that Fort's anger evaporated.

"I have a great respect for you, sir; but a greater love for Noel, and nothing in this world will prevent me trying to give my life to her."

A smile quivered over Pierson's face. "If you try, then I can but pray that you will fail."

Fort did not answer, and went out.

He walked slowly away from the bungalow, with his head down, sore, angry, and yet-relieved. He knew where he stood; nor did he feel that he had been worsted—those strictures had not touched him. Convicted of immorality, he remained conscious of private justifications, in a way that human beings have. Only one little corner of memory, unseen and uncriticised by his opponent, troubled him. He pardoned himself the rest; the one thing he did not pardon was the fact that he had known Noel before his liaison with Leila commenced; had even let Leila sweep him away on, an evening when he had been in Noel's company. For that he felt a real disgust with himself. And all the way back to the station he kept thinking: 'How could I? I deserve to lose her! Still, I shall try; but not now—not yet!' And, wearily enough, he took the train back to town.

CHAPTER III

Both girls rose early that last day, and went with their father to Communion. As Gratian had said to George: "It's nothing to me now, but it will mean a lot to him out there, as a memory of us. So I must go." And he had answered: "Quite right, my dear. Let him have all he can get of you both to-day. I'll keep out of the way, and be back the last thing at night." Their father's smile when he saw them waiting for him went straight to both their hearts. It was a delicious day, and the early freshness had not yet dried out of the air, when they were walking home to breakfast. Each girl had slipped a hand under his arm. 'It's like Moses or was it Aaron?' Noel thought absurdly Memory had complete hold of her. All the old days! Nursery hours on Sundays after tea, stories out of the huge Bible bound in mother-o'pearl, with photogravures of the Holy Land—palms, and hills, and goats, and little Eastern figures, and funny boats on the Sea of Galilee, and camels—always camels. The book would be on his knee, and they one on each arm of his chair, waiting eagerly for the pages to be turned so that a new picture came. And there would be the feel of his cheek, prickly against theirs; and the old names with the old glamour—to Gratian, Joshua, Daniel, Mordecai, Peter; to Noel Absalom because of his hair, and Haman because she liked the sound, and Ruth because she was pretty and John because he leaned on Jesus' breast. Neither of them cared for Job or David, and Elijah and Elisha they detested because they hated the name Eliza. And later days by firelight in the drawing-room, roasting chestnuts just before evening church, and telling ghost stories, and trying to make Daddy eat his share. And hours beside him at the piano, each eager for her special hymns—for Gratian, "Onward, Christian Soldiers," "Lead, Kindly Light," and "O God Our Help"; for Noel, "Nearer, My God, to Thee," the one with "The Hosts of Midian" in it, and "For Those in Peril on the Sea." And carols! Ah! And Choristers! Noel had loved one deeply—the word "chorister" was so enchanting; and because of his whiteness, and hair which had no grease on it, but stood up all bright; she had never spoken to him—a far worship, like that for a star. And always, always Daddy had been gentle; sometimes angry, but always gentle; and they sometimes not at all! And mixed up with it all, the dogs they had had, and the cats they had had, and the cockatoo, and the governesses, and their red cloaks, and the curates, and the pantomimes, and "Peter Pan," and "Alice in Wonderland"—Daddy sitting between them, so that one could snuggle up. And later, the school-days, the hockey, the prizes, the holidays, the rush into his arms; and the great and wonderful yearly exodus to far places, fishing and bathing; walks and drives; rides and climbs, always with him. And concerts and Shakespeare plays in the Christmas and Easter holidays; and the walk home through the streets—all lighted in those days—one on each side of him. And this was the end! They waited on him at breakfast: they kept stealing glances at him, photographing him in their minds. Gratian got her camera and did actually photograph him in the morning sunlight with Noel, without Noel, with the baby; against all regulations for the defence of the realm. It was Noel who suggested: "Daddy, let's take lunch out and go for all day on the cliffs, us three, and forget there's a war."

So easy to say, so difficult to do, with the boom of the guns travelling to their ears along the grass, mingled with the buzz of insects. Yet that hum of summer, the innumerable voices of tiny lives, gossamer things all as alive as they, and as important to their frail selves; and the white clouds, few and so slow-moving, and the remote strange purity which clings to the chalky downs, all this white and green and blue of land and sea had its peace, which crept into the spirits of those three alone with Nature, this once more, the last time for—who could say how long? They talked, by tacit agreement, of nothing but what had happened before the war began, while the flock of the blown dandelions drifted past. Pierson sat cross-legged on the grass, without his cap, suffering a little still from the stiffness of his unwonted garments. And the girls lay one on each side of him, half critical, and half admiring. Noel could not bear his collar.

"If you had a soft collar you'd be lovely, Daddy. Perhaps out there they'll let you take it off. It must be fearfully hot in Egypt. Oh! I wish I were going. I wish I were going everywhere in the world. Some day!" Presently he read to them, Murray's "Hippolytus" of Euripides. And now and then Gratian and he discussed a passage. But Noel lay silent, looking at the sky. Whenever his voice ceased, there was the song of the larks, and very faint, the distant mutter of the guns.

They stayed up there till past six, and it was time to go and have tea before Evening Service. Those hours in the baking sun had drawn virtue out of them; they were silent and melancholy all the evening. Noel was the first to go up to her bedroom. She went without saying good night—she knew her father would come to her room that last evening. George had not yet come in; and Gratian was left alone with Pierson in the drawing-room, round whose single lamp, in spite of close-drawn curtains, moths were circling: She moved over to him on the sofa.

"Dad, promise me not to worry about Nollie; we'll take care of her."

"She can only take care of herself, Gracie, and will she? Did you know that Captain Fort was here yesterday?"

"She told me."

"What is her feeling about him?"

"I don't think she knows. Nollie dreams along, and then suddenly rushes."

"I wish she were safe from that man."

"But, Dad, why? George likes him and so do I."

A big grey moth was fluttering against the lamp. Pierson got up and caught it in the curve of his palm. "Poor thing! You're like my Nollie; so soft, and dreamy, so feckless, so reckless." And going to the curtains, he thrust his hand through, and released the moth.

"Dad!" said Gratian suddenly, "we can only find out for ourselves, even if we do singe our wings in doing it. We've been reading James's 'Pragmatism.' George says the only chapter that's important is missing— the one on ethics, to show that what we do is not wrong till it's proved wrong by the result. I suppose he was afraid to deliver that lecture."

Pierson's face wore the smile which always came on it when he had to deal with George, the smile which said: "Ah, George, that's very clever; but I know."

"My dear," he said, "that doctrine is the most dangerous in the world. I am surprised at George."

"I don't think George is in danger, Dad."

"George is a man of wide experience and strong judgment and character; but think how fatal it would be for Nollie, my poor Nollie, whom a little gust can blow into the candle."

"All the same," said Gratian stubbornly, "I don't think anyone can be good or worth anything unless they judge for themselves and take risks."

Pierson went close to her; his face was quivering.

"Don't let us differ on this last night; I must go up to Nollie for a minute, and then to bed. I shan't see you to-morrow; you mustn't get up; I can bear parting better like this. And my train goes at eight. God bless you, Gracie; give George my love. I know, I have always known that he's a good man, though we do fight so. Good-bye, my darling."

He went out with his cheeks wet from Gratian's tears, and stood in the porch a minute to recover his composure. The shadow of the house stretched velvet and blunt over the rock-garden. A night-jar was spinning; the churring sound affected him oddly. The last English night-bird he would hear. England! What a night-to say good-bye! 'My country!' he thought; 'my beautiful country!' The dew was lying thick and silvery already on the little patch of grass-the last dew, the last scent of an English night. The call of a bugle floated out. "England!" he prayed; "God be about you!" A little sound answered from across the grass, like an old man's cough, and the scrape and rattle of a chain. A face emerged at the edge of the house's shadow; bearded and horned like that of Pan, it seemed to stare at him. And he saw the dim grey form of the garden goat, heard it scuttle round the stake to which it was tethered, as though alarmed at this visitor to its' domain.

He went up the half-flight of stairs to Noel's narrow little room, next the nursery. No voice answered his tap. It was dark, but he could see her at the window, leaning far out, with her chin on her hands.

"Nollie!"

She answered without turning: "Such a lovely night, Daddy. Come and look! I'd like to set the goat free, only he'd eat the rock plants. But it is his night, isn't it? He ought to be running and skipping in it: it's such a shame to tie things up. Did you never, feel wild in your heart, Daddy?"

"Always, I think, Nollie; too wild. It's been hard to tame oneself."

Noel slipped her hand through his arm. "Let's go and take the goat and skip together on the hills. If only we had a penny whistle! Did you hear the bugle? The bugle and the goat!"

Pierson pressed the hand against him.

"Nollie, be good while I'm away. You know what I don't want. I told you in my letter." He looked at her cheek, and dared say no more. Her face had its "fey" look again.

"Don't you feel," she said suddenly, "on a night like this, all the things, all the things—the stars have lives, Daddy, and the moon has a big life, and the shadows have, and the moths and the birds and the goats and the trees, and the flowers, and all of us—escaped? Oh! Daddy, why is there a war? And why are people so bound and so unhappy? Don't tell me it's God—don't!"

Pierson could not answer, for there came into his mind the Greek song he had been reading aloud that afternoon—

"O for a deep and dewy Spring, With runlets cold to draw and drink, And a great meadow blossoming, Long-grassed, and poplars in a ring, To rest me by the brink. O take me to the mountain, O, Past the great pines and through the wood, Up where the lean hounds softly go, A-whine for wild things' blood, And madly flies the dappled roe, O God, to shout and speed them there; An arrow by my chestnut hair Drawn tight and one keen glimmering spear Ah! if I could!"

All that in life had been to him unknown, of venture and wild savour; all the emotion he had stifled; the swift Pan he had denied; the sharp fruits, the burning suns, the dark pools, the unearthly moonlight, which were not of God—all came with the breath of that old song, and the look on the girl's face. And he covered his eyes.

Noel's hand tugged at his arm. "Isn't beauty terribly alive," she murmured, "like a lovely person? it makes you ache to kiss it."

His lips felt parched. "There is a beauty beyond all that," he said stubbornly.

"Where?"

"Holiness, duty, faith. O Nollie, my love!" But Noel's hand tightened on his arm.

"Shall I tell you what I should like?" she whispered. "To take God's hand and show Him things. I'm certain He's not seen everything."

A shudder went through Pierson, one of those queer sudden shivers, which come from a strange note in a voice, or a new sharp scent or sight.

"My dear, what things you say!"

"But He hasn't, and it's time He did. We'd creep, and peep, and see it all for once, as He can't in His churches. Daddy, oh! Daddy! I can't bear it any more; to think of them being killed on a night like this; killed and killed so that they never see it all again—never see it—never see it!" She sank down, and covered her face with her arms.

"I can't, I can't! Oh! take it all away, the cruelty! Why does it come—why the stars and the flowers, if God doesn't care any more than that?"

Horribly affected he stood bending over her, stroking her head. Then the habit of a hundred death-beds helped him. "Come, Nollie! This life is but a minute. We must all die."

"But not they—not so young!" She clung to his knees, and looked up. "Daddy, I don't want you to go; promise me to come back!"

The childishness of those words brought back his balance.

"My dear sweetheart, of course! Come, Nollie, get up. The sun's been too much for you."

Noel got up, and put her hands on her father's shoulders. "Forgive me for all my badness, and all my badness to come, especially all my badness to come!"

Pierson smiled. "I shall always forgive you, Nollie; but there won't be—there mustn't be any badness to come. I pray God to keep you, and make you like your mother."

"Mother never had a devil, like you and me."

He was silent from surprise. How did this child know the devil of wild feeling he had fought against year after year; until with the many years he had felt it weakening within him! She whispered on: "I don't hate my devil.

"Why should I?—it's part of me. Every day when the sun sets, I'll think of you, Daddy; and you might do the same—that'll keep me good. I shan't come to the station tomorrow, I should only cry. And I shan't say good-bye now. It's unlucky."

She flung her arms round him; and half smothered by that fervent embrace, he kissed her cheeks and hair. Freed of each other at last, he stood for a moment looking at her by the moonlight.

"There never was anyone more loving than you; Nollie!" he said quietly. "Remember my letter. And good night, my love!" Then, afraid to stay another second, he went quickly out of the dark little room....

George Laird, returning half an hour later, heard a voice saying softly: "George, George!"

Looking up, he saw a little white blur at the window, and Noel's face just visible.

"George, let the goat loose, just for to-night, to please me."

Something in that voice, and in the gesture of her stretched-out arm moved George in a queer way, although, as Pierson had once said, he had no music in his soul. He loosed the goat.

CHAPTER IV

1

In the weeks which succeeded Pierson's departure, Gratian and George often discussed Noel's conduct and position by the light of the Pragmatic theory. George held a suitably scientific view. Just as he would point out to his wife—in the physical world, creatures who diverged from the normal had to justify their divergence in competition with their environments, or else go under, so in the ethical world it was all a question of whether Nollie could make good her vagary. If she could, and grew in strength of character thereby, it was ipso facto all right, her vagary would be proved an advantage, and the world enriched. If not, the world by her failure to make good would be impoverished, and her vagary proved wrong. The orthodox and academies—he insisted—were always forgetting the adaptability of living organisms; how every action which was out of the ordinary, unconsciously modified all the other actions together with the outlook, and philosophy of the doer. "Of course Nollie was crazy," he said, "but when she did what she did, she at once began to think differently about life and morals. The deepest instinct we all have is the instinct that we must do what we must, and think that what we've done is really all right; in fact the—instinct of self-preservation. We're all fighting animals; and we feel in our bones that if we admit we're beaten—we are beaten; but that every fight we win, especially against odds, hardens those bones. But personally I don't think she can make good on her own."

Gratian, whose Pragmatism was not yet fully baked, responded doubtfully:

"No, I don't think she can. And if she could I'm not sure. But isn't Pragmatism a perfectly beastly word, George? It has no sense of humour in it at all."

"It is a bit thick, and in the hands of the young, deuced likely to become Prigmatism; but not with Nollie."

They watched the victim of their discussions with real anxiety. The knowledge that she would never be more sheltered than she was with them, at all events until she married, gravely impeded the formation of any judgment as to whether or no she could make good. Now and again there would come to Gratian who after all knew her sister better than George—the disquieting thought that whatever conclusion Noel led them to form, she would almost certainly force them to abandon sooner or later.

Three days after her father's departure Noel had declared that she wanted to work on the land. This George had promptly vetoed.

"You aren't strong enough yet, my dear: Wait till the harvest begins. Then you can go and help on the farm here. If you can stand that without damage, we'll think about it."

But the weather was wet and harvest late, and Noel had nothing much to do but attend to her baby, already well attended to by Nurse, and dream and brood, and now and then cook an omelette or do some housework for the sake of a gnawing conscience. Since Gratian and George were away in hospital all day, she was very much alone. Several times in the evenings Gratian tried to come at the core of her thoughts, Twice she flew the kite of Leila. The first time Noel only answered: "Yes, she's a brick." The second time, she said: "I don't want to think about her."

But, hardening her heart, Gratian went on: "Don't you think it's queer we've never heard from Captain Fort since he came down?"

In her calmest voice Noel answered: "Why should we, after being told that he wasn't liked?"

"Who told him that?"

"I told him, that Daddy didn't; but I expect Daddy said much worse things." She gave a little laugh, then softly added: "Daddy's wonderful, isn't he?"

"How?"

"The way he drives one to do the other thing. If he hadn't opposed my marriage to Cyril, you know, that wouldn't have happened, it just made all the difference. It stirred me up so fearfully." Gratian stared at her, astonished that she could see herself so clearly. Towards the end of August she had a letter from Fort.

"DEAR MRS. LAIRD,

"You know all about things, of course, except the one thing which to me is all important. I can't go on without knowing whether I have a chance with your sister. It is against your father's expressed wish that she should have anything to do with me, but I told him that I could not and would not promise not to ask her. I get my holiday at the end of this month, and am coming down to put it to the touch. It means more to me than you can possibly imagine.

"I am, dear Mrs. Laird,

"Your very faithful servant,

"JAMES FORT."

She discussed the letter with George, whose advice was: "Answer it politely, but say nothing; and nothing to Nollie. I think it would be a very good thing. Of course it's a bit of a make-shift—twice her age; but he's a genuine man, if not exactly brilliant."

Gratian answered almost sullenly: "I've always wanted the very best for Nollie."

George screwed up his steel-coloured eyes, as he might have looked at one on whom he had to operate. "Quite so," he said. "But you must remember, Gracie, that out of the swan she was, Nollie has made herself into a lame duck. Fifty per cent at least is off her value, socially. We must look at things as they are."

"Father is dead against it."

George smiled, on the point of saying: 'That makes me feel it must be a good thing!' But he subdued the impulse.

"I agree that we're bound by his absence not to further it actively. Still Nollie knows his wishes, and it's up to her and no one else. After all, she's no longer a child."

His advice was followed. But to write that polite letter, which said nothing, cost Gratian a sleepless night, and two or three hours' penmanship. She was very conscientious. Knowledge of this impending visit increased the anxiety with which she watched her sister, but the only inkling she obtained of Noel's state of mind was when the girl showed her a letter she had received from Thirza, asking her to come back to Kestrel. A postscript, in Uncle Bob's handwriting, added these words:

"We're getting quite fossilised down here; Eve's gone and left us again. We miss you and the youngster awfully. Come along down, Nollie there's a dear!"

"They're darlings," Noel said, "but I shan't go. I'm too restless, ever since Daddy went; you don't know how restless. This rain simply makes me want to die."

2

The weather improved next day, and at the end of that week harvest began. By what seemed to Noel a stroke of luck the farmer's binder was broken; he could not get it repaired, and wanted all the human binders he could get. That first day in the fields blistered her hands, burnt her face and neck, made every nerve and bone in her body ache; but was the happiest day she had spent for weeks, the happiest perhaps since Cyril Morland left her, over a year ago. She had a bath and went to bed the moment she got in.

Lying there nibbling chocolate and smoking a cigarette, she luxuriated in the weariness which had stilled her dreadful restlessness. Watching the smoke of her cigarette curl up against the sunset glow which filled her window, she mused: If only she could be tired out like this every day! She would be all right then, would lose the feeling of not knowing what she wanted, of being in a sort o of large box, with the lid slammed down, roaming round it like a dazed and homesick bee in an overturned tumbler; the feeling of being only half alive, of having a wing maimed so that she could only fly a little way, and must then drop.

She slept like a top that night. But the next day's work was real torture, and the third not much better. By the end of the week, however, she was no longer stiff.

Saturday was cloudless; a perfect day. The field she was working in lay on a slope. It was the last field to be cut, and the best wheat yet, with a glorious burnt shade in its gold and the ears blunt and full. She had got used now to the feel of the great sheaves in her arms, and the binding wisps drawn through her hand till she held them level, below the ears, ready for the twist. There was no new sensation in it now; just steady, rather dreamy work, to keep her place in the row, to the swish-swish of the cutter and the call of the driver to his horses at the turns; with continual little pauses, to straighten and rest her back a moment, and shake her head free from the flies, or suck her finger, sore from the constant pushing of the straw ends under. So the hours went on, rather hot and wearisome, yet with a feeling of something good being done, of a job getting surely to its end. And gradually the centre patch narrowed, and the sun slowly slanted down.

When they stopped for tea, instead of running home as usual, she drank it cold out of a flask she had brought, ate a bun and some chocolate, and lay down on her back against the hedge. She always avoided that group of her fellow workers round the tea-cans which the farmer's wife brought out. To avoid people, if she could, had become habitual to her now. They must know about her, or would soon if she gave them the chance. She had never lost consciousness of her ring-finger, expecting every eye to fall on it as a matter of course. Lying on her face, she puffed her cigarette into the grass, and watched a beetle, till one of the sheep-dogs, scouting for scraps, came up, and she fed him with her second bun. Having finished the bun, he tried to eat the beetle, and, when she rescued it, convinced that she had nothing more to give him, sneezed at her, and went away. Pressing the end of her cigarette out against the bank, she turned over. Already the driver was perched on his tiny seat, and his companion, whose business it was to free the falling corn, was getting up alongside. Swish-swish! It had begun again. She rose, stretched herself, and went back to her place in the row. The field would be finished to-night; she would have a lovely rest-all Sunday I Towards seven o'clock a narrow strip, not twenty yards broad, alone was left. This last half hour was what Noel dreaded. To-day it was worse, for the farmer had no cartridges left, and the rabbits were dealt with by hullabaloo and sticks and chasing dogs. Rabbits were vermin, of course, and ate the crops, and must be killed; besides, they were good food, and fetched two shillings apiece; all this she knew but to see the poor frightened things stealing out, pounced on, turned, shouted at, chased, rolled over by great swift dogs, fallen on by the boys and killed and carried with their limp grey bodies upside down, so dead and soft and helpless, always made her feel quite sick. She stood very still, trying not to see or hear, and in the corn opposite to her a rabbit stole along, crouched, and peeped. 'Oh!' she thought, 'come out here, bunny. I'll let you away—can't you see I will? It's your only chance. Come out!' But the rabbit crouched, and gazed, with its little cowed head poked forward, and its ears laid flat; it seemed trying to understand whether this still thing in front of it was the same as those others. With the thought, 'Of course it won't while I look at it,' Noel turned her head away. Out of the corner of her eye she could see a man standing a few yards off. The rabbit bolted out. Now the man would shout and turn it. But he did not, and the rabbit scuttled past him and away to the hedge. She heard a shout from the end of the row, saw a dog galloping. Too late! Hurrah! And clasping her hands, she looked at the man. It was Fort! With the queerest feeling—amazement, pleasure, the thrill of conspiracy, she saw him coming up to her.

"I did want that rabbit to get off," she sighed out; "I've been watching it. Thank you!"

He looked at her. "My goodness!" was all he said.

Noel's hands flew up to her cheeks. "Yes, I know; is my nose very red?"

"No; you're as lovely as Ruth, if she was lovely."

Swish-swish! The cutter came by; Noel started forward to her place in the row; but catching her arm, he said: "No, let me do this little bit. I haven't had a day in the fields since the war began. Talk to me while I'm binding."

She stood watching him. He made a different, stronger twist from hers, and took larger sheaves, so that she felt a sort of jealousy.

"I didn't know you knew about this sort of thing."

"Oh, Lord, yes! I had a farm once out West. Nothing like field-work, to make you feel good. I've been watching you; you bind jolly well."

Noel gave a sigh of pleasure.

"Where have you come from?" she asked.

"Straight from the station. I'm on my holiday." He looked up at her, and they both fell silent.

Swish-swish! The cutter was coming again. Noel went to the beginning of her portion of the falling corn, he to the end of it. They worked towards each other, and met before the cutter was on them a third time.

"Will you come in to supper?"

"I'd love to."

"Then let's go now, please. I don't want to see any more rabbits killed."

They spoke very little on the way to the bungalow, but she felt his eyes on her all the time. She left him with George and Gratian who had just come in, and went up for her bath.

Supper had been laid out in the verandah, and it was nearly dark before they had finished. In rhyme with the failing of the light Noel became more and more silent. When they went in, she ran up to her baby. She did not go down again, but as on the night before her father went away, stood at her window, leaning out. A dark night, no moon; in the starlight she could only just see the dim garden, where no goat was grazing. Now that her first excitement had worn off, this sudden reappearance of Fort filled her with nervous melancholy: She knew perfectly well what he had come for, she had always known. She had no certain knowledge of her own mind; but she knew that all these weeks she had been between his influence and her father's, listening to them, as it were, pleading with her. And, curiously, the pleading of each, instead of drawing her towards the pleader, had seemed dragging her away from him, driving her into the arms of the other. To the protection of one or the other she felt she must go; and it humiliated her to think that in all the world there was no other place for her. The wildness of that one night in the old Abbey seemed to have power to govern all her life to come. Why should that one night, that one act, have this uncanny power to drive her this way or that, to those arms or these? Must she, because of it, always need protection? Standing there in the dark it was almost as if they had come up behind her, with their pleadings; and a shiver ran down her back. She longed to turn on them, and cry out: "Go away; oh; go away! I don't want either of you; I just want to be left alone!" Then something, a moth perhaps, touched her neck. She gasped and shook herself. How silly!

She heard the back door round the corner of the house opening; a man's low voice down in the dark said:

"Who's the young lady that comes out in the fields?"

Another voice—one of the maids—answered:

"The Missis's sister."

"They say she's got a baby."

"Never you mind what she's got."

Noel heard the man's laugh. It seemed to her the most odious laugh she had ever heard. She thought swiftly and absurdly: 'I'll get away from all this.' The window was only a few feet up. She got out on to the ledge, let herself down, and dropped. There was a flower-bed below, quite soft, with a scent of geranium-leaves and earth. She brushed herself, and went tiptoeing across the gravel and the little front lawn, to the gate. The house was quite dark, quite silent. She walked on, down the road. 'Jolly!' she thought. 'Night after night we sleep, and never see the nights: sleep until we're called, and never see anything. If they want to catch me they'll have to run.' And she began running down the road in her evening frock and shoes, with nothing on her head. She stopped after going perhaps three hundred yards, by the edge of the wood. It was splendidly dark in there, and she groped her way from trunk to trunk, with a delicious, half-scared sense of adventure and novelty. She stopped at last by a thin trunk whose bark glimmered faintly. She felt it with her cheek, quite smooth—a birch tree; and, with her arms round it, she stood perfectly still. Wonderfully, magically silent, fresh and sweet-scented and dark! The little tree trembled suddenly within her arms, and she heard the low distant rumble, to which she had grown so accustomed—the guns, always at work, killing—killing men and killing trees, little trees perhaps like this within her arms, little trembling trees! Out there, in this dark night, there would not be a single unscarred tree like this smooth quivering thing, no fields of corn, not even a bush or a blade of grass, no leaves to rustle and smell sweet, not a bird, no little soft-footed night beasts, except the rats; and she shuddered, thinking of the Belgian soldier-painter. Holding the tree tight, she squeezed its smooth body against her. A rush of the same helpless, hopeless revolt and sorrow overtook her, which had wrung from her that passionate little outburst to her father, the night before he went away. Killed, torn, and bruised; burned, and killed, like Cyril! All the young things, like this little tree.

Rumble! Rumble! Quiver! Quiver! And all else so still, so sweet and still, and starry, up there through the leaves.... 'I can't bear it!' she thought. She pressed her lips, which the sun had warmed all day, against the satiny smooth bark. But the little tree stood within her arms insentient, quivering only to the long rumbles. With each of those dull mutterings, life and love were going out, like the flames of candles on a Christmas-tree, blown, one by one. To her eyes, accustomed by now to the darkness in there, the wood seemed slowly to be gathering a sort of life, as though it were a great thing watching her; a great thing with hundreds of limbs and eyes, and the power of breathing. The little tree, which had seemed so individual and friendly, ceased to be a comfort and became a part of the whole living wood, absorbed in itself, and coldly watching her, this intruder of the mischievous breed, the fatal breed which loosed those rumblings on the earth. Noel unlocked her arms, and recoiled. A bough scraped her neck, some leaves flew against her eyes; she stepped aside, tripped over a root, and fell. A bough had hit her too, and she lay a little dazed, quivering at such dark unfriendliness. She held her hands up to her face for the mere pleasure of seeing something a little less dark; it was childish, and absurd, but she was frightened. The wood seemed to have so many eyes, so many arms, and all unfriendly; it seemed waiting to give her other blows, other falls, and to guard her within its darkness until—! She got up, moved a few steps, and stood still, she had forgotten from where she had come in. And afraid of moving deeper into the unfriendly wood, she turned slowly round, trying to tell which way to go. It was all just one dark watching thing, of limbs on the ground and in the air. 'Any way,' she thought; 'any way of course will take me out!' And she groped forward, keeping her hands up to guard her face. It was silly, but she could not help the sinking, scattered feeling which comes to one bushed, or lost in a fog. If the wood had not been so dark, so,—alive! And for a second she had the senseless, terrifying thought of a child: 'What if I never get out!' Then she laughed at it, and stood still again, listening. There was no sound to guide her, no sound at all except that faint dull rumble, which seemed to come from every side, now. And the trees watched her. 'Ugh!' she thought; 'I hate this wood!' She saw it now, its snaky branches, its darkness, and great forms, as an abode of giants and witches. She groped and scrambled on again, tripped once more, and fell, hitting her forehead against a trunk. The blow dazed and sobered her. 'It's idiotic,' she thought; 'I'm a baby! I'll Just walk very slowly till I reach the edge. I know it isn't a large wood!' She turned deliberately to face each direction; solemnly selected that from which the muttering of the guns seemed to come, and started again, moving very slowly with her hands stretched out. Something rustled in the undergrowth, quite close; she saw a pair of green eyes shining. Her heart jumped into her mouth. The thing sprang—there was a swish of ferns and twigs, and silence. Noel clasped her breast. A poaching cat! And again she moved forward. But she had lost direction. 'I'm going round and round,' she thought. 'They always do.' And the sinking scattered feeling of the "bushed" clutched at her again. 'Shall I call?' she thought. 'I must be near the road. But it's so babyish.' She moved on again. Her foot struck something soft. A voice muttered a thick oath; a hand seized her ankle. She leaped, and dragged and wrenched it free; and, utterly unnerved, she screamed, and ran forward blindly.

CHAPTER V

No one could have so convinced a feeling as Jimmy Fort that he would be a 'bit of a makeshift' for Noel. He had spent the weeks after his interview with her father obsessed by her image, often saying to himself "It won't do. It's playing it too low down to try and get that child, when I know that, but for her trouble, I shouldn't have a chance." He had never had much opinion of his looks, but now he seemed to himself absurdly old and dried-up in this desert of a London. He loathed the Office job to which they had put him, and the whole atmosphere of officialdom. Another year of it, and he would shrivel like an old apple! He began to look at himself anxiously, taking stock of his physical assets now that he had this dream of young beauty. He would be forty next month, and she was nineteen! But there would be times too when he would feel that, with her, he could be as much of a "three-year-old" as the youngster she had loved. Having little hope of winning her, he took her "past" but lightly. Was it not that past which gave him what chance he had? On two things he was determined: He would not trade on her past. And if by any chance she took him, he would never show her that he remembered that she had one.

After writing to Gratian he had spent the week before his holiday began, in an attempt to renew the youthfulness of his appearance, which made him feel older, leaner, bonier and browner than ever. He got up early, rode in the rain, took Turkish baths, and did all manner of exercises; neither smoked nor drank, and went to bed early, exactly as if he had been going to ride a steeplechase. On the afternoon, when at last he left on that terrific pilgrimage, he gazed at his face with a sort of despair, it was so lean, and leather-coloured, and he counted almost a dozen grey hairs.

When he reached the bungalow, and was told that she was working in the corn-fields, he had for the first time a feeling that Fate was on his side. Such a meeting would be easier than any other! He had been watching her for several minutes before she saw him, with his heart beating more violently than it had ever beaten in the trenches; and that new feeling of hope stayed with him—all through the greeting, throughout supper, and even after she had left them and gone upstairs. Then, with the suddenness of a blind drawn down, it vanished, and he sat on, trying to talk, and slowly getting more and more silent and restless.

"Nollie gets so tired, working," Gratian said: He knew she meant it kindly but that she should say it at all was ominous. He got up at last, having lost hope of seeing Noel again, conscious too that he had answered the last three questions at random.

In the porch George said: "You'll come in to lunch tomorrow, won't you?"

"Oh, thanks, I'm afraid it'll bore you all."

"Not a bit. Nollie won't be so tired."

Again—so well meant. They were very kind. He looked up from the gate, trying to make out which her window might be; but all was dark. A little way down the road he stopped to light a cigarette; and, leaning against a gate, drew the smoke of it deep into his lungs, trying to assuage the ache in his heart. So it was hopeless! She had taken the first, the very first chance, to get away from him! She knew that he loved her, could not help knowing, for he had never been able to keep it out of his eyes and voice. If she had felt ever so little for him, she would not have avoided him this first evening. 'I'll go back to that desert,' he thought; 'I'm not going to whine and crawl. I'll go back, and bite on it; one must have some pride. Oh, why the hell am I crocked-up like this? If only I could get out to France again!' And then Noel's figure bent over the falling corn formed before him. 'I'll have one more try,' he thought; 'one more—tomorrow somewhere, I'll get to know for certain. And if I get what Leila's got I shall deserve it, I suppose. Poor Leila! Where is she? Back at High Constantia?' What was that? A cry—of terror—in that wood! Crossing to the edge, he called "Coo-ee!" and stood peering into its darkness. He heard the sound of bushes being brushed aside, and whistled. A figure came bursting out, almost into his arms.

"Hallo!" he said; "what's up?"

A voice gasped: "Oh! It's—it's nothing!"

He saw Noel. She had swayed back, and stood about a yard away. He could dimly see her covering her face with her arms. Feeling instinctively that she wanted to hide her fright, he said quietly:

"What luck! I was just passing. It's awfully dark."

"I—I got lost; and a man—caught my foot, in there!"

Moved beyond control by the little gulps and gasps of her breathing, he stepped forward and put his hands on her shoulders. He held her lightly, without speaking, terrified lest he should wound her pride.

"I-I got in there," she gasped, "and the trees—and I stumbled over a roan asleep, and he—"

"Yes, Yes, I know," he murmured, as if to a child. She had dropped her arms now, and he could see her face, with eyes unnaturally dilated, and lips quivering. Then moved again beyond control, he drew her so close that he could feel the throbbing of her heart, and put his lips to her forehead all wet with heat. She closed her eyes, gave a little choke, and buried her face against his coat.

"There, there, my darling!" he kept on saying. "There, there, my darling!" He could feel the snuggling of her cheek against his shoulder. He had got her—had got her! He was somehow certain that she would not draw back now. And in the wonder and ecstasy of that thought, all the world above her head, the stars in their courses, the wood which had frightened her, seemed miracles of beauty and fitness. By such fortune as had never come to man, he had got her! And he murmured over and over again:

"I love you!" She was resting perfectly quiet against him, while her heart ceased gradually to beat so fast. He could feel her cheek rubbing against his coat of Harris tweed. Suddenly she sniffed at it, and whispered:

"It smells good."

When summer sun has burned all Egypt, the white man looks eagerly each day for evening, whose rose-coloured veil melts opalescent into the dun drift, of the hills, and iridescent above, into the slowly deepening blue. Pierson stood gazing at the mystery of the desert from under the little group of palms and bougainvillea which formed the garden of the hospital. Even-song was in full voice: From the far wing a gramophone was grinding out a music-hall ditty; two aeroplanes, wheeling exactly like the buzzards of the desert, were letting drip the faint whir of their flight; metallic voices drifted from the Arab village; the wheels of the water-wells creaked; and every now and then a dry rustle was stirred from the palm-leaves by puffs of desert wind. On either hand an old road ran out, whose line could be marked by the little old watch-towers of another age. For how many hundred years had human life passed along it to East and West; the brown men and their camels, threading that immemorial track over the desert, which ever filled him with wonder, so still it was, so wide, so desolate, and every evening so beautiful! He sometimes felt that he could sit for ever looking at it; as though its cruel mysterious loveliness were—home; and yet he never looked at it without a spasm of homesickness.

So far his new work had brought him no nearer to the hearts of men. Or at least he did not feel it had. Both at the regimental base, and now in this hospital—an intermediate stage—waiting for the draft with which he would be going into Palestine, all had been very nice to him, friendly, and as it were indulgent; so might schoolboys have treated some well-intentioned dreamy master, or business men a harmless idealistic inventor who came visiting their offices. He had even the feeling that they were glad to have him about, just as they were glad to have their mascots and their regimental colours; but of heart-to-heart simple comradeship—it seemed they neither wanted it of him nor expected him to give it, so that he had a feeling that he would be forward and impertinent to offer it. Moreover, he no longer knew how. He was very lonely. 'When I come face to face with death,' he would think, 'it will be different. Death makes us all brothers. I may be of real use to them then.'

They brought him a letter while he stood there listening to that even-song, gazing at the old desert road.

"DARLING DAD,

"I do hope this will reach you before you move on to Palestine. You said in your last—at the end of September, so I hope you'll just get it. There is one great piece of news, which I'm afraid will hurt and trouble you; Nollie is married to Jimmy Fort. They were married down here this afternoon, and have just gone up to Town. They have to find a house of course. She has been very restless, lonely, and unhappy ever since you went, and I'm sure it is really for the best: She is quite another creature, and simply devoted, headlong. It's just like Nollie. She says she didn't know what she wanted, up to the last minute. But now she seems as if she could never want anything else.

"Dad dear, Nollie could never have made good by herself. It isn't her nature, and it's much better like this, I feel sure, and so does George. Of course it isn't ideal—and one wanted that for her; but she did break her wing, and he is so awfully good and devoted to her, though you didn't believe it, and perhaps won't, even now. The great thing is to feel her happy again, and know she's safe. Nollie is capable of great devotion; only she must be anchored. She was drifting all about; and one doesn't know what she might have done, in one of her moods. I do hope you won't grieve about it. She's dreadfully anxious about how you'll feel. I know it will be wretched for you, so far off; but do try and believe it's for the best.... She's out of danger; and she was really in a horrible position. It's so good for the baby, too, and only fair to him. I do think one must take things as they are, Dad dear. It was impossible to mend Nollie's wing. If she were a fighter, and gloried in it, or if she were the sort who would 'take the veil'—but she isn't either. So it is all right, Dad. She's writing to you herself. I'm sure Leila didn't want Jimmy Fort to be unhappy because he couldn't love her; or she would never have gone away. George sends you his love; we are both very well. And Nollie is looking splendid still, after her harvest work. All, all my love, Dad dear. Is there anything we can get, and send you? Do take care of your blessed self, and don't grieve about Nollie.

"GRATIAN."

A half-sheet of paper fluttered down; he picked it up from among the parched fibre of dead palm-leaves.

"DADDY DARLING,

"I've done it. Forgive me—I'm so happy.

"Your NOLLIE."

The desert shimmered, the palm-leaves rustled, and Pierson stood trying to master the emotion roused in him by those two letters. He felt no anger, not even vexation; he felt no sorrow, but a loneliness so utter and complete that he did not know how to bear it. It seemed as if some last link with life had' snapped. 'My girls are happy,' he thought. 'If I am not—what does it matter? If my faith and my convictions mean nothing to them—why should they follow? I must and will not feel lonely. I ought to have the sense of God present, to feel His hand in mine. If I cannot, what use am I—what use to the poor fellows in there, what use in all the world?'

An old native on a donkey went by, piping a Soudanese melody on a little wooden Arab flute. Pierson turned back into the hospital humming it. A nurse met him there.

"The poor boy at the end of A ward is sinking fast, sir; I expect he'd like to see you."

He went into A ward, and walked down between the beds to the west window end, where two screens had been put, to block off the cot. Another nurse, who was sitting beside it, rose at once.

"He's quite conscious," she whispered; "he can still speak a little. He's such a dear." A tear rolled down her cheek, and she passed out behind the screens. Pierson looked down at the boy; perhaps he was twenty, but the unshaven down on his cheeks was soft and almost colourless. His eyes were closed. He breathed regularly, and did not seem in pain; but there was about him that which told he was going; something resigned, already of the grave. The window was wide open, covered by mosquito-netting, and a tiny line of sunlight, slanting through across the foot of the cot, crept slowly backwards over the sheets and the boy's body, shortening as it crept. In the grey whiteness of the walls; the bed, the boy's face, just that pale yellow bar of sunlight, and one splash of red and blue from a little flag on the wall glowed out. At this cooler hour, the ward behind the screens was almost empty, and few sounds broke the stillness; but from without came that intermittent rustle of dry palm-leaves. Pierson waited in silence, watching the sun sink. If the boy might pass like this, it would be God's mercy. Then he saw the boy's eyes open, wonderfully clear eyes of the lighted grey which has dark rims; his lips moved, and Pierson bent down to hear.

"I'm goin' West, zurr." The whisper had a little soft burr; the lips quivered; a pucker as of a child formed on his face, and passed.

Through Pierson's mind there flashed the thought: 'O God! Let me be some help to him!'

"To God, my dear son!" he said.

A flicker of humour, of ironic question, passed over the boy's lips.

Terribly moved, Pierson knelt down, and began softly, fervently praying. His whispering mingled with the rustle of the palm-leaves, while the bar of sunlight crept up the body. In the boy's smile had been the whole of stoic doubt, of stoic acquiescence. It had met him with an unconscious challenge; had seemed to know so much. Pierson took his hand, which lay outside the sheet. The boy's lips moved, as though in thanks; he drew a long feeble breath, as if to suck in the thread of sunlight; and his eyes closed. Pierson bent over the hand. When he looked up the boy was dead. He kissed his forehead and went quietly out.

The sun had set, and he walked away from the hospital to a hillock beyond the track on the desert's edge, and stood looking at the afterglow. The sun and the boy—together they had gone West, into that wide glowing nothingness.

The muezzin call to sunset prayer in the Arab village came to him clear and sharp, while he sat there, unutterably lonely. Why had that smile so moved him? Other death smiles had been like this evening smile on the desert hills—a glowing peace, a promise of heaven. But the boy's smile had said: 'Waste no breath on me—you cannot help. Who knows—who knows? I have no hope, no faith; but I am adventuring. Good-bye!' Poor boy! He had braved all things, and moved out uncertain, yet undaunted! Was that, then, the uttermost truth, was faith a smaller thing? But from that strange notion he recoiled with horror. 'In faith I have lived, in faith I will die!' he thought, 'God helping me!' And the breeze, ruffling the desert sand, blew the grains against the palms of his hands, outstretched above the warm earth.

John Galsworthy – A Short Biography

John Galsworthy, eldest son of John Galsworthy (1817-1904), a solicitor and company director of Old Jewry, London, and Blanche Bailey (1835-1915), daughter of Charles Bartleet, a needlemaker in Redditch. His father's ancestors originated in Wembury, near Plymouth in England, and Galsworthy, for whom family origins were of significant importance, maintained a close connection with Devon. His more immediate family were considerably wealthy and well established in the shipping industry, and owned a fine estate in Kingston-upon-Thames called Parkfield, where Galsworthy was born on the 14th August 1867. At the age of nine he began education at Saugeen, a Bournemouth preparatory school, before starting at Harrow school in 1881 where he remained until 1886, distinguishing himself as an athlete.

His education at Harrow being successful enough to gain him entrance to Oxford, he began at New College to read law and gained a second-class degree with honours in 1889. Following Lincoln's Inn he was called to the bar in 1890. Despite this recognition he realised that he was not keen to actually begin practising law and so he resolved instead to look after the family's shipping business while specialising himself in Marine Law. This decision saw him take to the seas to destinations such as Vancouver, Island and South AFrica, though it was at the age of twenty-five on one particular journey to Australia, motivated by an (unfulfilled) intention to meet Robert Louis Stevenson on Samoa that he would being to realise fully his literary interests: though he was not considering becoming a writer at this time, his enjoyment of literature was enough to encourage an attempt at meeting a great writer and eventually enabled one of the most significant encounters of his life. He made the journey with his friend Edward Sanderson and, though he missed Stevenson, he met Joseph Conrad, a fellow future author famed for his novels which were often nautically themed. At the time Conrad was the first mate of the sailing-ship Torrens moored in the harbour of Adelaide, Australia; still very much focused on his ship-borne career, he was yet to begin his writing in earnest.

Indeed, though neither knew at the time, both Conrad and Galsworthy were at similar junctures in their lives, their time spent as sea acting as a transitional period during which each found their literary calling. It is perhaps owning to this unknown common ground that they became close friends. During his time on the Torrens Galsworthy recorded several details, offering a frank and valuable characterisation of Conrad while also illuminating his own experiences as a student of Marine Law.

"I supposed to be studying navigation for the Admiralty Bar, would every day work out the position of the ship with the captain. On one side of the saloon table we would sit and check our observations with those of Conrad, who from the other side of the table would look at us a little quizzically."

On his return to England and the cessation of his nautical voyaging, Galsworthy began an affair with the wife of his first cousin, Major Arthur John Galsworthy. Ada Nemesis Pearson Cooper (1864-1956), the daughter of Emanuel Copper, an obstetrician from Norwich, remained married to the Major for ten years and the affair remained secret for its duration. In order to conceal the affair they took considerable pains to avoid suspicion. One such tactic was to stay in a secluded farmhouse called Wingstone in the village on Manaton on Dartmoor, in Devon. In Galsworthy's decision to choose Devon as the location for their clandestine rendezvous we see evidence of Galsworthy's affection for the place of his father's origin. It was only when, in 1905, she divorced the Major that their affair became known following their marriage on 23rd September of that year.

Galsworthy now took to writing sometime after having met Conrad and his career began in earnest when, in 1897, his first work, From the Four Winds, a volume of short stories, was published under the pseudonym John Sinjohn. He succeeded this in 1898 with Jocelyn, his first novel, and then his second in 1900, Villa Rubein. In 1901 he published a second volume of short stories, A Man of Devon, which was the last of his work to be published under pseudonym. The first of his work to be published under his own name was The Island Pharisees in 1904, a novel of social observation, seasoned with flashes of satire and propaganda. His decision to write under his own name is arguably owing to the recent death of his father, either as a mark of respect to his name or because now he was able to publish freely without incurring the possibility of paternal disappointment at his choice of career. It also marked a shift in his professionalism; he had hitherto published with small, independent publishers, but The Island Pharisees was published by Heinemann, a far more established House and one with whom he remained for the duration of his writing career.

He arguably cemented his position and maturity as a writer when, in 1906, he saw the publication of both his first major play, The Silver Box, and the novel The Man of Property. Each was published to considerable critical acclaim, and to achieve both in such a short space of time was impressive. the Silver Box concerns the imbalance in the justice system with regards to criminals of differing class by contrasting the treatment of a poor thief and a rich thief, both of whom stole silver cigarette cases but for very different reasons. The complexity of individual experience when not dealt with in public is highlighted and questioned in a bravely critical manner; despite the clear issues it raises with class and privilege, the final night was attended by the Price and Princess of Wales. The Man of Property was the first novel in the famous The Forsyte Saga, a trilogy of novels with an 'interlude' between each one, written between 1906 and 1921. Dealing with the questions of status, class and materialism, The Man of Property introduces us to the Forsyte family, particularly Soames Forsyte, who is acutely aware of his status as 'new money' and equally keen to assert himself as a wealthy man. Jealous of his wife and desperate to own things in order to confirm his wealth to those observing him, he engineers a plan to keep his wife from her friends which backfires spectacularly when, instead of cutting her off, all Soames achieves is enabling her to have an affair. This drives Soames to terrible actions with terrible consequences, which Galsworthy depicts with confidence.

Very typically Edwardian, the novel focuses on conflict between property and art, and to a certain degree much of its emotional power is drawn from Galsworthy's own life, particularly his affair with Ada. Their rendezvous in the countryside of Devon mirror the manner in which Forsyte seeks to relocate his wife and; though theirs was a much healthier relationship, there are clear similarities. By examining the fragile nature of the class system and those moving within it Galsworthy offered an important perspective on the relationships between material wealth, personal happiness and obsession, and the manner in which these change over time. His contemporaries widely regarded the publication of this novel as marking the end of Victorianism. His friend Conrad praised it as "indubitably a piece of art" and, though the notoriously risqué D.H. Lawrence lamented the novel's timidity in the face of sexuality and sensuality, he considered it potentially "a very great novel, a very great satire".

Though he continued to write both plays and novels, it was his work as a playwright for which he was most celebrated by his contemporaries. Indeed, his next novel, The Country House, seems uncharacteristically unfocused, its satirical view of those belonging to the country set comparatively unremarkable and weakly characterised, while at times the tone of satire becomes one of ironic detachment. In 1909 he published Fraternity, an exploration of of the various connections between urban society and the social classes therein, though its representation of lower-class Londoners is utterly unconvincing and ill-informed. Remaining with the subject of the landed gentry and the society surrounding it, in 1915 he published The Freelands, which does not stray far from conservative discussions of capitalism, the rural economy and their interrelationship.

His drama, however, featured a convincingly muted realism, directed at a relatively small, educated and politically-aware audience. His social agenda is prevalent here too, and is represented in a simple and static manner producing arresting instances of high drama. This talent for creating moments of captivating theatre is complimented by an instinctual sense of balance enabling his narratives to vacillate between their emotional high- and low-points, ultimately reaching conclusive equilibrium. This is particularly evident in one of his most popular plays, Strife, published in 1909 and examining the antagonists in a strike at a Cornish tin mine. In this, and in 1910's Justice, he approaches his subject with sympathy, irony and balance, which establishes a position of narrative authority while garnering the audiences trust that he is representing his characters and their motives justly. Justice condemns the use of solitary confinement in prisons, a reformist agenda which caught the liberality of his contemporary audiences along with the home secretary, Winston Churchill. Despite he was careful to disassociate himself with politics and professed himself apolitical, he and his work were nevertheless aligned with the views of the Liberal establishment. He spent much of the duration of the First World War working in a field hospital in France as an orderly having been passed over for military service.

Despite the popularity and brilliance of his work, it was only in 1920 that he had his first true commercial success with The Skin Game, a melodrama dealing with ethics, property and class. The play was adapted by Alfred Hitchcock in 1931. Galsworthy, meanwhile, had turned down a knighthood in 1918, considering his work not sufficient to be made a knight of the realm. He did, however, accept the Belgian Palmes d'Or in the following year. In 1920 he published the second novel in the Forsyte Saga, In Chancery, in which he resumes many of the themes of the first novel, focusing on the marital disharmony between Soames Forsyte and his wife. Katherine Mansfield considered it "a fascinating, brilliant book" in her review in The Atheneum. Then, in 1921, he was elected as the PEN International Literary Club's first president. The concluding novel to The Forsyte Saga, To Let was published in 1921 with a kind of peace being found between Forsyte and his now-ex wife, though he is left contemplating his losses and his greed. More ironic treatment of class confusions followed in Loyalties, bringing with it more popular success which lasted until 1926 and Escape, the last of his popular plays. Though he enjoyed popular success it was inconsistent and relatively small. His Collected Plays was published in 1929.

Over the course of time the appreciation of his work has gradually shifted from his plays to his novels, and particularly the detail and intricacy of his chronicle of English social difference, tension and pretension in The Forsyte Saga. Its success encouraged Galsworthy to revisit Soames Forsyte in a second trilogy, A Modern Comedy, which follows Soames's obsessive love of his daughter Fleur. In its three volumes, The White Monkey (1924), The Silver Spoon (1936) and Swan Song (1928) he examines the English commercial upper-middle class and its ideologies, its instinct to possess as its only way of distinguishing itself manifested in the poisonous materialism of Soames. Interestingly, this emergent social class which he so vehemently criticises is the very class from which he emerged. He witnessed first-hand its insularity, its chauvinism, its restrictive and oppressive morality, its stubborn imperialism and its materialism, and it is this experience which enables him to write so comfortably about it. Swan Song is widely considered among the best of Galsworthy's writing for the depth of its exploration of society and its heightened emotional subtlety. In 1929 he was appointed to the Order of Merit, despite having turned down a knighthood earlier. He spent his last years writing a third trilogy, End of the Chapter, beginning in 1931 with Maid in Waiting, Flowering Wilderness in 1932 and concluding with Over The River in 1933. These are significantly less coherent works and are indicative of his deteriorating health. Indeed, in 1932 he was awarded the Nobel Prize, though he was too ill to attend the ceremony.

Throughout the course of his career he received honorary degrees from the universities of St Andrews (1922), Manchester (1927), Dublin (1929), Cambridge (1930), Sheffield (1930), Oxford (1931), and Princeton (1931). In 1926 New College, Oxford, elected him as an honourary fellow. In photographs he is portrayed as handsome, fastidiously dressed and dignified. He was unusually compassionate and this saw him involved in several charitable and humane causes throughout the course of his life, including penal reforms, attacks on theatrical censorship and campaigning for animal rights. Though he spent the majority of the final seven years of his life at his home in Bury, West Sussex, it was at his home in Hampstead, London, that he died of a brain tumour on 31st January, 1933, six weeks after having been too ill to attend the ceremony in honour of his receiving the Nobel Prize. According to demands made in his will he was cremated and his ashes scattered over the South Downs from an aeroplane. Also in his will was his wish to leave cottages to several of his astonished tenants. He is memorialised in Highgate 'New' Cemetery and in the cloisters of New College, Oxford, where he was an honourary fellow.

John Galsworthy – A Concise Bibliography

From the Four Winds, 1897 (as John Sinjohn)
Jocelyn, 1898 (as John Sinjohn)
Villa Rubein, 1900 (as John Sinjohn)
A Man of Devon, 1901 (as John Sinjohn)
The Island Pharisees, 1904
The Silver Box, 1906 (his first play)
The Man of Property, 1906 – First book of The Forsyte Saga (1922)
The Country House, 1907
A Commentary, 1908
Fraternity, 1909
A Justification for the Censorship of Plays, 1909
Strife, 1909
Fraternity, 1909
Joy, 1909
Justice, 1910
A Motley, 1910
The Spirit of Punishment, 1910
Horses in Mines, 1910
The Patrician, 1911
The Little Dream, 1911
The Pigeon, 1912
The Eldest Son, 1912
Quality, 1912
Moods, Songs, and Doggerels, 1912
For Love of Beasts, 1912
The Inn of Tranquillity, 1912
The Dark Flower, 1913
The Fugitive, 1913
The Mob, 1914
The Freelands, 1915
The Little Man, 1915
A Bit o' Love, 1915
A Sheaf, 1916
The Apple Tree, 1916
The Foundations, 1917
Beyond, 1917
Five Tales, 1918
Indian Summer of a Forsyte, 1918 – First interlude of The Forsyte Saga
Saint's Progress, 1919
Addresses in America, 1912
In Chancery, 1920 – Second book of The Forsyte Saga
Awakening, 1920 – Second interlude of The Forsyte Saga

The Skin Game, 1920
To Let, 1921 – Third book of The Forsyte Saga
A Family Man, 1922
The Little Man, 1922
Loyalties, 1922
Windows, 1922
Captures, 1923
Abracadabra, 1924
The Forest, 1924
Old English, 1924
The White Monkey, 1924 – First book of A Modern Comedy
The Show, 1925
Escape, 1926
The Silver Spoon, 1926 – Second book of A Modern Comedy
Verses New and Old, 1926
Castles in Spain, 1927
A Silent Wooing, 1927 – First Interlude of A Modern Comedy
Passers By, 1927 – Second Interlude of A Modern Comedy
Swan Song, 1928 – Third book of A Modern Comedy
The Manaton Edition, 1923–26 (collection, 30 vols.)
Exiled, 1929
The Roof, 1929
On Forsyte 'Change, 1930
Two Essays on Conrad, 1930
Soames and the Flag, 1930
The Creation of Character in Literature, 1931 (The Romanes Lecture for 1931).
Maid in Waiting, 1931 – First book of End of the Chapter (1934)
Forty Poems, 1932
Flowering Wilderness, 1932 – Second book of End of the Chapter
Autobiographical Letters of Galsworthy: A Correspondence with Frank Harris, 1933
One More River (originally Over the River), 1933 – Third book of End of the Chapter
The Grove Edition, 1927–34 (collection, 27 Vols.)
Collected Poems, 1934
Punch and Go, 1935
The Life and Letters, 1935
The Winter Garden, 1935
Forsytes, Pendyces and Others, 1935
Selected Short Stories, 1935
Glimpses and Reflections, 1937

www.ingramcontent.com/pod-product-compliance
Lightning Source LLC
Chambersburg PA
CBHW061211170626
46809CB00003B/1319